THE MILKWEED TRIPTYCH: BOOK ONE

BITTER SEEDS

IAN TREGILLIS

orbit

www.orbitbooks.net

ORBIT

First published in the United States in 2010 by Tor
First published in Great Britain in 2012 by Orbit

A CIP catalogue record for this book
is available from the British Library.

ISBN 978-0-356-50169-7

Typeset in Baskerville by M Rules
Printed and bound in Great Britain by
Clays Ltd, St Ives plc

Papers used by Orbit are from well-managed forests
and other responsible sources.

MIX
Paper from
responsible sources
FSC® C104740

Orbit
An imprint of
Little, Brown Book Group
100 Victoria Embankment
London EC4Y 0DY

An Hachette UK Company
www.hachette.co.uk

www.orbitbooks.net

To Zoë, with love

Behold ye among the heathen, and regard, and wonder marvelously: for I will work a work in your days, which ye will not believe, though it be told you.

HABAKKUK 1:5 (KJV)

There are no great men, only great challenges that ordinary men are forced by circumstances to meet.

ADMIRAL WILLIAM HALSEY

Behold: I give you the Overman.

FRIEDRICH NIETZSCHE

PROLOGUE

23 October 1920
11 kilometers southwest of Weimar, Germany

Murder on the wind: crows and ravens wheeled beneath a heavy sky, like spots of ink splashed across a leaden canvas. They soared over leafless forests, crumbling villages, abandoned fields of barleycorn and wheat. The fields had gone to seed; village chimneys stood dormant and cold. There would be no waste here, no food free for the taking.

And so the ravens moved on.

For years they had watched armies surge across the continent with the ebb and flow of war, waltzing to the music of empire. They had dined on the detritus of warfare, feasted on the warriors themselves. But now the dance was over, the trenches empty, the bones picked clean.

And so the ravens moved on.

They rode a wind redolent of wet leaves and the promise of a cleansing frost. There had been a time when the winds had smelled of bitter almonds and other scents engineered for a different kind of cleansing. Like an illness, the taint of war extended far from the battlefields where those toxic winds had blown.

And so the ravens moved on.

Far below, a spot of motion and color became a beacon on the still and muted landscape. A strawberry roan strained at the harness of a hay wagon. Hay meant farmers; farmers meant food. The ravens spiraled down for a closer look at this wagon and its driver.

The driver tapped the mare with the tip of his whip. She snorted, exhaling great gouts of steam as the wagon wheels squelched through the butterscotch mud of a rutted farm track. The driver's breath steamed, too, in the late afternoon chill as he rubbed his hands together. He shivered. So did the children nestled in the hay behind him. Autumn had descended upon Europe with cold-hearted glee in this first full year after the Great War, threatening still leaner times ahead.

He craned his neck to glance at the children. It would do nobody any good if they succumbed to the cold before he delivered them to the orphanage.

Every bump in the road set the smallest child to coughing. The towheaded boy of five or six years had dull eyes and sunken cheeks that spoke of hunger in the belly, and a wheeze that spoke of dampness in the lungs. He shivered, hacking himself raw each time the wagon thumped over a root or stone. Tufts of hay fluttered down from where he had stuffed his threadbare woolen shirt and trousers for warmth.

The other two children clung to each other under a pile of hay, their bones distinct under hunger-taut skin. But the gypsy blood of some distant relation had infused the siblings with a hint of olive coloring that fended off the pallor that had claimed the sickly boy. The older of the pair, a gangly boy of six or seven, wrapped his arms around his sister, trying vainly to protect her from the chill. The sloe-eyed girl hardly noticed, her dark gaze never wavering from the coughing boy.

The driver turned his attention back to the road. He'd made this journey several times, and the orphans he ferried were much the same from one trip to the next. Quiet. Frightened. Sometimes they wept. But there was something different about the gypsy girl. He shivered again.

The road wove through a dark forest of oak and ash. Acorns crunched beneath the wagon wheels. Gnarled trees grasped at the sky. The boughs creaked in the wind, as though commenting upon the passage of the wagon in some ancient, inhuman language.

The driver nudged his mare into a sharp turn at a crossroads. Soon the trees thinned out and the road skirted the edge of a wide clearing. A whitewashed three-story house and a cluster of smaller buildings on the far side of the clearing suggested the country estate of a wealthy family, or perhaps a prosperous farm untouched by war. Once upon a time, the scions of a moneyed clan had indeed taken their holidays here, but times had changed, and now this place was neither estate nor farm.

A sign suspended on two tall flagpoles arced over the crushed-gravel lane that veered for the house. In precise Gothic lettering painted upon rough-hewn birch wood, it declared that these were the grounds of the Children's Home for Human Enlightenment.

The sign neither mentioned hope nor counseled its abandonment. But in the driver's opinion, it should have.

Months had passed since the farm was given a new life, but the purpose of this place was unclear. Tales told of a flickering electric-blue glow in the windows at night, the pervasive whiff of ozone, muffled screams, and always – always – the loamy shit-smell of freshly turned soil. But the countless rumors did agree on one thing: Herr Doktor von Westarp paid well for healthy children.

And that was enough for the driver in these lean gray years that came tumbling from the Armistice. He had children of his own to feed at home, but the war had produced a bounty of parentless ragamuffins willing to trust anybody who promised a warm meal.

A field came into view behind the house. Row upon row of earthen mounds dotted it, tiny piles of black dirt not much larger than a sack of grain. Off in the distance a tall man in overalls heaped soil upon a new mound. Influenza, it was claimed, had ravaged the foundling home.

Ravens lined the eaves of every building, watching the workman, with inky black eyes. A few settled on the ground nearby. They picked at a mound, tugging at something under the dirt, until the workman chased them off.

The wagon creaked to a halt not far from the house. The mare snorted. The driver climbed down. He lifted the children and set them on their feet as a short balding man emerged from the house. He wore a gentleman's tweeds under the long white coat of a tradesman, wire-rimmed spectacles, and a precisely groomed mustache.

'*Herr Doktor,*' said the driver.

'*Ja,*' said the well-dressed man. He pulled a cream-colored handkerchief from a coat pocket. It turned the color of rust as he wiped his hands clean. He nodded at the children. 'What have you brought me this time?'

'You're still paying, yes?'

The doctor said nothing. He pulled the girl's arms, testing

her muscle tone and the resilience of her skin tissues. Unceremoniously and without warning he yanked up her dirt-crusted frock to cup his hand between her legs. Her brother he grabbed roughly by the jaw, pulling his mouth open to peer inside. The youngsters' heads received the closest scrutiny. The doctor traced every contour of their skulls, muttering to himself as he did so.

Finally he looked up at the driver, still prodding and pulling at the new arrivals. 'They look thin. Hungry.'

'Of course they're hungry. But they're healthy. That's what you want, isn't it?'

The adults haggled. The driver saw the girl step behind the doctor to give the towheaded boy a quick shove. He stumbled in the mud. The impact unleashed another volley of coughs and spasms. He rested on all fours, spittle trailing from his lips.

The doctor broke off in midsentence, his head snapping around to watch the boy. 'What is this? That boy is ill. Look! He's weak.'

'It's the weather,' the driver mumbled. 'Makes everyone cough.'

'I'll pay you for the other two, but not this one,' said the doctor. 'I'm not wasting my time on him.' He waved the workman over from the field. The tall man joined the adults and children with long loping strides.

'This one is too ill,' said the doctor. 'Take him.'

The workman put his hand on the sickly child's shoulder and led him away. They disappeared behind a shed.

Money changed hands. The driver checked his horse and wagon for the return trip, eager to be away, but he kept one eye on the girl.

'Come,' said the doctor, beckoning once to the siblings with a hooked finger. He turned for the house. The older boy followed. His sister stayed behind, her eyes fixed on where the workman and sick boy had disappeared.

Clang. A sharp noise rang out from behind the shed, like the blade of a shovel hitting something hard, followed by the softer *bump-slump* as of a grain sack dropping into soft earth. A storm of black wings slapped the air as a flock of ravens took for the sky.

The gypsy girl hurried to regain her brother. The corner of her mouth twisted up in a private little smile as she took his hand.

The driver thought about that smile all the way home.

Fewer mouths meant more food to go around.

23 October 1920
St. Pancras, London, England

The promise of a cleansing frost extended west, across the Channel, where the ravens of Albion felt it keenly. They knew, with the craftiness of their kind, that the easiest path to food was to steal it from others. So they circled over the city, content to leave the hard work to the scavengers below, animal and human alike.

A group of children moved through the shadows and alleys with direction and purpose, led by a boy in a blue mackintosh. The ravens followed. From their high perches along the eaves of the surrounding houses, they watched the boy in blue lead his companions to the low brick wall around a winter garden. They watched the children shimmy over the wall. And they watched the gardener watching the children through the drapes of a second-story window.

*

His name was John Stephenson, and as a captain in the nascent Royal Flying Corps, he had spent the first several years of the Great War flying over enemy territory with a camera mounted beneath his Bristol F2A. That ended with a burst of Austrian anti-aircraft fire. He crashed in No-Man's Land. After a long, agonizing ride in a horse-drawn ambulance, he awoke in a Red Cross field hospital, mostly intact but minus his left arm.

He'd disregarded the injury and served the Crown by staying with the Corps. Analyzing photographs required eyes and brains, not arms. By war's end, he'd been coordinating the surveillance balloons and reconnaissance flights.

He'd spent years poring over blurry photographs with a jeweler's loupe, studying bird's-eye views of trenches, troop movements, and gun emplacements. But now he watched from above while a half dozen hooligans uprooted the winter rye. He would have flown downstairs and knocked their skulls together, but for the boy in the blue mackintosh. He couldn't have been more than ten years old, but there he was, excoriating the others to respect Stephenson's property even as they ransacked his garden.

Odd little duckling, that one.

This wasn't vandalism at work. It was hunger. But the rye was little more than a ground cover for keeping out winter-hardy weeds. And the beets and carrots hadn't been in the ground long. The scavenging turned ugly.

A girl rooting through the deepest corner of the garden discovered a tomato excluded from the autumn crop because it had fallen and bruised. She beamed at the shriveled half-white mass. The largest boy in the group, a little monster with beady pig-eyes, grabbed her arm with both hands.

'Give it,' he said, wrenching her skin as though wringing out a towel.

She cried out, but didn't let go of her treasure. The other children watched, transfixed in the midst of looting.

'Give it,' repeated the bully. The girl whimpered.

The boy in blue stepped forward. 'Sod off,' he said. 'Let her go.'

'Make me.'

The boy wasn't small, per se, but the bully was much larger. If they tussled, the outcome was inevitable.

The others watched with silent anticipation. The girl cried. Ravens called for blood.

'Fine.' The boy rummaged in the soil along the wall behind a row of winter rye. Several moments passed. 'Here,' he said, regaining his feet. One hand he kept behind his back, but with the other he offered another tomato left over from the autumn crop. It was little more than a bag of mush inside a tough papery skin. Probably a worthy find by the standards of these children. 'You can have this one if you let her alone.'

The bully held out one hand, but didn't release the sniffling girl. A reddish wheal circled her forearm where he'd twisted the flesh. He wiggled his fingers. 'Give it.'

'All right,' said the smaller boy. Then he lobbed the food high overhead.

The bully pushed the girl away and craned his head back, intent on catching his prize.

The first stone caught him in the throat. The second thunked against his ear as he sprawled backwards. He was down and crying before the tomato splattered in the dirt.

The smaller boy had excellent aim. He'd ended the fight before it began.

Bloody hell.

Stephenson expected the thrower to jump the bully, to press

the advantage. He'd seen it in the war, the way months of hard living could alloy hunger with fear and anger, making natural the most beastly behavior. But instead the boy turned his back on the bully to check on the girl. The matter, in his mind, was settled.

Not so for the bully. Lying in the dirt, face streaked with tears and snot, he watched the thrower with something shapeless and dark churning in his eyes.

Stephenson had seen this before, too. Rage looked the same in any soul, old or young. He left the window and ran downstairs before his garden became an exhibition hall. The bully had gained his feet when Stephenson opened the door.

One of the children yelled, 'Leg it!'

The children swarmed the low brick wall where they'd entered. Some needed a boost to get over it, including the girl. The boy who had felled the bully stayed behind, pushing the stragglers atop the wall.

Seeing this reinforced Stephenson's initial reaction. There was something special about this boy. He was shrewd, with a profound sense of honor, and a vicious fighter, too. With proper tutelage ...

Stephenson called out. 'Wait! Not so fast.'

The boy turned. He watched Stephenson approach with an air of bored disinterest. He'd been caught and didn't pretend otherwise.

'What's your name, lad?'

The boy's gaze flickered between Stephenson's eyes and the empty sleeve pinned to his shoulder.

'I'm Stephenson. Captain, in point of fact.' The wind tossed Stephenson's sleeve, waving it like a flag.

The boy considered this. He stuck his chin out, saying, 'Raybould Marsh, sir.'

'You're quite a clever lad, aren't you, Master Marsh?'

'That's what my mum says, sir.'

Stephenson didn't bother to ask after the father. Another casualty of Britain's lost generation, he gauged.

'And why aren't you in school right now?'

Many children had abandoned school during the war, and after, to help support families bereft of fathers and older brothers. The boy wasn't working, yet he wasn't exactly a hooligan, either. And he had a home, by the sound of it, which was likely more than some of his cohorts had.

The boy shrugged. His body language said, *Don't much care for school.* His mouth said, 'What will you do to me?'

'Are you hungry? Getting enough to eat at home?'

The boy shook his head, then nodded.

'What's your mum do?'

'Seamstress.'

'She works hard, I gather.'

The boy nodded again.

'To address your question: Your friends have visited extensive damage upon my plantings, so I'm pressing you into service. Know anything about gardening?'

'No.'

'Might have known not to expect much from my winter garden if you had, eh?'

The boy said nothing.

'Very well, then. Starting tomorrow, you'll get a bob for each day spent replanting. Which you will take home to your hardworking mother.'

'Yes, sir.' The boy sounded glum, but his eyes gleamed.

'We'll have to do something about your attitude toward education, as well.'

'That's what my mum says, sir.'

Stephenson shooed away the ravens picking at the spilled food. They screeched to each other as they rode a cold wind, shadows upon a blackening sky.

23 October 1920
Bestwood-on-Trent, Nottinghamshire, England

Rooks, crows, jackdaws, and ravens scoured the island from south to north on their search for food. And, in the manner of their continental cousins, they were ever-present.

Except for one glade deep in the Midlands, at the heart of the ancestral holdings of the jarls of Æthelred. In some distant epoch, the skin of the world here had peeled back to reveal the great granite bones of the earth, from which spat forth a hot spring: water touched with fire and stone. No ravens had ventured there since before the Norsemen had arrived to cleave the island with their Danelaw.

Time passed. Generations of men came and went, lived and died around the spring. The jarls became earls, then dukes. The Norsemen became Normen, then Britons. They fought Saxons; they fought Saracens; they fought the Kaiser. But the land outlived them all with elemental constancy.

Throughout the centuries, blackbirds shunned the glade and its phantoms. But the great manor downstream of the spring evoked no such reservations. And so they perched on the spires of Bestwood, watching and listening.

'Hell and damnation! Where is that boy?'

Malcolm, the steward of Bestwood, hurried to catch up to the twelfth Duke of Aelred as he banged through the house. Servants fled the stomp of the duke's boots like starlings fleeing a falcon's cry.

The kitchen staff jumped to attention when the duke entered with his majordomo.

'Has William been here?'

Heads shook all around.

'Are you certain? My grandson hasn't been here?'

Mrs. Toomre, Bestwood's head cook, was a whip-thin woman with ashen hair. She stepped forward and curtsied.

'Yes, Your Grace.'

The duke's gaze made a slow tour of the kitchen. A heavy silence fell over the room while veins throbbed at the corners of his jaw, the high-water mark of his anger. He turned on his heels and marched out. Malcolm released the breath he'd been holding. He was determined to prevent madness from claiming another Beauclerk.

'Well? Off you go. Help His Grace.' Mrs. Toomre waved off the rest of her staff. 'Scoot.'

When the room had cleared and the others were out of earshot, she hoisted up the dumbwaiter. She worked slowly so that the pulleys didn't creak. When William's dome of coppery-red hair dawned over the transom, she leaned over and hefted him out with arms made strong by decades of manual labor. The boy was tall for an eight-year-old, taller even than his older brother.

'There you are. None the worse for wear, I hope.' She pulled a peppermint stick from a pocket in her apron. He snatched it.

Malcolm bowed ever so slightly. 'Master William. Still enjoying our game, I trust?'

The boy nodded, smiling around his treat. He smelled like

parsnips and old beef tallow from hiding in the dumbwaiter all afternoon.

Mrs. Toomre pulled the steward into a corner. 'We can't keep this up forever,' she whispered. She wrung her hands on her apron, adding, 'What if the duke caught us?'

'We needn't do so forever. Just until dark. His Grace will have to postpone then.'

'But what do we do tomorrow?'

'Tomorrow we prepare a poultice of hobnailed liver for His Grace's hangover, and begin again.'

Mrs. Toomre frowned. But just then the stomping resumed, and with renewed vigor. She pushed William toward Mr. Malcolm. 'Quick!'

He took the boy's hand and pulled him through the larder. Gravel crunched underfoot as they scooted out of the house through the deliverymen's door, headed for the stable, trailing white clouds of breath in the cool air. Malcolm had pressed most of the household staff into aiding the search for William, so the stable was empty. The duke kept his horses here as well as his motor car. The converted stable reeked of petrol and manure.

Mr. Malcolm opened a cabinet. 'In here, young master.'

William, giggling, stepped inside the cabinet as Mr. Malcolm held it open. He wrapped himself in the leather overcoat his grandfather wore when motoring.

'Quiet as a mouse,' the older man whispered, 'as the duke creeps around the house. Isn't that right?'

The child nodded, still giggling. Malcolm felt relieved to see him still enjoying the game. Hiding the boy would become much harder if he were frightened.

'Remember how we play this game?'

'Quiet and still, all the same,' said the boy.

'Good lad.' Malcolm tweaked William's nose with the pad of his thumb and shut the cabinet. A sliver of light shone on the boy's face. The cabinet doors didn't join together properly. 'I'll return to fetch you soon.'

The duke, William's grandfather, had gone on many long expeditions about the grounds with his own son over the years. Grouse hunting, he'd claimed, though he seldom took a gun. The only thing Mr. Malcolm knew for certain was that they'd spent much time in the glade upstream from the house. The same glade where the staff refused to venture, citing visions and noises. Years after the duke's heir – William's father – had produced two sons of his own, he'd taken to spending time in the glade alone. He returned to the manor at all hours, wild-eyed and unkempt, mumbling hoarsely of blood and prices unpaid. This lasted until he went to France and died fighting the Hun.

The duke's grandsons moved to Bestwood soon after. They were too young to remember their father very well, so the move was uneventful. Aubrey, the older son and heir apparent, received the grooming expected of a Peer of the Realm. The duke showed little interest in his younger grandson. And it had stayed that way for several years.

Until two days previously, when he had asked Malcolm to find hunting clothes that might fit William. Malcolm didn't know what happened in the glade, or what the duke did there. But he felt honor-bound to protect William from it.

Malcolm left William standing in the cabinet only to find the duke standing in the far doorway, blocking his egress. His Grace had seen everything.

He glared at Malcolm. The majordomo resisted the urge to squirm under the force of that gaze. The silence stretched between them. The duke approached until the two men stood nearly nose to nose.

'Mr. Malcolm,' he said. 'Tell the staff to return to their duties. Then fetch a coat for the boy and retrieve the carpetbag from my study.' His breath, sour with juniper berries, brushed across Malcolm's face. It stung the eyes, made him squint.

Malcolm had no recourse but to do as he was told. The duke had flushed out his grandson by the time he returned bearing a thick dun-colored pullover for William and the duke's paisley carpetbag. Malcolm made brief eye contact with William before taking his leave of the duke.

'I'm sorry,' he mouthed.

William's grandfather took him by the hand. The ridges of the fine white scars arrayed across his palm tickled the soft skin on the back of William's hand.

'Come,' he said. 'It's time you saw the estate.'

'I've already seen the grounds, Papa.'

The old man cuffed the boy on the ear hard enough to make his eyes water. 'No, you haven't.'

They walked around the house, to the brook that gurgled through the gardens. They followed it upstream, crashing through the occasional thicket. Eventually the crenellations and spires of Bestwood disappeared behind a row of hillocks crowned with proud stands of yew and English oak. They traced the brook to a cleft within a lichen-scarred boulder in a small clearing.

Though hemmed about by trees on every side, the glade was quiet and free of birdsong. The screeches and caws of the large black birds that crisscrossed the sky over the estate barely echoed in the distance. William hadn't paid the birds any heed, but now their absence felt strange.

Several bundles of kindling had been piled alongside the boulder. From within the carpetbag the duke produced a canister of matches and a folding pocketknife with a handle fashioned from a segment of deer antler. He built a fire and motioned William to his side.

'Show me your hand, boy.'

William did. His grandfather took it in a solid grip, pulled the boy's arm straight, and sliced William's palm with his pocketknife. William screamed and tried to pull away, but his grandfather didn't release him until the blood trickled down William's wrist to stain the cuff of his pullover. The old man nodded in satisfaction as the hot tickle pulsed along William's hand and dripped to the earth.

William scooted backwards, afraid of what his grandfather might do next. He wanted to go home, back to Mr. Malcolm and Mrs. Toomre, but he was lost and couldn't see through his tears.

His grandfather spoke again. But now he spoke a language that William couldn't understand, more wails and gurgles than words. Inhuman noises from a human vessel.

It lulled the boy into an uneasy stupor, like a fever dream. The fire's warmth dried the tears on his face. A shadow fell across the glade; the world tipped sideways.

And then the fire spoke.

ONE

2 February 1939
Tarragona, Spain

Lieutenant-Commander Raybould Marsh, formerly of His Majesty's Royal Navy and currently of the Secret Intelligence Service, rode a flatbed truck through ruined olive groves while a civil war raged not many miles away. He secretly carried two fake passports, two train tickets to Lisbon, vouchers for berths on a steamer bound for Ireland, and one thousand pounds sterling. And he was bored.

He'd been riding all morning. The truck passed yet another of the derelict farmhouses dotting the Catalonian landscape. Some had burned to the ground. Others stared back at him with empty windows for eyes, half-naked where the plaster had sloughed to the ground under erratic rows of bullet holes. Wind sighed through open doorways.

Sometimes the farmers and their families had been buried in the very fields they tended, as evidenced by the mounds. And sometimes they had been left to rot, as evidenced by the birds. Marsh envied the farmers their families, but not their ends.

The land had fared no better than the farmers at the hands of armed factions. Artillery had pocked the fields and rained shrapnel upon centuries-old olive groves. In places, near the largest craters, the tang of cordite still wafted from broken earth.

At one point, the truck had to swerve around the charred hulk of a Soviet-issue T-38 tank straddling the road. It looked like an inverted soup tureen on treads but was based, Marsh noted with pride and amusement, upon the Vickers. It was a common sight. Abandoned Republican matériel littered the countryside. Most of Spain had long since fallen to the Nationalists; now they mounted their final offensive, grinding north through Catalonia to strangle the final Republican strongholds.

Officially, Britain had chosen to stay on the sidelines of the Spanish conflict. But the imminent victory of Franco's Nationalists and their Fascist allies was raising eyebrows back home. Marsh's section within the SIS, or MI6 as some people preferred to call it, was tasked with gathering information about Germany's feverish rearmament over the past few years. So when a defector had contacted the British consulate claiming to have information about something new the Nazis were field-testing in Spain, Marsh got tapped for an 'Iberian holiday,' as the old man put it.

'Holiday,' Marsh repeated to himself. Stephenson had a wry sense of humor.

The truck labored out of the valley into Tarragona, briefly passing through the shadow of a Roman aqueduct that straddled the foothills. A coastal plain spread out before Marsh as they topped the final rise. Orange and pomegranate groves, untended by virtue of winter and war, dotted the seaward slopes of the hills overlooking the city. At the right time of year, the groves might have perfumed the wind with their blossoms. Today the wind smelled of petrol, dust, and the distant sea.

Below the groves sprawled the city: a jumble of bright stucco, wide plazas, and even the occasional gingko-lined avenue left behind by long-dead Romans. One could see where medieval Spanish city planning had collided with and absorbed the remnants of an older empire. On the whole, Tarragona was well-preserved, having fallen to the Nationalists three weeks earlier after token resistance.

Somewhere in that mess waited Marsh's informant.

Between the city and the horizon stretched the great blue-green expanse of the Mediterranean Sea. It sparkled under the winter sun. Most years enjoyed frequent winter rains that tamped down the dust. This season had been too sporadic, and today the winds blew inland, so the breeze coming off the sea spread an ocher haze across the bowl of the city.

Farther west, whitecaps massaged the coastline where a trawler steamed out of port. Marsh was too far away to smell the fear and desperation, to feel the press of bodies, to hear the din on the docks as families clamored for passage to Mexico and South America. Those refugees not willing to risk capture in the Pyrenees while fleeing to France, and who could afford otherwise, instead mobbed the ports. For now, Franco's Nationalists were busy formalizing their control of the country. But when that was done, the reprisals would begin.

The dirt road became cracked macadam as they descended into the city. Marsh shifted his weight when the macadam turned into uneven cobblestones. It had been a long couple of days since he'd crossed the border from Portugal.

His ride pulled to a stop in the shadow of a medieval cathedral. The driver banged his fist on the outside of his door. Marsh grabbed his rucksack and hopped down, gritting his teeth against the twinge of pain in his knee.

'*Gracias,*' he said. He paid the driver the promised amount, a small fortune by the standards of a poor farmer even in peacetime. The driver took the cash and rumbled away without another word, leaving Marsh to cough in a plume of exhaust.

I'd spend it quickly if I were you.

Marsh set off for the cathedral. As far as the driver knew, it was his destination. And so he'd relate, if anybody should happen to ask him about his passenger. The cathedral loomed over the circular Plaza Imperial, and from there it was a short walk to the Hotel Alexandria. Marsh had memorized the layout of the city before leaving London. Walking massaged the ache from his knee.

The narrow side streets were quiet and devoid of crowds, a fact for which he was thankful. He wore the heavy boots of a farmer, a flannel shirt under his overalls, and a kerchief tied around his neck in the local style. But he also wore the skin of an Englishman, colored pale by years of rain, rather than a complexion earned through a life of outdoor labor. But most folks weren't terribly observant. With a little luck and discretion, his garb would plant the proper suggestion in people's eyes; as long as he drew no extra attention to himself, their minds would fill in the expected details.

It was livelier on the plaza. The handfuls of people he passed in the wide open space shuffled through their lives under a cloud of dread and anticipation. Strident Art Deco placards touted General Franco's cause from every available surface. (*Unidad! Unidad! Unidad!*) The Nationalists' propaganda machine had wasted no time.

The cathedral bells chimed sext: midday. Marsh quickened his pace. The plan was to make contact at noon.

Krasnopolsky, an ethnic Pole born in the German enclave of

Danzig, had come to Spain attached to a unit of Fascist forces supporting the Nationalist cause. Whatever his work entailed, he'd done it without protest for years. Until he decided, quite spontaneously, to defect. But the Nationalists' victory was merely a matter of time, meaning that his new enemies had the country locked up tight. Betraying them so late in the game was a bloody stupid move.

Thus he had contacted the British consulate in Lisbon. In return for assistance leaving the country, he'd share his knowledge of a new technology the Schutzstaffel had deployed against the Republicans. Franco, moved by a fit of despotic largesse, had given the Third Reich carte blanche to use Spain as a military proving ground. In that manner, the Luftwaffe had debuted its carpet-bombing technique in Guernica. MI6 wanted to know about anything else the Jerries had developed over the past few years.

Which was why Marsh carried virtually enough money to purchase his own steamer, if it came to that. He'd stay at Krasnopolsky's side all the way back to Great Britain.

The Hotel Alexandria was a narrow five-story building wedged between larger apartment blocks. Its balconies hung over the street in pairs jutting from the canary-yellow façade. The building had only the single entrance. Less than ideal.

The lobby was a mishmash of ugly modernist décor and Spanish imperialism. It looked like the result of a half-hearted makeover. Clean, bare spots high on the yellowed plaster marked the places where paintings had hung, most likely of King Alfonso and his family. Through a doorway to the left, a handful of men and women talked quietly in what passed for the Alexandria's bar.

Marsh threaded his way toward the reception desk through a maze of angular Bauhaus furniture and potted ferns. But he abandoned his intent to ring Krasnopolsky's room when he caught sight of the lone figure sitting at the rear of the lobby, in the shadows of the staircase.

The man perched on the edge of a chaise longue, smoking, with a suitcase next to him and a slim leather valise on his lap. He stamped out his cigarette and lit a new one with shaky hands. Judging by the number of cigarette butts in the ashtray next to the chaise, he'd been waiting there, in *public*, since well before noon.

Marsh cringed. He'd marked Krasnopolsky instantly. The man was an idiot with no conception of tradecraft.

He purchased a newspaper from the front desk, then took a seat in a high-backed leather chair next to Krasnopolsky's nest. The other man looked at him, did a double take, and shifted his feet.

MI6 had no photographs of Krasnopolsky; they'd had to produce the doctored passport based on the man's description of himself. He'd overstated his looks. He was a tall fellow, even sitting down, and skeleton-thin with an aquiline nose and ears like sails. If he were to stand in the corner of a dark room, Marsh imagined, he might be mistaken for a coat-rack.

Marsh paged through the paper, thoroughly ignoring Krasnopolsky. He waited until it looked like the defector wasn't quite so ready to flee.

'Pardon me, sir,' said Marsh in Spanish, 'but do you happen to know if the trains are running to Seville?'

Krasnopolsky jumped. '*Bitte?*'

Marsh repeated his question, more quietly, in German.

'Oh. Who knows? They're less reliable every day. The trains, I mean.'

'Yes. But General Franco will fix that soon.'

'Took you long enough,' Krasnopolsky whispered. 'I've been waiting all morning.'

Marsh responded in kind. 'In that case, you're a fool. You were supposed to wait in your room.'

'Do you have my papers?'

Marsh took a deep breath. 'Look, friend.' He tried to clamp down on the irritation creeping into his voice. 'Why don't we go back to your room and talk privately. Hmmm?'

Krasnopolsky lit another cigarette from the butt of the previous one. Italian issue. Marsh wondered how anyone could tolerate those acrid little monstrosities.

'I've already checked out. I'm safer in public. I need those papers.'

'What do you mean, safer in public?'

Krasnopolsky drew on the cigarette, watching the crowd. Pale discolorations mottled the skin of his fingers.

'Look, we're not a sodding travel agency,' said Marsh. 'You haven't given me a reason to help you yet.'

Krasnopolsky said nothing.

'You're wasting my time.' Marsh stood. 'I'm leaving.'

Krasnopolsky sighed. Plumes of gray smoke jetted from his nostrils. 'Karl Heinrich von Westarp.'

Marsh sat again, enveloped in a bluish cloud. 'What?'

'Not what. Who. Doctor von Westarp.'

'He's the reason you left?'

'Not him. His children. Von Westarp's children.'

'His kids?'

Krasnopolsky shook his head. He opened his mouth to elaborate just as a glass shattered in the bar. His mouth clacked shut. The skin on his knuckles turned pale as he tightened his grip on the valise.

'What was that?'

Dear God. This is hopeless. 'You need to relax. Let's get something to calm you down,' said Marsh, pointing to the side doorway that led to the bar. He pulled the man to his feet and marshaled him through the lobby.

After getting Krasnopolsky settled at a corner table, Marsh went to the bar and ordered a glass of Spanish red. Then he thought better of it and ordered the entire bottle instead. The barman swept up the last of the broken glass, grumbling about having to retrieve the wine from the cellar.

Marsh waited at the bar, keeping an eye on Krasnopolsky while eavesdropping on conversations. The question on everybody's mind was how things would change once Franco was formally in power.

The barman plunked a bottle in front of Marsh. Marsh was digging cash out of his pocket when he felt the surge of heat wash across his back. Somebody screamed.

'Dios mío!'

A cry went up: *'Fuego! Fuego!'*

Marsh spun. The rear corner of the hotel bar, steeped in shadows just moments earlier, now shone in the light from flames racing up the walls. *No! It can't be—*

Marsh dodged the people fleeing the fire, fighting upstream like a salmon. But he stopped in his tracks when he saw the source of the flames.

Krasnopolsky blazed at the center of the conflagration like a human salamander. New flames burst forth from everything he touched as he flailed around the room, wailing like a banshee. Air shimmered in waves around him; it seared the inside of Marsh's nose. The metal snaps on Marsh's overalls scorched his shirt, sizzled against his chest. The room stank of charred pork.

The burning man collapsed in a heap of bone and ash. Marsh glimpsed a half-incinerated valise on the burning floor. He gritted his teeth and kicked it away. The rubber soles of his boots became tacky, squelching on the floor as he danced away from the fire. He tossed aside a fern and dumped the pot of soil on the valise to smother the flames.

Then he snatched what little remained of Krasnopolsky's valise and fled the burning hotel.

3 February 1939
Girona, Spain

Artillery concussions boomed through the river valleys and almond orchards surrounding Girona. *That's the sound of one's enemies caught between the hammer and the anvil,* Klaus mused. With pride he added, *And we are the anvil.*

The besieged stronghold was Franco's final stop on his sweep through Catalonia. Once Girona fell, finishing the ground war would become a mere formality.

'They would have sent fighters after me today, if they had any planes left. I'm sure of it.' Rudolf's hair shone like copper in the sun as he chucked Klaus on the shoulder. 'Can you imagine that? I wish they did have an air force left. That would look spectacular on film!'

'T-t-t-t—,' said Kammler.

'Rudolf running away again? I've already seen that in person. Why would I watch it on film?' Klaus laughed. 'The doctor would prefer you actually confront our enemies. Like the rest of us do,' he added with a gesture that encompassed himself, Heike, and even drooling Kammler.

Kammler again: 'G-g-g—'

'Up yours,' said Rudolf. 'All of you.'

They rode at the vanguard of a small caravan, bouncing along in silence but for the occasional outburst of stuttering nonsense from Kammler. His handler, Hauptsturmführer Buhler, had unbuckled the leash around Kammler's neck, so now the muscle-bound imbecile had reverted to his harmless and somewhat pitiable state. Klaus wondered what the cameramen and techni-cians in the other trucks talked about in their off-time.

The road back to their farmhouse wended through a vast olive plantation. Rows of trees marched all the way from the edge of the hills overlooking the town to within a dozen yards of the house. The hills themselves had turned brown in spots, owing to a dry winter. Overhead, a fingernail moon hung in a powder-blue sky. A cool, damp breeze gusted up from the river valley.

The north and east sides of the plantation had been shattered by misaimed artillery. The ongoing siege slowly chewed up more of the plantation each time another shell went off course. *A shame*, thought Klaus. *I like olives.*

They pulled up in front of a wide two-story farmhouse built in the style of a Roman villa. The family that had owned it must have been rather prosperous. When he had first arrived here, Klaus wondered if the family had also owned the almond groves that blanketed the surrounding hillsides. Not that it mattered. The Reichsbehörde had needed a base of operations from which to field-test Doctor von Westarp's work, and so the family had disappeared.

The others climbed out of the truck and filed into the house. Klaus paused a moment to scan the wide windows on the second floor, hoping to catch a glimpse of his sister. He worried about her when he was gone all day.

He doffed the straw hat he wore and rubbed at his scalp with the stumps of his two missing fingers as he entered the house. He reached inside his shirt, undid the clasp, and disconnected the pencil-thick bundle of wires that extended from several points on his skull to the battery harness at his waist. The braided wires dangled over his shoulder like a Chinaman's queue.

They had left their crisp Schutzstaffel uniforms back at the Reichsbehörde when they came to Spain, opting instead for the locals' more inconspicuous overalls, kerchiefs, and floppy wide-brimmed hats. If nothing else, their disguises conveniently hid the wires. But the coarse peasant apparel tended to snag the wires' cloth insulation, sometimes catching painfully when Klaus moved quickly or unwisely.

Klaus followed Rudolf past the makeshift darkroom – once a child's bedroom – where the cameramen stacked the film canisters from the day's work. One canister was larger and bulkier than the others; the technicians always dispensed with it first. Heike's ability necessitated a special camera and special film to record her activities.

The cameramen looked down as he approached. They unloaded an Agfa eight-millimeter reel with conspicuous silence and diligence. The defector had put them all on edge. Doctor Von Westarp was half-inclined to use the remaining cameramen for target practice, and they knew it.

Klaus pushed through the crowded farmhouse, toward the laboratory and debriefing room, eager to remove his battery harness. Over the previous decade, the engineers had made great strides with the batteries, and they had outdone themselves with the lithium-ion design. But after a long day in the field, it still felt like he'd hung a lead brick on his belt. The sooner he handed over his harness, the sooner he could try to quell the spasms in his back.

The technicians would gauge charge depletion in the batteries and reference that against the activity documented by the cameramen. Klaus would detail his exploits slipping through Republican fortifications and pushing land mines into the earth. Any information of military value he'd gleaned would be passed – after appropriate sanitization to obscure the nature of its source – to the Reich's allies converging on Girona. The arrangement was a quid pro quo in return for Franco's permission to operate in Spain.

The door to the debriefing room swung open as Klaus lay his hand on the knob. He confronted a pair of eyes so pale and unfeeling, they might have been chiseled from ice. Reinhardt stepped into the corridor.

Von Westarp was there, too. He wore a dark lab coat with a dusting of dandruff on the shoulders from his graying tonsure. 'Excellent work,' said the doctor, reaching up to clasp Reinhardt's shoulder. 'Today, I feel pride.'

Reinhardt smiled, his eyes glistening. Klaus and Rudolf saluted as Von Westarp brushed past. 'Herr Doktor!'

The doctor glanced at them through his fish-eye glasses. It felt like being stuck under a microscope. He spared nothing but a sniff of disdain for them as he entered the laboratory. Klaus glimpsed one of the Twins strapped to a table as the doctor slammed the door behind him.

Klaus and Rudolf shared a look. Klaus shrugged.

Rudolf turned toward Reinhardt. 'Where the hell have you been the past few days?'

'Serving the Reich. Carrying out my orders.'

Rudolf stared.

'I don't believe you,' said Klaus.

'Ask your sister.'

The whine of a drill erupted from the makeshift laboratory. Simultaneously, a long, low moan emanated from a different room across the corridor. The moans became screams as the stink of hot bone wafted from the lab.

The trio moved farther down the corridor in order to better hear each other.

Rudolf shook his head. 'Your mouth is full of shit. What orders?'

Reinhardt shrugged nonchalantly, but his eyes still glistened with pride. 'I was sent to plug a leak. The defector is no longer a problem.'

'You? They sent *you*?' Rudolf tossed his hands in the air. 'This is insanity. You have as much finesse as an incendiary bomb.'

Reinhardt's mission meant he was the first of von Westarp's projects to be deemed complete, fully mature. Klaus had expected to garner that honor for himself. While he considered the consequences of Reinhardt's *de facto* promotion, Heike sidled up the corridor, eyes on the floor and silent like a visible ghost.

Reinhardt spread his arms. 'Darling!'

Klaus heard the intake of breath when Heike looked up. She blinked eyes of Prussian blue, then dropped her head again, hiding her face behind long corn silk tresses.

'No welcome-back kiss?'

She tried to pass. Reinhardt blocked her. 'I think you missed me. Worried about me.' His fingers brushed the curve of her ear as he tucked back a lock of her hair. Heike shuddered.

'Do you get cold at night?' he whispered in her ear. 'I can fix that.'

She looked up. Reinhardt leaned closer. She spat. His head snapped back.

Klaus snorted with laughter. Heike slipped around Reinhardt and hurried toward the debriefing room.

'You'd do well to show me a little kindness now and then, Liebling!' he shouted, flicking away the spittle under his eye.

Rudolf shook his head again. 'I cannot believe they chose *you*.'

Since Heike had claimed the debriefing room, and since von Westarp and the technicians were preoccupied in the laboratory, Klaus would have to wait to turn in his battery. He went upstairs to find his sister.

Gretel hadn't moved since that morning, when she'd dragged a table under the picture window along the colonnaded verandah. The window afforded a view of olive groves, the Ter and Onyar rivers off in the distance, and plumes of smoke rising from the valley below. Although if she had chosen the window for the scenery, it didn't show. Her attention to the book propped on her lap was absolute. Just as it had been when Klaus departed that morning.

She sat with bare feet propped on the edge of another chair, wiggling her toes, the hem of a patchwork peasant dress draped across her bony ankles. A long braid of raven-black hair hung past each shoulder. Wires snaked down from her skull, twirled around her braids, and disappeared in the folds of her dress where the fabric occluded the bulge of a harness. The window silhouetted the profile of her face, the high cheekbones and hatchet nose. Within arm's reach on the table stood a stack of books, teapot, cup, and saucer.

'I'm back,' he said. 'Did you have a good day?'

Gretel turned a page. She didn't say anything.

'How are you feeling?'

Her teacup clinked on its saucer as a massive artillery barrage, much closer than the last, shook the building. The saucer danced across the table. Gretel, still absorbed in the works of the modernist poets, reached out with one arm and absently caught it just before it tipped over the edge.

When she moved, the frayed insulation on her wires snagged the collar of her dress.

'Are you in pain? If the batteries are uncomfortable, you could talk to . . . The doctor is here . . .'

She ignored him. Gretel had become increasingly distant in the years since her ability had manifested itself with visions of the future. He left her to her poetry.

Rudolf watched the exchange from the doorway, cloaked in a quivering rage. The news of Reinhardt's promotion had gone down poorly. He shoulder-checked Klaus as he stomped to Gretel's seat.

'Is this how you spend your time? Reading?'

Turning a page, she yawned.

'Is this all you do while we're out there' – he jabbed a finger at the window – 'facing bullets and bombs?'

From his vantage in the doorway, Klaus saw one corner of Gretel's mouth twitch up in the hint of a smile. He frowned.

Rudolf continued, 'Years of work to harness your willpower, and to what end? So that you can study poetry? I can't imagine why the doctor keeps you alive. Even the imbecile Kammler is more useful than you. And your brother, at least he overcame that mongrel blood in your veins.'

'Hey!' Klaus made to intercept Rudolf's tirade, but Reinhardt caught his arm. He liked a good fight.

Rudolf's feet left the floor. Hovering next to her table, he said, 'Look! He made us great.' He spread his arms and pirouetted above the floor. 'He made us gods!' He landed. 'But then there's *you*. A disgusting waste.'

Gretel noted the place in her book, set it on the table, then downed the rest of her tea. She scooted her chair back and stretched. Her back popped.

'What,' Reinhardt muttered, 'is your sister doing?'

Klaus shook his head. But then Gretel dropped to all fours, and his unease became full-blown dread. Klaus fumbled for his wire. He plugged it into the battery on his waist and clicked the latch.

Gretel crawled under the table.

The scent of singed pine curled up from the floorboards beneath Reinhardt's boots as he invoked his *Willenskräfte*, his willpower.

Rudolf laughed. 'That's right! Crawl away, mongrel, crawl away to your doghouse.'

Gretel curled up, knees to chest, and clamped her hands over her ears.

The taste of copper flooded Klaus's mouth as he accepted the surge of electricity into his brain. The Götterelektron energized his Willenskräfte, turning him insubstantial at the same moment Reinhardt armored himself in a searing blue nimbus.

Rudolf saw them and frowned. 'What—?'

WHUMP!

The explosion sent shrapnel winging harmlessly through Klaus's ghost-body. Debris from the errant mortar shell vaporized in Reinhardt's corona. He defended himself with a burst of heat that ignited the wooden floorboards.

The smoke drifted through the hole where the window and part of the roof had been. Klaus's ears rang.

He rematerialized. Then he realized it wasn't ringing he heard, but screaming from throughout the farmhouse. A figure lay on the floor, streaked in blood and clothed in burnt tatters, hands clasping its face.

'Gretel!'

She clambered out of her makeshift bomb shelter and dusted herself off. Klaus exhaled with relief.

The room fell silent but for the crackle of flames, and screams that trailed off into sobs. Rudolf shuddered.

Gretel kneeled next to him and took his hands. Shrapnel had reduced his face to so much meat. His breath came in explosive gasps.

She leaned close. Like a lover, she caressed his ruined face, kissed his cheek, whispered in his ear. A single word passed her blood-smeared lips:

'Incoming.'

She stood. The hem of her dress draped across Rudolf's face as she stepped over him. Then she sauntered out of the burning room, trailing the flying man's blood.

Rudolf stopped shuddering. He died on the spot. Just as Gretel had known he would.

4 February 1939
Barcelona, Spain

The cashier wrinkled his nose. After a day and a half on the road, the smell of incinerated hotel still infused Marsh's clothes. It even wafted out of his hair. He expected to find soot streaked on his face when he finally used a real washroom. And he couldn't work up enough saliva to clear the smoked-pork taste from his mouth.

Marsh let the cashier glimpse the bundle of cash under his hand. The distaste on the other man's face turned into greed. He licked his lips. After a moment's hesitation, he nodded. Marsh slid his hand across the counter. With that, he traded every pound and peseta for a berth on the last British steamer out of Barcelona.

Marsh shook his head. *Nearly a grand for something that shouldn't cost one pony. Thank you, Franco.* It would have been easier to use the tickets intended for Krasnopolsky, but someone had been watching him; given the fool's conduct, Marsh couldn't risk adhering to the original travel plan.

And now Krasnopolsky was dead, reduced to so much ash in the span of a few heartbeats, along with most of the information he carried. During his journey from Tarragona, Marsh had emptied the unburned scraps from the valise into an envelope along with the cash and Krasnopolsky's passport. There wasn't much left: the lower-left corners from a half dozen pages of a memo or report, written in German; half a photograph; and a jumble of acetate strips. The strips were all that remained of an eight-millimeter filmstrip. The film had been coiled on a reel, but when the valise ignited, a portion of the film had melted and disintegrated, rendering the rest a jumbled mess of confetti.

Marsh had pored over it all a dozen times. The legible pages contained no mention of a Doctor von Westarp or children. The visible portion of the photograph showed an unremarkable farmhouse. And the scraps of film were unintelligible to his naked eyes.

Marsh took the proffered voucher and retreated back through the crowd mobbing the ticket window. A breeze mingled fear, seaweed, rotting fish, and diesel fuel into a stomach-churning mélange. Every port in Catalonia must have been staggering under the influx of refugees as the Nationalists made their final push into the Pyrenees.

He headed for his pier, scanning the crowd as he went. There wasn't much time before his ship departed, but Marsh wanted to

find something first. He watched a portly well-dressed man pushing a hand truck piled high with luggage. The man stopped on
the boardwalk to pull a pair of eyeglasses from his pocket.

Aha, thought Marsh. *Those should do the trick.*

The man frowned at his ticket, then looked around in search
of a placard. Marsh orchestrated his collision with the hand truck
to make it appear as though he'd been too intent on his own
ticket to notice it. Luggage clattered to the boardwalk.

'*Hijo de puta!*'

'*Lo siento! Lo siento, señor.*'

Marsh swiped the eyeglasses while helping the man gather his
things. '*Lo siento muchísimo.*' The man departed with a crack about
burying Marsh's heart in a hole so deep, the Virgin Mary
couldn't find it.

A piercing shriek echoed throughout the port. The steam
whistle on Marsh's ship, making its penultimate boarding call.
People scurried up the gangplank in ones, twos, and threes.
Marsh needed to get going, but his curiosity couldn't be contained any longer.

A stack of cargo crates formed a passable shelter from the
wind and crowds. Marsh hid behind the crates, crouched on a
coil of rope. He pulled an acetate fragment from the envelope
inside his shirt. What the fire hadn't destroyed outright it had
made very brittle, so he took great care when handling the crisp
film. Using the eyeglasses as a makeshift magnifier, he strained to
identify the images.

Twenty frames of a brick wall. The second fragment showed
an empty field. The third showed two men in Schutzstaffel uniforms kneeling over an empty container and smiling. The fourth
fragment showed a machine gun nest and the long view down a
firing range.

The fifth showed an anti-aircraft gun hovering above the same range. Marsh shook his head. Too many hours on the road and not enough sleep. But when he looked again, it truly did look like the eighty-eight was floating in midair. No evidence of an explosion, either, though it was hard to tell from a few frames of heat-damaged film.

What on God's green Earth were you mixed up with, Krasnopolsky?

The fragments crackled against each other when he dropped them back in the envelope. Once the envelope was secured inside his shirt once more, he stood as though he'd merely ducked behind the crates to tie his shoes.

A gypsy woman stared at him from across the boardwalk with wide plum-dark eyes. She'd been beaten. The skin around one of her eyes looked like the rind of an aubergine; the corner of her mouth quirked up where her split lip had scabbed over.

Marsh frowned. He sized up her companion, a man with the same olive skin as the woman. Brother? Husband? A tall fellow, but not problematically so. *Enjoy beating up women, do you?* Marsh cracked his knuckles as he started for the pair.

Another breeze rolled off the harbor. It tugged up the kerchief tied over her hair and fluttered the braids hanging past her shoulders.

And jostled the wires connected to her head.

Marsh stopped. He looked again.

Wires. In her head.

The wind died, and the kerchief covered her hair again.

She winked at him.

Her companion said something. She turned away. Marsh made to follow them before they disappeared in the throng.

The whistle on his steamer blew two short, impatient bursts. Final call. He looked over his shoulder. The last few stragglers dashed up the gangplank under the watchful scowl of the porter.

When he turned back, the woman was gone.

'Gretel, please.' Klaus tugged at his sister's hand. 'We have to go.'

Exasperation crept into his voice, though he tried to suppress it. In addition to Rudolf, two technicians had died when the errant mortar shell hit the house. A doctor had also died in the fire during the confused scramble to evacuate. One of the Twins nearly perished, too, before Reinhardt strode through the fire and released her from the restraints on the operating table. Standartenführer Pabst made the decision then and there to terminate training operations in Spain. There was no point in risking further Reichsbehörde assets to another 'accident.' They had their field results; it was time to go home.

'Sorry, brother.' Gretel turned and smiled. The swollen skin around her eye stretched tight. 'I'll be good.'

Pabst had belted her with a savage backhand across the jaw when he learned of Rudolf's death. It was her duty, her purpose, to warn them of such dangers, he'd screamed. And, like the incantations of a mad alchemist, her laughter had transmuted his rage to violence, his open hand to a fist.

Reinhardt wasn't punished for burning down the house.

'What were you staring at?'

'Daydreams. Posies and gravestones.'

Klaus sighed. 'Our pier is this way,' he said, pulling her through the crowd.

TWO

Brittle scraps of acetate fluttered across Stephenson's desk as he paged through Marsh's report. The charred edges of the document fragments littered the wide expanse of cherrywood with black flakes and smears of carbon. Ashes skittered along the desk and drifted to the carpet at Marsh's feet every time Stephenson exhaled. They smelled of woodsmoke and scorched leather.

Marsh rocked on the balls of his feet. Stephenson had been at it for a good half hour.

Somewhere down on the street the *rat-a-tat* syncopation of a two-stroke engine drifted out of the white noise of a London morning. A motorbike, probably a Villiers, zipping along Victoria Street, Marsh gauged. Stephenson's window didn't afford a grand view, mostly just the buildings across Broadway, but from here on the fifth floor of SIS headquarters, it was possible to glimpse the late-winter sun on the trees of St. James' Park several streets over.

'Hmmm.'

Marsh looked back to his mentor. Stephenson opened a side drawer and produced a jeweler's loupe, a holdover from his days as a photo recon analyst during the Great War. He examined a random sampling of film scraps with quiet concentration. One by one he held them up toward the window in his single hand, squinting through the magnifying lens. Marsh scooted aside so as not to block what little natural light the window provided.

Marsh sighed. He pressed the backs of his fingers to his neck and cracked his knuckles against his jaw. Stephenson cleared his throat; Marsh dropped his hands.

Years of polishing had imbued the wood-paneled walls with a satiny finish that reflected the soft glow of lamplight. The walls matched the bookcases, and Stephenson's desk. Above the wainscoting hung maps; photographs of a young, two-armed Stephenson in flying leathers; and a few of his wife, Corrie's, watercolors.

Stephenson had married a Yank from Tennessee. She tended to paint landscapes and nature studies from memory, evoking the rolling hills of her home. Marsh's mentor derived a strange amusement from decorating his office with images of plants foreign to a country of gardeners.

'Well,' said Stephenson at last, still squinting at the film scraps, 'I'm quite impressed. When you cock something up, you do it good and proper.'

'Sir?'

'I sent you to Spain to run a simple errand.'

'Sir—'

'Somebody just swans in and torches your contact and where are you, hmmm? Off getting pissed in the pub.'

'Sir, it's not as if some pikey came traipsing along with a bucket of kerosene—'

'Hmm. This is interesting.' Stephenson held up one of the scraps. 'What do you make of this one?'

Marsh took the film in one hand and the loupe in the other. The fragment contained less than a dozen frames, several of which had been darkened by heat damage. A sequence of eight or nine frames – a fraction of a second – showed a woman standing in front of a brick wall, and then just the brick wall, with no transition from one frame to the next. She was nude except for the belt at her waist connected to her head by what appeared to be wires.

'Looks like they stopped the camera.' He handed the items back to Stephenson. 'Or perhaps this was spliced together from various sources.' He pointed at the film scrap. 'Those things in her head. That's what I saw in Barcelona. Different woman, though.' He shrugged. 'It's not the only oddity in the film, sir.'

Stephenson waved him toward a chair upholstered in button-tufted chintz. As Marsh took the load off his feet, the old man opened another desk drawer and pulled out a bottle and two glasses.

'Brandy?'

'Please.' Marsh sank farther into the chair.

'I imagine you could use it.'

A knock sounded at the door while Stephenson poured. He called, 'Yes, Marjorie.'

His secretary peeked inside. 'Sir, Commander Pryce from the Admiralty wants – Oh! You're back.'

Marsh nodded at her. 'Hi, Margie.' She seemed pleased to see him. But she was a married woman, and that caused a pang of loneliness.

'Whatever it is, he'll have to wait,' said Stephenson.

'Sir, he said—'

'Not now. I'll call him back.'

She nodded and withdrew.

As the head of circulating section T (short for 'technological surprise'), Stephenson was responsible for gathering intelligence pertaining to military technologies under development within Nazi Germany. Although the section itself was only a few years old, it descended from the historical roots of the organization prior to the Great War, when foreign espionage was the purview of the Admiralty, focused primarily on gauging the strength of the Imperial German Navy. Politically savvy Stephenson therefore maintained close ties with the Admiralty, not least because C, the head of SIS, was a career naval officer.

Marsh accepted one of the glasses. Stephenson held his up: 'To safe travels, and safe returns.' *Clink*. This ritual had become their custom. Insofar as Stephenson had been a father to Marsh, tradecraft was the family business.

'This one turned out to be more complicated than we realized,' said Stephenson, settling back into his own chair. Marsh grimaced. It was the nearest thing to an apology he'd ever heard out of the old man. And that made him uneasy.

Stephenson gestured at the desk with his glass. 'So. What should we do with this mess?'

'It might be possible to copy the remaining frames and to splice together a rough approximation of the original film. That's what I'd do.'

Stephenson nodded. 'I'll put out a few feelers. We'll need somebody good, somebody who can keep his mouth shut. It may take a while. And the photograph?'

'Could be anywhere. Probably useless, at least until we know more.'

Stephenson nodded. 'And what of the documents?'

Marsh shrugged. 'Difficult to say. One gets the impression that they're excerpts from medical reports.'

'Your man did mention a doctor, I note,' said Stephenson, sifting through Marsh's report again. 'Von Westarp? Medical doctor, presumably.' He put the loupe back in his desk and produced a packet of cigarettes. An American brand, Lucky Strike.

Over the *skritch* of Stephenson's match, Marsh added, 'He also said something about children. Got rather worked up about it. Peculiar.'

Around the cigarette dangling from his lips, Stephenson asked, 'And what, I wonder, does one thing have to do with the other?'

'My thoughts exactly, sir.'

The two men watched in quiet contemplation as shadows slowly inched along the street. The tip of Stephenson's cigarette flared marigold orange in the growing darkness.

He stamped it out in a marble ashtray and turned on another lamp. 'Right, then. First things first. I'm opening a new file. Until we resolve this issue, or it resolves itself, refer to this matter under the rubric "Milkweed."' At this last he nodded at the wall over Marsh's head.

Marsh craned his neck. Another of Corrie's watercolors hung over the chair. 'Understood.'

'And as for Milkweed, there are a few people who ought to be apprised of this. If I can call them together on short notice, are you free this evening, Marsh?'

'Yes, sir.'

'Excellent. I'll ring you.'

Stephenson's car, a gleaming cream-colored Rolls Royce Mulliner, rolled up at half seven. A gray cloud roiled out when

Marsh entered. The interior smelled of leather and Lucky Strikes. Stephenson rapped the roof once Marsh was settled, signaling his driver to proceed.

From Marsh's home in Walworth they drove west. The Rolls thumped as they crossed onto the steel spans of Lambeth Bridge. Stephenson's driver swung the car north on Millbank when they passed beneath a granite obelisk and its pineapple finial at the far side of the Thames.

Soon Victoria Tower loomed out of the night, a square stone giant wrapped in fog and lamplight. They passed the Perpendicular Gothic filigrees of Westminster Palace: Tudor details on a classic body, as somebody once said. Marsh noted the gradations where the crumbling Yorkshire limestone was being replaced with honey-colored clipsham.

They skirted Parliament Square, passed the Cenotaph, and continued north onto Whitehall.

'Sir, where are we going?'

Stephenson turned. 'Do you know what I miss the most about the old days?'

'Your arm?'

'Ha. Cheeky lad,' said the older man. 'No. Back then, we didn't have so many damnable meetings. Now it's all we ever do.' His eyes twinkled. 'This one's a bit above your regular pay grade, I'm afraid. I trust you won't mind, just this once.'

Oh, hell. That meant sitting in a room full of tossers who would discount Marsh the moment he opened his mouth. He'd had quite enough of that at university.

The car passed through the narrow arch of a long, low screen into the courtyard of a pseudo-Palladian three-story brick building. The Admiralty.

Marsh followed Stephenson through a side door into a

neoclassical rabbit warren. Their footsteps echoed through marble colonnades, twisting stairwells, and narrow corridors. At length the older man stopped before a single door of simple walnut. He knocked.

A pale man – *any one of countless bureaucrats in this lightless den,* Marsh thought – ushered them into a dark room. Marsh smelled brandy and the mustiness of old paper when he stepped inside. A pair of brass lamps with jade-green lampshades stood on twin davenports flanking the room. The lamps cast their illumination in tight circles near the center of the room, leaving the periphery in deep shadows.

Fabric rustled in one corner of the room, as of somebody shifting in a chair. Elsewhere somebody suffered a coughing fit. Deep shadows, but not empty.

'About time, Stephenson.' A man with a great aquiline nose glanced at his pocket watch. Marsh recognized the Earl Stanhope, First Lord of the Admiralty.

Marsh leaned toward Stephenson. 'Sir,' he whispered, 'may I ask what I'm doing here?'

'I'd like you to tell these gentlemen' – his gesture encompassed the room, shadows and all – 'about your experience in Spain.'

'It's all in my report, sir.'

'Yes ... but I believe they should hear it straight from you. Indulge me.'

Marsh did. He took care to emphasize the peculiar nature of the fire, its rapidity as well as the conspicuous absence of petrol, oil, and other smells. For their part, his audience appeared to take the story in stride. But Marsh felt a subtle disdain in the silence, a tacit acknowledgment among these men that he was not one of them. Still, they listened without interruption until:

'What do you mean this fellow was on fire?'

'Blazing like the Crystal Palace. Spouting flames which quickly spread from his body to the furniture to the walls, and in moments the entire hotel was ablaze. In other words, he was on fire.'

Stephenson touched Marsh's arm as if to say, *Easy, lad. Don't get your dander up*. Marsh wrapped up with his arrival in Barcelona, describing the film fragments and the Frankensteined gypsy girl.

The flare of a match briefly silhouetted the profile of a rotund man in the corner as he lit a cigar. Before the light faded, Marsh also glimpsed Commander Pryce, and Admiral Sir Hugh Sinclair, who was Stephenson's superior and the head of SIS.

Sinclair spoke up next. 'Leaving aside the more improbable portions of this tale . . .' He trailed off into another coughing fit before continuing. 'What do you make of this, Stephenson?'

Stephenson's shrug was a peculiar lopsided gesture on the one-armed man. 'I don't know what to make of it, sir. But I'd say we have a bloody great problem on our hands.' He enumerated the points of his argument on his fingers. 'First, we know Krasnopolsky witnessed things that frightened him half-dead. Second, he died in a fire that arose quite spontaneously. If Commander Marsh says there was no external fuel, I assure you gentlemen there was none. And third, the circumstantial evidence on the film suggests the Jerries have tapped into something rather unnatural.'

Unnatural. The old man's comment jarred something loose at the back of Marsh's mind. The half-forgotten memory of a drunken misadventure back at university. He'd long since attributed the hazy recollections of that night to drink – he had been rather pissed. But now recent events conspired to resurrect the memory, casting it in a new light.

It took Marsh back to Oxford, and a long night spent

searching the Bodleian for anthropodermic volumes with an irre-pressible friend. A grisly night, but harmless ... until Will found the object of his quest and read aloud from it. Marsh crossed his arms, warding off a frisson of disquiet. He'd never returned to the Bodleian after that night. Nor had they ever spoken about it. One sensed that Will had committed a whopping great indis-cretion, even by his standards.

Unnatural. Marsh had comforted himself with hopeful self-delusion, disregarding the whole affair as a faulty memory and perhaps a lesson on the perils of drinking to excess. Except, of course, Will had been sober as a deacon. And now as he listened to Stephenson and reflected upon the events in Spain, Marsh confronted the possibility that his memory was unscathed.

Marsh returned his attention to the conversation at hand. Somebody had turned on another lamp. The room had split in two factions: those who believed Stephenson and Marsh were crazy, and those who believed they were merely mistaken. Arguments flew back and forth until Admiral Sinclair clapped his hands for silence.

'Gentlemen! This is leading nowhere. I'll issue an all-section directive to flag and compile any information regarding this von Westarp character. Until we know more, there is nothing we can do. I suggest we table the issue.'

Marsh's thoughts were still in Oxford. 'That's a mistake,' he blurted.

Stephenson coughed, the corners of his mouth turned up behind his hand. *He loves it when I make an ass of myself.*

Somebody muttered something about 'Stephenson's pet gorilla,' Marsh's nickname back at SIS. They saw him as a rough fellow, brutish, and – because of his class – no doubt endowed with disgraceful manners. A gorilla.

The Admiral leaned forward, fixing Marsh with a cold stare.

He coughed again into his handkerchief before responding. 'I beg your pardon, *Commander?*'

'Forgive me, sir, but I was there. And I'm telling you, the Jerries are on to something here. If we wait on this, it'll be too late to do anything.'

'Well, then,' chimed the First Lord. 'Thank you so very much for sharing your vast wisdom and expertise.' He shifted in his chair, turning his attention fully on his peers. A none-too-subtle indication that Marsh was dismissed and disregarded.

Thinking of Will, Marsh murmured to Stephenson, 'We need to recruit specialists.'

'Specialists?'

Well, hell. In for a penny, in for a pound, thought Marsh. He nodded at Stephenson. The old man regarded his protégé through narrowed eyes.

'Yes,' said Marsh. 'Experts in the unnatural.'

There was no point in Marsh announcing the idea. But Stephenson had the respect of these men, and so he voiced Marsh's suggestion as though it were his own.

The room erupted in pandemonium.

'Right, then. We'll just open our doors to every crank we can muster, shall we? Press them into service?'

'—may as well issue faerie wands to the troops while we're at it—'

'—off his rocker—'

'—wasting our time—'

The rotund man in the shadows cleared his throat. 'Hmm. Let the man have his say.'

Marsh recognized the voice. *And what the hell is* he *doing here? He holds no office . . . although if war breaks out on the continent, Stanhope may be ousted.*

Stephenson looked at Marsh. 'What do you have in mind?'

Marsh shook his head. 'First let me talk to somebody. Discreetly. Then I'll get back to you.'

7 March 1939
Reichsbehörde für die Erweiterung germanischen Potenzials

Klaus abandoned his plan to actively humiliate Reinhardt at the award ceremony after learning none other than Reichsführer-SS Heinrich Himmler would pin the Spanish Cross on Doctor von Westarp's chest. Had it been a lower-level functionary presiding over the ceremony, Klaus would have gone ahead and knocked Reinhardt down a few rungs. But embarrassing Reinhardt on today of all days would also mean disgracing the doctor in front of his patron. Contemplating the inevitable retribution was enough to make Klaus tremble. Instead, he resolved to outperform Reinhardt during the day's demonstrations.

All of which he kept to himself while marching behind Reinhardt, alongside Heike and Hauptsturmführer Buhler. The imbecile Kammler shambled along at the end of his leash. Theirs were the visually spectacular abilities, and thus they led the procession. Reinhardt in front, of course, because in the doctor's eyes, he was complete: the pinnacle of his achievement.

We'll see about that, thought Klaus.

Behind them, his sister marched alongside the Twins. Her power, like that of the identical psionicists, had a quiet potency that didn't lend itself to pomp and flash. Although Gretel had survived the errant shell in Spain without a scratch: she had known exactly where to huddle, and when. But like the Twins', her demonstration was scheduled later in the day.

Klaus sneaked a glance at her. Like the rest of them, she wore a crisp, perfect new uniform. But in one hand she also carried a bent, ragged, black-and-white umbrella. The old thing jarred with her uniform. It seemed so out of place that for a moment he couldn't help but check the sky. But the day had dawned clear and blue and bright. So bright, in fact, that sunlight glinted on the newly created insignia pinned to their collars: SS *siegrunen* cleaving a skull, like lightning bolts energizing the Willenskräfte.

The munitions range where the most rigorous skill testing took place had been transformed into a makeshift parade ground. White-coated technicians had taken up shovels and filled the craters. Everything received a new coat of paint. Bunting hung from every sill, swastika flags from every eave.

The doctor had started the program that eventually became the Reichsbehörde on his family farm. It was fitting, then, that the dozen buildings now comprised by the complex huddled around the original house. The wood-and-brick farmhouse with blue trim was the nexus of the Reichsbehörde. The doctor lived on the third floor, where he enjoyed an unobstructed view of the surrounding training grounds. Klaus and the doctor's other children lived in his shadow, on the second floor. And the original laboratory still occupied the first floor, although it had fallen into disuse as the complex had expanded. The other buildings – the laboratories, barracks for the mundane troops, machine shops, chemical huts, toolsheds, the icehouse and pump house – flanked the farmhouse, forming the arms of a U.

The farm's greatest virtue was its isolation. It was surrounded on all sides by oak and ash trees.

Klaus and his companions marched to the center of the training grounds, turned in formation, and came to a halt in front of the riser where the doctor sat with his two distinguished visitors.

For all the pomp, it was a small ceremony. Only Himmler, the doctor's patron of many years, and one of his subordinates, SS-Obergruppenführer Greifelt, had arrived from Berlin. The nascent Götterelektrongruppe was the Reich's greatest weapon. As such, its true nature·was, for the time being, a closely guarded secret. The mundane troops attached to the REGP knew a single untoward comment could land them in contempt of the Gestapo.

Klaus had never seen Himmler in person. He was surprised to find the Reichsführer was a chinless baby-faced man.

Klaus and the others stood at attention while Himmler heaped glowing praise upon the doctor's lifelong dedication to the pursuit of knowledge. It had begun with the doctor's brief flirtation with the Thule Society twenty years earlier. But while the theosophical underpinnings of the Society's belief in the vanished 'Aryan supermen of lost Atlantis' had resonated with many, the doctor had quickly rejected the society's meaningless preoccupation with mysticism and struck out on his own. His guiding stars were science and rationality, and between them he charted a course not for pointlessly lamenting lost greatness, but actively recreating it. And so he built his orphanage, reasoning that children were closest to the wellspring of greatness, the least corrupted by everyday existence.

He believed in human potential, thought Klaus, *and so he created us.*

Back then, Klaus and the others had been little more than striplings. Formless bricks of clay waiting to be molded by the potter and tempered by the kiln. Klaus occasionally wondered, with idle curiosity, if he and Gretel once had other siblings.

The orphanage had been in place for years when Himmler and von Westarp were introduced by a former colleague in the Thule Society. Doctor von Westarp's eminently practical approach earned an enthusiastic supporter in Himmler. Thus, when Himmler became the leader of the SS, one of his first actions was to create the Institut Menschlichen Vorsprung, the Institute of Human Advancement, to house the doctor's research. He also made the doctor an SS-Oberführer, senior colonel, enabling him to work without interference.

A few years later, the IMV became the Reichsbehörde für die Erweiterung germanischen Potenzials, the Reich's Authority for the Advancement of Germanic Potential. For administrative purposes, Himmler shoehorned this into the RKF Hauptamt because on paper, von Westarp's research fell under Greifelt's purview: the 'strengthening of Germanism.' But this was an administrative formality, and in reality, the doctor continued to report directly to the Reichsführer.

And today the doctor's many years of work had come to fruition. He had transformed a handful of mewling babes into the vanguard of a new SS, men and women so great that a new unit of the Verfügungstruppe had been created for them, complete with their own insigne. Today von Westarp's children became officers of the new Götterelektrongruppe. And so, Himmler concluded, the spiritual and intellectual father of the REGP deserved the Reich's gratitude and its highest honor.

Hollow-cheeked Greifelt listened to these remarks with alternating looks of boredom and puzzlement. He had never been to the REGP, had never seen the doctor's work. Klaus suspected that Himmler had discouraged any such visits. Greifelt was a technocrat, an accountant in soldier's garb.

Herr Doktor von Westarp became the first recipient of the Spanish Cross, First Class, for superior contributions to the struggle against communism in Spain: sword-bearing eagles surrounding a golden Iron Cross, at the center of which diamonds ringed an opal swastika. It sent splinters of sunlight across the grounds every time the doctor's chest swelled with pride.

His children received the much smaller bronze Victory in Spain medals intended for members of the Condor Legion.

Then it came time for the demonstrations. Today the doctor could revel in the glory of his achievements, as his children personally showcased their abilities to the doctor's patron and putative superior officer for the first time. The show would also serve as a rehearsal for the private demonstration planned for the Führer's fiftieth birthday next month.

Reinhardt strode across the munitions range while two technicians readied the bipod of an MG 34 machine rifle. He cloaked himself in flames and motioned for them to begin.

Reinhardt stood at attention, head high and chin thrust out, unfazed by the ammunition vaporizing against his chest. The bullets disappeared as violet coruscations within a man-shaped corona of blue fire. Himmler's expression went blank. He adjusted his round wire-rimmed glasses and leaned over to say something to the doctor. The doctor nodded. Greifelt's mouth and eyes went wide. He gaped at Reinhardt, unblinking, even after Doctor von Westarp helped him to his seat.

In true combat, the barrage would have knocked Reinhardt on his ass. Klaus had seen it – and laughed – many times. Although the salamander's willpower could subvert lead, strip it of its strength and render it harmless to flesh, it could not subvert momentum. The stream of superheated vapor would have sent him sprawling across the parade ground, mussing his hair and new uniform.

But that would have been undignified. Reinhardt had demanded a concrete slug be buried in the ground, with tungsten-alloy stirrups for his toes. And lately whatever Reinhardt demanded, he received.

A shame. Sabotaging the stirrups would have been simplicity itself. On a different day, a less auspicious day, Klaus would have done it without reservation.

The doctor gave the order to cease fire. The machine gunner stopped. The last echoes of gunfire died away, and then quiet befell the parade ground but for the ticking of the rifle barrel and the *whoosh* of superheated air in Reinhardt's updraft.

The flames disappeared. Reinhardt looked as though he hadn't moved a hair, although now the chest of his uniform exhibited the metallic sheen of vapor-deposited lead. Perhaps as much as a kilogram. His dignity might have been preserved, but the uniform was ruined anyway.

Greifelt marveled at the sight of the bullet slag. He cocked his head toward the doctor, though he continued to stare at Reinhardt. His voice small and uncertain, he murmured, 'But why wasn't his uniform scorched away?'

Reinhardt presumed to answer for the doctor. 'Because I willed it not to be so, Herr Obergruppenführer.'

It was the same reason Klaus didn't fall through the earth when he became insubstantial: because doing so would contradict his Willenskräfte. Some things were trickier than others in this matter of the mind. Klaus's lungs did not absorb oxygen in their ghost state. Heike had yet to fully master her own Willenskräfte, to make her ability encompass her clothing as well as her body.

Unlike Reinhardt, Klaus required no tricks to preserve his dignity. The bullets winged through his wraith-body and shredded the wall behind him. Their momentum presented no problems. And when the barrage ended, his uniform was pristine.

Yet Himmler seemed less pleased than he had been with Reinhardt's presentation. He did not return Klaus's sharp salute when the demonstration ended. Instead he leaned over to whisper to the doctor again. The doctor shook his head.

He's concerned because my skin is too dark for an Aryan, thought Klaus. *A mongrel shouldn't be able to do what I can*. It was maddening, and disappointing, but he knew his chance to prove himself would come soon enough.

Buhler cringed behind Kammler during their turn in front of the gun. Kammler's face turned red and his eyes bulged slightly as Buhler savaged his leash. 'Wall. *Wall!*' Lead splattered against an invisible barrier and tinkled to the fire-glazed earth at Kammler's feet.

Rudolf's ability had never lent itself directly to dodging bullets – at least, he hadn't yet mastered it before the accident – but the sight of him swooping over the range would have gone over extremely well.

Stupefied, Greifelt broke out of his trance. His lips moved, but he made no sound. Formality failed him. 'My God,' he said. 'I can't believe what I'm seeing.'

Himmler slapped von Westarp on the back. 'You've done it, my friend. You've created a new breed of man.'

The doctor's chest swelled. He smiled. *Smiled*. 'Watch it all. Watch my children at work.' He pointed to the truck rumbling onto the field.

It puttered to a stop. A layer of cotton duck, mottled green and brown like a forest canopy, hung over the ribs of the cargo bed. A pair of mundane troops from the LSSAH hopped out of the cab. They threw the tailgate open with a *clang*. A half dozen men climbed out of the truck, shivering in the breeze, blinking at the sun. Unkempt, threadbare, emaciated. Jews, Communists,

Roma, and other enemies of the state from one of the labor camps. The truck pulled away.

Klaus, Reinhardt, and Heike joined Kammler and his handler on the field. Heike unsheathed her knife. Reinhardt blew her a kiss. She vanished, leaving her uniform suspended in midair.

The prisoners scattered.

Buhler pointed to the fastest one. 'Hurl!' An invisible hand slapped the fugitive across the field. He landed atop another of the condemned men. They crumpled to the ground in a tangle of broken bones.

Flames engulfed another man before he'd run ten yards.

Heike disrobed amidst the chaos. The last of her clothing hit the ground as Reinhardt torched another fugitive.

Over the years, they'd killed many in training. But in all that time, Klaus mused, Reinhardt had never once looked a victim in the eye. Klaus knew how to make a much better show for the doctor and his guests. Normally he crept up to his targets like a wraith, then finished them quietly. Knives were easier, but they weren't impressive. And today was Doctor von Westarp's day.

He sought out one of the Roma prisoners, a particularly filthy wretch with olive-colored flesh like Klaus and Gretel. He tackled the man and kneeled on his chest. The bastard kept squirming, so Klaus grabbed his throat and put his weight on it.

'Close your eyes,' he whispered. 'I'll make it quick.'

In the end, the man still resisted. After glancing to ensure he had the dignitaries' attention, Klaus reached into the man's chest. He hooked the aorta with two fingers, feeling life pulsing from a fluttering heart. His victim flailed again when Klaus severed the artery.

The final kill fell to Heike.

Her breaths gave her away, diaphanous vapor clouds that

materialized as they left her body. But her training took hold, and the traitorous exhalations came less and less frequently. Klaus's own demonstration still had his chest heaving; it took no great leap of imagination to feel the fire in Heike's lungs as she stalked the prisoner.

The last puffs of her breath drifted away. His eyes darted back and forth as he turned, half-crouched and panting, in slow circles. A feral intensity limned his eyes with white. Clever beast: he watched the ground, trying to track her, but Reinhardt's demonstration had annealed the earth, scorched it into a crude ceramic.

His back arched, and his head tipped back. Slender Heike exhaled as she grappled with him. He wrestled with a hole in the mist, a ghost wreathed in her own breath. The outline of the knife moved toward his throat, but in his flailing, he caught her wrist. She struggled; he was stronger. He thrust out her arm and bent double, flipping her over his back.

'Hoompf . . .' The impact knocked the wind from her lungs and jostled the plug from her battery harness. Heike reappeared, sprawled on her back at the prisoner's feet. A hint of blue tinged her lips and cheeks, and the chill had stippled her naked body with gooseflesh.

Reinhardt tensed, singeing the fine hairs on the back of Klaus's neck and hands. Years of witnessing such unplanned reappearances during her training sessions had fueled his all-consuming obsession with Heike.

The prisoner dashed for the forest on the far side of the complex.

'Stop him!' von Westarp shrieked.

There was little chance of the prisoner escaping; far less chance that he'd get word of what he'd seen to somebody who mattered. But that was beside the point.

'Kill him now! He embarrasses me!'

A furrow of flames rent the earth in pursuit of the fleeing prisoner, but then he turned the corner and disappeared out of sight behind the barracks.

Ha! Klaus could cut straight through one of the laboratories to catch the prisoner, and then *he* would be von Westarp's favorite.

Obergruppenführer Greifelt cowered behind crossed forearms and screamed as Klaus charged through him. Klaus headed along a diagonal for the far end of the laboratory, to intercept the prisoner as he passed through the gap between the buildings on the long sprint across the clearing. He'd ghosted through the sound-proofed walls and the polished steel surgical table in the operating theater before it occurred to him to check the gauge on his harness.

The needle rested in the red.

'Scheisse!' He skidded to a halt against the far wall of the theater. The bricks gouged his palms.

By the time Klaus emerged outside, the prisoner had nearly entered the trees near the pump house. His path put him back in view of those assembled on the firing range. Apparently Reinhardt had depleted his battery, too, because the running man didn't burst into flames. Not so the telekinetic imbecile. Buhler gesticulated at the escaping prisoner with one hand as he yanked on Kammler's leash with the other. 'Crush! Crush!'

The prisoner slammed to a halt as though he'd hit a glass wall. His body folded up, bones crackling like china.

But Kammler, in his simpleminded zeal, also crushed the pump house. The building disappeared in an implosion of splintered timbers and powdered brick. A plume of spring water erupted through the debris. Gretel unfurled her umbrella, looking amused. It rained on the Reichsbehörde.

Himmler and Greifelt left soon after that, soggy and shaken.

And though Doctor von Westarp kept his medal, he punished them all.

Heike received the worst of his rage. Her screams emanated from the laboratory. They trailed off after a while, either because he'd made his point or because her vocal cords had given out.

The doctor locked Reinhardt in the icehouse.

Klaus's part in the debacle won him a day in the crate. Mewling apologies did no good. Von Westarp stripped him of his harness before kicking him inside the coffin-sized box. Steel bolts clanged into place. Klaus pounded on the lid. Claustrophobia turned the trickle of breathable air rank. He grappled with the urge to hyperventilate, meting out his breaths against the rhythm of his heart. The knowledge that he'd disappointed the doctor created a nausea that threatened to overwhelm him.

Later that night, Pabst gave Gretel new bruises. 'It is your duty!' – thud – 'to warn us!' – slap – 'of such problems!'

Her laughter echoed through darkness and coffins.

8 March 1939
Soho, London, England

Winter had receded in recent days, as though resting up for a big finale. But as a rule, the Hart and Hearth kept its fireplace stoked from October to April. Which was one reason Lord William Beauclerk found it a fine place for a proper tête-à-tête with old friends.

Firelight shimmered on the polished oak beams and cast fluid shadows across the ridges and swirls of horsehair plaster in the ceiling. With an occasional pop that launched a whiff of pine into the room, the sound and smell of the fire melded with the fog of conversation and tobacco.

Six o'clock, so the place was filling quickly with a solid cross section of the working class, just off work and stopping for a pint on the way home. Loudmouthed tradesmen, lorry drivers, a newspaper vendor with ink-stained fingers. Also a few artists and playwrights. And a lovely pair of shopgirls at the next table. The frumpier one had her back to Will; her companion wore an embroidered cloche over a bob of auburn hair and a dusting of freckles on milk-pale skin.

The Hart had a cozy little snug. He made a mental note to invite the bird for a private drink later. Working-class women, he'd found, could be less reserved with their affections than those from other stations in life. Another factor in Will's fondness for the Hart. Although his brother had become a bit of a prig lately, prone to worrying about bastards turning up on the doorstep.

Aubrey could go on at length about what was proper and improper and the responsibilities that came with Will's station in life. To hear him tell it, Will would destroy the country by having it off with a shopgirl. Will had little patience for Aubrey's obsession with noblesse oblige.

He preferred the company in places like this, though he sometimes felt conspicuous. Somewhere along the line he'd taken to wearing a bowler, almost as a form of camouflage. But his shirt cost more than some of these people earned in a week. Thus he'd learned over the years to twist his vowels, leaving behind burrs and clipped syllables in order to emulate the regional accent of the Midlands. Will had grown up listening to how the staff at Bestwood spoke.

The door opened. A cold draft followed Marsh into the pub, tousling close-cropped hair the color of wet sand. A forest-green cable-knit turtleneck and gray corduroys covered his solid build. Marsh wasn't exactly short, or blocky, either, though he sometimes came across as such. It was an illusion created by the way he carried himself, and a face more suited to a boxer than a scholar. But he reminded Will of nothing so much as a coiled spring. Not in the sense of being high-strung or nervous: quite the opposite. But Will had always sensed something inside the man, tightly controlled but powerful.

Marsh ordered at the bar, then leaned against the brass rail while waiting for his pint. When Marsh entered a room, he studied it as though it were a puzzle to be solved. He'd had that mannerism forever – the peculiar way his eyes moved, absorbing every detail. He did it now, examining the pub and the lounge with caramel-colored eyes.

But Will had taken a table in the corner of a dark, smoky pub. He lifted his head. 'Pip.' Will had christened Marsh with that nickname during their first year at university together.

Marsh didn't hear him. Will stood, repeating, 'Pip! Over here.' He lifted his hand to wave, but rapped his knuckles on a stag head in the process. 'Oh, sodding.' Tea slopped out of its cup when he bumped the table. 'Hell.'

Will sucked on his knuckles. The shopgirls tittered.

The commotion drew Marsh's attention. The corners of his eyes crinkled in a smile. He approached Will's table.

'Good to see you, Will.' They clasped hands. Marsh had a brawler's hands: thick fingers with round puckered knuckles and a solid grip. Will's hands were more slender. Their handshake creased the thin white scars that spiderwebbed Will's palm. Not painful, but unpleasant.

'And you'n all, mate.'

The other man cocked an eyebrow. Marsh rankled when

people adopted a more common mode around him. At university, he'd worked to achieve a more refined diction of his own.

'Apologies,' said Will, slipping back into his normal enunciations. He had, perhaps, laid it on a bit. 'I'd forgotten. Force of habit, you know.'

Marsh grinned. He nodded at the teapot and empty cup. 'Buy you something stronger?'

Will shook his head. 'I'd settle for just a slice of lemon, honestly. You'd think there's a war.' Will sighed theatrically. 'Alas. I'll soldier on.'

'Still not drinking, eh? It's comforting to know you still cling to your affectations.'

'Your billfold can thank old granddad for my peculiarities.'

'Every one? The mind reels.'

Will laughed. 'It does indeed.'

'And how's your brother?' asked Marsh, taking a seat.

'His Grace has made something of a holy terror of himself in the House of Lords. Fancies himself a crusader these days.'

'Socialist?' Marsh looked at him in mild alarm. 'Hasn't gone pink, has he?'

'Oh, no. He's not a Bolshie.' Will dismissed the concern, waving his long fingers in a languid circle. 'Merely decided he's the champion of the common man. Taken the plight of the Spaniards to heart, or some such.'

At the mention of Spain, Marsh looked rather serious for a moment. 'Good for him. Someone ought.'

'A bit late, I fear. I'll relay your greetings, yes?' A formality, of course.

'Please do,' said Marsh. He sipped at his pint, eyes scanning the room behind Will.

'Well then,' said Will, 'to the matter at hand.'

Marsh continued to stare past Will's shoulder.

'I said,' Will repeated, 'to the matter at hand.'

'What?' Marsh looked like he'd just been poleaxed.

Will dangled one long arm over the back of his chair and chanced a look. Marsh's attention had landed on the freckled coquette. *Aha.* 'Delightful girl.'

'Hmm?' Marsh tried to hide the flush in his cheeks by taking a long draw on his pint. 'I suppose she is.'

With casual disinterest, Will asked, 'Shall I wave her over?'

'No, no,' said Marsh, shaking his head. But then he fixed Will with a sly look. 'You don't fool me. I'll wager you were planning to invite her to the snug for a private drink, weren't you?'

'I don't know what you mean, sir,' said Will in mock indignation. 'Aubrey would have a proper fit.'

'Oh?'

'She's a charming little turtledove, make no mistake. But Aubrey has developed an alarming tendency to frown upon – ahem – dalliances.'

Marsh opened his mouth slightly and tipped his head back. 'Ah . . .'

'He believes in the dignity of the working classes – plight of the working man and all that. But not in their breeding. Can't wait for me to settle down with somebody perfectly dreadful as fits my station.'

'Oh dear.'

'Yes.'

'Next you'll tell me he's pushing you to join some perfectly respectable profession and give up the gadabout's life. As also fits your station.'

'I'd be a perfectly respectable captain right now if not for these flat feet. Centuries of inbreeding, you know.'

'What will you do?'

'Aubrey has made noise of endowing a charity. Perhaps I'll join his crusade.'

'Doesn't sound like your line of work, Will.'

'No. Still, what can we do? Now, you said you wanted to pick my brain about something. My brain, addled and inbred as 'tis, is at your disposal.'

'Ah. Well, then, speaking of your grandfather—' Marsh lowered his voice. '—I have some questions about his hobby.'

Will scooted his chair closer to the fire to ward off a sudden chill. He had unwillingly shared his grandfather's 'hobby' for over a decade before the wretched old warlock finally drank himself to death.

'I . . . I don't follow you, Pip.' An unconvincing deflection, and Will knew it.

'Back at university, you read from a book . . .'

'Ah.' Will sighed, knowing he couldn't dodge the issue. 'The Bodleian. I'd rather hoped you were too pissed to remember that night.'

'I nearly was. I'd discounted it as a drunken memory.'

'Better to leave it that way. It was years ago. Ancient history. Why bring it up now?'

Marsh fell quiet for a moment. A distant look danced across his eyes as he watched some private memory unfold. 'Recently I saw something . . . strange.'

Will shook his head. 'The world is a strange place, Pip. I'm sorry, but I truly can't help you. It's better for everybody if you forget anything I might have said or done in my careless youth.'

Marsh sipped at his pint. When Marsh spoke again, Will could feel that coiled spring pushing a new intensity into his voice. 'I wouldn't have brought this up if it wasn't important.'

Will knew he'd never get Marsh to drop the subject. He pinched the bridge of his nose, fighting off a sudden weariness. When he opened his eyes, Marsh was studying the scars on his hand. Will poured himself another cup of tea as a distraction. 'Very well. What do you want to know?'

'That thing you can do. Is it dangerous?'

The question was so absurd, so unexpected, that it caught Will by surprise. The dread and tension he'd felt came out in one loud, barking laugh. The shopgirls turned to stare at him before resuming their quiet conversation.

'Dangerous? That's your question? If you're seeking a new hobby, Pip, you're better off juggling rabid badgers on a street corner. You might even make a few quid.'

But the jovial tone didn't lighten Marsh's countenance. He spoke again, more quietly. 'That hobby . . . could it kill somebody? Hypothetically.'

'*Kill* somebody?' Will thought back to his grandfather and his dimly remembered father. 'Yes, hypothetically.'

'Could that be done deliberately?'

'I dislike the direction this conversation has taken.'

'I'm not asking how. Just if.'

'In the strictest sense? Yes, it's possible. But nobody would ever *do* it. Regardless of the circumstances.' In response to Marsh's quizzical expression, Will elaborated. 'There are rules about this sort of thing. It's rather complicated. Suffice it to say that invoking the Eidolons to kill a human being would be unwise to a degree I cannot express. Taboo does not begin to cover it.'

Marsh's fingertip spiraled through the beads of condensation on his glass, pulling them together into a single droplet that slithered down to the coaster. He pressed one hand to his jaw, cracked his knuckles, then did the same with the other hand. It meant he was thinking.

'You must forgive my directness, Pip, but just what are you dancing around?'

Marsh nursed his beer. He set it down, centering it on a little cork circle with great attention. Will concentrated to pull Marsh's voice from the pub din.

'You understand this can't go beyond the two of us.'

In spite of his better judgment, Will was intrigued. He agreed with a solemn dip of the head.

'What would you say if you heard tell of a man bursting into flames? Spontaneously. No warning.'

Will stared at him for a long moment. He refilled his cup. He took a long sip, thinking. The tea had gone tepid.

'Fire, you say?'

'Like a Roman candle.'

Now this *was* fascinating. Macabre, but fascinating. Will felt like a character in a penny dreadful. 'How extraordinary. This is the strange thing you witnessed?'

Marsh said nothing, his face blank.

'I know what you're thinking,' said Will, 'but it's rather baroque, don't you think? If I wanted someone dead, there are many easier ways to go about it.' He took a sip of cold tea before continuing. 'Besides which, it's irrelevant. The fact that we're still here tells me it wasn't done by a, ah, hobbyist.' Will disliked using the proper term, *warlock*, in casual conversation.

Marsh looked intrigued by this, but Will didn't elaborate. 'That's a no, then.'

'If you're asking whether I could be wrong, then yes. But that's my opinion.' Will shrugged. 'Such as it is.'

A melancholy half smile creased Marsh's face. 'It's top-drawer, Will. Cheers, mate.'

'Very good, then.' Will tapped his teacup to Marsh's pint. They drank in companionable silence.

Marsh's eyes fixed on the amber depths of his half-empty pint as though scrying. He doodled on the table in streaks of condensation and spilled tea. Will recognized the posture of a man grappling with an unsolved riddle.

He'd had a bad tooth once. The ache swelled until it followed him everywhere, intruded on every facet of his waking life, ceaselessly demanded his attention until he solved the problem and had the accursed thing removed. Unanswered questions rankled Marsh in the same way.

'Mmm.' Marsh set his glass down quickly, foam trickling down his chin. 'One last thing, before I forget.'

'Another mystery? Aren't you quite the sphinx tonight. I may come to regret it later, but I confess I can hardly (no worries, love)—' The frumpier shopgirl knocked Will's chair when she stood to make her way to the ladies' convenience. '—contain my curiosity. Do tell.'

'It may be a while, but I might have something in a few months. Would you be willing to take a look at something, provide your expert opinion on it?'

'That depends, Pip. Look at what, exactly?'

'Better if I don't say right now.' Marsh shrugged. 'It may turn out to be nothing. Are you interested?'

Part of Will wanted to recoil from the offer. The old training, the indoctrination, rose to the fore. Discussing these matters with outsiders was never done, under any circumstances. But he was torn. It would be a welcome respite from working for Aubrey. And he'd already broken ranks, back at Oxford; the damage was long done. A little consultation. What harm could it do?

Will made his decision. 'I am, as ever, your most humble and obedient servant.'

In a far lighter tone, Marsh said, 'Excuse me a moment?'

Will nodded. His friend went off to use the loo, sidling through the crowd that had swelled over the past half hour. Will cocked his arm over the back of his chair. The coquette's friend hadn't yet returned.

'We've been abandoned,' he said.

The woman in the cloche frowned. 'Hmm?'

'I said,' he repeated over the din, 'that our friends have abandoned us.'

'Oh.' The barest of smiles flitted across her face. Her eyes went back to watching the room.

Will sighed. He tried again. 'May I join you?'

She didn't say anything. He joined her. She frowned.

Marsh returned, looking puzzled and then startled when he saw Will sitting with her.

'It's just that my dashing companion and I—' He indicated Marsh with a little flourish of the wrist. '—have been discussing the most peculiar matters. Cosmic matters, no less. But now that's finished and a little light conversation would be the perfect aperitif before supper.'

She cocked an eyebrow at them both, sizing them up.

'Oh, I know, he isn't much to look at.' Marsh glared at him. The woman had a musical laugh, like a carillonneur practicing the scales.

Will continued, 'But that's his modus operandi, you see. Lulling people into a false security. He's quite the devil, I assure you.' He tapped the side of his nose. 'The PM's right-hand man.'

'Does every champion of the Crown blush so freely?'

'*Au contraire.* That's how a discerning eye knows he's the true item.' Will winked. 'Strength through humility, you know. What you're seeing is a rare grace.'

'I see.' She nodded slowly, lips pursed in exaggerated reverence. 'How impressive.'

'William Beauclerk.' He offered his hand to her across the table.

'Olivia Turnbull.' She brushed his fingers with a perfunctory tug. Will slumped in his chair. It took a blunt rejection to sting so sharply. Typically he was more successful with the fairer sex. Typically he usually didn't sound like such a toff when he tried. *Blast.*

The brunt of her gaze fell on Marsh, eyebrows arched in amusement. 'Does your crimson companion have a name?'

'Raybould Marsh. Um.' Marsh held out his hand. She took it. 'Just Marsh, if you prefer.'

'Liv. Delighted.'

'Likewise,' said Marsh, looking poleaxed again.

THREE

3 August 1939
Reichsbehörde für die Erweiterung germanischen Potenzials

Spring and summer brought a host of changes to the Reichsbehörde during the run-up to war. Nobody called it that, of course, but Klaus could see how the little things added up into one coherent picture.

It had begun soon after Spain, when training regimens across the board went to live-fire exercises twice per week. And the training periods with nonlethal combatants doubled in length. 'For endurance,' said the doctor.

Around the time that greenery returned to the surrounding forests, the Reichsbehörde received its first-ever visitors from the Oberkommando der Wehrmacht. But the officers from the military high command didn't come for demonstrations. They came to speak with Gretel. Throughout the spring and well into summer, she attended numerous meetings with the doctor, Standartenführer Pabst, and the officers from the OKW. She never revealed what went on in those closed-door sessions, but Klaus suspected they were strategy discussions. Why else would the Reich's military leadership spend so much time with a precog?

Gretel had been meeting with the OKW off and on for two months when the training regimens underwent more upheaval. Another first: the members of the Götterelektrongruppe started training in teams, no longer as solo operatives. They trained in pairs, trios, and quartets, practiced for every scenario imaginable.

And then – as if the writing on the wall weren't clear enough – an OKW officer took the Twins away on the first day of August. That implied the Reich anticipated a need for rapid ultrasecure communications. No doubt one of the Twins would be ensconced in OKW headquarters for the duration of the war. The other sister's destination was a popular topic of speculation in the mess hall.

'I hear she's going to France,' said one of the mundane troops. They tended to sit together at meals, segregating themselves from Doctor von Westarp's more abrasive children. But Klaus preferred their company to Reinhardt's bluster, and they liked him more than most.

A second man shook his head. He speared a mushroom, popped it in his mouth, and said, 'England.'

Klaus slid aside to make room for Heike. She took a seat next to him, nodding her thanks. They shared a connection through their powers, which although different had similar applications. Heike and Klaus both trained for infiltration, observation, and assassination. Recently they'd begun training in tandem. He took a small measure of comfort in the knowledge that Heike's mastery of her Willenskräfte didn't yet equal his own.

None of the mundanes objected to her company. Conversation faltered for a moment while they admired her. When she wasn't invisible, Heike was endowed with a head-turning beauty. The portrait of Aryan perfection. And Heike was easy company. She even ate quietly.

A third soldier picked up the conversational thread. Around a mouthful of potato, he said, 'England? That's ridiculous. She'll be in Moscow by the end of the week.'

Crumbs flew as he spoke. Klaus smelled cabbage and sausage on the man's breath.

'If you're that curious,' said the second man, 'you know who to ask.' A mischievous grin spread across his face. 'Tell you what. I'll give you a Reichsmark for trying. I'll even double it if Gretel gives you a straight answer.' The soldiers laughed.

'And maybe she'll gamble with us later. We'll make a fortune!' They pounded the table in their laughter.

'I like playing cards.' Gretel stood in the doorway, dinner tray in hand.

The laughter stopped. The soldiers fell silent, suddenly fixated on their dinners. Their heads inched lower over their plates when she approached. Heike had been ignoring the mundanes, but Klaus felt the quiver of tension from her direction as well.

'Can my brother play, too?'

The trio of mundanes abandoned their meals. 'Have to inventory the armory,' muttered one. 'I'll join you,' said another. In moments they were gone.

One of Gretel's long braids tickled Klaus as she settled beside him. She took the fork and half-eaten piece of cake one soldier had left behind. 'Mmm. Chocolate.'

She didn't, Klaus noticed, have any food on her tray. It was stacked with magazines. On top was an old issue of *Time*, an American publication he recognized from the infirmary's reading collection. She was reading about the abdication of Edward VIII and his subsequent wedding.

'Why are you reading that? That's old news.'

'Every girl dreams of her wedding day, brother.'

Klaus finished off his stew before it cooled. He nibbled on Gretel's purloined cake while talking with Heike.

'They're changing the obstacle course again.' Klaus could breeze through obstructions easily enough. But other tasks, such as navigating while inside a wall, still presented challenges.

'Yes,' said Heike. She rubbed her shoulder. Klaus recognized the dark bruises on her clavicle: wax bullets. She hadn't graduated to the live-fire exercises yet. 'And they've hung bells on everything.'

'I think we'll get deployed soon,' he said.

Heike shrugged. 'Some of us.' After that she fell silent again. Her meal consisted mostly of salad with just a little bread on the side. Heike ate greens at every meal.

Klaus and Gretel were finishing the last of the cake when Reinhardt entered. He smiled when he saw Heike. 'Ah! There you are, Liebling.'

Heike deflated. She unleashed a long sigh as she set down her cutlery.

Reinhardt crossed the room to lay a hand on Heike's shoulder. 'I'm disappointed. I'd hoped that tonight we'd dine alone together.'

Heike tossed the dishes of her unfinished meal back on her tray. She stood, and with another brief nod to Klaus, swept out of the hall. Reinhardt crossed his arms, leaning back against the table as he watched her go.

After she was gone, he said, 'You know, Klaus, we're uniquely positioned to help each other, you and I.'

'Is that so?' Klaus almost preferred Reinhardt when he wasn't trying to be charming. The artifice was both irritating and unconvincing.

'Oh, yes. It's no secret that things are changing here. I'll wager even stupid Kammler can see it.'

'Hmmmm.'

'It's only a matter of time before I'm promoted. But I'm afraid your career faces certain—' He cleared his throat, with a meaningful glance at Gretel. '—handicaps.'

Klaus looked at his sister, who didn't react to the insult. 'What's your point?' he asked.

Reinhardt spread his hands in the air. 'All I'm saying is that you could use friends in high places. And when I've moved on, I won't forget the friends I've left behind.' He shrugged. 'Heike respects you, though I can't imagine why. Put in a good word for me, talk her out of this silly and frankly tedious resistance, and I'll return the favor when the time comes.'

You pig, thought Klaus. 'Somehow I doubt that.'

'It's true,' chimed Gretel. 'He'll get what he wants, eventually. She won't resist him forever.'

Reinhardt nodded, pleased by Gretel's prediction. 'Listen to your sister, Klaus.' He waved a finger in the air as he walked away. 'My offer stands.'

Gretel flipped through her magazine, still reading. 'I like flowers very much,' she said to nobody in particular. 'I think I'd want to be married in a garden.'

4 August 1939
St. Pancras, London, England

Marsh brought a bouquet of forget-me-nots and red carnations when he took Liv to dinner a week after meeting her at the Hart and Hearth. A month after that, she sneaked him into her garret at the boarding house, where they made love during a window-cracking hailstorm. A day after that, Marsh finagled a two-month advance out of Stephenson, added it to the cash he'd already saved, rode the Tube to Knightsbridge station, and bought a ring at Harrods.

He presented it to Liv on her birthday. They set the wedding for Marsh's birthday.

Liv, like Marsh, preferred a small ceremony. She was visibly moved when Stephenson and his wife, Corrie, offered to host it in their garden; she understood the significance of that place in her future husband's life.

Although he wasn't particularly religious, Marsh had taken to attending Sunday services with Liv. The Church of England vicar who had baptized Liv and eulogized her father agreed to preside over the nuptials.

The day had dawned gloomy and overcast, but the good fortune that had attended their courtship from the start saw fit to give them a blue sky by early afternoon. Corrie had draped the garden wall with ivy garlands and streamers of crepe paper. Marsh sucked in a sudden breath when Stephenson escorted Liv into the garden under an arbor strewn with hyacinths and roses. The sunlight on her milky skin and simple white gown made her luminous.

Will gasped. 'You've outdone yourself,' he whispered.

'You have it, right?' said Marsh.

'Have what, Pip?'

Marsh turned. Will winked.

'You're terrible,' said Marsh as he turned back to admire his approaching bride. The Stephensons' tiny garden seemed ten leagues long. He'd never seen the old man move so slowly. But he knew he'd forever hold behind his eyelids the image of Liv under roses with daffodils in her hair.

'One of us has to be. Your bride is a perniciously civilizing influence.'

Marsh cast about for a retort, but then Liv and Stephenson joined them, and all he could think was, *I'm getting married. This is real. I'm marrying this amazing, stunning woman. She's marrying me.*

It was a simple ceremony, brief as it was small. Liv, like Marsh, had little in the way of family. In addition to Will and the Stephensons, the only guests were Liv's mother and a maiden aunt from Williton. Liv's auntie didn't approve of Marsh, but she teared up and tossed rice just like the rest.

Marsh and Liv took their first dance barefoot in the grass while listening to a scratchy recording of Vera Lynn. He kissed his wife, touched her, inhaled her.

'I wish we could stay like this forever,' he said.

'Hold me, fool,' she said, head on his shoulder.

Stephenson produced a bottle of champagne and seven flutes. Will waited until everybody held a glass before raising his own.

'Raybould and I first met at university, meaning I've known him longer than most, with two notable exceptions.' Will nodded at the Stephensons as he said this.

Then he turned to Liv's mother. 'Mrs. Turnbull, I imagine you find yourself wondering, "Who is this charming, clever, handsome, and fascinating man?"' She nodded meekly, looking delighted but nervous. 'It is my great pleasure to put your mind at ease, madam.' Will took her hand, kissed it, and said, 'My name is William Edward Guthrie Beauclerk, and I am pleased to be at your service.' Laughter. 'But perhaps you also wonder about this strange man who has stolen your daughter's heart.' Nervous smiles from mother and auntie. 'My first impression of Pip was that he was coarse, neither handsome nor clever, utterly lacking in passion, rudderless, and without direction in life. But I give you my solemn word, madam, that I was utterly mistaken in every regard. Well, most.' More laughter. Marsh's face ached as he struggled not to grin like a fool.

Next, Will turned to address Liv. 'Now, Olivia, all joking aside. I've known your husband for more than a decade, but in all that time I've seen him speechless exactly once. And that was when he met you, my dear. It takes a remarkable person to defeat Pip's quicksilver mind. You're more than a match for him, and in that, you've won him forever. Trust me. I know the man.'

Then it was Stephenson's turn for a shorter and gruffer toast: 'This is the second time you've made a mess of my garden, lad. I trust you won't make a habit of this.' Marsh laughed, looking at his feet to hide the blush creeping into his face.

Stephenson turned to Liv. 'You're a delightful lady, Olivia, and far too good for him. I only wish he'd met you sooner. Much, much sooner.' She laughed, too, her face shimmering with tears.

They drank. Will barely touched the champagne to his lips, and spit it back in the flute when he thought nobody was looking. He shrugged awkwardly when he caught Marsh watching him. But Marsh was too preoccupied to feel anything other than amusement.

The little garden party stretched into evening. Marsh danced with his mother-in-law, and Liv's auntie, and Corrie, but mostly with his wife. As the sky turned pink in the west, Will offered to take Liv's bleary-eyed mother and yawning aunt back to their hotel. Corrie took Liv inside to wrap up a watercolor of her choosing.

Alone in the garden, Stephenson and Marsh clinked their glasses together. 'You've done well,' said Stephenson.

'I know,' said Marsh, staring after his wife as she entered the house.

Stephenson drained his champagne in one gulp. When Corrie shut the door, he said quietly, 'You've had a lot on your mind, but I hope you haven't forgotten about Milkweed.'

Inwardly, Marsh sighed. 'No.'

'Good. Because the film's ready for an audience.'

'Took long enough.'

Stephenson agreed. He nodded toward the back gate, where Will had departed with Liv's family. 'Still think your specialist will shed some light for us?'

6 August 1939
Westminster, London, England

'Oy! Keep yer bleedin' fingers off that goddamn film, Yer Highness!'

Will jumped away from the projector as if an adder, rather than acetate, were coiled about the reel. He lowered himself into a chair facing the far end of the room, where a Scot in gray overalls continued to curse while struggling to unfurl a screen.

'My apologies,' Will murmured. He'd been through a lot in the past hour; he didn't feel quite himself. His knees had gone wobbly and he hadn't quite regained his balance.

Pausing before he launched another volley of curses at the tripod, the Scot asked, 'Why the hell is he here?'

'Because he's our local expert,' said Marsh.

The man with the projector screen snorted. 'He is, eh? That's just bloody wonderful,' he muttered.

'Don't mind him.' Marsh joined Will at the table. 'How are you feeling? You look . . . pale.'

'Well, it's rather a lot to take in, isn't it?'

Marsh's message had been vague, saying only that he'd very much appreciate Will's opinion on a matter. Will had suspected it might have had something to do with their conversation in the Hart and Hearth back in February, the evening they'd both met Liv. But, having already agreed to provide his assistance, and being more than a little curious, he cheerfully attended this strange meeting in the Broadway Buildings. The concrete edifice stood a couple of streets south of St. James' Park, just down from the eponymous Tube station, and a ten-minute walk from Buckingham Palace. Will had dismissed it as an uninspired government building.

He hadn't known it housed SIS headquarters.

Or that his dear friend, for whom he'd stood as best man not a week earlier, was a spy.

As for Stephenson, Will had always regarded Marsh's putative father as a bristly but harmless codger. But the old man had seemed anything but harmless when he'd shoved a copy of the Official Secrets Act in Will's face. Technically – as Will now understood, thanks to Stephenson's rather alarming speech – the Act was law within the United Kingdom, so he was bound by its provisions whether he knew it or not. This may have been Stephenson's attempt to comfort a bewildered newcomer. It didn't. But by making Will sign a sworn oath that he would abide by the terms of the OSA, he'd guaranteed that Will would pay attention and take the matter seriously.

The Scot finished with the screen. He returned to the front of the room, where he took up the eight-millimeter film reel and started threading it through the projector.

Will asked, 'Pip, how long have you been an agent of the Crown?' He rubbed his palms on his knees, slowly warming to the subject.

Marsh gave him a guilty half smile. 'Since leaving the Navy.'

'Ah. I see. And all the time I believed you worked for the Foreign Office . . .'

'I'm afraid so.'

'Ah. Recruited you out of the Navy, did they?'

'No, it was before that.'

'Oxford?'

Marsh hesitated. He started to answer, but stopped when the door opened. Stephenson entered, carrying a file folder. The old man latched the door behind him.

Ah, thought Will. *So that's it.*

'It was a long time ago,' said Marsh.

'Does your blushing bride know about this?'

Stephenson and Marsh shared a quick, fraught glance at each other. Something unsaid passed between them. Will knew with certainty he'd just resurrected an uncomfortable topic. But the moment passed before he could find a way to gracefully rescind the question. Stephenson joined the gruff fellow at the projector, where they spoke quietly.

His eyes on Stephenson's back, Marsh said, 'Look, Will. Were it the least bit possible, Liv would know all. But she's safer the less she knows. And I will do anything – *anything* – to protect her.' Again Will felt that sense of a powerful spring uncoiling inside Marsh, a warning tremor of intensity. Marsh pointed at the projector. 'Which in fact is why we're here.'

'I think we're ready,' said Stephenson. 'Time for you to get these gentlemen up to speed, Commander.' He walked along the wall, pulling every window shade until the room would have been dark if not for the light of a single lamp.

The announcement created opposing reactions inside Will. He shook off the tremor of unease, the sensation of a last chance slipping away. *If I leave now*, he thought, *I've seen no secrets and there's no harm done.* But as childish as it may have been, he also felt a tingle of excitement. *William Edward Guthrie Beauclerk, special consultant to His Majesty's spies!*

And as far as breaking ranks with the other warlocks went, he'd already done that at the Bodleian, years ago. It may have been a foolish thing to do, but the damage was already done. By helping Marsh now, Will could turn that foolish indiscretion into something good.

The Scot took a chair on the other side of Marsh. Marsh scooted his own chair back a bit so that he could address Will and the other man.

'First things first,' he said. 'Will, meet James Lorimer. Lorimer, meet Lord William Beauclerk.'

Will offered his hand. 'A pleasure.'

'Aye.'

As they shook hands, Will noticed mottled discolorations on Lorimer's fingers. The man was older than he or Marsh, too, closer to Stephenson's age. Perhaps his late forties. He enjoyed the occasional cigar, too. The smell wafted from him, and his thick black beard was dusted with ashes.

Will couldn't help but look down at himself: the Savile Row shirt of sea-island cotton, the double-breasted suit, the pocket watch. Perhaps the breast-pocket silk had been a step too far in this company. He could see Lorimer making the same evaluation as they looked each other over. Then again, Will hadn't known what to expect of this meeting.

Marsh continued. 'Lorimer knows part of this story, and you know a different part of it, Will, though you may not realize it.' And then he launched into an incredible tale: sneaking into wartime Spain to meet a Nazi defector; spontaneous human combustion; a half-charred filmstrip; a gypsy woman with wires in her hair.

Had it been somebody else telling the story, Will would have laughed it off as a fevered hallucination. Instead he had to accept the notion that in another century Marsh would have been the real-life hero of a Rudyard Kipling adventure.

What am I doing here?

'And that is how we recruited Lorimer into our little family,' said Marsh, gesturing at the Scot. 'He was a sergeant back in the Great War, connected with the Army Film and Photographic Unit. Later he went to work for the General Post Office Film Unit. We needed somebody who could reconstruct the Tarragona film. Somebody good.'

Lorimer said, 'Reconstruction's a bold claim. You haven't seen the end result, boy. Stitched it together as best I could, but there's a fair bit missing. Had to make wild guesses in some parts. Even so, that film . . .' He trailed off, shaking his head. Then he pointed at Will. 'Remind me again. What's His Highness doing here?'

Marsh said, 'Stephenson and I feel, based on what little we've seen, that Jerry is on to something unnatural. Having seen the entire film, you may agree.' Lorimer canted his head, as if to say *perhaps*. 'To best deal with this, we need an expert in the unnatural. Will is a, ah . . .'

'Oh, for heaven's sake, Pip. Let's get over heavy ground lightly, shall we?' Will turned to face Lorimer and Stephenson behind him. He took a deep breath. 'My grandfather was a warlock. My father, too. While I didn't follow in the family hobby, I have had the training.'

Lorimer looked disgusted. 'This is unbelievable. Five months. Five months I've worked on that sodding filmstrip, nightmares for free, and for what? So that you can hand it off to this chinless wonder.' He stood.

Stephenson laid his one hand on the man's shoulder. 'Sit down.' Lorimer took his seat again, grumbling. 'We didn't hire you for your beliefs. You're here as a film expert, and as such, you'll do your goddamn job.'

Will recoiled. The old man had a steely core, unpleasantly like his grandfather.

'It's no hoax,' said Marsh. 'I've seen it.' The look in his eyes was clouded and distant. Will knew he was back at the Bodleian. Marsh shook his head, as though clearing his thoughts. He pointed to Stephenson's file folder. 'Is that what I think it is?'

Stephenson took a seat at the head of the table. He flipped open the dossier and slid it in front of Will, Marsh, and Lorimer. 'This is everything we have on Doctor Karl Heinrich von Westarp.'

It was, Will noticed, a rather thin file. A single photograph clipped to the top page depicted a grainy black-and-white head shot of a man showing the first hints of baldness. He wore round wire-rimmed spectacles and a thin mustache. The graininess made Will think the image had been enlarged from a portion of a larger photo.

'Born in Weimar, Germany, April 13, 1872. Only child to Gottfried and Marlissa von Westarp. Wealthy family, owned quite a bit of land. Father died in 1899; mother died in 1915. He was apparently self-taught in his youth, and attended the University of Heidelberg starting in his mid-twenties, from 1896 through 1902. Quite the scholar. Studied philosophy, chemistry, physiology, and history. Wrote a well-received treatise on Nietzsche. Didn't obtain his letters in history, however. He may have had a falling out with the faculty.

'After Heidelberg, von Westarp came to Britain to study medicine at King's College, London. Stayed there until 1908 before returning to Germany.'

Marsh sat up. 'He was here.'

Will said, 'Thirty years ago, Pip.'

'This,' said Stephenson, tapping the photograph, 'is our only image of the man. Class photo from King's, taken on the day their medical degrees were conferred.

'After that, our man disappears for the next ten years. We've been unable to turn up any sign of him prior to autumn of 1918, when he popped up again in Munich. Where he became one of the founding members of the Thule-Gesellschaft.'

Marsh whistled. 'I'll be damned.'

Will shook his head, knowing he'd just missed something important. He looked back and forth between Stephenson and Marsh. 'I'm a bit lost here, gents.'

'Thule Society. Bunch of Teutonic occultists,' said Marsh. 'And anti-Communists, and anti-Semites.'

Upon hearing this explanation, Lorimer took on a more contemplative demeanor. His eyebrows pulled together in a small frown. Will remembered that Lorimer was the only person in the room who had so far seen the reconstructed Tarragona filmstrip.

'But von Westarp didn't stay with the Thulies very long. Had a falling out with them, too, within a year.'

'Do we know what caused this rift?'

'No. All we know for certain is that by 1920 he had returned to Weimar, and converted his family estate to a foundling home.'

'A *what*?'

Stephenson read from a card in the folder. 'Yes. The Children's Home for Human Enlightenment.'

Marsh cracked his knuckles, thinking. Almost to himself, he said, '"His children. Von Westarp's children." Krasnopolsky mentioned them.'

A wave of unease came over Will, closely followed by the memory of a long-disregarded myth. 'Why the sudden interest in children? What prompted this?'

Stephenson shrugged. 'Unknown. But our assets in the area have uncovered announcements in the local papers dating from around that time. Warnings of an outbreak of Spanish flu at an orphanage just outside of Weimar, warning people to stay away.'

'Is that true?' Will asked as he studied the doctor's photograph. Perhaps it was an artifact of the grainy reproduction, but the man seemed to regard the camera with a cold, almost clinical expression. Even on what should have been a joyful occasion. 'Was there such an outbreak?'

'Impossible to say. Von Westarp ran the orphanage as a private enterprise, funded with his own money. There are no public records. No death certificates.'

'So he was taking in kids,' said Lorimer, 'but at the same time he didn't want outside visitors.'

Marsh added, 'And he ran the whole thing on a country estate, family land. Plenty of room for hiding things.'

Lorimer voiced the key question. 'What was he doing?'

'Isolating them,' Will murmured, almost to himself. 'Seeking the ur-language.' The others glanced at him, expecting elaboration. Stephenson appeared particularly keen to know Will's thoughts. But Will was preoccupied with legends and myths, hoary old tales of the first warlocks.

'Whatever it was, the orphanage ran quietly for most of a decade. Until '29, when Himmler gifted von Westarp with the rank of SS-Oberführer.' Stephenson closed the file. 'Here ends the lesson. Now let's see what Krasnopolsky died to bring us.'

Lorimer stood. He turned off the lamp, plunging the room into darkness before the clattering projector tossed a bright white square on the screen and the wall behind it. Lorimer nudged the projector, centering it.

The film began with the Crown seal, and this notice:

MILKWEED / GRACKLE

MOST SECRET

UNAUTHORISED DISSEMINATION OF THE
INFORMATION CONTAINED IN THIS FILM
CONSTITUTES TREASON AGAINST THE UNITED
KINGDOM OF GREAT BRITAIN AND NORTHERN
IRELAND AS DEFINED BY PARLIAMENT IN THE
OFFICIAL SECRETS ACT OF 1920. PUNISHMENT UP TO
AND INCLUDING EXECUTION MAY RESULT.

MILKWEED / GRACKLE

Well, thought Will, *I'm in it now.*

The room strobed dark and light so quickly that Will's eyes ached in the effort to keep up. A parade of images flashed on the screen, sandwiched in moments of darkness. The dark frames were placeholders, he realized, representing the portions of film damaged by fire. After the reel spooled past the outer-most layers where fire had done the most damage, the dark stretches grew shorter. But not enough to make viewing easy or comfortable.

Will struggled to absorb the surreal tableaux. A shirtless man hovering twenty feet above an orchard. Half a second of nothing but a brick wall, then a nude woman standing before it with no transition. A young man with pale eyes laying his hand on an anvil, the film shimmering, the metal sagging. Another man standing halfway inside a wall, like a ghost. A muscular fellow on a leash (a *leash?*) scowling at a mortar emplacement that imploded upon itself. The ghost man standing in front of a chattering machine gun. The leashed man scowling at an upside-down tank. A soldier throwing something at the anvil man, and a flash.

The subjects of the film wore belts with dark leads running up to their skulls. Each and every one of them. Repeated viewings didn't make it any less horrifying.

They watched the film again. And again. And again.

Will was so wrapped up trying to assemble the images into a single story — trying to conceive of how von Westarp had achieved these unnatural results — that it wasn't until the third viewing he noticed an obvious problem.

'There's no sound,' he said, breaking the silence.

'Of course there's no bleedin' sound,' said Lorimer. 'It's a silent fucking filmstrip.'

'That's a shame,' said Will. When Marsh asked him why, he elaborated. 'If we could *hear* those proceedings, it would be a great boon. Alas, that's not an option.'

'So you do think this is supernatural?'

'Are you not watching the same film as I, Pip? Because I believe I just witnessed a flying man. A *flying man*. That is not natural.'

Stephenson said, 'What are those things they wear? The belts, and the implants.'

Will shook his head. 'Honestly, I haven't the faintest idea. This is a form of the craft utterly unknown to me. But I'd like to know how it works.' It looked like magic without blood. Was that even possible?

Marsh looked at Stephenson, then back to Will. 'You'll do it, then? You'll help us?'

'I am at your service,' said Will.

'Welcome to Milkweed,' said Stephenson.

FOUR

The Götterelektrongruppe sped through a moonlit forest in a six-wheeled Panzerspähwagen. Klaus rode in the back, along with a massive store of replacement batteries. The road swerved around hills and dipped through gullies. The armored scout car had minimal suspension; every bump in the road jostled the occupants as they sped along.

A two-hundred-meter-wide swath of old-growth forest and underbrush disappeared in their wake, flattened and incinerated in an orgy of willpower. On the left, impenetrable stands of beech and spruce disappeared behind the bulwark of blue fire racing alongside the truck. On the right, centuries-old oaks and sapling firs disintegrated as though ripped apart by a giant thresher.

The car was designed for a crew of five; they numbered six. Reinhardt and Kammler sat in front, crammed next to their driver. Buhler huddled behind Kammler, in the gunner's seat. His leg jounced up and down as he yanked on the imbecile's leash. Gretel was in the rear, next to Klaus, where the radio operator normally sat. She sat with her head tipped back, eyes closed but looking ahead.

Reinhardt and Kammler drained their packs with wild, amphetamine-fueled abandon. Klaus relayed new batteries up front as his comrades swapped out the depleted packs. At first they had stopped every few kilometers to change the batteries. After a while they had found a rhythm, though, and now they moved like clockwork.

They were the tip of the spear. By morning, the three Panzerkorps of German Army Group A would barrel through the newly opened forest, circumventing the Maginot Line and tearing into France's soft, undefended interior.

Their leaders called it Operation Sichelschnitt: the cut of the sickle.

The engine rumble made a contrabass counterpoint to the white noise *whoosh* of fire and imploding wood stock. Outside, the night smelled like the workshop of an overzealous carpenter, singed sawdust and pulped lumber. It stank inside the car. Kammler had crapped himself.

'Crush. Crush. Crush,' Buhler rasped. Hours of screaming, then chanting, the same mantra had given his voice the texture of sandpaper.

At some point during the night, they crossed from Belgium into France, though even with a map it was impossible to tell when or where.

Gretel sat up. She said, 'Fortification, two minutes ahead. Sentries will hear us forty seconds from now.' Klaus shifted his weight as their driver, a combat driving specialist reassigned from the elite LSSAH unit of the Waffen-SS, applied the brakes. 'Seventy seconds from now. Ninety.' The truck puttered to a stop. 'The sentries will not hear us,' Gretel concluded.

She turned, smirking. 'But Hauptsturmführer Buhler will fall in a thistle when he goes to piss in the woods.'

'Crazy bitch. You say that every time we stop. You're trying to make me hold it all night.'

She shrugged.

Everyone climbed out. Buhler handed Kammler's leash over to the driver, who wrinkled his nose. The crackle of underbrush receded as Buhler strode off to relieve himself. Reinhardt leaned against the cab. He lifted a cigarette to his mouth with trembling hands. The amphetamines had him wound so tightly, he almost vibrated. Moonlight shone in the whites of his eyes. A tiny orange flame momentarily engulfed the tip of the cigarette. Klaus knew that the cigarette wouldn't mask the taste in Reinhardt's mouth.

The heavy fortifications – the *grands ouvrages* – of the Maginot Line didn't extend through the Ardennes. The forest had long been considered impassable with heavy armor. And so it had been, until tonight.

But the French had sprinkled smaller fortifications – *petits ouvrages* – through the portion of forest that extended across the border. These, too, had to be destroyed to ensure the flawless roll-out of the Blitzkrieg. Klaus's ability was useless for clearing timberland. But he had no equal for clearing fortifications.

Klaus hefted a pack from the overloaded car. He checked the contents. Thirty kilograms of PETN were sufficient to tear open the heaviest *ouvrage* like a tin can. But when detonated *inside* the steel-plated walls, it would turn the fort into a meat grinder.

Gretel joined him as he double-checked the gauge on his battery harness. She pointed. 'That way. Follow the gully until you reach the clearing. You'll find the fort in the crook between two hills.'

'How are you feeling?' Klaus asked. 'Do you need a new battery yet?' She didn't say anything.

Klaus had advocated a plan where Gretel stayed behind, away from the battlefront, relaying her directions via the Twins. But in order to plumb the next twelve hours and shepherd them safely to the other side, she first had to twine her future with their own. Or so she insisted.

Twined futures hadn't helped Rudolf.

'Why don't you stay with the truck? It'll be safer than—'

She raised a hand, cutting him off. She cocked her head. A moment later the rustle of underbrush and a muffled 'Damn it!' drifted out of the silent forest.

'Thistle,' she said. Klaus sighed.

A stream of invective preceded Buhler all the way back to the truck. 'Crazy fucking mongrel whore,' it concluded.

They regrouped. Reinhardt crushed out his cigarette. Buhler took Kammler's leash again. 'Stay here,' he ordered the driver. The pale-faced zealot saluted.

They tromped off along the gully that Gretel had pointed out. Klaus led with his sister at his side. Behind them followed Reinhardt, Buhler, and Kammler. Run-off from recent spring rains splashed beneath their boots. They pushed through a thicket the hard way – Reinhardt and Kammler were too wound up on amphetamines to perform subtleties of Willenskräfte.

They crawled on their stomachs just under the lip of the ravine as the underbrush gave way to a tiny clearing. An *ouvrage* loomed before them in the shadows. It looked like an inverted breadbox pimpled along the top with retractable machine gun turrets.

Klaus adjusted the straps over his shoulders. He reached for the clasp on his battery harness.

'Wait,' Gretel whispered. 'Let the sentries pass.'

She patted him on the side. He looked at her. Occasionally,

when meeting her gaze, he saw something coiled up in her madness, steely and cold. But tonight the moonlight stilled the depths behind her eyes. She smiled. A real smile, with even a hint of warmth.

Her hand lingered. 'Go now, brother.'

Klaus took a deep breath and plugged in. The taste of copper flooded his mouth. He crested the streambed and headed for the fort. Nine inches of steel and concrete ghosted through his eyeballs, his bones, his thumping heart. The French fortifications presented as much resistance to Klaus as an open window presented the wind.

Smaller forts like this could house a few hundred fighting men, depending on the internal configuration. This one was shaped like a T. A subterranean garrison at the long end of the central tunnel probably held two hundred men or more. But it was the middle of the night, and most of the troops slept through Klaus's silent infiltration. He entered at the top of the T, between the two gun turrets.

He set the first demolition charge at the mouth of the tunnel sloping down to the barracks. He set the timer for one minute before moving toward the far end of the fort.

The pair of yawning soldiers up in the turret didn't notice him until they heard the *thump* as he dropped another bundle of explosives at their feet. This one Klaus set on a fifteen-second delay.

The gunners jumped down. At first they stared at him, bleary-eyed and confused. Comprehension slowly dawned as they took in his uniform.

'Intruder! Intruder!' One raised an alarm while the other tried to shoot Klaus. The bullets passed through him and pinged off the wall.

Klaus ignored them. He returned the way he had come, and was just passing the tunnel entrance when an explosion ripped through the turret behind him. The concussion reverberated throughout the building. The quickest soldiers came up from the garrison just in time to meet the shock wave from the shaped charge that Klaus had planted. Smoke filled the passageways.

Klaus dropped the rest of his ordnance under the second turret before exiting through the wall. The third blast shook the earth as he rematerialized outside.

Gasping fresh air into his lungs, he called the all clear.

Reinhardt, Buhler, and Kammler came charging up.

'I said, all clear. What's going on?'

Reinhardt said, 'Gretel said you needed help.'

'What?'

'Said you screwed up. Again.'

'I did no such thing. Look! It's done.' Plumes of oily smoke roiled out of the view slots in the turrets at either end of the casemate.

When they returned to their hiding spot in the streambed, it was empty.

Klaus looked around. 'Where's my sister?'

'Must be waiting back at the truck.'

But Gretel wasn't there. Only the driver, who jumped to attention upon their return. Buhler flew into a rage.

Oh, Gretel, what have you done? She'd run away, and now she was alone in what would soon be a war zone.

Klaus wondered what would become of him. Doctor von Westarp and Standartenführer Pabst would naturally assume he had been complicit in his sister's defection. The night's first twinges of fear squeezed his chest.

But even more than fear, he felt resentment. Gretel had

wandered off, probably chasing her own amusement, unconcerned by the situation it created for him.

He slumped against the side of the truck, hands crammed into his pockets. Paper crinkled where there had been none before. He unfolded the note.

His eyes traced the loops and swirls of Gretel's spidery copperplate. *Dear Brother*, it began.

10 May 1940
Soho, London, England

'Oh, damn.'

Will tried to set down the telephone hand piece but instead tossed it on the desk when it slipped out of his hand. It clattered against the Bakelite cradle and set the bells inside to humming. The gauze bandage wrapped around his hand made him awkward; the cotton packed against his palm made it difficult to grip things. Especially with sweaty fingertips.

Opening the window had admitted no end of traffic noise, the rumble of omnibuses and taxis, but not the slightest hint of breeze. It did, however, give the tobacco smoke somewhere to go after it seeped up through the loose floorboards from the Hart and Hearth down below. The biggest gaps bordered the broad stonework chimney that extended from the pub's hearth through the second story and up to the roof above. The chimney, a welcome source of heat in winter, imposed itself on the broom-closet office like a tidal wave of stone frozen in the moment before breaking.

He'd frittered the day away working for his brother's charity, as he did several times per week. The work put a public face on

his support of the war effort, at a time when most able-bodied
men his age had joined up. They'd been able to lease the space
over the pub cheaply because Will was the only person willing to
brave the creaking staircase and endure an afternoon in the
hotbox, as Will tended to think of it. Still, he preferred the space
above the pub to working out of the home, or from the club. It
offered seclusion when Will chose to pursue his own little project
for the war effort.

Most of a year had passed since they'd screened that
damnable film for him. And they'd made very little progress since
then. Von Westarp's methods remained opaque as ever, the
whereabouts of his 'children' unknown.

But Will felt confident, and proud, that he could change that.
Soon after joining the Milkweed effort – a grandiose name for
four men with nothing to do – Will had returned home to
Bestwood. He'd stayed there just long enough to collect a few of
his grandfather's papers before returning to London.

Will's language skills, once rusty through years of neglect, had
improved in the past nine months. And now he felt ready to propose his idea to Marsh, when the fellow returned from France.

Today, however, he'd spent doing real work for the charity
rather than poring over grandfather's lexicons. Aubrey thought
it might be wise to devote fund-raising toward the victory garden
program. Will had promised to get a few heavy hitters on board,
give the whole thing a higher profile. And so he'd spent hours on
the telephone.

Or would have. A strange day all around. Half the time, the
lines were jammed. The other half of the time, it seemed nobody
could be bothered to answer the telephone. Like the entire city
had nipped out for a moment and never come back. He hadn't
heard any laughter or snippets of conversation drifting up from

the pub, either, as he usually did. Even the traffic was more subdued today, as though burdened with a peculiar self-consciousness.

The telephone rang. *Finally*, Will thought.

'Good afternoon.'

'Will?' said a tentative voice with a common accent.

'Olivia! This is a surprise. What can I do for you, my dear?'

'I'm rather embarrassed to have to ask this of you, but Raybould isn't home yet. I rang the neighbors and even John and Corrie, but I'm afraid nobody's home.' She sounded nervous. That made Will nervous.

'Let me assure you it is impossible to impose upon me. So have at it.'

'I think—' She paused, sucked in a breath. '—I'm having the baby. Could you ride to the hospital with me?'

'Oh.' Liv's words sank in. 'Oh!' He jumped out of his chair, knocking it over. 'I'll be there at once!'

She must have heard the commotion, because she let loose with her musical laugh. The laugh he admired so much.

'Relax, Will. It's not happening this instant. But do get here soon, please?'

'Quick as I'm able.'

'Cheers.'

Two thoughts tumbled through Will's mind as he gathered up his bowler and briefcase. *A baby! I'll be an uncle, in spirit if not in fact.* But then, on the heels of that excitement, an itch of concern at the back of his mind. *Why aren't you home yet, Pip? Why would you miss this? You were supposed to be back this morning.*

Down on the street he hurried in the direction of Piccadilly, where he'd be sure to hail a cab if he couldn't find one sooner. A vigorous constitutional was the balm for an unsettled mind. Or so his grandfather used to say, the miserable old bastard. Pain twinged through Will's hand.

He passed the Queen's Theatre and turned right on Shaftesbury. The usual West End hustle-bustle, the press of too many people and too little sidewalk, didn't materialize as he ventured through the theater district. It was too early in the day for the shows, and hence for the taxis.

Quite a few men were across the Channel right now, of course. The few people he did pass shuffled around him shrouded in nervous energy, clutching newspapers or looking at him without seeing him. He passed the marquees of the Apollo and the Lyric, garish adverts in a long expanse of somber brick. Calendulas lined flower boxes on the sills of upper stories, fiery eruptions of red and yellow in a gray marble canyon.

He found the missing crowds when he reached Piccadilly. Men and women mobbed a newsstand three-deep. The stand was a tiny thing wedged between a jeweler's and a tobacconist, facing the Shaftesbury Memorial in the center of the circus. The fountain itself stood unadorned, the statue of Anteros having been removed to safety in the countryside soon after the outbreak of war the previous autumn.

Will nudged his way to the front of the crowd swarming the newsstand.

'Hi, hi, paper man.' Coins jingled in his palm. 'Give us a – hell.'

Will dropped a shilling's worth of change atop the vendor's stack of papers. Several pence rolled off and tinkled underfoot. The *Times*'s headline told him why it had been such an odd day, why such a pall hung over the streets, and why Marsh hadn't made it home: the Jerries had invaded France. The Phony War was over.

He hopped from the curb into the traffic whirling around the circus. Brakes screeched. To the colorful invective of a cabbie he replied with a fiver and an address in Walworth, south of the river. Will absorbed the salient details from the paper during the ride: blitzkrieg; French forces in disarray; PM Chamberlain stepping down.

Marsh had gone to France a little over a week ago on business for MI6. But as far as his wife knew, he'd gone to America with a delegation from the Foreign Secretary's Office, in hopes of procuring more support from the Yanks. A perfectly safe, if somewhat hopeless, mission.

Will left the paper in the taxi. He thrust another handful of bills at the driver, and told him to wait. He bounded through the front gate of a two-and-a-half-story mock Tudor house. *Rapraprap.* He rapped again. *Raprapraprap.*

Liv answered. The frown tugging at her mouth and eyes disappeared when she saw him. Pregnancy in its final stages had rounded out her face, put a flush into creamy skin.

'Hi, Will. Thanks for coming.'

'Liv, my dear, terribly sorry to be so late, beastly of me, I know, particularly in your time of need, had something of a bother finding a cab.' It came out more rushed than he'd intended. He took a breath.

She ushered him inside. He squeezed past the bulge of her belly straining at the blue wool of her WAAF uniform.

'Goodness. Don't tell me they still have you chained to a switchboard all day?'

'It's better than sitting here, waiting.'

Will wasn't surprised that Liv had held her situation as long as she had. Liv was a force of nature when she wanted to be. And, of course, her husband's employer had connections. Typically,

WAAFs, Wrens, and other women who found themselves PWP – pregnant without permission – got sent home for the duration. It happened commonly: 'Up with a lark, to bed with a Wren,' as the saying went.

'Nobody would fault you if you chose to evacuate. Pip least of all.'

Liv shook her head, hands resting on her stomach. 'Not until he gets to meet our baby.'

Our baby. You and Pip. But if life had turned out differently . . . Will shoved the pang of envy aside, sobered by thoughts of France. *It may be* your *baby from now on, Liv.*

He closed the door for her, nudging it past an end table with his bandaged hand. A bowl of water and a folded wool blanket sat on the table, for covering the door in case of gas attacks.

'Oh, my. What happened to your hand, Will?'

'This?' He flexed his hand, checked that blood hadn't seeped through the new bandages. 'Bashed it with a spade,' he lied. 'Aubrey's gone on a tear about the victory gardens right now. Bloody sharp, those things.' He tapped the side of his nose. 'It's Hitler's master plan, you know. Do us all in with gardening mishaps.'

'Hmm.' She looked upstairs, her hand still on her stomach. 'I haven't finished packing. My suitcase is in the—' She teetered for a moment. —'oof . . .' Will jumped to her side. 'In the bedroom,' she finished.

Will led her to a chair in the den. 'You rest. I'll pack your things. Think of me as your Passepartout.'

He dashed up the stairs and found the bedroom immediately. It was a small house. A suitcase sat open on the bed. It felt a bit voyeuristic rummaging through Liv's and Marsh's things, but he tried not to dwell on that. Especially while he packed her undergarments. Will made something of a mess as he tried to be quick without leaving anything obvious behind. He grabbed a toothbrush from the bathroom on the way back down, hoping it was Liv's.

Back downstairs, he found Liv composing a note for her husband. She smiled as she wrote it.

Will took several careful breaths so that he could put as much nonchalance into his voice as he could muster. 'Heard from Pip, have you?'

She shook her head, signing the note.

'Still in America, getting the Yanks to lend a hand?'

She nodded. 'Yes.'

'Well.' He hefted the case again. 'Your carriage awaits,' he said, offering his arm.

'I'm not infirm, Will.' Color crept down the curve of her neck, where a few strands of auburn hair had pulled free of her bun.

'No, but you're walking for two.'

Back in the cab, the newspaper reinforced Will's concern that Liv was about to give birth unaware that her husband was trapped in a war zone. The neighborhood blurred past them. Getting Liv to the hospital had become a matter of personal honor for the driver.

Liv said, 'Did we remember to lock the door?'

'I'm quite certain we did. Trust your Passepartout. Speaking of which, will you have enough around the house? With the little one to feed? Do you need extra ration books? It's no trouble. My brother—'

'I'm not going to *cheat*, Will.'

'No, no. Of course not. But you'll let me know if you need anything, won't you?'

She patted her stomach. 'We'll be fine.'

But what if it's just the two of you from now on?

The conversation ranged to baby names (Will suggested Malcolm, for a boy), mutual acquaintances, and whether America would enter the war.

They pulled up at a hospital in the shadow of London Bridge. As the driver carried Liv's case to the entrance, Will helped her out of the cab: 'Please remember, Liv. If you're ever in need of anything, don't hesitate to say. Leaning on His Grace is my God-given talent.'

She looked at him with suspicion in her eyes. But then another contraction hit, and the issue was dropped.

10 May 1940
Mézières, France

Stealing a motorbike turned out to be a bit like *riding* one. The skill came back quickly, Marsh found.

A violet spark leapt between two strands of copper as Marsh touched them together. It made the alley smell of ozone. He spat out bits of rubber, tasting blood; he'd stripped the wires with his teeth. The BMW sputtered once, then died. He tweaked the throttle on the second try. The sputtering relaxed into the regular *brum-pum-pum-pum* of a four-stroke.

He inched out of the alleyway into chaos. Cars, trucks, carts, bicycles, and pedestrians glutted the narrow cobbled street. Word of the invasion had spread, and like the orders from a field commander, it had mobilized an army of refugees. An opening appeared ahead of a truck. Marsh gunned the throttle. He darted past the truck and spun the bike around. Gravel kicked up by his U-turn rained on the refugees and their vehicles. In return he received the blare of horns and a few gestures.

The more panic gripped France, the harder it would be for Marsh to get an accurate picture of what had happened. On the other hand, the chaos made it easy to steal a motorbike without attracting notice.

Getting out of Mézières required driving against the flow of traffic. The avenues were little more than glorified cow paths, best used for guiding livestock. They predated motor cars and weren't conducive to a spontaneous evacuation. Marsh treated the traffic like an obstacle course. After one close call with the steaming grille of an overheated farm truck, he made the outskirts of the hamlet.

Good thing Liv didn't see that. He imagined the way her fingers danced along her belly when she was startled, the way she used his first name when she was upset.

Once on the open road, he opened the throttle as far as it would go. He sped east, toward the Ardennes Forest, and the advancing German armor.

Probably best she doesn't know about any of this.

Another invasion front had also opened up to the north, in the low countries of Belgium and the Netherlands, but that came as no great surprise. France and Britain had put such an offensive at the center of their strategy for dealing with the inevitable German invasion. The British Expeditionary Forces and their French counterparts were positioned for exactly this contingency. But it was the penetration of the supposedly impassable Ardennes – in large numbers and with heavy armor, by some accounts – that had caught the French off guard. And thus interested Marsh.

The French had taken the impenetrability of the forest for

granted. So much so that they'd incorporated it into the Maginot Line, treating it like a natural extension of their defenses. Cutting through the Ardennes enabled the Jerry panzers to circumvent the fortifications and press into France against a paltry armed resistance.

Marsh's stomach lurched. Both wheels left the road for an instant as he topped a swell in the road. The BMW flexed under his weight as it touched down at the bottom of the rise. He fought to keep it upright on a track made soft by a week of late spring rains.

The rains of recent days had coaxed a quiet exuberance from the land. Beech and oak trees had shrugged off their lethargy and erupted into new foliage. The woods smelled of new life, a clean start. Marsh blew through patches of sunlight and shadow on the sun-dappled road so quickly that his eyes couldn't adjust. He squinted, but it didn't help him see into the shadows along the roadsides.

It occurred to him he had no idea how far west the Jerries had advanced. The shadows might have hidden anything. He wrenched the throttle again.

The road skirted a field. A farmer directing a horse-drawn plow waved at him.

The sleepiest and most isolated outposts hadn't received the news yet. They'd find out soon enough. Perhaps when they woke up under a swastika.

It was only by accident that Marsh himself had heard the account that piqued his interest.

Outwardly, the Low Countries maintained a policy of strict neutrality. They refused to prepare openly for a German invasion, for fear of provoking one. Secretly, however, they had been negotiating with the Anglo-French Entente for over eight months.

Some of these talks took place in small, unremarkable villages throughout the countryside in order to preserve their privacy. Stephenson had tapped Marsh for liaison duty during the latest round of arrangements between the various intelligence services.

It wasn't part of T-section's duties. But the old man had exercised his clout to get Marsh put on the job, on the slim chance their colleagues from other nations had information about von Westarp or the Reichsbehörde. Marsh knew it was a desperation move, because Milkweed was starved for information. Nine months was far too long to go without new developments.

Still, Stephenson's decision was little appreciated by Marsh. It meant leaving his wife, lying to her, days before their first child's birth. It meant listening to French blustering and Belgian dithering when instead he could have been waiting on Liv, serenading her, making her laugh.

But then the reports had come. Marsh had been sitting next to his French counterpart when a breathless gendarme burst in the room. Everyone knew what it meant.

The gendarme had hurried across the room, kneeled between Marsh and his counterpart, and whispered more loudly than was prudent, owing perhaps to fear or adrenaline. His report bleached the color from the other man's face.

Then Marsh's counterpart had stood, announcing through the thick brush of his handlebar mustache: 'Gentlemen. The Germans are moving.'

But the gendarme had phrased it differently. *The Germans have burned through Ardennes.*

Perhaps it was a colloquialism.

Perhaps not.

But *something* unusual had happened.

More refugees glutted the road as Marsh neared another

village. He eased off the throttle. A single maniac racing *toward* the front was bound to raise eyebrows. They watched him as he passed. In their eyes he saw uncertainty and fear braided together.

He turned down a street filled with the warm-yeast smell of fresh bread. Marsh's stomach gurgled. Some people chose not to run. Where could they run? The German war machine was just a few hours away, and moving fast. Invasion or no, people still had to eat.

The bike jittered over irregular paving stones, needling his irritation. *In and out. A quick look around, then back to Liv. That's all.* The quicker, the better.

As he crested into the valley on the far side of the village, he caught a whiff of something swampy. The Meuse, farther down the valley. If the Germans stopped to regroup, the river would be a likely place to do so. If he wanted to see the Ardennes first-hand, he'd have to find a way around.

He sped up again. The road descended into a wide green basin quilted with checkerboard fields and hedges, torn down the middle by the dark, sinuous Meuse. Farther down, the steeples and clock towers of Sedan shone in the sun. The chiming of a carillon echoed across the valley.

The morning's meeting had disbanded immediately after the gendarme delivered his news. But before fleeing to the Channel, Marsh had paused just long enough to send a report.

Two words, fired into the ether with a machine gun burst of dots and dashes: 'Crowing monarch.'

The first word flagged the message for Stephenson.

The second implied a connection to Milkweed.

The association with that morning's invasion would, Marsh hoped, be self-evident.

After that he struck the transmitter and vacated his room at the inn, intent on getting back to Britain. But then he saw the motorbike leaning against the alley fence. Free for the taking.

The petrol gauge reported the tank three-quarters empty. Enough to reach the Ardennes, but not enough margin to get out again, too. He slowed once again as he entered Sedan, eyes peeled for a chance to refuel the bike. If he were fleeing the invasion, he'd make damn sure his truck had a spare petrol canister.

The world had become steadily more surreal as he sped toward the Ardennes. Sedan was no exception. News of the invasion must have reached a town of this size. Yet for every person hurrying out of town, somebody else clung to daily routine. Aproned shopkeepers swept the sidewalks outside their establishments while people assembled for morning Mass. Quite a few people, in fact.

Their eyes and bodies radiated anxiety. They moved quickly, skittishly, like songbirds expecting a house cat to leap out of the bushes at any moment. And they studied their surroundings intensely. The passage of a stranger drew a great deal of attention. Wary gazes followed him as he threaded the town.

Marsh stopped at the first alley he could find, a lane wedged between an apothecary and a tailor. It was so narrow that he had to dismount before entering.

A woman sat by herself at the café across the street, reading a book. The fog of panic settling on Sedan didn't touch her. It wasn't even clear if the café was open for business; either way, she looked serene, unmoved. She glanced up as Marsh hopped off the motorbike. She looked down again when he noticed her, hiding her face behind long hair and the fringe of her kerchief. Marsh pushed the bike into the alley. He stowed it behind a rubbish bin.

He peered around the corner before emerging. People on the street paid him no attention, intent as they were either on fleeing the Germans or clinging to the comfort of routine. The woman at the café twirled a finger through one black braid while she read.

The lightheaded feeling of déjà vu swirled through him, made him dizzy. Marsh watched himself watching this same woman, as if he'd done it before. Something about the hair, the kerchief—

Wires.

He'd seen her before. In Spain. At first he hadn't recognized her, she'd been so badly beaten previously. Which had caught his attention the first time around. The ferocity of her bruises had made her stand out amongst all the other refugees at the port.

And, of course, she had the wires in her head. Just like the subjects of the Tarragona film.

Am I losing my mind? How is this possible? What the hell is she doing here?

She looked up again. Marsh ducked back in the shadows, thinking. He abandoned his attempt to visit the Ardennes.

A windblown newspaper rustled down the alley. Marsh tucked it under his arm. He waited until more refugees passed down the street in front of the café. When a Peugeot piled high with a family's belongings shielded him from her view, he darted out of the alley and into the apothecary.

The apothecary filled his order with quaking hands. His attention almost never touched on Marsh, hovering instead on the steady stream of traffic past his shop.

Marsh tried to keep the slow traffic between himself and the café as he worked his way up the street. He circled the building and crossed the street out of sight from the café. He sidled up the avenue with the newspaper draped over his Enfield revolver.

A short baroque wrought-iron fence ringed the café. Marsh stepped over it rather than risk a creaky gate. He wove around tables set with glass vases and spring daisies that shone white and yellow in the late-morning sun. He approached the woman's table from behind.

The corner of her mouth quirked up when he sat down.

In French, he whispered, 'There's a gun pointed at you under this table. Try anything, anything at all, and I'll put a bullet in your gut.'

She turned a page, not looking up. 'No, you won't.'

She spoke English tinged with a German accent. Her voice was throatier than he'd expected from one so petite.

'Try me,' he said. 'Who are you?'

'No.' She shook her head, smirking. 'The real question is who are *you*, Raybould Marsh?'

Shit. He fumbled the revolver, nearly shot her in the leg before he regained himself. His liaison work for the Entente had been under a false name. Even Krasnopolsky hadn't known his name, back in Spain over a year ago.

Before he could gather his wits to press further, she dog-eared the page and set the book down. It was a collection of poems by T. S. Eliot: *Prufrock and Other Observations.*

'I suppose you'll want to drug me now.' She nodded at the pocket where he'd placed the vial and cloth from the apothecary. She had large dark eyes.

What the hell is going on? Who is *this girl?* She carried herself with a supreme confidence that shook him.

Marsh struggled to keep the unease from his voice. 'We're leaving now. Together.' To make his point, he gave her a glimpse of the gun. She stuck her tongue at him.

He stood. He took her arm as though helping her up.

'Wait.' She grabbed the daisy from the vase on her table. 'For later,' she said.

Marsh escorted her from the café, his arm around her waist. She sighed, as if content. He pulled her into an alley, expecting a struggle. But she didn't fight him. Nor did she resist when he rolled the newspaper, stuffed it with cotton from the apothecary, and applied the diethyl ether he'd purchased. He'd prepared to do it all one-handed while restraining her.

Instead she waited placidly for him to apply the ether cone over her mouth and nose. She winked at him before slumping into his arms. Her head rolled sideways, revealing a wire taped to her neck. It extended under her blouse.

He carried her to the street. He flagged down a passing car. 'Help! Help, please. My wife is very ill.'

Keeping her unconscious during the relay race back to Britain was a challenge. People frowned upon a man who drugged his wife. But he'd anticipated this, so he'd also purchased chloral hydrate. Slipping it into her water – 'Drink up, dear, you're not feeling well' – worked best. People always plied the ill with fluids. Things got easier after he met a regiment from the BEF and could abandon the artifice. Still, he watched her for the entire journey.

Who was she? She knew him. She had *waited* for him.

Had they been watching him since Spain? He fought the urge to hunch his shoulders, to gouge away the target etched between his shoulder blades. Then he thought of Jerry spies staking out his life. Perhaps they were watching Liv this very moment. He clenched his jaw until he felt a headache coming on. Anger and frustration made his face feel hot.

They crossed the Channel in the cargo hold of a Dutch

merchant ship running supplies for the BEF. As soon as he had privacy, he untied the kerchief over her hair. He traced the wire bundle from a bulge at her waist – probably a belt like those in the film – up her back, neck, and into her scalp. At the back of her head it split into four smaller wires, each connected directly to a different location on her skull. When he sifted through the hair on her scalp, thick black locks that smelled of sweat and dirt and wood smoke, he found her skull riddled with a monstrous assortment of surgical scars.

What was she?

He needed a closer look at her belt, too, but couldn't achieve that without stripping her naked. It would have to wait until he got her to Milkweed.

The mysterious woman woke again during the passage across the Channel, perhaps roused by the choppy waves knocking on the hull beneath them. Marsh reached out to dose her with more ether.

'Wait.' She grabbed his wrist.

His skin tingled under the intense warmth of her fingertips.

She fished in the folds of her dress for the café daisy. 'Congratulations.' She handed it to him, adding, 'It's a girl.'

Then she pulled his hand to her face and passed out again.

FIVE

Marsh arrived home before sunrise. But for the chatter of song-birds ushering in the dawn, the city was quiet in this hour when the distinction between night and morning lost its meaning. The blackout kept the streets dark.

Though Liv had been sleeping fitfully in the past few weeks, he didn't want to ring the bell and risk waking her. He fumbled through his pockets, seeking his house key. Several moments passed, during which he envisioned the key jostling out of his pocket during his motorcycle ride (had that been just yesterday morning?), his encounter with the girl, or during the bumpy Channel crossing. He even started to wonder if the girl had picked his pocket, but then his fingers brushed the cold metal.

The door swung open, sending bright light spilling down the steps and into the street, when he pushed the key into the lock.

The door was unlocked. It hadn't been latched. And the lights were still on.

Exhaustion resisted him as he forced his mind into focus again. Too many hours on constant alert had frayed his nerves, but a single thought burned through the fog in his mind. Just hours ago he'd been speculating about Jerry spies watching him and Liv.

A set-up. Oh, God, how did I miss this for so long?

Marsh slammed the door behind him. 'Liv? Liv!' His voice echoed through a quiet house. He trotted from room to room. She wasn't in the den; she wasn't in the kitchen. He went to the garden, hoping that perhaps there'd been an air raid alert and she'd simply fallen asleep in the Anderson shelter. But she wasn't there, either.

Back inside, he bounded up the narrow stairs two at a time. The bedroom was a scene of disarray: the drawers of Liv's wardrobe stood open, and her clothes were strewn across the bed and floor.

Scenarios, event sequences, spooled out in his head. He captured the girl in France ... her handlers contacted assets in London ... they snatched Liv in retaliation.

No, no, no, no. It made no sense.

But if the girl knew him, she probably knew something about this, too.

I'll yank those goddamn wires from her head one by one.

Marsh had the telephone in hand, ringing Stephenson, when he found the note: *Darling – Labor started. Have gone to hospital with Will. Love, Liv. xx P.S. Stop worrying, you lovely fool!*

She'd taken the time to leave a message, knowing how terribly he'd fret if he came home to an empty house.

The sudden release of tension left his knees weak. Marsh slumped against the wall, not knowing whether to laugh or cry. He did a little of both.

Hailing a cab at this hour was out of the question. Marsh covered the first two miles to the hospital on foot. He would have run the rest of the way, too, but for an alert ARP warden just coming off his watch at dawn when he heard the echo of Marsh's footsteps down the street.

'Olivia Marsh? Olivia Marsh?' At the hospital he chanted her name like a mantra, confronting people with it. A nurse directed him to the room Liv shared with two more new mothers.

Liv slept propped up in bed, her head tipped to one side and her mouth slightly open. Sweat had plastered her hair to her forehead, but now it had evaporated, leaving her bangs frizzy, disheveled. Dark bags hung beneath her eyes. Her face was round and puffy.

She'd never been more beautiful.

And in the crook of one arm, held close to her chest, nestled a bundle of pink swaddling.

Marsh tiptoed across the room to Liv's bedside. He leaned over her, tugging as gently as he could on the folds of blanket to get a first look at his baby.

'Hi, you,' said Liv in a hoarse voice. She smiled. It was an exhausted smile, but it touched her half-open eyes. 'You're home.'

Marsh kissed her sweat-salted lips. 'I'm so sorry I wasn't home sooner. I'm so sorry.'

Liv lifted the bundle. 'Meet your daughter.'

His baby felt lighter than a snowflake. Her tiny face was bright red, and her eyes and mouth were scrunched together under folds of baby fat. Wisps of pale hair traced across her perfect scalp like gossamer.

She smelled marvelously. She smelled like family. Her silken skin tickled Marsh's lips. He hadn't shaved, so he took care not to let his whiskers scratch his daughter. Nothing would *ever* hurt her. He'd tear the world apart, brick by brick, if he had to.

Liv scooted over on the narrow bed. Marsh lay on his side, cradling their daughter between them.

'You look absolutely manic,' she said. 'I left a note.'

'I found it. Eventually.'

'I'm glad you're home.'

'Me, too.' He kissed his daughter and his wife again. 'Me, too.'

In spite of his exhaustion, hours passed before the cogs in his head finally ground to a stop so he could sleep.

Congratulations. It's a girl.

11 May 1940
Westminster, London, England

The invasion of France forced Will's hand. He'd planned to pitch his idea to Marsh before approaching Stephenson. But Marsh was stuck somewhere in France with the Jerries closing in. Will had to speak with the old man at once.

To hell with von Westarp. They needed to find Marsh, and Will knew how to do it.

Will tried SIS HQ first, knowing Stephenson hadn't finished moving his office to Milkweed's new space in the Old Admiralty. The old man had used his clout to turn Milkweed into a semi-autonomous agency isolated from the rest of SIS. By declining the promotion his seniority deserved after Admiral Sinclair died, Stephenson gained a few favors from Lieutenant Colonel Menzies, the new C.

But Stephenson wasn't in the Broadway Buildings. Will decided to cut through the forty acres of St. James' Park on foot, because walking to the Admiralty was easier than riding the Tube to Charing Cross and then backtracking.

He exited the park directly across Horse Guards' Road from the Admiralty. He found Lorimer having a smoke on the steps. It appeared the Scot was having a rest. But then Will saw that Lorimer was studying something in his lap. It looked like a belt with a strange battery attached to it.

A smoldering cigar hung from the corner of Lorimer's mouth. The man smoked less frequently these days; good tobacco was hard to come by. Lorimer looked up as Will approached. He removed the cigar from his mouth with fingers discolored by long exposure to developing reagents.

'Missed the excitement, Yer Highness.'

'So I gather. I can't find Stephenson.'

Lorimer jerked a thumb over his shoulder. 'Just returned from meeting the new PM.' He paused to puff on his cigar, then added, 'He took the film with him.'

'Ah.' The old man hadn't wasted any time briefing Churchill on Milkweed. 'Good. I need to speak with him about Marsh.'

Another puff. 'They're in the cellar.'

'They?'

'Marsh, Stephenson, and the prisoner.'

'He's back?' Giddy relief flooded through Will, followed by confusion. 'Wait. Prisoner?'

Lorimer waved off the question while he took another puff. 'Have Marsh explain it to you. I'm busy.' He focused his attention back on the battery, turning it this way and that.

'I certainly intend to,' said Will. He bounded up the stairs two at a time. Near the top, he paused, patted his pockets, and turned. 'Oh, damn. Hi, Lorimer, I wonder if you'd part with a cigar?'

'You don't smoke.'

'Heavens, no. Dreadful habit. Can't abide it.'

'I had a shit time getting my hands on these.'

'Ah. Well. It's for a good cause. Morale, you know.'

Lorimer fished another cigar from the breast pocket of his overalls. He handed it over, grumbling. 'My last.'

'Brilliant.' Will tipped his hat to Lorimer. 'Cheers.'

The space beneath the Old Admiralty was a rabbit warren of vaulted brick tunnels that intersected in groined arches. They extended almost to St. James' in the west, under Whitehall in the east, and practically to the Admiralty Arch in the north. The fortified section had less character, gray concrete corridors lit with naked lightbulbs that cast severe shadows.

Will found Marsh and Stephenson standing outside one of the storage rooms at the end of a long corridor. The pair spoke quietly, occasionally peering through the square window of glass and wire mesh set high in the steel door.

Marsh was saying to Stephenson, 'And then she gave me this.' He twirled a daisy in his fingers. The crumpled flower had seen better days. A petal fluttered to the concrete at Stephenson's feet like a bit of crepe paper.

Will cocked an eyebrow as he took in the flower. 'You devil, you. I see it clearly now: a trail of broken hearts across France, winsome milkmaids and Parisian grandes dames.'

Stephenson ignored him. 'She didn't say anything else?' he asked, again staring through the grille.

'No. I dosed her after that. Hi, Will. And nothing of the sort. It's—'

'I should hope not,' said Will. With a little flourish he produced the cigar and popped it into Marsh's mouth.

Marsh jerked back in alarm, yanked the cigar from his mouth. 'Blech.' He spat. Marsh didn't smoke. 'A simple "congratulations" would suffice. Blech.'

Will laughed. 'I'd get used to this if I were you. I believe it's traditional.' He pounded Marsh on the back.

Stephenson indulged in a little chuckle. 'He's right.'

'So,' said Will, 'boy or girl?'

'Girl,' said Marsh. He smiled, but the hard light highlighted the dark papery skin under Marsh's eyes. It made him look gaunt. And his hair was mussed. The poor fellow looked as though his last sleep had been several days ago. In a haystack.

'You look awful,' said Will.

'I've heard.' He started to turn toward the window again, but then the stopped and turned. 'Thanks for getting Liv to the hospital, Will. I can't thank you enough.'

'It was nothing, Pip. I was glad to help, and as it happened your neighbors had left her high and dry.'

Marsh nodded more thanks, but a strange look passed between him and Stephenson as he did so.

Looking back and forth between them, Will asked, 'And what, pray tell, has kept you from your loving wife? You made a rather hasty exit from the Continent, I gather.'

Marsh summarized the events of the past several days. Just as he'd done with his Spanish adventure, he made it all sound routine: secret meetings, speeding toward the German army, capturing a foreign agent.

After Marsh wrapped up his story, Will pointed at the window through which Stephenson had been peering. 'Our new guest?' Stephenson nodded. Will peeked inside the makeshift brig.

The storeroom was empty but for a cot. A woman lay across it, hair fanned about her head like a sable halo. Darker-skinned than he'd expected. She had bony ankles.

'Heavy sleeper, is she?'

'I dosed her as we entered the city. Better if she doesn't know where we are.'

At this, Will rolled his head back, feeling dense – *Ah, of course. I'm hopeless.* Again he caught the glance flickering between Stephenson and Marsh.

'I sense you chaps are hiding a bloody great secret.'

'She knows things, Will.'

'Things?'

'She knew my name. And that we'd just had a girl.'

Air whistled through Will's teeth as he inhaled. Though he was a tyro in this business, he understood Marsh's liaison work for the Entente, and meeting Krasnopolsky, had both been carried out under false identities. And if those had been compromised—

'A mole?'

'Or,' said Stephenson quietly, 'we have to consider the possibility that somebody has been watching Marsh. Perhaps watching each of us.'

The news made Will feel naked, exposed. He suppressed the urge to glance over his shoulder, but only just. 'Why? And since when?'

'Since Spain would be the logical conclusion,' said Marsh. He pointed through the window. 'And there's more. Look. She has the wires.'

'No?'

Marsh nodded. Will's palms slapped the door as he pressed himself to the window for a closer look. 'I'll be damned.' He couldn't see anything under all the hair. 'I don't recognize her,' he said.

'She's not in the Tarragona film,' said Stephenson.

Oh, hell. Nothing for it, then. 'Ah. Well. Speaking of that, and since I have you both here – though you ought to be home right now, my friend – that's something I wanted to discuss.'

Stephenson said, 'At last. You have an answer for us?'

'No and yes. As to what von Westarp has done, and how, I still can't say.' Stephenson frowned. Will continued, before Stephenson could object: 'But! There's a way to find out. It's a bit drastic ... In fact, I came looking for you,' he said, pointing to Stephenson, 'to suggest instead using this approach to find Pip in France.' He grinned at Marsh. 'Glad we didn't have to.'

'How *do* you propose we obtain this information?'

'Simplicity itself,' said Will, expressing a confidence he didn't feel. 'We ask the Eidolons.'

'Who the hell are the Eidolons?'

'Not *who*, Pip. *What*.' In response to blank stares, Will elaborated. 'A warlock doesn't perform magic. A warlock isn't a magician. A warlock is a negotiator. A warlock changes the world around him by petitioning an Eidolon to circumvent the laws of nature. The Eidolons, being entities that exist ... outside ... of space and time, acknowledge no such laws.' He looked at Marsh. 'That night in the Bodleian? The thing you felt was the passage of an Eidolon not quite noticing us.'

'Jesus Christ,' said Marsh.

'I fail to see how this helps us,' said Stephenson.

Will said, 'It's clear from the film that whatever von Westarp has done, it's quite unnatural. That means the Eidolons are involved. But the most vexing thing about that film is how it shows no evidence of the negotiations. Which has made his methodology a deuce to unravel.'

'So,' said Marsh, warming to the subject, 'we just ask these Eidolons to tell us how the Jerries are doing it?'

'More or less.'

'It can't possibly be that simple.'

It won't be so bad, if I'm properly prepared.

Will rubbed his aching hand and shrugged. 'Mostly.' He pointed at the makeshift brig. 'In fact, our little guest is a boon. Having her on hand could simplify things.'

'We've got Lorimer at work on her belt,' said Marsh.

Stephenson nodded. 'Set it up, Beauclerk. I want it done as soon as you can. And you,' he said, squeezing Marsh's shoulder, 'go home. That's an order.'

Will slapped him on the back again. 'I'll walk out with you.'

Marsh pulled him aside when they reached the top of the stairs. 'I need to ask something of you.'

'I am, as always, your servant. What can I do?'

'Look, Will,' said Marsh, looking at his feet. 'First, I'll always be grateful to you for looking after Liv while I was away. But now I need you to keep your distance from my family. Just until . . .' Marsh made a vague gesture that encompassed their surroundings. '. . . until this is over and things go back to normal.'

Will took a step back, feeling slapped. 'Why?'

'Because if they're watching us, we have to keep as separate as possible.' Marsh raised his voice, perhaps even without realizing it. His eyes flashed. 'I can't protect my wife and daughter with you leading the Jerries straight to the bloody house. When I arrived this morning, the door was unlatched. Practically wide open. Was that you?'

The question, and the accusation veiled within, caught Will off guard. 'I, I don't know. Perhaps—'

'Well, it was you, or it was the Jerries rummaging through my house after you'd taken Liv. Didn't occur to you to watch your surroundings, did it?'

'I stood for you at your bloody wedding.' The words came out forcefully, propelled by bitterness and hurt. 'I *introduced* you.' Will's voice echoed in the corridor. 'You wouldn't *have* Liv if it weren't for me.'

Liv deserved better than to be cloistered from the world. She would suffocate. If Will understood that, why couldn't Marsh? The man didn't know what he had. Will spat, 'She isn't a china doll and she isn't a trophy. Were she my wife, I'd have the respect to warn her of danger.'

Marsh's eyes narrowed, and he pulled himself to his full height. Though he was still shorter than Will, his anger gave him a palpable force of presence. Will had never seen him truly angry; he immediately regretted his words. Marsh tamped down on the fire in his eyes with visible effort, leaving just a smoldering irritation there.

'Stephenson's arranging to have one or two men from SIS keep an eye on Liv and the baby, to find our watchers. Anything more runs the risk of drawing attention to Milkweed. Including your visits.'

'Haven't I at least earned the privilege of meeting your daughter?' Will's question acted like a bellows blowing fresh air on hot coals.

But Marsh swallowed the anger again. This time he shrugged, as though physically shaking it off. 'The war will be over soon, and then things will go back to the way they were.' He patted Will on the arm. 'Honest.'

Will knew that pressing the issue would only start a row when Marsh clearly wanted to avoid one. He resigned himself to hoping for a quick end to the war, so that he could visit with Liv again and meet Marsh's daughter. Someday he'd get to be an uncle. 'Can you at least relay my congratulations and best wishes to Liv?'

'Of course.' Marsh tried to lighten the mood. 'By the by, does Lorimer know you stole one of his cigars?'

Will played along, though he didn't feel like it.

12 May 1940
0°41'13" East, 50°26'9" North

It creaked and it sweat, this submersible coffin.

Every few minutes another bead of water rolled down the hull, leaving behind a trail that glistened like tears on the face of some iron leviathan. The droplets formed around the welds and rivets where the hull plates joined together. The submariners called it sweat; they said it was condensation from inside the boat.

But to Klaus's eyes it looked like the English Channel bleeding through the steel skin of Unterseeboot-115.

It was nearly as cramped as the box that Doctor von Westarp used to punish him. The crew – made more crowded than usual, and therefore more churlish, by Klaus's presence – breathed one another's breath, breathed air tainted with a hydrocarbon cloy of diesel that lingered long after the engines had been switched to electric power for silent running. He could have escaped the constriction by drawing upon the Götterelektron, but that would have meant dipping into the store of extra batteries they carried. And Gretel had been vague on why they were necessary.

He needed to rest. Though how anyone could sleep on a U-boat defied imagination. Every time he closed his eyes, another creak or groan echoed through the boat. And then his eyes would pop open, and he'd watch another bead of water rolling down the hull, and he'd be achingly aware of the ocean poised overhead to crush them at any moment.

He wished the submariners hadn't told him about the mine-fields. The Channel had already claimed several U-boats; the coast of Scotland was a safer insertion point. But this route was faster, and the Reich's commanders had every reason to expect a successful mission: Gretel had foreseen it. Or so she led them to believe. But as for the ultimate fate of the submarine, she had also kept that vague. This mission might include a three-mile swim to shore, and it would be just like Gretel not to mention it.

He squeezed his eyes shut, concentrated on breathing. He forced himself to relax, to take in air with a slow, relaxing rhythm.

The hull groaned as the boat sliced through the sea, changing depth once again.

Three days since he'd had any sleep. Before long, he'd start hallucinating.

Klaus pulled the crumpled paper from the breast pocket of his uniform. Soon he'd have to change clothes, but as long as he could get away with it, he wore his uniform. The Göt-terelektrongruppe insignia on his collar raised eyebrows and more than a few confused glances among the crew. They hadn't learned to fear it yet. Not so with his rank insignia. He was an SS-Obersturmführer. That, at least, these submariners under-stood.

He unfolded the note he had found in his pocket on the night of the Ardennes offensive.

Dear Brother: By the time you relay the contents of this note to Standartenführer Pabst, I will be in the custody of our enemies . . .

12 May 1940
Milkweed Headquarters, London, England

'Have you come to take me to the ball?'

'Get up.'

Marsh hauled the prisoner to her feet from where she'd been sitting cross-legged on the cot. He pulled her arms behind her back. So thin were her wrists that the handcuffs, twin bracelets of cold iron, hung loosely on her feverish skin.

She craned her neck to peer at him over her shoulder. 'No flowers?'

With his hand between her shoulder blades, he nudged her out of the cell. The ridge of the wire beneath her frock rolled away from the pressure of his fingers.

'But you presented a bouquet to Olivia when you first took her to dinner.'

The twisted, unexpected invasion of privacy riled him. Were the prisoner a man, Marsh wouldn't have hesitated to give him a little shove. And the prisoner, unable to catch himself, would have taken a tumble on hard concrete. A petty thing, perhaps, but it would make the point.

Threaten my family, will you?

But at that moment, looking up at him with faux innocence, she seemed so fragile. He remembered the bruises on her face when he'd first glimpsed her in Barcelona. Marsh also remembered the surgical scars. She'd been treated terribly, and she was too small to defend herself.

How could she have known about the corsage? A lucky guess, perhaps ... but she also knew Liv's name, and about the baby. And she had known Marsh was carrying ether in his pocket ... *And* she wore the same kind of battery harness seen in the Tarragona film.

Was she a mentalist of some sort? A mind reader?

Perhaps she couldn't stop herself from saying the things she did. Perhaps she'd blurted out something she saw in somebody's mind, some dark secret, and received a beating in return.

'How do you know the things you do?'

Her eyes widened in a caricature of harmlessness.

He tried a different tack. 'You act like you know me. Perhaps you also know that you're better off here than you were with your companions.'

Silence.

'We just want to understand what von Westarp did to you, and why.'

When she wanted, the woman had one hell of a poker face. It slid into place now, an expressionless mask.

He sighed. 'Don't ever mention my wife again.' As he took her elbow and led her toward the stairs, he added, 'Or my son.'

She twisted around to look at him again, a frown tugging her eyebrows together.

'Aha.' Marsh snapped his fingers. 'Gotcha.'

Her eyes narrowed; her expression frosted over.

Milkweed enjoyed a fair bit of seclusion in this disused corner of the Old Admiralty. It more or less had its own stairwell between the cellar and the second floor. Which meant that Marsh could get the prisoner upstairs without piquing unwanted interest. He kept a firm grip on her forearm – enough to prevent her from running, not enough to bruise her – as he escorted her past the offices that Stephenson had wrangled for the project. Several still stood empty but for gunmetal-gray filing cabinets and second-rate wooden desks adorned with typewriters that predated the Great War. Most rooms either had no furniture at all, or had been used for storage.

By day, these rooms along the rear of the building enjoyed a view of St. James' Park. Sunset over the park shone through a gap in the blackout curtains. Marsh pulled the prisoner aside and fixed that.

At Stephenson's insistence, they gathered in one of the smaller, interior rooms. Easier to keep out prying eyes and ears. Will had indicated that the location was immaterial.

Lorimer was there already, as was Stephenson. Marsh set the girl on a stool in a corner farthest from the doorway. He unlocked her handcuffs, pulled her arms around to the front, and then fastened one wrist to the pipe of a radiator. She watched the others with bored indifference.

Stephenson caught Marsh's eye, inclined his head toward the prisoner. *Get anything out of her?*

Marsh gave his head a minute shake as he closed the door. *Nothing, sir.*

Lorimer had determined that the object on her belt was indeed a battery, but of a sort he'd never seen. How it worked and why it was jacked into her skull remained a grotesque mystery. For the time being, it sat unmolested in Stephenson's vault until Milkweed could recruit a few science boffins to help Lorimer reverse-engineer the thing.

Getting a doctor to study the prisoner had been easier. Stephenson arranged the examination under the cover story that she was a rescued victim from the camps. The doctor blanched when he saw what had been done to her, but he studied the woman at length. But the purpose of the wires, and the significance of their locations on her skull, confounded him. He'd claimed there was no meaningful pattern to her scars. It was as though somebody had tried countless different combinations at random.

Many of the scars, he'd said, had formed long before the girl had stopped growing.

Von Westarp's children.

Lorimer came over. He slapped Marsh on the back. 'I hear congratulations are in order.' The prisoner turned to watch them. Marsh looked from Lorimer, to her, and back. The Scot nodded, taking the hint. 'You owe us a celebratory pint,' he whispered.

The prisoner watched everything. Marsh wondered if she knew what they had planned.

Will hurried in, carrying a moth-eaten paisley carpetbag in one hand and a briefcase in the other. He tossed the carpetbag in the corner. It clunked to the floor with the ring of metal on wood.

'Sorry, sorry gentlemen. Sorry I'm late.'

'Nice bag, Will. I didn't know you collect antiques.'

Will doffed his bowler and shrugged out of his suit coat. He hung them both on a rack behind the door. Then he unbuttoned his sleeves. Rolling them up, he said, 'That ugly thing? That's the reason I'm late, actually.'

Marsh leaned down to open the bag, but Will waved him off. 'Hi, hi, no need for that.'

'Then what's it for?'

'If everything goes well,' said Will, 'nothing.'

'And if it doesn't?'

Will's sigh – loud, explosive – dispelled the atmosphere of good humor that normally surrounded him. An angry Will was so rare that at first Marsh didn't recognize the scowl. Will snapped: 'Is a smidgen of optimism so much to ask for, or has that gone on the rationing list, too?' His shoulders slumped. 'Apologies. I haven't slept.' Sounding more like his usual self, he concluded with a feeble smile, 'As to the bag, best not to trouble ourselves with such matters.'

Stephenson joined the others. They huddled together as though part of a rugby scrum. Marsh took care to keep one eye on the prisoner as he listened to Stephenson whisper:

'I don't like this. Why does she need to be here?'

Will said, 'Far easier to query the Eidolons about von Westarp's handiwork if I can point to an example.'

'I still hate it. This thing you can do is our only leg up right now. You want to parade it in front of her.'

'Aye,' Lorimer said.

Will laughed quietly. 'Unless that film is a great hoax, she has seen this all before. Trust me.'

Stephenson frowned, then nodded. The four men emerged from their huddle. Marsh checked the prisoner. She cocked an eyebrow at him with a playful look in her eyes.

From the briefcase Will produced a dish, a tin of safety matches, a bundle of dry twigs, and a sheaf of yellowed papers. The pages were curled and even cracked in places. Will set the sticks atop the dish in the middle of the floor.

'How does this ritual work?' Stephenson asked.

'No. Not a ritual.' Will fixed the old man with a stare, looking serious. 'Negotiation.'

Stephenson shrugged. 'Whatever you want to call it.'

'Hear me now. Rituals and ceremonies are a load of made-up pageantry played out by loonies in robes dancing around bonfires on the solstice. A negotiation is the means of getting something done, for a price.'

Marsh interrupted: 'What kind of price?'

Will waved off the question. 'A trifle. "By the pricking of my thumbs," and all that.' But his gaze flicked to the carpetbag, and for a moment something akin to worry or concern creased his face.

But then his expression lightened. He exclaimed, 'Ah! Speaking of which.' He rummaged in his pockets for a moment before producing a clean white handkerchief and a safety pin. He crossed the room to join Marsh and the prisoner. Will extended his hand, as if asking her to dance, and gave her a little bow. 'Your hand, my dear.'

The prisoner seemed unimpressed.

Marsh asked, 'What are you doing?'

'I need a sample of her blood,' said Will. To the prisoner, he added, 'I'll only take a drop.'

Marsh took her by the wrist and raised her free hand toward Will. Her skin still felt warm to the touch. Will deftly nicked the woman's thumb with his pin. A scarlet bead emerged from the pad of her thumb. Will dabbed at it with the handkerchief, then inspected the small rust-colored stain. He held it up for all to see.

'Yes,' he said. 'This will be sufficient.'

The woman watched it all with an air of bored detachment. But then again, if their suspicions were correct, she had seen scenes like this many times before.

Will returned to the center of the room. 'Now. The principle is very simple. First, we have to catch the attention of an Eidolon. Once we've done that, we negotiate with it. Since we're merely asking for information, and not seeking to circumvent natural law, the price will be minor.'

Marsh frowned. 'Will, it can't possibly be that easy.'

'Ah. Well. There is a catch. The Eidolons don't have the same relationship to the universe that we do. In some sense, they *are* the universe – intelligent manifestations of it. You don't expect them to speak the King's English, do you?' He thumped the stack of papers. 'This is my grandfather's lexicon. The lingua franca of the Eidolons is a very, very ancient language. We call it Enochian.'

Stephenson lowered his voice. 'I still maintain this dictionary of yours is our single advantage at present.'

'She won't pick up a word of it. None of you will. You're far too old.' Marsh cocked his head at this, but Will didn't elaborate. 'Enochian is much too archaic for our lexicons to include terms for modern things like wires, batteries, and brain surgery. And I'm quite certain no warlock has ever had need to express the concept of, well, whatever's been done to her. Trust me. The odds of success are much higher if I can simply show her to the Eidolon.' He brandished the bloodstained handkerchief. 'Which is why I needed this.'

He folded his long, gangly legs beneath himself and sat on the floor. 'Make yourselves comfortable, gentlemen.'

Marsh opted to stand. So did Stephenson and Lorimer.

Will arranged the twigs into a small mound on the dish. 'This part isn't strictly necessary,' he said, 'but it's how I was trained. Helps me focus.' He lit a match and touched it to the kindling. The flame licked at the wood. 'Be warned that once we catch the attention of an Eidolon, things might seem a bit odd.'

'Odd?'

'It's tempting to say that reality warps around the presence of an Eidolon, but that's not quite right. If anything, they're more real than we are. So rather, reality follows them. Orbits them. Things become more real than you might otherwise be used to. It can be unsettling.'

Marsh shuddered, remembering the Bod. And *that* had merely been the *passage* of an Eidolon; it hadn't dallied. He asked, 'What should we expect?'

'Hard to know. Phantom smells, sounds, visions. Maybe nothing. It's different every time. Now shush.'

Aromatic cedar smoke trickled up from the burning tinders. It stung the eyes. Will stared into the flames.

Marsh pressed the backs of his fingers up against the smooth curve of his jaw. He cracked his knuckles, waiting for something to happen.

Will breathed deeply, sighed, then pulled an antler-handled jackknife from a trouser pocket. He raked the unfolded blade across the thin pale ridges that lined his palm. Blood welled up from the laceration. It trickled between his knuckles when he clenched his fist.

His lips moved. He mouthed the words, rather than give voice to them. The room was silent but for the crackling flames and the creak of floorboards underfoot when Marsh shifted his weight.

Will spoke.

The man sitting there was, as far as Marsh could tell, the same old Will. But the sounds coming out of him were not. These were not natural sounds.

Rather – they weren't natural for a human throat. It ranged from a bass deeper than anything Will could have produced within his body to shrieks and whistles that weren't heard so much as known.

And then, as had happened one night in Oxford, the room pitched like the deck of a sloop in high seas. Marsh staggered. He leaned against a nonexistent cant in the floor. He wondered how any of this could possibly be captured on film. Is this why it seemed so incomplete?

And then the fire spoke. It was the same language, but now unfiltered through a human vessel.

Enochian was the wail of dying stars, the whisper of galaxies winging through the void, the gurgle of primordial oceans, the crackle of a cooling planet, the thunder of creation. And beneath it all, a simmering undercurrent of malevolence.

We are pollution, a stain within the cosmos, Marsh realized. *And we are not welcome here.*

132   *Ian Tregillis*

Within the altered logic of that room, the reason for Will's self-injury became evident. Spilled blood carried the promise of eradication. *It catches their attention.*

Marsh retreated from the fire on trembling legs. The gypsy woman clenched his arm. Her icy façade had melted away, and in its place hung the visage of a terrified girl. She'd gone pale; she trembled. Her back was pressed to the wall, as though she tried to push herself out of the room.

An awareness suffused the room, the suffocating pressure of a vast intelligence. Something looked at Marsh. Saw him. He grappled with a primal urge to run, to hide, to render himself unknown and unnoticed once more. But hiding was impossible. The Eidolon was everywhere. Every*thing.*

It must have looked at the prisoner, too, because her fingernails drew blood.

My God, Will . . . How can you negotiate with something like this?

Somehow he did. Will conversed with it, like a microbe and a man sharing a common tongue. His attention stayed on the fire, but Marsh knew that in reality – reality? – the Eidolon was everywhere. Inside every atom.

Will rifled through the sheaf of pages on his lap. 'It appears I'm somewhat rustier than I'd realized,' he muttered. When he reached the end of the pile, he started again, flipping through the papers more frantically.

The Eidolon's presence rendered every silence an eternity in a perfect, lightless universe.

Marsh tried to look at his watch. He couldn't tell if it was running in the proper direction.

Will stopped halfway through the pile. 'Oh, dear.' He set down the sheaf of papers with shaking hands.

'Will?'

Very quietly, he said, 'Pip.'

'What did it say?'

'Do us a favor.'

'What is it?'

'I need you to open the bag.'

'What?'

'The bag, please.'

Marsh staggered across the room and zipped open the carpet-bag. It was stuffed with towels and bandages. Nestled beneath the linens were a thin leather cord, a wooden bit riddled with bite marks, and a pair of gardening shears.

'Will?'

'The Eidolon's price,' said Will, 'is a fingertip.'

'Like hell it is,' said Lorimer. 'Tell that thing to lick my nadgers, Yer Highness.'

'Are you out of your mind, Will?'

'I can't do it myself.'

'Then I'd say it won't be done.'

'The price has been negotiated. It will be paid.'

'The hell it will! Tell it to sod off.'

'My friends.' Will spoke in a rigidly neutral tone. The strain of maintaining his composure and concentration showed in the beads of moisture on his forehead. 'One does not renege on these negotiations.'

'Don't be a damn fool,' said Stephenson.

Will made a gesture that encompassed the room, and by extension, the Eidolon. 'My friends. Do you truly want to double-cross it?' In the same strained monotone, he continued, 'The price *will* be paid, regardless of our desires to the contrary.' His voice wavered. 'Mine in particular. At best we can control the circumstances of the payment.' He looked at

Marsh. 'And I'm asking you, Pip, to help me. I can't do it myself.'

'Will—'

'It's waiting. Please. Don't make it worse.'

Marsh felt as though he were trapped inside a fever dream. He watched himself take up the cord, bit, and shears. The curved blades of the shears scraped across the floorboards as he fought for balance on the swaying floor. The noise fell into a gulf created by the Eidolon's presence. Everything sounded hollow and insubstantial.

'I'm not staying for this shite,' said Lorimer. 'I'll find some ice.'

Stephenson barked, 'Get the brandy from my desk, too.'

'No!' said Will. 'Sir. I can't, ah, I have to be of sound mind to finish our transaction.'

Marsh looked between Stephenson and Will. 'Look, Will, I know it goes against your grain, but perhaps you should consider bending your principles this—'

'No. Let's just get it done.'

Marsh struggled to cross the inconstant room.

The floorboards rattled with a heavy *thump*, as if struck with something large.

'STOP!'

Everyone jumped.

Marsh halted in his tracks. 'What was that?'

'You heard it, too?' asked Stephenson.

'Ignore it. It's a side effect of the Eidolon, just as I warned you,' said Will. 'Makes us hear and see things. Real things. And my wish to make this stop right now is very real.'

Lorimer paused on his way out the door. 'Oy! What are you smiling at, lassie?'

Indeed, the prisoner's terror had evaporated. Now she sat in the corner with a cat–canary smirk on her face. Both corners of her mouth curled up. She looked even more satisfied than she had at the café. If anything, she looked . . . giddy.

Still in a dream, Marsh kneeled next to his friend. Since Will was left-handed, Marsh looped the leather cord just above the last knuckle on the smallest finger on Will's right hand. He pulled it as tight as he could, until the flesh underneath turned bone-white and the tip of Will's finger turned purple. Will winced.

As he tied off the cord, Marsh said, 'I'm sorry about what I said yesterday.'

'No apology necessary.' Just for a moment, the impish glint returned to Will's eyes. 'But if we're doing apologies, then this is as good a time as any to confess that I rather fancy your wife.'

Marsh smiled. 'I know, Will.'

'But I give you my solemn word I'd never do anything to hurt either of you.'

'I know that, too, Will.'

Marsh tested the knot. It held. He put his hand on Will's shoulder. 'Are you absolutely certain about this? We can find another way.'

'I'm certain. And no, we can't. Just please do it quickly. Please.'

'I promise.' Marsh handed over the wooden bit.

Will stuck it in his mouth. He closed his eyes, set his hand on the floor toward Marsh, and turned away.

Marsh crouched so as to put his weight on the shears and make the cut as quickly as possible. The metal blades reflected the angry orange light of the embers. He centered Will's finger-tip between the blades, made certain they would land above the tourniquet.

He counted. *One. Two—*

Three things happened at once. The blades crunched together

at the center of Will's finger. Will screamed. And the blood trickling down Marsh's arm, where the prisoner had gripped him,
caught the Eidolon's attention. It noticed Marsh again.

This time, it took a closer look.

Marsh's ego crumbled under the scrutiny of a boundless intellect. It fixated on his blood. It looked at him, in him, through
him, from within the very space he occupied. He smelled the iron
in Will's blood; saw those same atoms forged deep in the heart of
a dying star; felt the pressure of starlight on him; heard the quiet
patter of a fingertip hitting the floor, Will's sobs, and the popping
of novae. It studied the trajectory of Marsh's life, peered into
every dark corner . . .

The Eidolon withdrew. The fire spoke again.

Will clutched the mangled hand to his chest and coughed out
the bit. It dropped past his slack lips, trailing threads of spittle.
Will gaped at Marsh, trembling and looking paler than anybody
should.

'My God,' he said. 'They've given you a name.'

'Will? Are you—?'

Will waved him off. He pushed himself upright. Now his
speech didn't sound quite so impossible as it did before, riddled
as it was with utterly human sobbing and trembling. But he managed to respond to the Eidolon, and held up the bloodied
handkerchief with his undamaged hand.

The suffocating presence focused on the handkerchief, and
then oozed across the room to the prisoner. She trembled. The
sense of malice loomed over Marsh while the Eidolon inspected
her.

The back-and-forth between Will and the Eidolon continued
for moments or perhaps millennia. Marsh didn't bother to look
at his watch.

Will reverted to English. 'No!'

The presence receded from the room. In the eternity between one heartbeat and the next, it was gone. The room returned to normal, but for the blood misted on the floorboards alongside Will's fingertip.

Marsh crouched next to Will again. He took his friend by the shoulders. 'Will, we have to get you to a doctor.'

Stephenson came forward. 'What happened? What did it tell you?'

'He's going into shock,' said Lorimer, who entered carrying a bottle of brandy, though no ice.

Stephenson held him back. 'First things first. What did you learn?'

Will struggled to enunciate through his chattering teeth. 'Nothing.'

'It failed? Don't tell me this was all for naught.'

'No . . . it worked. But . . . the Jerries . . . whatever they're doing, the Eidolons have no part in it. It isn't magic. I don't know what it is.' His eyes rolled back in his head. He passed out.

The prisoner let loose with a self-satisfied, 'Hmmmph.'

Stephenson motioned at Marsh. 'Get her out of here! Lorimer, help me with Beauclerk.'

'Get up.' Marsh took the girl by the elbow as Lorimer and Stephenson draped Will's arms over their shoulders and carried him out of the room.

What a fiasco. Will had lost a finger, and for what? They hadn't learned a damn thing about what the Jerries were doing at von Westarp's farm.

She paused, staring into the room where earlier Marsh had adjusted the blackout curtains. Now the room was properly shadowed. Though it felt like the negotiation had gone for days, it had lasted only long enough for the sun to set. A blackout violation was the last thing they needed.

Marsh pulled the prisoner aside and double-checked the curtains. He took her elbow again.

'Hmmm,' she said, looking pensive.

Marsh frowned. 'What?'

'It hasn't worked yet,' she said, almost to herself. 'But I understand now.'

Marsh pried, but she said nothing more while he escorted her back to her cell.

SIX

13 May 1940
Whitehall, London, England

Klaus arrived in London at Victoria Station, and from there took the Underground.

His counterfeit lieutenant-commander uniform enabled him to slip through crowds as easily as the Götterelektron enabled him to slip through a French fortress. It rendered him a ghost, or perhaps invisible like Heike. People saw the uniform, not the man within.

Perhaps that meant they didn't notice Klaus's reluctance to speak, or the wig that was entirely too light for the color of this skin. Instead they might have noticed the unusual tailoring around the collar, or the way his uniform rode high across the shoulders as though he were caught in the middle of a prolonged shrug.

The wig and the strange tailoring were, of course, necessary for hiding his wires. But it still felt buffoonish. The wig itched, and caused him to sweat, not just from heat but also for fear it drew attention to him.

Although, in the frenzy of the past few days, there hadn't been time to procure one that looked halfway real. The Royal Navy uniform had been a lucky break, one of the few suitable uniforms available on short notice and which would fit Klaus after several rapid alterations.

Demolishing forest pillboxes in the middle of the night was one thing. But walking through throngs of the enemy while they pointed and laughed? This was different. If the crowds turned on him – and they would, if he revealed himself – his batteries wouldn't last long enough for him to evade capture forever.

Presumably, Gretel had anticipated these difficulties. Presumably, she cared, insofar as they interfered with her own designs. Whatever *those* were.

The Underground screeched to a halt at Charing Cross. When Klaus emerged on the platform, he saw a placard had been pasted to the tiled wall beside the ticket window. SPOT ON SIGHT, it read. ENEMY UNIFORMS. Beneath this, on the left, a color sketch depicted a Reich parachutist accurately down to the soles of his boots. The depiction of the Wehrmacht infantryman on the right was similarly detailed.

A strange, eerie feeling came over Klaus. It was an odd thing to see something so familiar in such a hostile place. But he also felt energized by it. Here he was, walking undetected among the enemy. Reinhardt wasn't the only one fit for his own missions.

Klaus evaded the crowds on the platform and jogged up the stairs to the street above. Until less than two years ago, Klaus had never set foot outside the Fatherland. Now he stood in the heart of the enemy capital.

A short walk took him to a roundabout with a tall column in the center. He used the time to study the city and its inhabitants. London was a dank city, full of dour-looking people plodding along under a colorless sky. Today a persistent drizzle had blown in from the Atlantic; the sky had been pissing down rain ever since Klaus boarded the train in Eastbourne early that morning. Mist shrouded everything, branding marble edifices and granite façades with dark blotches. It dripped from cornices and quoins, parapets and posts. Statues wept tears of condensed fog.

Rainwater hissed under the wheels of passing vehicles, amplifying the traffic noise and filling the streets with a persistent static thrum. Each auto, he noticed, had been outfitted with a blackout grille over the headlamps. The water penetrated everything; even the sidewalk smelled of damp stone. A cool rivulet trickled under Klaus's collar.

Chest-high stacks of mud-colored sandbags flanked the entrances to buildings. Businessmen carried gleaming metal helmets along with their attaché cases and newspapers. A girl selling flowers from a stand on the corner kept the haversack of a gas mask slung over her shoulder. Most people carried such a bag. Even schoolchildren.

This was a nation doggedly clinging to normalcy while it prepared for the worst. Klaus sensed an atmosphere of grim determination, of shared destiny, when he stood among these people.

A man hailed a taxicab across the street. The taxis here were ugly, boxy things. They looked like hearses. Klaus understood the idea, though he'd never ridden a taxi before. He imitated the man across the street, raising an arm and whistling as another of the black cabs sped past. It chuddered to a halt.

Klaus climbed in, weighing his words carefully. He opted for the shortest possible conversation. 'Admiralty,' he said.

The driver glanced over the seat, white eyebrows cocked high on his forehead. A tangle of spidery red capillaries etched his gin-blossom nose. 'Beg pardon, sir?'

Klaus enunciated every letter: 'Admiralty.'

The driver cast a glance over the seat. 'You all right, sir? You don't sound well.'

Scheisse.

Unlike Reinhardt, Klaus hadn't perfected his English.

Klaus glared at the driver and gestured through the windshield. 'Go,' he commanded.

The driver shrugged. He put the car in gear. 'Very good, sir. Next stop, the Admiralty.'

Though he had long since committed the contents to memory, Klaus took advantage of the ride to review his sister's note once more. He unfolded the paper, leaning against the acceleration as the cab sped around a corner.

. . . Come for me on the thirteenth of May—

The cab stopped. 'There we go,' said the driver over the *clunk* of the parking brake.

Klaus looked up. '—What?' He barely caught himself in time, and phrased the question in English.

'We're here, sir. The Admiralty, like you asked.'

'Already?' The word slipped out before he could stop, before he could concentrate on pronouncing it like a Briton.

The driver's face creased in confusion. 'Yes, sir.'

And indeed, they idled across the street from the front gate of a U-shaped brick building. A taller addition farther down the road was a jumble of white stone and dark red brick. The complex was larger than he'd expected.

The entire ride hadn't taken two minutes. Yet in that time Klaus had branded himself as a stranger who spoke with an accent and as a sailor who didn't know the location of the Admiralty. He'd made more work for himself. But it couldn't be carried out right here.

Klaus pointed down the street. 'Please let me off there, around the corner,' he said. He didn't obsess over his accent.

The driver looked confused, but didn't object. 'As you wish, sir.' The car lurched to another stop a few moments later, this time out of sight of the Admiralty complex.

Klaus pretended to go through the motions of pulling out a billfold. He counted bills, stalling until the driver turned forward again. When he did, Klaus reached through the seat to squeeze the man's heart still. Klaus leaned the body against the door so it wouldn't topple forward and bump the horn.

Fuck Reinhardt, anyway.

He climbed out and closed the door, trying but failing to spit the taste of electrified metal from his mouth.

The drizzle had seeped into his uniform by the time he crossed the street and hurried back to the Admiralty on foot. The taxi had saved him neither time nor discomfort.

A sentry saluted as Klaus passed through the gate. Klaus traversed a courtyard toward what appeared to be the main entrance. After returning another salute to the sentries flanking a sandbag revetment, he entered the Admiralty unchallenged. Nobody asked for his identity card; they took the uniform at face value. That wouldn't have happened at a Schutzstaffel building.

Britain was a stupid, backward place.

. . . Find me in the cellar. They will keep me locked in a storage room . . .

Klaus strode the corridors, searching for a stairwell. But if the Admiralty complex had seemed large and imposing from the outside, it was far more confusing inside. It gave the sense of having come together organically, without any overarching plan. Narrow corridors kinked with senseless doglegs meandered through the building; some were lined with doors down both sides, while others sported none. Some of the panels in the walls looked like doors, but were not. And there were doors that didn't look like doors at all, and which caught Klaus by surprise when they opened suddenly to discharge sailors and bureaucrats.

The need to pretend he belonged here, that he knew where he was going, hindered Klaus's search. A man with a single lieutenant's bar on each shoulder saluted as Klaus passed. Klaus returned the salute, a moment late and not nearly so crisply. The younger officer didn't react; perhaps he was accustomed to contempt from his superiors.

The first stairwell Klaus found went up, to the floor above, but not down to the cellar.

Gretel had this all planned out because she'd foreseen it. Naturally, she hadn't bothered to draw a map or give him specific directions.

Klaus considered forgoing stairs altogether, instead dropping straight through the floor into the cellar below. Assuming there *was* a cellar directly beneath him. If he was wrong, there was a very real chance he'd end up falling through the earth. He'd use up his one lungful of breath long before he popped out in some other part of the globe. He'd suffocate, die, rematerialize, and perhaps fossilize deep underground, a puzzle for future archaeologists.

He abandoned the notion. The search resumed amid mounting frustration.

'. . . You don't get it, Pip. The Eidolons don't *do* that. It's quite unheard of.'

'They must have names for things, Will.'

Two men – civilians, by their dress – turned the corner at the far end of the corridor. The taller and better-dressed one, a pale fellow with red hair like Rudolf, wore a gauze bandage wrapped about one of his fingers. Seepage had stained the pristine white cotton with blotches of rust. The sight elicited a sympathetic throb from the phantom ache in Klaus's missing fingers.

The shorter one was a coarse fellow, judging by his face. A pugilist, perhaps. He looked up momentarily as Klaus passed. Klaus nodded at him, hoping it would pass for a companionable gesture between countrymen. The man turned to his injured companion, listening to his response.

'Names for things, concepts, yes. But not for *people*. That's akin to naming the individual ants in an anthill.'

'Who was that bloke? Did he look familiar to you?'

Klaus called up his Willenskräfte to chance a shortcut.

'New recruit, perhaps. Look, getting back to the point, I can't impress upon you enough how peculiar . . .'

Klaus released his breath when he rematerialized around the corner.

'I'm not inclined,' said Marsh, 'to put stock in the pronouncements of something so malevolent. Just look at how it toyed with you.' He frowned. 'Sorry, Will, but it did.'

Nausea and light-headedness welled up again when Will nodded. Merely blunting the worst edge of the pain in his hand had required filling his stomach with aspirin. Any more, and he was bound to sick up. The naval medic had wanted to ply Will with something stronger, but Will had insisted that the troops needed every ampule far more than he did.

'Your distrust is well-placed. But there was no price associated with the name. The Eidolon stated it as fact, rather than as a ploy. And that's what makes it notable.'

'What does it mean? The name, I mean?'

'I haven't a clue.' Will shrugged, instantly regretting it. The pain redoubled its efforts, lancing from the missing tip of his finger all the way up his arm. 'There's nothing similar in Grandad's lexicon.'

Marsh stopped. His eyes widened. 'Bloody hell.'

Will added, 'Relax. That by itself isn't cause for alarm. Even the best lexicons are notoriously incomplete—'

Marsh spun, looking back up the corridor from where they had come. 'How could I be so dim?'

'What?'

'Of course he looked familiar. I've seen him in the sodding film!'

'What are you talking about?'

'It's one of them. They're here.'

Will whirled around to look, but the corridor was empty. He staggered. His knees still felt soft, watery from the previous day's ordeal. 'Are you certain? Perhaps it's just a residual oddity, a phantom leftover from our little experiment yesterday.' Will didn't believe it either as the words came out of his mouth. He wished he did. The Jerries on that film were downright terrifying customers.

Marsh dashed down the corridor, toward where the intruder had been heading. Over his shoulder he yelled, 'Raise the alarm, Will!'

Klaus pressed deeper into the Admiralty. If he still had his bearings correct, he was working toward the rear of the building. The place was a goddamned maze. Perhaps that's why the British made excellent sailors. They had to be navigational geniuses just to get around on land.

. . . They will keep me locked in a storage room. I will be granted a cot, however, and so will be cheerful and well-rested upon your arrival . . .

The soft scrape of enamel on enamel vibrated through Klaus's jaw as his teeth ground together. *Why do you do this to me, Gretel?* he wondered. *Your comfort won't matter at all if I can't* find *you.*

Fewer people walked these corridors. Some of the rooms were empty, looking like they had recently been vacated. Thick black folds of opaque fabric covered the windows. One room turned out to be a landing where a wooden balustrade spiraled up from the floor below. *Finally.*

Three men came up the stairs as Klaus reached the top. Two wore naval uniforms, the third a tweed suit. Klaus squeezed past them as they gained the landing. Relieved at having found the cellar, he forgot himself and momentarily disregarded the bars on the oldest man's shoulders.

'I say!' said the younger of the two officers.

The older – a commander, and therefore superior to Klaus's counterfeit rank – cleared his throat. He grabbed Klaus's shoulder and spun him around.

'Stop him!'

The brawler came barreling around the corner. The three men on the staircase turned at the commotion.

'Stop that man! He's a Jerry spy!'

Klaus dropped through the stairwell.

A hue and cry spread through the building. News of the intruder spread faster than Will could race through the corridors raising the alarm himself. It was like touching a match to dry tinder: after that initial spark, it assumed a life of its own. Most of the occupants of the Old Admiralty didn't know about Milkweed, or its purpose, but that was immaterial. There was a spy on the premises.

But none of the outsiders knew what to expect.

Will banged on the door to Lorimer's makeshift darkroom. 'Lorimer! Open up!'

It opened a few moments later, after much cursing, banging, and sloshing came from inside. Lorimer poked his head out, blinking widely as his eyes adjusted to the bright light of the hallway. 'What the hell is wrong with you?'

'I need to borrow you for a bit.'

'I'm busy.'

'Change of plans.' Will grabbed him by the shoulder and pulled him outside. 'It's an emergency,' he added.

Lorimer slammed the door. 'Don't bleed on me.'

Will leaned close. 'We have an intruder. One of *them*.' He answered the question in Lorimer's eyes with a whisper: 'I think he's here for the girl.'

Lorimer exhaled. 'Christ on a bloody camel.'

'Marsh has gone after the fellow – tall chap, about my height, darkish skin like the girl, dressed like an officer. So have a number of others, but they won't be expecting any, ah, tricks. Go help Marsh. He was headed for the cellar.'

'Wonderful.' The Scot muttered to himself as he ran off. 'We'll all burn to death like Hindu widows . . .'

A trio of matelots stampeded down the hall after Lorimer. Will pressed himself against the wall so as not to get flattened. He still bumped shoulders with one of the men as they charged past, evoking a renewed agony from his finger. Rather than join the commotion and chaos, Will opted for a different tactic.

The mob of pursuers expected to trap and catch the fellow indoors. But if he truly was one of von Westarp's kiddies, there was every chance he might disappear from sight, or burn through the walls, or cause them to fly apart, or Lord knew what. And if he joined forces with that strange woman and the store of knowledge in her head? They'd have little trouble getting away.

Will headed for a side door. Imagining how Marsh might have tackled the problem prompted him to approach Horse Guards' Road, along the park. *If it were me on the run, I'd come out this way, rather than risk drawing more attention to myself right there on Whitehall.*

Dusk had fallen. If there hadn't been a blackout in effect, the gas lamps in the park would have shone in little halos of mist left over from the day's long drizzle. Instead the only illumination came from the moon as it peeked through receding clouds overhead and a misty fog on the ground. The result was a pale diffuse light that bleached the color from the world. Quiet, too, but for the traffic humming around Trafalgar.

Will crossed the road and entered the park. It smelled humid with new spring growth; the soil squelched underfoot. Looking back at the Admiralty, he could just pick out the row of windows apportioned to Milkweed. Blackout curtains rendered every window opaque. Night-time in the city had been a romantic yet oft-times lonely affair since September.

Rather than stand out in the open like a proper fool, he pushed into the park, where the shadows were even deeper. In better times, it would have been possible to glimpse Buckingham Palace at the far end of the Mall. He stepped carefully, lest he take a tumble in one of the trenches dug for the sake of filling sandbags. Many of the parks had been turned over to gardening and home defense.

He crouched behind a mulberry tree, peering across to the Admiralty. A mallard called, down by the lake. Tires screeched and a horn blared somewhere nearby. Even in wartime, daily life in the wider world went on.

Mist seeped through the fine-spun cotton of Will's shirt. The damp Savile Row fabric cooled his skin where it had been warm with the perspiration of fear and excitement. At first it felt refreshing, then bracing. But it turned into clamminess as the minutes dragged on with nary a sign of activity across the street.

Did I expect to find somebody out here, or did I just run away from danger?

Though he was loath to sacrifice his hard-earned night vision, shivering and boredom prompted him to abandon his hiding spot. It wasn't until he had crossed the road again that he noticed the silhouette of somebody crouched alongside the building. The lurker darted around the corner of the Admiralty building.

Aha! You may be the smartest fellow in the room, Pip, but I'm no slouch either.

'Stop! You there, stop!' Will gave chase, following the shabby-looking fellow around the corner.

The man spun. He reared back, regarding Will with the wide unblinking eyes of a madman. Late middle-aged, Will guessed, with a slight paunch. Perhaps dismissing the fellow as a madman was uncharitable; he might have been a shell-shocked Tommy from the previous war. The chap's scar supported that notion. A long pink wrinkle stretched from the corner of his left eye down around his jaw and across his neck through an otherwise full beard.

'Will?'

Will stopped. He didn't recognize this fellow, nor did he recognize the gravel-and-whiskey voice. His voice, his footsteps, his breaths, even the rasp of his beard across the collar of his shirt echoed as if coming from the bottom of a deep well. It was hollow and hyperreal at once.

'Do I know you?' asked Will.

The man's eyes glimmered, as if with tears. 'I wish—'

And then, between one beat of Will's heart and the next, the man disappeared. He didn't scamper away, didn't hide in the shadows, but disappeared.

'Shit.' Will's knees gave out. He slumped against rough bricks of Admiralty House. 'Shit.' Part of him wished, at that particular moment, that he carried a flask.

Phantom visions, indeed.

Ooomf.

Klaus rematerialized a split second before landing in the cellar. He tucked in and exhaled, exactly as he'd been trained. His knees and shoulder absorbed most of the momentum as he rolled on a hard concrete floor. He leapt to his feet at the intersection of two long brick corridors lined with vaulted arches, like catacombs. Rows of identical steel doorways receded in both directions.

Why couldn't she draw a map?

Upstairs: 'What in the Lord's name just happened?'

'Dear God.'

'Out of my way!'

'Good heavens, I—'

'Step aside! Get out of my way!'

The brawler charged down the stairs. He must have shoved through the knot of officers on the landing. An ensign and the commander that Klaus had neglected to salute came tumbling down the stairs after him, like boulders in a rockslide.

He yelled again as he caught sight of Klaus. 'You! Stop! There's only one way out of here.'

Klaus picked a direction at random. 'Gretel! Where are you?'

Shouts and footsteps echoed throughout the cellar as his pursuers split up to trap him.

It went against his training, not to mention his better

judgment, to go so long without checking the gauge on his battery harness. But the harness was concealed beneath his uniform, and he couldn't easily dispense with it while being pursued. Plus, the disguise would be essential to their journey back to the shore.

Luckily for Klaus, most of the doors were suited with tiny windows, so he didn't have to waste the charge on his battery by peeking into each room. Several of the rooms were dark, however, so he'd had to reach inside to trip with light switches. Gretel wasn't to be found in any of these rooms, nor did she respond when he called her name, if she was nearby.

He zigzagged through the cellar with the civilian who had first recognized him relentlessly on his heels.

The German bastard was fast, and clever. Each time Marsh or somebody else got within arm's reach, or dived for him, he'd jump through a wall, or through the men themselves. Marsh managed to stay with him, though it meant running an obstacle course created by the other men.

The dodging and bumping, twisting and jumping, revived the ache in Marsh's knee. It pulsed hot, threatening to give out at any moment. *Not now. Not now.*

There was a bulge under his quarry's shirt, near his waist. Much like the woman. Marsh noticed the way he kept reaching for it, almost as if out of habit, every time he pulled his little trick.

The prisoner's battery had a gauge on it.

You want to check your battery ... Marsh stumbled, wrapped in his own thoughts. 'Ooof.' He crashed against a brick wall as the Jerry clipped through another corner. *The battery is your weakness.*

Marsh played the hunch. When another knot of pursuers neared the intruder, he yelled, 'His wire! Go for the wire!'

The German raised a hand to the back of his head, reflexively protecting himself even though it was unnecessary. He slipped through the crowd and disappeared around another corner.

Aha, thought Marsh. *Gotcha.*

At last.

Klaus spied his sister lying on a cot inside a small storeroom. 'Gretel!' He ghosted through the door. It clanged a few seconds later as his pursuer pounded on it.

Gretel blinked her eyes, yawned, and stretched.

'Gretel, get up. Are you hurt?'

'I was having the loveliest dream.' She sat up. Over the banging on the door, she added, 'You interrupted it, brother.'

Klaus took advantage of his pursuer's delay to swap out his battery. In his haste, he fumbled with the buttons on his uniform, unable to grip them properly with his mangled hand. Gretel undid the buttons and pulled his shirt. She grabbed a spare battery from his harness, strapped it into the empty spot on her own harness, and plugged in. Klaus pulled the wire from his depleted pack and reconnected it to the other spare.

A *k-chink* from the door lock announced that his pursuer had found the key to Gretel's cell. Klaus grabbed his sister's hand.

'You must not release my hand until I tell you. And hold your breath. Do you understand?'

She patted his cheek. 'So serious.'

That was the closest he'd get to a yes.

The Götterelektron coursed into his mind as the door groaned open on rusty hinges. Klaus imagined himself an overflowing vessel, imagined the Götterelektron spilling over into Gretel, carrying his Willenskräfte along with it.

If they went out through the wall of her cell, they'd come out underground. They had to get back up to ground level first.

Klaus pulled his sister through the doorway and the bruiser standing in it to block them. The man jumped back in shock and tumbled to the floor, though to his credit he didn't unleash a girl-ish scream as Obergruppenführer Greifelt had.

They rematerialized again once they passed him, to conserve the battery. This one would drain even faster, because two bodies drew from it now.

Gretel blew a kiss over her shoulder. 'Farewell, my darling, until we meet again.'

Marsh flinched. He couldn't help it.

The intruder charged him as soon as he wrenched the door open. Marsh had been braced for a fight, but when the bloke came at him, he tensed for a collision because his body took over and reacted on the basis of prior life experience. Even though he knew damn well what this fellow had in mind.

Face to face, eye to eye, and then – just for a blink – they occu-pied the same space.

It had been different with the Eidolon. That thing existed in the gaps between everywhere and between everywhen, sidling through the mortar of the universe. To say that he and the Eidolon had occupied the same space was imprecise, like saying that the bricks of a retaining wall and the mortar within it were one and the same.

The memory alone left Marsh feeling naked, skinless, formless, and insignificant.

The Nazi passed through him without evoking any sensation. Not even an itch. Like he truly wasn't there.

He and his girlfriend – *Gretel*, he called her *Gretel* – were just people. Damned unusual people, perhaps, but in the end they were people. Will was right. The Eidolons had nothing to do with this. Marsh saw that with the benefit of his inside-out view during the instant when the intruder and prisoner ghosted through him.

He still jumped, though. He couldn't help it.

On instinct, he tried to spin about and grab the girl's wire, but his hand breezed through her neck. It surprised him, tipped him off balance. He sprawled on the floor.

Gretel glanced over her shoulder. She blew a kiss, announcing, 'Farewell, my darling, until we meet again.'

Marsh jumped to his feet and gave chase. But unlike the escaping duo, he had to dodge the others trying to block, grab, and tackle them. The fugitives acknowledged no obstacles in their dash for the stairs.

'Clear out! Clear the corridor!'

He closed the gap on the long straightaway to the bottom flight. A number of others – Marsh glimpsed Lorimer there – planned to take the fugitives on the stairs, and so this stretch of corridor was empty.

Sprinting to catch up to the pair, he became aware of a new sound amidst the pandemonium.

Panting.

If Marsh had needed a further assurance that the figures he chased were merely a man and a woman, and not supernatural entities, this would have cinched it.

Running just a pace behind them, striving to bridge the last few feet and snag the girl while the pair was momentarily substantial, he could see the flush on their faces, hear their breath.

Of course! You can't breathe when you're a ghost.

'Clear the bloody stairs!'

Marsh barged through the crowd on the stairwell, but far slower than those he chased. The fugitives reached the top and made their exit through the wall. He came up short, slamming against the same wall. His mind raced along with his heartbeat as he crouched with hands to knees, catching his own breath.

Now I understand the rules.

Klaus couldn't evade pursuit quite so nimbly with his sister in tow. They breezed through the men and their outstretched arms like ghosts in a haunted forest.

Smaller Gretel couldn't match his strides. He half pulled, half lifted her up the stairwell as they bounded up to the ground floor. Once up top, he pulled her through the outer wall. They passed into cool, moist air. After the noise and chaos inside, Klaus found nightfall in London disarmingly sedate.

It became more difficult to pull Gretel along once they re-materialized. As a ghost, she offered no resistance to his tugs. But as a physical entity with a physical body, she could not, or simply would not, match his sense of urgency. She stumbled along behind him as he led her across a street to an open green space.

'Stop! You there, stop!'

Klaus halted, spun. The challenge had emanated from across the street, back from where they had come, but he couldn't see anybody in the mist and moonlight. It seemed to have originated from around the corner of the building they'd just escaped. Klaus sighed.

'I don't think that was meant for us,' he said, eyes still scanning the street. 'Let's go while we still can.'

Klaus turned. And found Gretel face-to-face with a stranger.

'It's you.' Gretel smiled. 'You came for me.'

'It's *you*,' said the stranger. His gravelly voice betrayed no joy as he said it. One side of his face had been badly burned; his beard hid the worst of it, but a puckered furrow ran from the corner of his left eye to the edge of his jaw and across his throat.

In a strange way, the man reminded Klaus of his sister. The constant shadow behind Gretel's eyes, the madness there, was a vestige of things seen and known, things not meant for either. Klaus recognized the same look, the same shadow, behind this man's eyes. This was a man who had seen things. A man burdened by knowledge.

Klaus took her wrist again, tried to pull her away from this madman. 'Gretel, do you know him? Who—?'

Between one word and the next, the man disappeared. Much as Heike might have done. Klaus spun, searching for the mystery man, or an ambush. But the park was quiet.

A ghost?

Klaus shook his head, sighed. England was a strange place. He'd had enough of it.

Gretel still stared at the spot where the apparition had disappeared. He tugged on her wrist.

'We need to keep moving,' said Klaus.

She smiled. Beamed. 'It's going to work.'

'What's going to work?'

But she wouldn't say.

After that, evading capture was a tedious but trivial affair. It took most of the night, but Gretel guided them back to the southern seashore without incident. They waited for their rendezvous, shivering in the dark amongst nets, green-glass net floats, traps, and fishing boats. Smooth round pebbles covered the beach, and they tinkled like glass beads underfoot. A rowboat came for them just before dawn. It ferried them to the shape looming out of the water like a shark fin in the predawn light. Brother and sister descended the hatch into dark, cramped Unterseeboot-115 as the sun rose over the English Channel.

SEVEN

14 May 1940
Milkweed Headquarters, London, England

Stephenson had already worked himself into something just short of a foam-flecked tirade by the time Will arrived. Will glanced over at Lorimer and Marsh for a show of solidarity, knowing he was in for the brunt of it. They stood silent and motionless. Stephenson let loose as soon as Will closed the office door behind him.

'How the *hell* did he know where to find her?'

Cigarette ash swirled around Stephenson as he paced. He used the cigarette like a baton, gesturing at his troops like a displeased commandant. Little white flakes settled on his suit and tie like dandruff.

He turned on Will. 'And *you*! What in God's name were you thinking? You insisted the prisoner wouldn't see anything she hadn't already seen. And then you bollixed everything up by *tipping our hand to the enemy*.'

Will found himself standing at attention. Stephenson's tirade evoked his grandfather's rages. *I won't hide. I won't.* He rubbed the palm of his hand. At least Stephenson wasn't drunk.

'She – I mean, I – it was the only thing that made sense,' said Will. 'The only sensible explanation was that the Jerries had been communing with the Eidolons.' One of his grandfather's worst habits, the most infuriating and belittling, had been the way he'd blame Will for his own irrational mistakes. Will pushed back. 'Implicitly or not, you'd made that assumption when you brought me on board. I was working within the parameters you gave me.'

In the corner of his eye, he saw Marsh stiffen.

Bad move.

'My faulty assumption was that you could think for yourself, Beauclerk.' Stephenson dragged on his cigarette again before continuing. 'As for their escape, how did he find her so easily?'

'Not through the Eidolons. However they did it, it was through human means.'

'Do you honestly think,' Stephenson said quietly, 'that bastard was human?'

Will preferred him when he bellowed. He understood eruptions of temper; quiet rages unsettled him. Marsh's patron had an iron presence that gave his gray gaze the intensity of a hammer blow.

Marsh piped up. 'As a matter of fact, sir, I'm more sure of it now than ever before.' He'd known Stephenson most of his life, and so he didn't quail before Stephenson's fury. 'They have fears and weaknesses just like the rest of us. Vulnerabilities.' His eyes went distant and unfocused for a moment. 'Will's right, sir. This has nothing to do with the Eidolons.'

'Back to my question: How did he find her?'

'The girl did know a great many things,' said Marsh.

'Your point?'

Marsh shrugged, shook his head. Will watched the gears turning behind his friend's eyes, watched him sorting through puzzle pieces that didn't quite fit together. 'At least we know her name now,' Marsh added. 'Gretel.'

'Wonderful! In that case, I'd say we have this locked up tight. I'll just pop on down to the Prime Minister, shall I? "No worries, sir, the Jerries caught us with our knickers down, but we have a single name now, so victory is assured." Is that what you'd like me to tell him?'

Will tried not to breathe.

'How the hell were we supposed to catch that minger?' Now Lorimer pushed back. 'Can't fight against something like that.'

Stephenson went very still, as though frozen in place with a veneer of ice. 'Allow me to remind you gentlemen that our mandate, as handed directly to me by the Prime Minister himself, is to do exactly that.' One by one he stared them down as he continued. He stood nose to nose with Lorimer. 'It is our job to *find* ways to fight them.' He moved in front of Marsh. 'It is our job to thwart them at every turn.' Tobacco breath puffed across Will's face when Stephenson stood before him to conclude, 'And it is our job to do so discreetly. It is *not* our job to go flashing our knickers to everyone we meet.'

Stephenson finally sat down behind his desk. He'd moved his office, including some of the furniture and most of the watercolors, into the Old Admiralty. Leadership of MI6's T-section now rested on other shoulders. The old man had parlayed all his political capital into the oversight of an obscure four-man operation.

'We need more men, sir,' said Marsh.

'And there, at least, is one area where your world-class cockup might benefit us.'

'Sir?'

Pain returned to Will's fingertip. Phantom limb syndrome, the doctors called it. Aspirin no longer took the edge off his pain. He checked the bandages while Marsh's appeal echoed in his ears. *We need more men.*

'How many people witnessed your fumble yesterday?'

'Hard to say, sir. A dozen. Perhaps more.'

'More,' chimed Lorimer. 'At least that many saw him bring the lass upstairs after he found her. And they ran *through* that many again . . .' He trailed off, head shaking.

'Congratulations,' said Stephenson. He turned toward Marsh. 'Your request for additional men and matériel has been granted. Those witnesses are your new recruits.'

'I don't understand?' Will received the hammer-blow stare again in response to his question.

Marsh answered for Stephenson. 'It's damage control, Will. They saw something that we were supposed to keep under lock and key. Literally and figuratively. They know our secret and we need the men, so it makes sense to recruit them into Milkweed.'

'They already have stations,' said Lorimer. 'What'll we do, form up a press-gang?'

Stephenson opened a desk drawer. He produced a bundle of papers wrapped with a black ribbon. 'No need. These will suffice.' He split the bunch between Will, Marsh, and Lorimer. Each page was embossed with the full Royal Arms, making it equivalent to a decree from His Majesty. 'Find your witnesses. Give them these. Doubtless some of them have already talked. So work fast.' He nodded at Lorimer. 'Be prepared to show the film in a day or two.'

Lorimer nodded. 'Aye.'

Rusty spots marred the pristine white cotton tied around the stub of Will's finger. They served as a strong reminder that he wasn't up to snuff. He'd been foolish to volunteer his services. He wasn't a competent negotiator; he was lucky the Eidolon's price hadn't been far worse.

Will divided his stack of papers in two. He handed one half to Marsh and Lorimer each. 'I rather think this is a better job for you chaps.'

'We need to do this as quickly as possible, Will.'

'I fear that spies and soldiers won't ever be enough.' He held up his bandaged hand. 'And my contribution to this effort has been less than exemplary thus far. We need true experts, not a dilettante like myself.'

He turned to Stephenson. 'With your leave, I'd like to do a little recruiting of a different sort.'

'You'll need those papers.'

Will shook his head. 'They wouldn't do the least bit of good. The men I have in mind aren't easily intimidated or impressed. Otherwise, they'd have perished long ago.' To Lorimer, he said, 'We *can* fight von Westarp's people. If we have the proper men for the job.'

Stephenson nodded. 'Go to it, all three of you.'

Lorimer stayed behind while the others filed out of Stephenson's office. As Will closed the door, he heard Lorimer saying, 'There may be a way to fight them. But I won't know until I've disassembled the lass's battery . . .'

Marsh accompanied Will on his way outside. 'Think you'll have any luck?'

'Depends on what you mean. Good or bad?'

Marsh smirked. He scrutinized the face of everyone they passed. Will realized he was doing the same.

'I'd wager our luck is destined to change soon enough. Law of averages, you know.'

They exited the Admiralty, past sandbag revetments and

sodden marines. The drizzle had stopped overnight, but now it was raining stair-rods. Water sluiced between the stones in the courtyard and poured in little runnels from the brims of the sentries' helmets.

Will opened his umbrella, careful not to jostle his injured hand. Marsh nodded at the bandages.

'How's it feeling?'

'This?' Will steeled himself for pain before flexing his hand. 'A minor inconvenience,' he lied. 'I'll be right as rain before you know it.'

'It's an awful thing, Will. I wish I hadn't done it.'

'Hi, hi, none of that. We do what we must. Ha! That's a rather fitting epitaph, come to think of it.'

Marsh grimaced. 'You may be right.'

'Keep your eyes and ears open. I might have something for you in a week or two.'

'Where are you going?'

'First, home. Then for a bit of a ramble through the country, I expect.'

'Take care of yourself, Will.'

'You, too, Pip.'

Marsh went back inside. Will ventured into the downpour. He slogged up Whitehall toward Trafalgar until he succeeded in hailing a cab. It took him to the Kensington flat Will rented with the allowance siphoned from his brother Aubrey every few months.

Will packed a suitcase with the essentials for what he guessed would be a fortnight of travel. Then he gathered up what he had of his grandfather's papers. A hasty inspection while waiting for another taxi confirmed his expectations. The information he sought wasn't there.

From St. Pancras Station, he called ahead to Bestwood. A car met him when he arrived in Nottinghamshire.

15 May 1940
Bestwood-on-Trent, Nottinghamshire, England

'What the devil are you doing here?'

'And a very good morning to you, too, Your Grace.'

Will looked up from where he sat cross-legged on a Turkish silk rug in the midst of a pile of books and papers he'd pulled from the shelves. It was just after dawn, the sun peeking through the gap between earth and leaden sky. Sunlight poured like honey across the polished rosewood and leather of his grandfather's library, evoking a lustrous shimmer from the rug. His brother stood in the doorway.

'How long have you been here?'

'Got in yesterday evening.'

'Already making a mess of the place, I see.'

'I'm looking for something.'

'I can tell.'

Aubrey strode into the study. Four years Will's senior, the thirteenth Duke of Aelred was fully six inches shorter and fifty pounds heavier than his brother. Whereas atavistic Will had inherited the fiery hair and pale eyes of long-dead Danish marauders, Aubrey had picked up a simpler combination of hazel eyes and mouse-brown hair. Which already showed signs of thinning. The brothers were no more alike in appearance than they were in temperament.

Even at this uncivilized hour of the day, Aubrey dressed as though expecting His Majesty to call at any moment. His tie alone probably cost more than all the linens in Marsh's house combined. Will, on the other hand, was quite content in his bathrobe.

Aubrey lifted the lid on the silver carafe sitting on the tea service Will had taken to the library. He sniffed. 'You had the kitchen staff brew up coffee?'

'No. Tried making it myself. I really can't recommend it. Terrible stuff. Cold now, I'm afraid.'

'You've wasted it, haven't you. Typical. There is a war on, William.'

'So I've heard.'

'Are you staying long?' asked Aubrey in a nonchalant tone that belied the preferred answer. He circled Will's nest on the floor, looking for other misdeeds and affronts. Will half expected him to don a white glove and inspect the room for dust, the prig.

'I'll be far and away as soon as I find some of grandfather's papers. You wouldn't know where Mr. Malcolm packed them, would you?'

'I thought you'd taken them.'

'Not all.'

Aubrey stopped before the diamond-shaped leaded-glass windowpanes overlooking the garden. A pair of ravens cawed to each other from the boughs of a yew. He turned. 'What are you so keen to find?'

Secretive men engaged in secretive practices, thought Will. Warlocks excelled at maintaining a low profile. In the oldest families, like Will's, the knowledge had been whispered down bloodlines for centuries. But on occasion warlocks had been known to exchange tidbits of Enochian, like folk musicians trading old songs and melodies. Any warlock worth his salt kept a journal. If grandfather had ever noted where he'd acquired such tidbits, that information would be in his journal.

Will stood. 'The war has put me much in mind of father lately. Thought perhaps that grandfather's journals might shed some light on him. I don't remember father at all, though I suppose you do.'

'I didn't know grandfather kept a journal.'

Grandfather had always taken great care to shield Aubrey from the strange disciplines he practiced with Will. Will's older brother was blissfully ignorant of Eidolons, Enochian, and all the rest. *Lucky, lucky.*

Will shrugged. 'Perhaps I'm wasting my time.'

'I should say – What did you do to your hand, William?'

'Gardening accident.'

Aubrey cocked an eyebrow. 'That's odd. From what I've heard, you abandoned the foundation and left the victory gardens to others.'

'Be assured,' said Will, 'that planting the seeds of victory is my one and only concern.'

'I'll send someone to help you sort through the things Mr. Malcolm packed away after grandfather's death. You'll need it. There's an entire room on the third floor.'

'Smashing. Oh – I'll need one of the cars, too.'

Aubrey rolled his eyes.

Will brought the Humber Snipe to a halt and killed the engine. He checked the name in the journal again before placing the book in the glove box along with the map. He'd had to stop for directions at two pubs and a filling station before he found this place.

He climbed out and donned his bowler. Silence lay thick upon this clearing and its modest little cottage. It swallowed the *clunk* of the car door and the *tink-tink-tink* of the Humber's cooling engine. Wind didn't whisper through these oaks; instead it tiptoed through the boughs.

And no birdsong, Will noted.

The cottage's roof sagged in the center. It put the wooden shingles out of true. Green and yellow moss grew in the gaps, alongside sprigs of purple foxglove and belladonna. The door rattled when Will knocked.

The man who answered the door was older than Will, old enough to be his father, but still too young to be a contemporary of his grandfather.

Bloodlines.

'Mr. Shapley?'

The man looked past Will at the car. He frowned. 'Who are you?'

'My name is William Beauclerk,' said Will, extending his good hand, 'and I'm pleased to make your acquaintance, sir.' Surreptitiously, he inspected the man's hand as they shook. It was ribbed, front and back, with a network of white ridges and pink wheals.

'For if I'm not mistaken, your father and my grandfather were colleagues.'

29 May 1940
Walworth, London, England

As hopes of a decisive victory in France deteriorated, so, too, did hopes of quiet and efficient damage control after the fiasco of Gretel's escape. Just as the Jerries' lightning advance through the

Ardennes had caught the French and British defenders unaware, her rescue caught Milkweed off guard and unprepared to extinguish the firestorm of rumor and speculation left in her wake.

In the fortnight following the debacle, Marsh and Lorimer found the spectacle indelibly seared into the witnesses' memories. Explaining away what they'd seen was impossible. Simultaneously, the bulk of the British Expeditionary Force found itself in an untenable position, squeezed between two German army groups. One advanced south into France via the Low Countries; the other raced west from its penetration point in the Ardennes.

The defenders adopted a new strategy. They retreated to the Atlantic coast for evacuation across the Channel. The ranks of those awaiting rescue at Dunkirk swelled daily.

As did the ranks of Milkweed. Within a week of the escape, Marsh and company had together conscripted thirty-one people into their ranks. They showed the Tarragona film twice. The witnesses they recruited included numerous officers and enlisted from His Majesty's Navy, a handful of fighting men from other services, and one accountant who'd had the misfortune of being at the wrong place at the wrong time. Stephenson also took the opportunity to enlist a handful of scientists and engineers to assist Lorimer in his analysis of the battery.

But it wasn't enough. Milkweed needed a strategy for quashing the rumors. One that would kill the issue.

The King declared Sunday, May 26 – which also happened to be the first day of the Dunkirk evacuation – a national day of prayer. Most Sundays, Liv sang in the choir. But on that day, Liv and Marsh had joined the congregants overflowing from the chapel into the surrounding churchyard. They'd been unable to hear a word of the vicar's sermon, by virtue of distance and the cacophony of church bells shaking off the nation's pent-up anxiety.

After the service, Marsh kissed Liv and baby Agnes good-bye, returned to work, and together with Stephenson he selected a fellow countryman for execution.

Lieutenant F. P. Cattermole was a middling and undistinguished officer who offered Milkweed no skills that hadn't already been acquired through other personnel. He hadn't witnessed the escape. But he had heard about it secondhand, and he was a prolific rumormonger.

And, it turned out, he was also a madman, a drunkard, and a fifth columnist seeking to lower morale by spreading Jerry propaganda.

The veracity of the charges was immaterial. Far more important was the grim seriousness with which they were dealt. On the morning of May 29, Cattermole, Milkweed's sacrificial lamb, became the first man hanged under the week-old Treachery Act of 1940, mere days after his 'discovery' as a Nazi collaborator within the Admiralty.

Marsh knew it was a necessary evil. But it didn't alter the fact he'd condemned an innocent man.

Others who had heard of the events second- and thirdhand were now strongly disinclined to share what they had heard, and equally disinclined to pay the rumors any heed at all. They were, after all, nothing but the outlandish fabrications of a Jerry spy. As evidenced by the fact that what Cattermole had described – a man walking through walls? – was impossible.

Marsh stopped at a florist on the way home that evening. 'I'm home, Liv,' he called as he kicked off his shoes. He paused to straighten the framed watercolor hanging in the vestibule; it had been a wedding gift from Corrie Stephenson.

He bumped the end table, knocking to the floor a leaflet from the Ministry of Information and the War Office: *If the Invader Comes.* Liv had set it next to the bowl of water and the blankets. *Hide your food. Hide your maps. Lock up your bicycles. Leave nothing for the Germans.*

Her voice, all chimes and flutes, called from the kitchen. 'In here.'

He went through the den. Liv had put the bassinet there, so as to keep an eye on Agnes while preparing dinner.

Their daughter was a pudgy scrunch-faced bundle in pink swaddling. He brushed her forehead with his lips, as lightly as he could so as not to wake her. She smelled of talcum and baby. He swelled his lungs with the scent of his daughter. If there existed a more potent anodyne for an unsettled mind, Marsh couldn't imagine what it might be. He stood there, wishing he didn't have to breathe, didn't have to release her essence.

The thought of breathing reminded him of the man who rescued Gretel, and speculations about his vulnerabilities. He shook his head, banished the memory.

'Papa's home,' he whispered.

Agnes mewled and shifted, crumpling her face into a new pattern of wrinkles. Her blanket undulated in little fits and starts, powered by the spasmodic motions of her arms and legs before she settled again.

'Papa missed you.'

He watched her for another minute before going to the kitchen. Liv stood at the sink with her back to him, chopping vegetables for a Woolton pie – something new recommended by the Ministry of Food – as she sang along to the music on the wireless.

He wrapped one arm about her waist, pulled her close, and kissed the nape of her neck as he thrust the bouquet before her with his other arm. 'Ta-da,' he said through the fringes of chest-nut hair stuck to his lips.

'Oh! They're lovely.' She took the bouquet of daffodils, snap-dragons, and delphinia.

She twisted in his embrace. 'Thank you,' she said, kissing him. He pulled her closer. She was soft and warm.

'You're shaking,' she said. 'Are you getting ill?'

'Just cold. Hold me a bit.'

She did. Liv read his face when she came up for air. One of her slender eyebrows arched up, as though rearing back for a better look at him. Her face wasn't so round as it had been just before Agnes was born, but still not yet so thin as it had been when they'd first met. She still carried some of Agnes on her.

'Hmm.'

'What?'

'Are the flowers for me or for you?'

'What do you mean?'

'You're feeling guilty about something.'

When had she burrowed inside him like that? This was part of Liv's magic, the way she saw into him, saw the man inside him. She'd done it since the moment they met, as though she'd made a study of him all his life.

'Of course they're for you, dove.' Marsh sighed. He shook his head. 'Bad day at work.'

She didn't ask. She didn't need to.

'So they are for you, then.' She poked a finger in his stomach. 'Cheeky.'

He jumped. 'Never.' Somewhere inside him, storm clouds thinned, turned from coal to lead.

'Hmm,' she said. With the vegetable knife she trimmed the flower stems. Then she plucked a glass preserves jar from the

narrow shelf above the sink. Water sprayed in every direction, jet-
ting from the spout, when she filled the jar. It darkened her
blouse, shone like diamond droplets on her eyelashes.

She frowned, blinked at him. 'I wish you'd mend that.'

'I'll do it now.' He opened the cabinet beneath the sink. She
arranged the bouquet on the windowsill overlooking the back
garden where the Anderson bomb shelter and Marsh's shed
crowded together. She bumped his head with her hip, ever so
carefully, as she did. A breeze swirled through the open window
to tug at the petals.

He touched the back of her knee, rested his hand on the curve
of her calf. 'Someday, Liv, you'll have a real vase. You won't be
using jam jars forever.'

'I think it's cozy.'

Marsh's toolbox jangled as he pulled it out from under the
sink. The sink needed mending on a regular basis.

Agnes cried. Her wails, surprising in their intensity from a
package so small, drowned out the wireless.

Liv lifted Agnes from the bassinet. She hugged the blanketed
bundle to her chest, swaying on her feet in time with the music.
'Shhh, shhh.'

She sang along with Vera Lynn on the wireless, lulling Agnes
to rest. 'We'll meet again, don't know where, don't know
when . . .' Marsh hummed while pulling the faucet apart.

'Tsk, tsk.' Liv cooed to their daughter. 'Your father couldn't
carry a tune in a bucket. What should we do with him? Should
we keep him?'

'What's that, pretty girl?' She leaned her head toward little
Agnes resting against her shoulder, as though listening to a whisper. She fixed Marsh with a long sly look. 'Yes, I suppose he is. In
a rugged sort of way.' One of her tresses bounced across the pale

curve of her neck as she shrugged. 'If one goes for that sort of thing.'

Despite himself, Marsh smiled.

'What else should you know about your father? Hmmm. What a curious girl you are. Now let me think.' She put a finger of her free hand to the corner of her mouth and frowned, eyebrows hanging low over her eyes.

'Well, he is rather sharp. Or so his friends tell me.'

Marsh replaced the washer, chuckling to himself. Somewhere, the sun burned through storm clouds and gloom. He felt inside the valve seat with the tip of his finger. It was worn and rough.

'There's the problem,' he muttered to himself. 'Have to replace that.' Until he did, it would keep chewing up washers, forcing him to replace them regularly.

'And occasionally,' said Liv, 'he shows a glimmer of usefulness about the home. Not often, however.'

He tightened everything, reopened the valve beneath the sink, and tested the faucet. Water gushed from the spout and nowhere else.

'On second thought,' Liv said to their unconscious daughter, 'let's keep him round a bit longer.'

Marsh embraced her. They swayed to the music. Quietly, he asked, 'How long until we eat?'

'A little while.'

'In that case, I'll go out to the shed. Try to get something done before it's too dark.' He kissed Liv on the cheek. 'It's past warm enough to get the tomatoes in the ground, and I should do it soon. Otherwise, it'll be a long wait for a proper salad this summer.'

'Go, you. I'll call when it's time to eat.'

Music floated through the open window all the way to Marsh's shed, though it was too faint to make out. He hummed the Vera Lynn song to himself as he worked. *We'll meet again . . . don't know where . . . don't know when . . .*

He inspected the tomato vines, checking for hornworms and fungus. Just as he'd been taught when he was very young. He'd been putting the plants out every morning to harden them in preparation for transplanting to the garden. In another day or two, they'd be ready to stay out overnight.

Crash. From inside came the noise of a shattered dish.

'Liv?'

He stepped out of the shed. Agnes wailed again.

'Liv?'

'Raybould? Raybould, come here!'

He dropped the plant he'd been working with and dashed back to the house, picturing a ghostly man attacking his family. Liv looked pale and drawn where she knelt in front of the wireless in the den, Agnes clutched to her chest. She reached for him, pulled him to her. Now she was the one to shiver.

'—intensive Luftwaffe bombing, torpedoes, and artillery barrages from the First Panzer Division onshore. Royal Navy destroyers lost during the evacuation include the *Grafton*, the *Grenade*, the *Wakeful*, the *Basilisk*, the *Havant*, and the *Keith*.' The molasses-smooth baritone of Alvar Lidell paused, as though the announcer were turning a page.

'They're saying they've abandoned the evacuation,' said Liv, squeezing Marsh's hand. 'They won't, will they?'

The news continued: 'Vice Admiral Ramsey today announced that despite a most difficult situation, a total of over twenty-eight thousand fighting men have been evacuated since Sunday.'

Left unsaid, of course, was the number of men left behind on the beaches of Dunkirk. Nor was there any count of civilian craft obliterated by the Luftwaffe, though the toll on the ragtag flotilla must have been very high.

They listened through the night. The BBC gave no such numbers. If it knew them, it wasn't likely to report. But Marsh, who had been there not three weeks earlier, knew the combined total French and BEF roster spread across northern France approached half a million men.

He didn't share this with Liv. There was no need. By sunrise, a grim reality dawned on the world, leaving Marsh to wonder what sort of future Agnes would inherit.

Britain had lost an army.

INTERLUDE

They arrived in numbers that blackened the sky, and at the beaches, they feasted.

Amidst sand and iron, surf and steel, ravens gorged on the dead. The first few hours were best, before sunlight and seawater fouled the meat. But soon the carrion reek attracted more than birds. New men arrived to clear the beaches. The ravens, scavengers themselves, watched while these new men picked what they could from the dead. Derelict armaments. Cigarettes. Pocket watches.

And when the dead turned noisome with rot, the men used their clattering machines to excavate trenches and pile the bodies. The fires burned for a day, a night, and a day.

More men arrived, with still more machines. They amassed at the shore, facing west, while a fleet of boats and barges assembled in estuaries up and down the coast. Like some great predator poised to lunge upon its prey, this assembly fixated on the island across the Channel.

Large predators, the ravens knew, brought down large prey. Large prey meant a bounty of carrion.

And so the ravens stayed, and watched.

New shapes darkened the sky that summer. Wave upon wave of these fliers screamed over the water in angry gray wedges of aluminum and glass. Other machines, flown by other men, leapt into the sky to meet them. This was a new kind of dance, a ballet not yet seen in the surge of armies and waltz of empires.

And so the ravens stayed, and watched.

Twined contrails traced sigils in the bright blue sky over the island. The attackers swarmed around the lattice masts dotting the coast like honeybees drawn to sunflowers. One by one, the towers fell, rendering the defenders blind. It was as though their eyes had been plucked out in homage to some ancient myth.

The battles moved inland, beyond the horizon, deeper over the island every week. Each day saw fewer defenders taking to the sky than the day before. The crows and ravens here had it harder than their Continental cousins, for the mounting dead were crushed under timber and brick and so did not make for easy picking.

Sensing its time had come, the army on the coast roused itself and focused on the island with renewed vigor.

And so the ravens stayed, and watched.

But then, at the height of summer, the weather in the Channel . . . *changed*.

The fog – improbably thick – appeared within hours. It heeded neither sun nor wind. Distant shores disappeared, shrouded in persistent gloom. Sunlight could not dispel the haze that wreathed the island.

Phantoms writhed within the cloud bank. Fleeting patterns of light and shadow, noises like voices too faint to make out, lingering scents that evoked empty memories.

The phantoms danced within the water, too. The waves on the Channel assumed impossible geometries: pyramidal waves sliced past one another like serrated saw teeth; towering, needled-tipped spindles whirled through the troughs between the waves; whitecapped breakers defied time and gravity like immense crystal sculptures.

But although these elements rendered the crossing impassable to all manner of ship and landing craft, they did not gird the heavens. The bombs continued to fall. And fall they did, in numbers too great to count.

That autumn, the ravens of Albion abandoned the Tower of London.

EIGHT

31 August 1940
Paddington, London, England

An air of white-knuckled desperation had settled over the platforms at Paddington Station. It put Marsh in mind of Barcelona. But there the mass of refugees swarming the port had comprised entire families fleeing the Nationalist victory. Here the atmosphere was charged with heartache as parents said good-bye to their children.

It simply wasn't possible to evacuate all of London. A long, hard summer had put billet space in the countryside at a premium.

Marsh carried Agnes, wedging gaps in the crowd for Liv, who maneuvered Agnes's pram. Every child at the station wore a pasteboard tag clipped to his or her clothing. Sunlight fell on Agnes's tag and illuminated her evacuee number: 21417. She'd drawn a high number in the evacuation lottery. Her parents had suffered several sleepless weeks waiting to see if they would send their baby girl away before the relentless Blitz caught up with them. The long bellows of their daughter's anti-gas helmet dangled over the side of the pram as Liv navigated the crowd.

Every child had a gas mask. Many carried, or dragged, canvas
duffel bags brimming with blankets and clothes. Rag dolls peeked
from a few sacks. A box of lead soldiers spilled onto the platform
when one boy dropped his bag. Marsh fended off the throng and
helped him gather his toys.

Marsh hated crowds. He hated the prickly feeling that took
root between his shoulder blades when Liv and Agnes went out.
It had been that way for months, ever since he'd come to suspect
the Jerries were watching his family. And now they were about to
send Agnes from the city. She'd be away from the bombs, but
she'd also be where Jerry could watch her and her father couldn't.

A man lost his footing and lurched out of the throng. He
approached too closely, too quickly, and nearly crashed into
Agnes. Simmering resentment, something Marsh had carried for
weeks without fully realizing it, boiled over. Months of frustration
at being unable to *do* anything sought release. Marsh's elbow
caught the man under the jaw and snapped his head back.

'Guhh—'

Marsh glared into the widened eyes of the coughing man.
'You need to step back, friend.'

The man did, clutching his neck as he did so. His companion,
most likely his wife, glared at Liv as she wheeled past the pair.
Marsh raised his arms to fend off others rushing to claim the spot
he cleared for Liv on the platform. He hip-checked a woman
who tried to barge in with her own pram.

The assisted private-evacuation program had taken on a frantic quality after the Luftwaffe had systematically destroyed the
Chain Home radar stations lining Britain's coast. With that elec-
tronic fence out of commission, the Luftwaffe had been free to
obliterate the RAF Fighter Command sector stations in the
southeast. The ops rooms had fallen even more quickly than the

radar masts. The methodical dismantling of Britain's air defenses had proceeded with such inexorable logic that it seemed directed by a higher intelligence. Now the bombs fell on London day and night, and two months into this Blitz, the evacuations to the country couldn't proceed quickly enough.

The overseas evacuation scheme was a failure. Less than a fortnight ago, a U-boat had torpedoed the *City of Benares* and killed ninety-plus children bound for Canada.

The smell of wet paint mingled with the stink of panic and sweat on the train platform. Marsh kept it all at bay with the scent of Agnes. When the invaders came – and they would, everyone knew, just as soon as the odd weather in the Channel cleared up – they would be hard-pressed to find a single signpost, milepost, or placard that might help them gain their bearings. More than a few pubs whose names might have provided a clue to geography had been repainted and rechristened in the process. Every train platform in the nation had likewise received new coats of paint. Only the schedules printed in tiny lettering and posted in glass cases at select locations within the station offered any useful information at all.

All of which had made finding the proper train rather difficult. But now here they were, waiting to meet the lady from the Women's Voluntary Services who would escort Agnes to the countryside.

Liv's aunt Margaret was a billeting officer in Williton, and had reluctantly agreed to care for Agnes herself. The most recent, and therefore most stringent, regulations governing the evacuation forbade mothers from accompanying their children, even infants. Evacuation space was reserved strictly for children and pregnant women.

Marsh nudged his wife. 'Look,' he said, pointing at a row of expectant mothers. All were clearly in the final months of their pregnancies. He had to speak up so she could hear him. 'That must be the Williton Balloon Barrage.'

Liv grimaced, but the play on words didn't ease the tightness at the corners of her eyes. 'You've been spending too much time with Will.' Her gaze flitted over the crowd. 'How will we find her in this mess?'

'I'd hoped she'd find us instead.'

'I can take Agnes if you want to have a look about.'

'No,' said Marsh, shaking his head. 'Let's not split up. Not yet.'

'It's only temporary,' she said, repeating their mantra of recent days. By repeating it constantly, Marsh could almost convince himself it was true, as though he could sculpt reality with the force of his belief.

'She'll be safer out of the city.' Another mantra.

Agnes mewled. Marsh bounced her in his arms. 'Liv,' he said. 'Maybe you should get on the train, too. Margaret will have no choice but to find space if you show up on her doorstep. She's a billeting officer, after all.'

'Oh, heavens, no. No, no, my dears,' said a voice in the crowd.

Marsh and Liv turned to face a wizened little woman. She carried a clipboard in one hand and an infant on her hip. Wisps of graying hair waved under the brim of her hat and from where they had worked loose from her bun. She wore wool socks that had fallen down below the hem of her dress, one higher than the other. Her mouth was full of crooked yellow teeth that looked ready to tumble over, like gravestones in an untended churchyard.

Were they expected to entrust their daughter's well-being to this harridan?

Marsh squeezed his daughter as tightly as he dared without rousing her. This lady from the WVS wouldn't be inclined to do them any more favors if Agnes got cranky even before the ride to Williton.

'I beg your pardon?' he asked.

The woman clucked her tongue. 'Terrible, what Hitler's done, making parents say good-bye to their little ones like this.' She shook her head. 'But there's no room.'

'Room?' Marsh tensed. Heat flushed through his face. The entire situation was fucking ridiculous. 'Sod the room. My girl is only four months old!' The woman's mouth formed a little O as she stepped back.

Liv laid her hand on Marsh's arm. She gave him a reassuring squeeze. More quietly, she said, 'You're from WVS? Agnes is going to stay with my aunt in Williton.'

'Yes.' The lady peered at Agnes's tag, then consulted a list, deftly handling the yearling on her hip and the clipboard at the same time. '21417 ... 21417 ... Agnes Marsh?'

Liv nodded.

The woman checked something off on the clipboard. 'Don't you worry yourselves one jot. I'll personally deliver little Agnes safe and sound to the waiting arms of your auntie. And what a doll she is, too.'

Reluctantly, Marsh gave one last squeeze and kiss to the bundle in his arms. 'I love you, Agnes,' he whispered. He held her close, filling his awareness with her scent, where he intended to hold it until his daughter came home again. Then he handed Agnes to his wife. He asked, 'Isn't there any chance at all you could let Liv go along, too?'

'Raybould, we've been through this—'

'I'd feel immeasurably better if I knew she were safe.'

The WVS harridan clucked her tongue. 'Oh, my dears, I'm so sorry.'

Marsh pressed the issue while Liv said her own good-bye to Agnes. 'You clearly need the help.' He nodded at the yearling on the woman's hip. 'How will you care for him *and* Agnes, not to mention their things?' He indicated the pram and the bulky anti-gas helmet.

The woman laughed. 'Oh, my. It's more than just these two.' She pointed across the platform to where a group of children ranging from toddlers to perhaps ten years old received hugs and kisses from weeping parents. A train porter and three more ladies from the WVS watched uncomfortably over the good-byes.

'But there's enough of us to make do,' the WVS woman continued. She smiled, again revealing those graveyard teeth. 'Haven't lost one yet.'

'I should bloody well hope not.' The Stukas had been known to strafe trains now and then. Every parent knew it.

The WVS woman's lips moved silently for a moment while she studied Marsh's face, as though searching for some way to reassure him or deflect his irritation. Part of him felt badly. She probably received a great deal of abuse. The billeting officers had it worst, but anybody working in the evacuation program was bound to become the focus of strangers' frustration. Before he could assume a softer tone and apologize, she shrugged slightly and held her free arm out to Liv and Agnes.

'Come, dear, let's introduce Agnes to the rest. And perhaps while we're doing that, your husband can help the porter load little Agnes's things on the train.'

Marsh pushed the pram behind the trio to the group of young evacuees and distraught parents. With a bit of shoving and cursing, he and the porter managed to make room in the luggage car for the pram, helmet, and a suitcase of clothing and diapers for Agnes.

The whistle blew. After a final kiss and hug, Liv handed their one and only daughter over to this group of strangers. The runny-nosed evacuees and their meager group of escorts boarded the train. The WVS lady took a window seat and held Agnes up for Marsh and Liv to see as the engine chuffed away down the tracks.

He put his arm around Liv. She rested her head on his shoulder. They watched the tracks until the train whistle faded in the distance.

31 August 1940
Dover, England

The first thing Will noticed was the sunlight. It moved like a living thing.

He stood with Stephenson at the coast, not a dozen strides from where the earth plunged straight down along the famous chalk cliffs of Dover. A gust of wind eddied around Will's legs, rippling the hem of his topcoat, snapping it like a flag. The wind smelled of brine and, impossibly, Mr. Malcolm's shaving lotion.

Will shivered. The stump of his missing finger throbbed with pain. He paced, fidgeting to ward off the chill. Something grabbed his attention, a sense of something odd glimpsed in the corner of his eye. He looked at the long shadow his body carved from the sunrise.

It hadn't moved.

The edges of his shadow rippled, oozed into tendrils of light that choked off the darkness. Will's new shadow grew via the same process in reverse. Repulsion flooded through him while the darkness spread out from his shoes, slithering across the grass before settling into a natural shape.

He shivered again and looked at the sea. The sun hung low in the southeast, round and red like a bullet hole in the sky. The light shone through the English Channel. The Channel was filled with Eidolons. Something unnatural happened to the light inside that non-euclidean fog.

Will glanced at Stephenson. The old man either hadn't noticed the strange light, or somehow managed to not care. His attention was entirely on the Channel, which he studied with binoculars. Weather spotters had reported the disturbance moving closer to shore every day.

Wind hummed through the barricades, pulled a persistent thrum from the coils of razor wire. Barricades like these lined the coast from Ramsgate to Plymouth. But this fence wasn't intended for keeping the Germans out. If invasion happened, no fleet would land here; the cliffs were far too high. No. This barricade had been built to keep people in. To prevent them from hurling themselves into the sea.

Three months had passed since the tragedy at Dunkirk. Two months since Milkweed's warlocks had first invoked the Eidolons to warp the weather in the Channel. And a fortnight had passed since the local police lost count of the suicides along the coast.

A uniformed constable waved at Will from up by the road. He didn't approach. The locals kept as far from the shoreline as they could. Will waved back.

'Sir,' he said. Stephenson let the binoculars hang on a leather strap around his neck. The interplay of sunlight and shadow trickled through the grass when he turned to look at Will. Will said, 'Our bobby is hailing us.'

'Don't forget,' said Stephenson from the corner of his mouth as they ambled up the gentle slope to the road. 'Should anybody ask, we're from the War Office. Got it?'

'War Office. Check.' Will hadn't the slightest idea how to portray himself that way. What did folks from the War Office talk about? Not bloody demons and supermen, that much was certain.

The bobby, a ruddy man with a pug nose, nodded to them as they approached his car. 'You see, sirs? Just like I told you. Something strange going on out there.'

'Hmmm,' said Stephenson.

'Do you think it's the Jerries doing this?'

'Hmmm,' said Will. It seemed the safest thing to say. Better than the truth: *No, son, we're the ones doing this.*

'Just got a call over the blower,' said the officer.

Waves of tension radiated from the poor fellow. Will couldn't help but feel an awed respect for the policeman's resolve. Doing his job day after day, trying to protect people while enduring constant exposure to that wrongness off the coast . . . He was a good man. Will wished he could have offered him some perspective, some sense of hope.

The bobby continued, 'Sounds like something you should see, if you can spare the time.'

Stephenson asked, 'What is it?'

The bobby hesitated. 'It's . . . well, hard to say. Not rightly sure. Better to see for yourselves.'

Will rode up front while Stephenson rode in back. They drove to a small village east of the Dover port. The sun shed a little of its unnatural taint as it climbed higher, no longer shining through the Eidolons.

They stopped at a primary school. Something cold and hard congealed in the pit of Will's stomach. A frightened teacher ushered them inside. The bobby introduced Stephenson and Will as being 'from the government.'

It was a small school, a handful of rooms. Will guessed that it normally accommodated no more than fifty or sixty children. But it was emptier than that owing to the evacuations. The remaining children either had drawn high numbers in the lottery, or their parents had refused to split up the family.

The teacher led them to a playground in back. Four children, three boys and a girl, sat on a swing set. They rocked in the breeze. They didn't blink and they didn't shift, except for their silent constantly moving lips.

'How long have they been like this?' the bobby asked.

'I rang the bell,' she said. 'They didn't come in, so I went out to collect them.'

Stephenson and Will shared a look. Will shrugged. Dreading what he'd find, he went over to get a closer look at the children.

The first thing he realized was that they all faced southeast, toward the coast.

The second thing he realized was that they weren't, in fact, silent. They were babbling. In synch.

He knelt in the sand to better hear them. It was baby talk, nonsense. But Will's trained ears heard something inhuman buried in the quiet prepubescent mumbling.

These children were trying to speak Enochian.

He stood. 'We have a problem.'

Stephenson joined him, leaving the constable and the teacher to their speculations about German bombers and chemical warfare.

'I know why the fog is moving inland,' said Will.

'What is it? What are they doing?'

'They're singing to the Eidolons.'

Stephenson mulled this over. He scratched his chin. 'Can we use this?'

The question knocked Will so off-kilter, it took a moment to regain his mental footing. 'Sir?'

'If they can speak to the Eidolons like you and the others do, perhaps they can participate in the defense.'

Will shook his head, appalled. 'Not without many years of training. These kids might have picked up bits and pieces, but they'll never be warlocks.' He frowned. 'They'll never be completely normal, either.'

'Hmm. Pity. We could have used the help.'

Will suddenly understood the purpose of this trip. Stephenson wanted a first-hand look at the supernatural blockade not out of concern for the effect it had on the surrounding countryside, but out of a businesslike need to evaluate its staying power.

Stephenson wanted to know how long they had until the warlocks faltered, until unnatural weather no longer kept the Germans at bay. Only survival mattered. Nothing else.

And in that moment, Will knew with a sick certainty that things would only grow worse. Stephenson knew damn well what it cost to make the Channel impassable, and to keep it so. But the old man didn't care. If he could be so callous toward the string of unintentional human tragedies arising along the coast, he could also turn a blind eye toward the very intentional tragedies the warlocks would no doubt commit in order to pay the Eidolons' blood prices.

Will had naively assumed limits had been placed on what the warlocks would be allowed to do. A budget of sorts, one they didn't dare overspend. But now he understood that the old man didn't care about the prices. If anything, he sanctioned them.

*

The ride back to London was long, Stephenson's questions exhausting. Will tried to sleep when he returned to his flat, but he couldn't banish the memory of those mumbling children. He didn't *want* to sleep with that image stuck in his head.

He wished he could have slept. Keeping the Channel blocked meant Milkweed's warlocks were on a tight rotation. And that meant another round of blood prices soon. And all of this had been the case before they'd realized the Eidolons were moving inland. Meaning they'd have to redouble their efforts. Somehow.

Will returned to Milkweed before dawn and spent the day working on the one aspect of the job that didn't fill him with dread. It did, however, leave him feeling lost at sea. After months of intensive study at the feet of some rather formidable fellows, he still couldn't translate the Eidolons' name for Marsh. Couldn't even take a stab at it. Neither could the others.

Will hurled his lexicon across the room. 'Damn it, damn it, damn it.' The binding splintered when it hit the wall, erupting into a blizzard of fluttering pages.

It was a copy, of course; none of the warlocks he'd recruited for Milkweed would let go of their invaluable originals. But their greed for new crumbs of Enochian had made them amenable to pooling their knowledge into a single master document. This master lexicon represented the culmination of centuries of Enochian scholarship by generations of Britain's warlocks. Nothing like it had ever been compiled before.

'Buy you a pint to settle your nerves?'

Marsh leaned in the doorway. His arms were crossed over his chest, and he had a look of concern on his face.

A pint? Well. Perhaps . . .

But Marsh merely meant it in jest. Of course.

'Ha. Cheeky sod. I'm knackered. I'd kill for a solid night's sleep, to be perfectly honest.'

'You look like you could sleep for days,' said Marsh.

'It's all these damnable air raid alerts. Getting so that a fellow can't get a night's rest any longer. You'd think the Luftwaffe had declared a war on sleep. You're looking a bit ragged yourself.'

'We sent Agnes away yesterday.'

'Oh, dear. It won't be forever.'

'Wondering what von Westarp's brood will do next, that's what keeps *me* awake at night.'

'We'll find out soon enough, Pip.'

'If we ever encounter them again.'

After those spectacular few days in May, their enemies had disappeared into the Reich. Since then, the listening posts of the Y-station network had turned up nothing pertaining to von Westarp's project. They'd all but vanished. It was nerve-racking.

'We will. And we'll have some surprises for them next time round, eh?'

'So I hope. Clever chap, that Lorimer,' said Marsh.

'He says the same of you, you know.'

Lorimer's team of engineers had spent the summer poring over Gretel's battery. They had a few ideas.

Will didn't understand any of it, but he didn't much care. He was doing his own bit for the war. He'd long ago abandoned any worry that he wasn't doing his share.

Marsh stopped leaning in the doorframe and entered. He picked up a few of the pages that had scattered across the floor. 'Can you slip away right now, or are you on board to relieve the next shift?'

'I'm not back on negotiations for another few days. In the meantime, I'm working on, ah, other things.'

'Lucky you, then. I'm sure that's a relief.'

Will held his tongue for a moment, searching for a diplomatic reply. 'Of sorts, I suppose. There are worse things than negotiations.' He experienced a momentary bout of light-headedness when he stood. Dizziness plagued him these days, as though he were perpetually stepping off a carousel. *And, oh, what a carnival life has become.*

He had to catch his balance on the edge of the desk when he tried to gather up a few of the pages.

'Are you quite sure you're well?' Marsh asked.

'Stood too quickly,' Will lied.

Marsh helped him gather up the loose papers. They worked in silence for a few moments, broken only by the rumblings of Enochian from the next room and a few measures of music. Something orchestral. Phantoms had become commonplace in the Old Admiralty building. At present things were relatively sedate, but for the illusory slant to the floor and the ghostly music. Often it was worse, such as those two days in August when the corridors had been filled with a peculiar mélange of wet sheepdog and overripe bananas. The week before that, a ghostly Siamese had stalked the corridors, occasionally pausing to cough up a phantom hairball.

And there wasn't a clock in the entire wing that ran properly, which was something of a nuisance.

But luckily for Milkweed, many of the Admiralty's offices and much of its personnel had been relocated to safer locales. This was the case with many government entities, even the BBC.

Marsh glanced at the writing on a few pages. 'This is the master lexicon.'

'Indeed.'

'Did it offend you?'

Will took the jumbled pile of papers that Marsh offered him and sighed. 'Frustrated, perhaps.' He shook off the maudlin sentiment. In what he hoped was a lighter tone, he asked, 'No matter. Did you have a question for me, Pip?'

The music became a percussive thrumming that rattled the floorboards like a giant heartbeat. Marsh said, 'Can we talk about it somewhere else?'

'Yes, please, by all means, let's.' Will glanced at his wristwatch out of habit, even though it was a useless gesture. 'I think I'm done for the day.' He set the jumble of papers on the desk and snatched his coat and bowler from the hooks behind the door.

'I'll give you a lift home.'

'Brilliant. Cheers.'

On their way out, Marsh paused outside the room where a triad of warlocks chanted at a shimmering column of smoke. The air in this room coated Will's tongue with the taste of mothballs. Two more warlocks sat in the corner, ready to join in immediately if the strain overcame one of the negotiators. Milkweed had already lost one warlock to heart attack. The hoary legends of master warlocks' immunity to death had proved untrue.

Will could identify the negotiators based on their scars: Hargreaves, White, and Grafton. One side of Hargreaves's face had the rough pink texture of extensive burn scarring; White had long ago lost much of his nose; pockmarks covered every inch of Grafton's skin above the collar, including his bald scalp. Shapley, a journeyman warlock like Will with scarred hands to match, sat in the corner next to Webber, who stared at the pair in the corridor with one blue and one milky eye.

Marsh shivered. Farther down the corridor, and out of earshot of the others, he asked, 'Will, how long can they keep it up?'

'Those chaps? They're the experts.'

'I mean all of them, together. All of you.'

'We'll hold on as long as we can.'

'But how long is that? Stephenson told me what you found in Dover. That the barricade is moving inland.'

It wasn't a topic the warlocks discussed openly amongst themselves. But there was no denying they had exhausted their ability to keep the cost of intervention low. The Eidolons' price grew with each renewal of the pact, like a tide rushing up the beach, quickly, terribly, and Will couldn't see the tide line. They were drowning, an inch at a time, and he was running up and down the beach with a child's toy spade and bucket.

Will remembered the suicides, the damaged children. Ancillary blood prices. Enochian realpolitik.

Will yanked at his tie to loosen the knot squeezing his throat. 'Another week. Perhaps ten days.'

They exited the Admiralty, passed the marine sentries and revetments. They crossed the courtyard beneath a cloudless ice-blue sky.

Marsh turned up the street. 'This way,' he said. Then he asked, 'What happens after that?'

'The Eidolons leave. The Channel reverts to its natural state.'

'Will, it could be weeks before the natural weather makes invasion impossible.'

'I know.' Will followed Marsh to a cream-colored Rolls. 'This is Stephenson's car.'

'He's up-country right now. Why let his petrol ration go to waste?'

Will indulged himself with an exhausted grin. 'You devil, you. He'll have your head for a chamber pot.'

'It was his idea.'

'Ah. I've half a mind to take a car back from Bestwood, to have something in the city. I cut a rather dashing figure in the Snipe, if I do say so myself.' Will concluded, 'Aubrey would have another fit, though.'

'I imagine he would.'

'He's right, I suppose. The best I could do with the Snipe is junk it in the street as an obstacle for Jerry.'

'You could become a tracker,' said Marsh. 'Sleep in your car, outside of the city at night.'

Will gave him another tired smile. They climbed in. 'Pity Stephenson didn't lend you his driver as well.'

'I'll tell him you said so.'

Marsh made a U-turn there on Whitehall. He drove north, toward Trafalgar. It meant he wanted to talk; it would have been shorter to go south. They passed the strongpoint erected inside Admiralty Arch. The machine gun emplacement guarded the long approach down the Mall toward Buckingham Palace. Will tugged on his tie again.

'We need more time, Will. We need new warlocks.'

After weeks of crisscrossing Great Britain and Ireland, Will had identified and contacted fewer than a dozen warlocks. He'd done everything short of picking up the island and shaking it. Several of the men he'd found had been too far gone, too ruined, to contribute.

'There are no more, Pip. We've turned every stone. I even went to the bloody Shetland Isles chasing the rumor of a legend of a folktale, but aside from some particularly bored-looked sheep, I found nothing of interest. I'm sorry, my friend, but there are no more.'

The shadow of a barrage balloon flashed over the Rolls as they rounded the square. The balloons had sprouted up by the thousands across London. They blotted out the sun in places, yet still seemed tiny when the Junkers and Messerschmitts came.

Marsh shook his head. 'I didn't say *more* warlocks. I said *new* warlocks. You and your colleagues need to start teaching Enochian to others.'

'It's not that simple.'

'I've discussed it with Stephenson. We'll recruit language savants from the other services. Perhaps they'll pick up just enough to—'

Will slapped his palm against the dashboard. The ever-present ache in the stump of his finger throbbed. 'I said it's not that simple.'

'Tell me.'

Will breathed deeply, fighting against the constriction in his chest. 'I had this very same conversation yesterday. Can't you have the old man explain it to you? Or one of the others?' By which he meant the warlocks.

'Stephenson won't understand it nearly so well as you do, and I don't know the others so well as I know you. I want to hear it from you.'

Do you know me, Pip? Lexicons and negotiations, actions and blood prices, there's my life for the past few months.

Will marshaled his thoughts. 'The problem is this: Learning Enochian requires exposure beginning at an early age. Adults cannot begin to learn Enochian. Only children can. The younger, the better.'

Marsh frowned. On a brief straightaway, he cracked his knuckles against his jaw, taking one hand at a time from the steering wheel. 'What happens when somebody does come to it as an adult? "Acceptable risk" doesn't mean what it used to, Will.'

'I'm bloody well aware of that. But I didn't say they *shouldn't* learn it. I said they *can't*.'

Marsh risked a sidelong glance at Will. 'Why?'

'We're surrounded with language, human language, from the moment we're born. Earlier, in fact, if you believe sound penetrates the womb. It ... corrupts us. But Enochian is the true universal language, truer and more pure than anything remotely human. Getting a fingerhold on it requires a certain amount of purity.'

'But you're learning from the others. Why isn't that impossible?'

'You can always widen or deepen a fingerhold, once you have that. The trick is getting that hold in the first place. And that can only be done as a child. I'll never amount to anything more than a journeyman, myself. Though I'm improving, thanks to the others. Grandfather started my lessons when I was eight – far too old. It's a miracle I absorbed any of it.'

'Stephenson told me about the children on the coast.'

Will nodded sadly. 'Proximity to Eidolons has been rumored to do that. But don't get your hopes up, Pip. Those children have been surrounded by human language. They're too tainted to learn Enochian without guidance. We don't have fifteen or twenty years to raise them into warlocks. And if you're considering stopgap measures, as I know you are, forget it.' He held up his hand, wiggled the stump of his missing finger. 'I will *not* expose children to blood prices. Full stop.'

They drove in silence for a few minutes. London had become a foreign city to Will. It was the collective effect of many little things, like the way ornamental wrought-iron railings around stairwells and gardens had disappeared into the foundries, and the X's taped across windowpanes. Not to mention the blocks where the Blitz had rendered homes and businesses into scrap heaps of construction debris.

'Will, there's something I don't understand.' Marsh maneuvered the Rolls through the narrow opening in a makeshift barricade of fence posts and sewer piping. Barricades like these would be closed off when the invasion came. Two middle-aged men, volunteers for the Home Guard, stood on either side of the barrier. Their denim overalls were too long; too-small steel helmets sat on their heads like forage caps; their rifles predated the Great War.

After they accelerated again, Marsh continued. 'If only children can learn Enochian, where did the lexicons come from? I know they're passed down the generations, but how did that begin? How did anything ever get transcribed?'

'Ah. You've grasped the very root of the matter. As I knew you would.'

'Tell me.'

'Well. The story goes that at some point in the Middle Ages – nobody can say exactly when – certain Church scholars and intellectuals of the day decided to trace the history of humanity back to its origin in the Garden of Eden. And so they sought the Adamical, pre-Deluge language.'

Marsh nodded. His eyes didn't leave the road, but Will knew he had Marsh's complete attention.

'Setting aside the medieval metaphysics for a moment, they reasoned that the oldest language would also be the most natural. Which is to say that in the absence of other influences, a person would naturally speak this language.'

'The absence of other influences?'

'Yes. So they did the obvious thing. They rounded up as many newborns as they could – it's best not to ask how – and raised them in strict isolation from all human contact and interaction.'

'Good Lord. That's barbaric.'

'Quite. But it worked. The only flaw in their experiment, of course, is that the ur-language isn't a human language at all.'

'My God,' said Marsh. Will knew he was thinking of his daughter.

They were nearing Will's flat, skimming along the south edge of the green expanse of Hyde Park along Kensington Road, when the light traffic slowed to a halt. Marsh idled Stephenson's Rolls into a queue of several other cars.

'Damned Jerries,' said Will. Bomb craters, the rubble of collapsed buildings, and unexploded ordnance were common traffic hazards of late.

They inched forward a bit at a time. Will expected to see a troop of sappers from the Royal Engineers setting up, as was often the case with bomb damage. Instead, a policeman directed the queue around a traffic smash-up.

An omnibus on a side street had blasted through the intersection with Kensington and smashed into the Victorian guardhouse at Alexandra Gate. It had clipped two cars, nearly flipping one, and pinning another to the guardhouse. The omnibus had ripped a deep furrow through the flowerbeds. Three of the four pillars on the guardhouse portico had come down, littering the grounds with chunks of granite. Will glimpsed two more policemen carrying a stretcher covered with a sheet away from the site of the pinned car just as Marsh cleared the congestion and sped up again.

Blood prices.

Will wondered who had arranged this one. He clawed at his necktie. He yanked his collar open, too. A shirt button *plinked* into his lap.

'Not far from your doorstep,' said Marsh. 'Perhaps it's for the best that you haven't driven the Snipe down from Bestwood.'

Will concentrated on breathing, the ebb and flow of air through his lungs. He wasn't drowning just yet. Not yet.

'You know, Pip ... I rather think I will take you up on that pint.'

Marsh looked at him sidewise. 'Honestly?'

'Please.'

Will didn't say anything else until Marsh found a pub with PLENTY OF BEER, BOTTLE & DRAUGHT chalked on the door. Marsh had to point it out twice. Will didn't hear him the first time, because he was too distracted by the crash of surf and an advancing tide.

1 September 1940
Reichsbehörde für die Erweiterung germanischen Potenzials

On Sundays, Klaus took breakfast with Doctor von Westarp.

His parlor on the third floor of the farmhouse overlooked the grounds of the REGP. The treetops of the distant forest shimmered green, yellow, and red in an early autumn breeze. Over the susurration of leaves, one could hear the stutter of a machine gun, the *whoosh* and crackle of fire, the *whumpf* of muffled land mine detonations, Buhler barking orders off in the distance. Gravel pattered against the windowpanes. It came from the immense sand pit that had been constructed on the west side of the complex.

It was quieter inside. The doctor demanded strict silence during meals. Extraneous noise caused indigestion, he insisted. Silence during the meal, followed by a symphony and one cup (precisely eight ounces) of coffee. That was the doctor's recipe for a vigorous constitution. But now Mahler's Sixth had ended, and the gramophone hissed while the needle skipped around the center of the disc. Klaus used a toast point to mop up the last of his breakfast. Today it had been quail eggs, salty Dutch bacon, lemon curd, and bitter coffee mixed with real cream.

The doctor commanded such esteem in the eyes of the Reich's leadership that he enjoyed the first pick of many spoils of war. And Klaus, having single-handedly rescued Gretel from enemy territory (therefore making possible the chain of successes that had inflated the doctor's prestige over the summer) enjoyed von Westarp's favor.

Skrreep. Von Westarp raised the gramophone needle, put the arm on its cradle, and gently lifted the disc with his fingertips. He tilted it this way and that, peering at it through his thick eye-glasses, inspecting it for dust and scratches with the same concentration he applied to subjects in his laboratory.

'I have a new task for you,' he said.

At last. A frisson of excitement ricocheted through Klaus, banishing the usual lethargy brought on by a fulfilling meal. He sat up. 'I'm ready.'

Emboldened by his success in May, Klaus had been agitating for another mission to England. Gretel's report regarding her experiences in enemy custody – though hard to believe at first – pointed the way to the conquest of Great Britain. Kill the sorcerers, and the island would fall. Klaus could do that easily.

But the high command had disregarded his suggestion. Gretel's advice had guided the Luftwaffe through the systematic elimination of Britain's air defenses. The island nation faced a deficit of fighting men, armaments, and morale. The OKW felt that Britain's final defenses would collapse under a sustained bombing campaign.

It was slow and inefficient. Klaus could fix the problem in a matter of days.

Von Westarp exhaled forcefully in short little bursts, clearing the gramophone disc of dust. The motes danced in the sunlight slanting through the tall windows. Between exhalations he added, almost as an afterthought, 'You must do this, or my reputation will suffer.'

'I would die to prevent that,' said Klaus. He was pleased with how genuine it sounded. Perhaps it was true.

'You will oversee the construction of new incubators.'

Incubators. The excitement disintegrated. Cold panic filled the void it left behind, as though Klaus had been stabbed with an icicle. The buzz of the Götterelektron filled his head. Klaus wanted to dematerialize, to become ephemeral so that he couldn't be imprisoned.

He had tried it once, years ago. His battery had lasted just long enough to whip the doctor into a frenzied rage. Two days later, Klaus had emerged from his box feeble with dehydration and sobbing for clemency.

A moment passed while the rest of the doctor's statement sank in. Klaus released the Götterelektron, ashamed of his weakness. He hoped the doctor hadn't noticed the way the dust had eddied through the space occupied by Klaus's body.

Klaus drained the last drops of coffee from his cup to wash away the taste of copper. He set it back on its saucer with the characteristic *clink* of fine Dresden porcelain.

'I don't understand.' Also genuine. Also true.

Von Westarp turned his attention to Klaus, eyes narrowed in irritation. 'The continuation of my work requires new incubators. You will see they are constructed promptly. You do remember your incubator, don't you?'

The doctor called it that because it incubated the Willenskräfte, willpower. Klaus called it a coffin box.

'Yes.'

'Tell the shop to build several of each type,' said the doctor. 'You have first-hand experience, so you will instruct them on the proper methods.' He slid the music disc into its sleeve. 'And note their progress closely.'

Klaus's incubator had been filled with hydraulic plates for squeezing the occupant. Reinhardt's incubator had been fitted with compressors, pumps, and coils of liquid refrigerant. Heike's incubator had been made of window glass, and ringed with lamps, mirrors, and lenses. Kammler's had been the largest, lined with knives and needles, with a single lever out of reach of the restraints.

Von Westarp shuffled across the room in the threadbare dressing gown he'd taken to calling his 'uniform.' He poured a new cup from the porcelain carafe on the table and scooped six heaping spoonfuls of sugar into his coffee. He took the coffee to the bay window overlooking the empire he'd built.

'They envy my success. They covet my standing with the Führer. You must watch them, lest my enemies sabotage me. You're the only one I trust.'

It was common for the doctor to change subjects like this. Such was the mark of a great mind, seeing connections that others found opaque. Common wisdom at the REGP.

But seeing him there at the window ... Klaus wondered if many great men shuffled around in their dressing gowns and obsessed over their bowel movements.

He was silent for too long as he considered this.

'Does this please you?' snapped von Westarp. 'The plotting of my enemies?'

'No, Herr Doctor!' The words came automatically. 'They won't dare act against you. I'll see to it.'

'Good. See the work is completed quickly.'

'It will be.' Klaus stood. He saluted. 'Thank you for breakfast, Herr Doctor.'

'Fetch your sister before you speak to the machinists,' said von Westarp, still gazing outside. Klaus recognized the black Mercedes coming up the long crushed-gravel drive. It belonged to General Field Marshal Keitel, the Führer's chief of staff on the OKW.

'At once.'

Von Westarp slurped at his coffee, waving him away with an impatient flutter of his free hand.

Klaus took his leave of the doctor and went downstairs. He passed the debriefing rooms on his way outside. From one of the rooms came a rhythmic panting and the squeak of wooden table legs across a tile floor as Pabst 'interrogated' one of the Twins. Her sister had been deployed to the Baltic states. Everything she learned about the Soviet occupation there would go straight to her double, unimpeded by the threat of Allied and Soviet listening posts intercepting the transmission.

The autumnal smell of wet leaves wafted across the training grounds. It would rain tonight. The grounds also smelled of diesel fuel and hot sand, from where Reinhardt trained for his mission to North Africa.

Britain's piddling deployments in Egypt and Sudan would fall quickly now that the Italians were on the move; their reinforcements had perished on the beaches of France, after all. But an Italian North Africa would put the Mediterranean in Mussolini's control. Reinhardt's talents – perfectly suited to the desert – would go a long way toward ensuring that didn't happen. He would also spearhead the inevitable advances into the oil fields of the Middle East.

News of the assignment had eased the foul mood that had enveloped Reinhardt since Klaus's elevation to von Westarp's favorite. For months, random objects had developed a tendency to erupt into flames in Klaus's presence.

Reinhardt's new boast was that he had learned how to reverse his ability, to pull heat *out* of something. It meant he could vitrify a swath of sand and cool it into a crude but passable roadbed in moments. Klaus watched. First, the air above the sandpit shimmered. Then the sand turned dark as the individual grains lost their cohesion and relaxed into slag. Dust and debris skittered along the ground past Reinhardt's boots, pulled along by the updraft. The furnace heat felt like sunburn on Klaus's face. The liquefied sand fractured and buckled as Reinhardt willed it cool. It made a hideous noise like the shattering of a million dinner plates.

The entire process took seconds. A Sonderkraftfahrzeug half track plowed forward, crossing from the solid earth of the training ground onto the simulated desert. The makeshift roadbed held. Without the benefit of Reinhardt's alchemy, the heavy armored vehicle would have sunk to its front axle.

But the result was akin to driving over a road paved with shards of glass. The front tires shredded explosively.

'Piss on Christ's wounds!' yelled Reinhardt.

'Perhaps you can regain the doctor's favor with comedy!' Klaus called.

'Piss on you, too,' said Reinhardt. The air around him started to shimmer again.

Klaus left. He passed the new pump house as he headed for the tree line at the far edge of the training ground.

The ground rumbled beneath his boots. He staggered. Slack-jawed Kammler shambled across a minefield, deflecting each detonation back into the earth with the force mirror of his willpower. His long leash snaked along the ground to where Buhler chanted at him through a megaphone.

Klaus found his sister strolling through the carpet of leaves under the oak and ash trees at the edge of the farm. She walked slowly, studying the ground before taking each step. Little blossoms of blue and white dusted her wild black hair with flower petals.

She went through phases. Back in Spain, it had been the modernist poets. This summer, she'd taken to collecting posies. But the weather was changing; Gretel would have to find a new hobby soon.

'Gretel.' She didn't look up. As usual.

Klaus joined her. Leaves and twigs crackled underfoot.

'Keitel is here. You shouldn't keep him waiting.'

'We have a few minutes.' She stopped and cocked her head, staring at nothing in particular. 'He has diarrhea.'

'The doctor will have something to say about that,' said Klaus. He offered his hand to guide her around a thornbush. Gretel took it, shifting the flowers she'd collected from one hand to the other.

'Come. We'll find a vase for those,' he said.

She gazed across the field to where Reinhardt raged.

'Poor junk man,' she said.

Klaus led her around the far side of the farm, toward where Keitel and von Westarp would be waiting. The route took them past the gunnery range that had become Heike's personal training ground. The guns here fired nonlethal wax bullets designed specially at the REGP, back in the days when it had been the IMV, the Human Advancement Institute. They wouldn't kill, but the pain was enough to make one wish they did. Klaus remembered his sessions on this range vividly, and he had the scars on his chest to ensure he'd never forget the lessons learned here.

Most of the others – Klaus, Reinhardt, even Kammler – had graduated beyond this facility years ago. Heike had yet to master it.

But she was getting close. She'd been training like a demon all summer. Ever since Klaus and Gretel had returned triumphantly from England. Reinhardt had been given an assignment even before that, back in Spain. And now one of the Twins had gone to Latvia. Soon even Kammler would be in the field, and Heike would be the last of von Westarp's children to be deemed complete. Nobody wanted to be the sole focus of his disappointment.

Heike stood at the bottom of the obstacle course. The wind teased her hair. Then she disappeared, uniform and all. Reinhardt had been quite upset when she achieved this breakthrough. He'd spent hours watching her train, relishing the moments when her concentration lapsed and he could glimpse, ever so briefly, her naked body.

The gunners opened up, releasing a hail of projectiles across the field every time a bell, chain, or flag indicated the passage of the invisible woman. Most of the bullets splattered harmlessly against the brick wall, but once or twice Klaus heard the 'Hoompf' as a round clipped Heike. But she maintained her concentration and didn't reappear.

'She's improving.' She'd be a formidable assassin. Nearly as good as Klaus when she came into her own.

'Don't you think?' he asked, turning back to Gretel.

The corner of Gretel's mouth quirked up, and the shadows returned to that place behind her eyes. Quietly, she said, 'Heike has her uses.'

Klaus sighed. There had been a time when that half smile filled him with dread. Now it just made him angry.

Gott. *She's going to fuck it up for me.*

'Don't do this, Gretel.'

She looked up. She blinked. She turned for the house.

Klaus grabbed her wrist and spun her toward him. Her arm was so thin and his grip so tight that his thumb and forefinger overlapped by more than a knuckle. Her skin was warm to the touch, though she'd spent the entire day outside. She stumbled, bumping into his chest. Her hair smelled of the purple bell-flowers dangling from her braids.

'Whatever you're thinking, don't. Things are going well now. Don't ruin this.'

'Are they? Are they truly?' She looked him in the eye. 'Do you enjoy building coffins, brother?'

He tried to hold her gaze, but flinched away. 'I'm tired of getting swept along in your wake.' He let go of her arm. 'Do something for *me* for a change.'

Gretel cocked her head, looking him up and down. Then she linked her arm in his and rested her head on his shoulder as he escorted her back inside.

'Twenty-one thousand. Four hundred. Seventeen,' she whispered.

21,417. Klaus wondered if that was supposed to mean something to him. He didn't ask.

NINE

10 September 1940
Soho, London, England

Will spent the afternoon at the Hart and Hearth, waiting to plant the bomb in his briefcase. He stared at the empty pint in his hand, listening to how it rang as he slid it back and forth along planks of polished beech. The glass clinked when he tapped it against the brass rail and asked the barman for another.

He wondered if the Nazis would commandeer the breweries when they arrived. He wondered if German beer differed greatly from British beer. Perhaps they'd build *biergartens*, too. That wouldn't be so bad.

Then again, if things went well tonight, the invasion would be postponed at least until spring. If not ... well, he'd have blood on his hands, no matter the outcome.

The barman refilled his glass. Will nodded his thanks. Drinking made it possible to endure the wait. *God bless you, Pip, for introducing me to the wonders of the pint.*

There had been a time when Will resisted such simple comforts. It seemed silly now. As much as he hated the man, he understood his grandfather differently these days.

His new drink had a thick head of foam. Will imagined it was sea foam, and that if he listened, he could hear the crash of advancing surf. It wouldn't stop until he drowned.

The Hart and Hearth that Will remembered so fondly had become a thing of the past. Gone were the roar of conversation, the clink of glasses, the shimmering firelight on the ceiling. The fireplace was dark. The drive to conserve fuel, even firewood, had trumped tradition.

People still came, people still drank, but the atmosphere had changed. They greeted each other a little too enthusiastically. They laughed a little too loudly. And they drank – when there was drink to be had – a little too seriously. It was the cumulative effect of months of living with a siege mentality.

These were the men and women who huddled in the shelters at night, got up the next morning, climbed over the rubble, and returned to work. Day after day after day. They came to the pubs for companionship, for the illusion of normalcy. But in truth, every person there was drinking alone, seeking the fortitude to make it through the night. Like Will.

He did his best not to notice them, or to be noticed. Rubbing elbows felt a bit ghoulish tonight.

As the afternoon wore on toward evening, Will saw many people glancing at pocket watches or the brass-and-mahogany grandmother clock in the corner. The barman clicked on the wireless a few minutes before six. It gave the valves time to warm up properly.

He rang the bell over the bar with two quick *clangs* on the hour. 'Six o'clock!' he announced.

The pub fell silent. Listening to the BBC six o'clock news was a national daily ritual. The patrons abandoned conversations and dart games to crowd the bar. A tradesman inadvertently kicked

Will's attaché case. Will held his breath as the case toppled over with a leaden *thump*. Nothing happened. Will, shaken but relieved, leaned the case against the bar, and shielded it from further offense.

Frank Phillips read news of the war. Luftwaffe raids had leveled the foundries in Shropshire, Lincolnshire, and Dorset. In Africa, General O'Connor's offensive against the Italians had begun to falter. He might have had a fighting chance with reinforcements, but of course there would be none. Fighting continued in Greece and Italian East Africa. Admiral Decoux, the Governor General of French Indochina, had granted the Japanese basing and transit rights throughout his territory. The tonnage of lend-lease shipments from the United States continued to decline, owing to ferocious wolf packs and a flagging commitment overseas. President Roosevelt's impassioned arguments for increasing aid to Great Britain were increasingly unpopular with the American people and its isolationist Congress.

Hitler's naval blockade was in some ways worse than the Blitz. Common knowledge said they'd stopped dyeing horsemeat green. It was no longer unsuitable for human consumption. The Ministry of Food denied this vocally.

Interest in the state of the outside world had been more keen in the spring, before Dunkirk, when Britain still believed it was in this war, and that victory could be had. These days, the state of the outside world was somewhat academic. The topic on everybody's mind, the subject of true interest, was the weather.

But Will didn't need the wireless to tell him about the weather in the Channel. He'd helped shape it. The fog had lifted, and a stillness had come upon the sea. The Eidolons had returned to their demesne, receded into the crawlspaces around time and space.

But the Met Office knew nothing of Eidolons and blood prices. It simply reported that the Channel was calm and clear. The unspoken corollary was that nothing stood between the south coast of England and the German invasion fleet in France. Will drained his glass and swallowed loudly, drowning out the gasps, the sobs of dismay.

Tonight, of all nights, the Jerries would come in droves. And not just bombers, but paratroopers, too, if Milkweed's gamble worked. The first tendrils of invasion.

The warlocks had concluded their marathon negotiation with the Eidolons; now they sought to begin anew from scratch. But the intervention would be costly. By unspoken agreement, none of the Milkweed warlocks worked near his home neighborhood tonight. It was easier that way.

Will had chosen the Hart and Hearth for two reasons. First, he knew he'd need the services of a public house before the night was through. Second, it had a shelter on the premises. This he knew through first-hand experience, having been stuck here during more than one raid.

He called for another pint. The world had gone fuzzy at the edges. He wanted to keep it like that until the work was done and his share of the blood price paid.

The barman left the wireless on after the BBC update ended. Jack Warner and Garrison Theatre filled the void in conversation. It was unnatural for a pub to be so quiet. As unnatural as a stove without a teakettle.

A number of patrons filed out in ones and twos. Probably those with families. Will begrudged them the excuse to leave.

It was a long wait spent keeping himself on the edge of numbness. But when the banshee wail of air raid sirens finally broke the monotony, he found they'd come too soon. He wasn't ready yet. He could still feel his fingers, his toes, the quickened beating of his heart.

The barman flung open the door behind the bar. A narrow staircase led down to the cellar. 'Right!' he called. 'Everybody down here!'

The patrons queued up behind the proprietor. Will tried to look natural as he lugged the attaché case, but it was quite heavy and threatened to overbalance him. Another door at the bottom of the stairwell opened on the cellar proper. An overpowering latrine stink wafted out of the shelter when the barman cranked this door open. Men and women covered their noses as they filed inside. Somebody, probably the barman's son, had forgotten to empty the pails and coal scuttles from the previous raid.

The air was cool and damp down here, but not enough to suppress the smell. Several cords' worth of firewood were stacked along one wall. Pillows, blankets, and thin mattresses had been laid out between rows of metal shelves. The shelves themselves were bare but for dwindling supplies of tinned meat and withered, eye-studded potatoes.

Will took a seat by the door. He counted nineteen souls in the shelter. Part of him was clinical, and obsessed over the mathematics. A simple calculation, he told himself. Dozens of lives for the sake of thousands. But most of him yearned to run away and drown in the surf.

Several faces he recognized, regulars like himself. He imagined they recognized him, too, as he'd been coming here for tea and atmosphere since long before the war. Before everything changed. Will remembered the evening he'd introduced Marsh and Liv, right upstairs. He wondered how many married couples over the years had met right here at the Hart and Hearth.

The ground shook. Tins rattled on the shelves.

He propped the attaché case on his lap. He waited for the others to hunker down for a long night. When it appeared they were settled and unlikely to surprise him, he cracked the case open, using the lid to shield the contents from casual onlookers. He'd already smeared his blood on the explosive charges, so that through him the Eidolons would gather new blood maps for nineteen souls: Will's share of the blood price. Will set the timer for ten minutes. Then he double-checked it, closed and locked the case, and slid it behind a pile of firewood.

Will waited as long as he dared – less than two minutes, to be sure, though it felt like eternity – until a moment when it seemed he'd been forgotten. He slipped out through the cellar door as quietly as he could.

He hoped that if anybody saw him, they'd presume he'd gone barmy and leave him to his fate. It happened on occasion; people went mad in the shelters. Above all, he prayed that nobody followed him outside. That would make for an awkward confrontation when the Hart and Hearth demolished itself. The blast would level the building. Tomorrow, the overworked rescue men combing through the debris for bodies wouldn't be bothered to notice that the damage pattern didn't match that of Jerry's bombs.

Whether or not his departure went unnoticed, nobody came after him. Running about outdoors during a raid was a fine way to get oneself killed.

Upstairs, he paused again to take in the pub one last time. He'd been sitting right over there, at the table under the stag head, when he first met Liv. The three of them, she and he and Marsh, had chatted there, one table over. Will shook his head, said his farewells, and pinched a bottle of gin from behind the bar. He'd earned it. He dropped the slender bottle into the deepest pocket of his coat. Then he stepped outside.

Chaos. Sirens echoed across the city while the thunder of ack-ack guns rattled windowpanes up and down the street. *Chuffchuffchuff. Chuffchuffchuffchuff.* A fireball illuminated the skyline to the north. The ground rippled. Paving stones clattered beneath Will's feet.

He took the first cross street, eager to put at least one street between himself and the pub. He tried to pick a direction that took him away from the heaviest concentration of bombing, but it was all around him.

The blackout had become a jumble of flickering shadows. Searchlights crisscrossed the sky, blazing through the smoke and occasionally flashing across a barrage balloon. When that happened, the reflected glare shone on the streets below like a few seconds of full moon. Meanwhile, a flurry of tracer rounds from a nearby battery cast shadows that slithered underfoot. The sky glowed orange with fire.

Will ran. The gin bottle knocked against his hip. The earth shook again, rattling the bones of London. When the bomb he'd planted became just another element of the pandemonium, he was several streets away and bounding down the stairs of the Tottenham Court Tube station. Several of the people taking shelter there looked up in surprise when they saw him. Clearly, said the looks on their faces, this latecomer was a madman.

How right they were.

Early the next morning, while the Hart and Hearth still burned, and while an invasion fleet sailed within sight of British soil, the Eidolons returned to the Channel.

*

12 September 1940
Reichsbehörde für die Erweiterung germanischen Potenzials

If you can spare a moment, Herr Doctor,' said Klaus, 'there's an issue with the new incubators.'

Von Westarp paced the length of the debriefing room. The breeze from his passage elicited a papery rustle from the dried wildflowers arranged in milk bottles on the sill.

He paused at the window long enough to glance outside again. 'She did this to humiliate me,' he said before launching into another circuit of the room. 'Where are they?' he asked nobody in particular.

The doctor had put his dressing gown aside long enough to squeeze back into his SS-Oberführer uniform. It didn't fit as it once had; the past year had been good to him. Klaus made a point not to look at the paunch straining at the doctor's belt and buttons.

'There is confusion regarding the equipment,' continued Klaus. 'I gave specific instructions to the machinists. Still, they've wasted time and resources requisitioning unnecessary supplies.'

Von Westarp reversed his circuit of the room. His boots pulverized a handful of wild rose petals that had fluttered to the floor. The air became sweeter and oilier as his continued pacing crushed blossoms knocked loose from Gretel's improvised drying racks.

Nobody had objected when she'd decided to use a corner of the debriefing room for her craft project. Her advice had led the Luftwaffe to dominate the skies over Britain; tolerating her eccentricities was the price for access to her precognition. For much of the summer, the ground floor of the farmhouse had smelled like a perfumery.

Reinhardt insisted it smelled like a Spanish whorehouse. He would know.

Klaus said, 'I confronted them. They claim to be working to your specifications.'

At the window again: 'I've been too lenient with her. Far too lenient.'

'But I'm certain,' Klaus concluded over the doctor's muttering, 'that a few words from you would clear this matter up immediately.'

The doctor squinted at him. 'What are you babbling about?'

'They've ordered the wrong equipment.'

'They've done no such thing! Why must you and your sister turn everything into an ordeal? Second-guessing my every instruction.'

The door opened. Standartenführer Pabst entered, pulling Gretel along with a strong grip at her elbow. Pabst shoved her toward a chair before joining the doctor at the window. They spoke in urgent whispers. Pabst and the doctor had been conferring much lately, though it seemed they agreed on little.

Her damp hair had left a trail of dark moisture spots down the back of her smock. Watertight plugs made from rubber and ceramic had been fitted over the connectors at the ends of her wires. A trail of white salt rime dusted the edges of her face, tracing a line along her forehead, across her ears, and under her jaw.

Pabst must have pulled her from the sensory deprivation tank without giving her time to wash. He and Doctor von Westarp had long since conceded, however reluctantly, that physical violence was of no use in controlling her. They'd resorted to more experimental punishments.

She'd been in the tank for over thirty hours. Von Westarp had locked her inside minutes after learning of the invasion fleet's destruction.

Klaus took the seat next to her at the conference table. Under his breath, he asked, 'How are you?'

'Well rested. Have you solved your matériel problem?'

He fished a handkerchief from his pocket and handed it to her while Pabst and von Westarp argued. He motioned at the edges of his face. She licked an edge of the handkerchief, then dabbed it along her forehead. The tank used concentrated magnesium salts in the water to increase buoyancy and thus mimic the sensation of weightlessness.

Left to his own devices, von Westarp would have left her in the tank much longer. Perhaps even a week, though she'd have succumbed to dehydration before that; rage made him careless. But General Keitel had called an emergency inquiry into her failure to warn the OKW of Operation Sea Lion's doom.

'What will you tell them, Gretel?'

She said something in response to his question, but Klaus couldn't hear it. Von Westarp announced, 'They're here.' Klaus glanced out the window to where a black Mercedes approached the farmhouse.

Von Westarp stood at one end of the conference table, Pabst at his right. 'Answer their questions and do as they say,' said the doctor. 'I will not be made a fool again.'

Gretel's disobedience used to be a private matter. A family affair. Such as when Rudolf had died. But now the Götterelektrongruppe was plugged into the vast apparatus of the Reich's war machine; privacy in failure and success did not exist. Gretel's failure was the doctor's failure.

Three men stomped into the room. General Field Marshal Keitel, the Führer's chief of staff on the OKW, was a silver-haired bull of a man. Klaus had never met the second man, but he wore the uniform of a Wehrmacht Heer generalleutnant. The toady man at Keitel's elbow, Major Schmid, was an opportunistic lickspittle, and grossly unqualified to head Luftwaffe Intelligence.

Also grossly outranked by his two companions, thought Klaus. *How did he weasel his way into this meeting?* Schmid was utterly dependent – almost pathetically so – upon Gretel for information. Who knew what might have happened had Schmid been forced to go it alone? If not for Gretel, Göring would still command the Luftwaffe. *Oh. He wants to know what will happen to him if my sister is out of the picture.*

What have you done, Gretel?

Keitel launched the inquiry as soon as he was seated. 'At 0500 yesterday morning, an invasion fleet launched from embarkation zones across coastal France, bound across clear seas for the south coast of England.' He stared, unblinking, at von Westarp while he recited these facts. 'At 0620, the advance forces sighted the coast. Spotters reported sudden heavy fog in the Channel at 0625. Contact with the fleet was lost at 0641.

'As of noon, all ships and barges remain missing. They are presumed lost with all hands.

'The combined losses to the Wehrmacht are incalculable.' He turned to face Gretel. 'I am here, as the Führer's representative, to know why this happened.'

Gretel watched the general with wide, innocent eyes. She said nothing.

'I demand to know why the OKW received no warnings.'

Gretel stayed silent. The corner of her mouth quirked up. Keitel went quite motionless, like a coiled spring. He didn't blink; he didn't breathe. He stared at her.

Oh, Gretel. Whatever you're doing, you have to stop. This is bigger than you and me. Klaus wished she could hear his thoughts. *These men think you're a traitor. These men will kill you. Even the doctor can't stop that.*

Keitel's face assumed ever darker shades of red as the silence stretched on.

Finally, Gretel spoke. 'In other words, you're wondering why I didn't save you from your own incompetence.'

The room was silent. The only sound came from the doctor, who made gurgling noises.

'What?' Keitel spoke so quietly that Klaus had to strain to hear him over the thudding of his own heart and the rush of blood through his ears. Klaus could see the general's pulse throbbing in the hollow of his throat.

'I can see the future,' she said in a conversational tone, 'but I can't perform miracles.'

Oh my God. They'll kill us all now, just for spite. Klaus risked a surreptitious glance at the gauge on his battery harness. It was low, but not so low he couldn't grab her and yank her through the wall if Keitel pulled his sidearm. He plugged in, careful to keep his movements hidden under the table.

Keitel stood. Klaus prepared to draw upon the Götterelektron. Von Westarp stood as well, imploring the general to, 'Wait!' and Klaus to, 'Make her behave!'

Gretel continued as though nothing had happened. 'Some things are inevitable, even to me. The destruction of the Reich doesn't have to be one of them.'

'The Ninth and Sixteenth Armies. GONE!' *Wham.* Keitel punctuated his statement with a fist to the table. 'Eleven divisions. GONE!' *Wham.* The floor shook under Keitel's rage. 'Half a million tons of shipping. GONE!' *Wham.* Across the room, on the windowsill, flower stems rattled inside milk bottles. 'Tanks. Artillery. Munitions. GONE! GONE! GONE!' *Wham. Wham. Wham.*

'And as I've told you,' said Gretel, meeting Keitel's fury with ice, 'it couldn't be helped.'

'Your duty was to warn us,' bellowed the Wehrmacht general-leutnant.

'What would you have done, had I warned you? I'll tell you, because I've seen it: You'd have postponed the invasion for another day. And still it would have failed. But the long-term implications would have been far worse than they are now. Today it is a loss, yes, but not our destruction.'

Keitel sat again. 'That's twice you've mentioned destruction.' A simple statement, testing the waters.

'Something is coming,' said Gretel.

'*What* is coming?' It was more an order than a question. Again, a simple statement, testing the waters.

'Our doom,' she said. The others fell silent while this prophecy sank in.

'The warlocks. This is their doing?' asked Pabst.

'Yes. They will destroy us all.' She shuddered, adding, 'I've seen it.'

'If this threat you describe is real,' said Keitel, 'what can be done about it?'

'There is a village in southwest England. Williton.' Shadows flickered behind her eyes when she uttered the name. 'You must destroy it if you wish to avert our fate.'

Schmid said, 'I've never heard of any such village.' To his superiors, he said, 'It's not listed on the strategic bombing survey. I'd know.'

Gretel acknowledged his presence for the first time since he entered. 'Oh, yes, Major Schmid's famous survey. You did such a fine job, identifying so many high-value targets all by yourself.' Gretel cocked an eyebrow. 'One wonders how a former clerk achieved such brilliance.'

Keitel shook his head, still flushed with fury. 'You did nothing to prevent the greatest defeat of this war. And now you insist we focus our efforts on an obscure, insignificant village. This is a waste of time.'

Gretel said, 'Williton is the key. Demolish it, leave nothing standing.'

Keitel stood again. 'We're finished here.' He headed for the door, the others in tow.

Klaus exhaled. They weren't, it appeared, going to kill her outright. But the doctor might, when all was said and done.

'Wait!' von Westarp followed them.

'Her madness is too far advanced,' said Keitel. 'She can't be trusted. You should put her down.'

While they argued, Gretel walked to the window. She pulled a few sprigs of the most well-preserved flowers from each bottle. She arranged the collection into a little bouquet of primrose and aster.

'Herr General Keitel,' she called. 'Your wife enjoys dried wildflowers, no?'

Keitel turned in the doorway, looking alarmed and impatient. 'What?'

Gretel said, 'Your wife.' She held the flowers up. 'When you go home this evening, give these to her. Tell her all will be well again.' She crossed the room to place the bundle in Keitel's hand. He towered over her. 'Reassure her,' she said. 'It wasn't her fault.'

He stared at her over the dried blossoms, as though taking the measure of her. Could he see the shadows behind her eyes as easily as Klaus?

'What do you know of Lisa?' he asked.

'All will be well again,' Gretel repeated. 'She will recover.'

He opened his mouth as if to say something else, but stopped. Then, without warning, he turned and exited. He didn't speak. Nor did he discard the flowers. His colleagues followed him out the door. The doctor joined them, as did Pabst.

Klaus waited until he and Gretel were alone. 'What was that all about?' he asked.

'His wife will miscarry this afternoon.' Gretel said it with the same bored disinterest she might have used to pronounce the day's soup not to her liking.

Klaus mulled this over. He was coming to understand that mad or not, Gretel did almost everything for a reason. He tried to see the world through her eyes, tried to think as she did. Cause and effect.

'That's why you've been picking flowers.' He didn't ask, because it wasn't a question. 'You knew he'd balk. But you also knew about his wife, and you knew how to exploit that situation to convince him to heed your advice.'

Gretel clucked her tongue. 'Such a devious brother I have.'

She blew loose petals and crumbled leaves from the table. Then she carried an armload of bottles from the windowsill to the table and began to rearrange the flowers.

Cause and effect.

'Why didn't you warn them?'

She concentrated on her wildflowers, saying nothing.

Cause and effect.

Klaus watched her try another arrangement, saying, 'If I asked, would you tell me what you're doing?'

'I'm arranging flowers. Perhaps you aren't so clever as I'd thought.'

'You know what I meant. Tell me, Gretel.'

'And allow you to be swept along in my wake? Never.'

Klaus stomped out of the room. He slammed the door.

The machine shop was a cacophony of drilling, hammering, welding, and sawing. It smelled of hot steel and oil. In addition to countermanding Klaus's directives regarding the supplies, the doctor had also increased his order. Now he wanted thirty incubators of each type.

Klaus remembered the day that the doctor first unveiled the devices. He had been perhaps eight or nine when the doctor first locked him inside his incubator. He'd screamed himself hoarse when the claustrophobia consumed him, pounded his fists raw. There was no room to move inside; it had been built especially for him, and modified accordingly as he grew over the years.

In those days, von Westarp had kept them all in the same room. When Klaus had become too exhausted to scream and carry on any longer, he listened to Rudolf, Heike, Kammler, and the rest cry all night long. Except Gretel, of course. Of all the children, she and she alone never cried. Not once that he could remember.

Klaus remembered something he hadn't thought about in years. There had been many more test subjects back then. So many, in fact, that the field behind the house was—

—And then Klaus knew why the doctor had ordered the machinists to requisition so much extraneous matériel. The gas lines, the lime, the earthmoving equipment. None of this was for building incubators. It was for the mass disposal of bodies.

The doctor was planning for a massive influx of test subjects. Too many to bury one at a time, as he'd done in the old days.

*

19 September 1940
Williton, England

Nine hours of bombing had erased the road to Williton, rendered it indistinguishable from the surrounding countryside. The churned and cratered earth still smoked in places. Here and there broken macadam peeked from the mud, but this only suggested a road, inasmuch as a shattered dish suggested a family dinner.

The undercarriage of the Rolls screeched as Marsh gunned the car over another hillock, causing debris to rake the belly of Stephenson's car. Then the suspension groaned when he forced the car to bounce across another cleft.

'What if she's cold?' said Liv, kneading a blanket in her fingers. It was pink, it had elephants and baby stains on it, and it smelled like Agnes. 'I hope she's not out in the cold.'

'She could be safe. They could be in a shelter.'

In London, one heard tell of folks emerging from their shelters with nary a scratch, only to find their neighborhoods flattened. Sometimes they had to wait for the rescue men to clear away debris before the door could be wedged open.

The little information doled out by the BBC suggested this would be unlikely. *Luftwaffe … Carpet bombing … Williton.* The details were hazy to Marsh. He'd been out the door on the way to beg, borrow, or steal Stephenson's car before Alvar Lidell had uttered four sentences. In the end, he stole it. As well as the petrol canister that Marsh tossed in the boot while Liv urged him to *hurry, God's sake, Agnes needed them, why couldn't he do it faster?*

'I hope she's not hungry. What if she's hungry? We didn't bring her food. We should go back and get her food.'

Marsh drove on, wishing for Williton to emerge from the smoke, whole and pristine. It didn't. He stopped the car when he couldn't cajole it over the debris any longer. He killed the engine. They climbed out.

Rubble. They stood on the shore of a sea of rubble that stretched to the horizon. Here and there men in wide-brimmed metal helmets like sun bonnets scrambled over the mounds. Searching, or carrying stretchers. Sunset glinted on one man's helmet, highlighting the letter *R* painted over the brim. But for the occasional rockslide of broken brick and masonry, the rescue men moved silently, like ghosts in somebody else's graveyard.

TNT and baby. Two scents that should never mingle.

Liv mumbled, 'She's cold. She's hungry and scared.'

'Where?' Marsh had never been to Williton, didn't know the village, didn't know where to find Liv's aunt.

They walked. Every block was a jumble of senseless images. Pulverized brick. A dented tea service. Shattered window glass. A Victorian fainting couch half-collapsed beneath a heap of charred timber. Jumbled masonry. A child's shoe. A bathtub. A cracked chimney, the bricks pulling apart in a snaggletoothed grimace. A family Bible. A dining room wall. A teacup.

What they didn't see were the telltale mounds of Anderson shelters.

That could have meant they'd sheltered in cellars. Cellars. Yes. Perhaps they were trapped inside. Underfoot, just feet away, waiting for somebody to free them. If he could find a cellar, find people alive and well and waiting to be dug out, then he'd know Agnes was safe somewhere, too.

'She wants her blanket,' said Liv.

The debris tore his trousers, gouged his knees. Window glass sliced his fingers. When he hurled the bricks aside, they landed with a crash and tinkle, oddly high-pitched for such heavy things. More bricks. More crashing.

He found a rhythm. Lift, hurl, crash. Blood and dust caked his hands. Lift. Hurl. Crash.

'Raybould.'

He couldn't spare Liv more than a glance. A trio of rescue men had joined her: one old, one pudgy, one pale. Good. More hands.

'Raybould,' she said again, less quietly this time.

They stood there, watching. Why weren't they helping him? He wrestled a length of timber from the wreckage. It perforated his hands with splinters.

Footsteps crunched through the debris. A hand rested heavily on his shoulder.

'It's over, son.'

Marsh tossed aside another piece of timber.

The rescue man crouched beside Marsh and squeezed his shoulder. 'That's our job,' he said. 'There's nothing you can do.'

Marsh's fingers wrapped themselves around something solid, a brick or piece of masonry. Lift. Hurl. Crash.

The hand on his shoulder moved to his elbow and tugged. 'Why don't you come with me. We'll get you some food.'

Marsh's fist closed around the corner of a brick.

'Come,' said the rescue man, standing up. 'It's over.'

'Nobody fucking tells me to abandon my daughter.'

'What's that?' The rescue man leaned forward. 'Why don't you stop for a moment so I can hear you better?'

Marsh launched to his feet as he spun. He put all his weight, all his rage, behind the thing in his fist.

It connected with the corner of the rescue man's mouth. Marsh felt something crack and give way. The man toppled backwards. His helmet clattered down a pile of debris. Marsh dropped the thing in his hand and leapt on him.

'I said nobody—' His fist connected again. '—fucking tells me—' Now the other fist. '—to abandon my *daughter*!'

A pair of arms wrapped around his waist and lifted. But Marsh's rage had been uncorked. He thrashed. He threw his head back, connecting with something that made a soft *crunch*. The grip on his waist loosened, but then more hands grabbed him from behind. He stamped down on the third man's instep and shoved his elbow back with as much force as he could muster, wrenching his shoulder as he did so.

'Oof …' The third man grunted, but didn't loosen his grip. He outweighed Marsh by a considerable margin, and so was able to pull him away.

The pain in Marsh's twisted shoulder and his lacerated hands became cracks in the dike restraining something immense and black. He didn't want to feel it, but it flooded through his defenses.

'Nobody …,' he panted. He sat in the mud because the words were too heavy. 'Tells me … Oh, God, Agnes. Where are you?' The last came out as a sob.

He looked to the man he'd hit. He appeared to be in his mid-sixties. Spittle and blood trailed from his lips. His mouth was dark red. The pale fellow crouched beside him, helped him up with one hand as he pressed a handkerchief to his nose with the other.

Mud seeped through Marsh's trousers. Cold. Wet. He wished the cold would seep into his heart and numb him.

'We sent her away,' said Liv.

She was sitting on what had been the front stoop of some-body's home. Marsh pulled himself up and joined her.

The rescue men gathered up their fallen companion. The man with the bloodied nose took one arm over his shoulders, and the pudgy man took the other. They limped away, casting glares and curses in Marsh's direction.

'Why did we send her away?' asked Liv, shivering.

Marsh draped an arm across her shoulders. She pulled away. They cried.

Night fell. The stars came out. Liv shivered again.

'You tried to send me away, too,' she said.

TEN

3 November 1940
Reichsbehörde für die Erweiterung germanischen Potenzials

The machine shop was a loud place. Klaus worked alone in an isolated corner, far in the back. Building incubators he could handle; the rest of the new construction projects left him feeling ill. He hated to think about the ovens.

He didn't realize somebody had approached him until the tip of the spanner turned orange. Wisps of smoke spiraled up from the blackened pinewood beneath the bolt he'd been tightening. Klaus dropped the tool when heat came surging down the handle into his hand. It slapped the floor like a dollop of taffy.

'Did I get your attention?'

Klaus turned, sucking at the new blisters on his palm. Reinhardt stood behind him, looking slightly amused.

'Haven't they sent you to Africa yet?'

'Not yet.'

The stink of melted linoleum emanated from where Klaus had dropped the tool. It glowed a dark red-black color as it sank into the floor. Klaus grabbed a pair of tongs from an adjacent workbench and dumped the spanner into a water barrel, creating clouds of steam.

'You could have yelled,' said Klaus. 'Or tapped my shoulder.'

'And risk startling you?' Reinhardt shook his head. 'That could have been dangerous. You're very jumpy.'

'Dangerous to whom, me or you?'

'I had your well-being in mind,' said Reinhardt. 'Do try to be gracious about it.'

Klaus fished the spanner from the barrel. The handle had warped, and the jaws had sagged out of true. Reinhardt's stunt had reduced it to so much mangled steel.

Klaus said, 'You've ruined it.'

'I'll melt it down if they wish to recast it.'

'What do you want? I'm busy.'

'Pabst wants to see us,' said Reinhardt.

'You and me? Now? Why?'

'I presume he wants to discuss the doctor's plan.'

'What plan is this?' asked Klaus, sucking at the burns on his palm again.

Reinhardt put on a wholly unconvincing show of forgetfulness. 'Oh, of course, this is the first you've heard of it. The doctor mentioned it over breakfast.'

You mean after breakfast, thought Klaus. *Doctor von Westarp wouldn't tolerate your chatter while he digested.*

'Whatever this entails,' he said, 'I hope it doesn't delay your deployment. That would be a shame.' Klaus used a clean rag to wipe the metal-and-sweat smell from his hands. It ripped the blisters open.

'No more a shame than after all these years, your best use is as a carpenter.'

'Do I have time to wash?'

'They're waiting now.'

'Of course they are,' said Klaus.

He followed Reinhardt to the farmhouse. They passed Heike
and Gretel, who were whispering in the niche beneath the stairs.
Whatever Gretel's grudge against the statuesque blond woman
might have been, it seemed to have passed.

Reinhardt leaned over the balustrade to blow a kiss at Heike.
She turned her back to him, shuddering.

Klaus caught a snippet of the conversation as he followed
Reinhardt up the stairs. '. . . disappointment is terribly profound,'
Gretel said.

Heike said, 'But my training. I've improved so much.'

'Perhaps. But in their eyes, it is not enough. They see only failure.' Gretel laid a hand on Heike's forearm. 'It is unfair.'

'What will I do?' Heike moaned.

The little he heard of this exchange surprised and startled
Klaus. He'd gathered that Pabst and the doctor were quite
pleased with Heike's recent breakthroughs. He made a mental
note to check on her later.

The second floor housed the rooms where Klaus and the
others slept. It was emptier these days. The Twins were gone, and
Kammler was off with the wolf packs, peeling apart the hulls of
American merchant marine ships and their escorts. The staircase
at the front of the building, for the doctor's official visitors, was
wide and grandiose. But Klaus and Reinhardt took the former
servants' stair instead.

The parlor hadn't changed since Klaus's last breakfast there,
prior to Gretel's failure to warn the fleet. The gaps amidst
leather-bound volumes on the shelves had moved around, and
now a new set of scribbles covered the doctor's blackboard, but

otherwise it was the same. The doctor's sanctorum, his workspace. Where his intellect reigned.

Pabst and von Westarp stood at the observation window, again speaking in hushed, urgent tones. Pabst turned when they entered. They saluted. He took a seat at the doctor's long dining table. Klaus and Reinhardt followed suit. The doctor remained at the window in his threadbare dressing gown, gazing outside with his arms crossed behind the small of his back.

Pabst spoke. 'The two of you await new deployments.'

'I'm ready at any time,' Reinhardt said.

'So am I,' Klaus added. 'I proved myself in England.'

Reinhardt laughed. 'I proved myself long before that.'

'You torched a hotel in a fallen city. Any imbecile with a box of matches could do that. *Kammler* could do that. I went straight to the enemy's heart and brought Gretel back alive. It wasn't so simple.'

'You went straight to the enemy's heart and went sightseeing! I would have known enough to strike while I was there. A killing blow, too, had it been me. I—'

'Enough!' shouted Pabst. 'Your deployments have been postponed. We need your combined talents here.'

Klaus looked at Reinhardt. *Please don't make us partners.* He wondered, not for the first time, if in a fight he could squeeze Reinhardt's heart, or scramble his brain, before Reinhardt burned him to death.

Reinhardt was watching him, too. Probably doing a similar calculation in his own head.

Pabst said, 'There are two issues.'

'What issues?' Klaus asked.

'The first comes from your sister. She has foreseen an assault upon the Reichsbehörde.'

Reinhardt objected. 'Herr Standartenführer. One must point out that neither the threat nor the source are particularly credible. It's hard to believe that anybody would be foolish enough to attack this place. But if they are? Let them,' he said. 'And Klaus's lunatic sister is untrustworthy. To the point of treason, if I may say so.'

'She's done more to advance the Reich's war effort than any other single person,' Klaus said.

'Is that so? Remind me. How many men died during the attempted invasion?'

Pabst slapped the table with his open palm. 'Quiet.' The doctor's tea service rattled on its platter. 'You are here to listen.'

He collected himself. 'Regardless of Gretel's recent performance,' Pabst continued, 'we will take her warning seriously. You will stay here until the threat has passed. Kammler has been recalled from the North Atlantic.'

Reinhardt muttered his assent. Klaus acknowledged the order.

'After that, the doctor has special plans for the pair of you.' The significance of the standartenführer's wording wasn't lost on Klaus, and he doubted Reinhardt missed it, either. As the head of the REGP, Doctor von Westarp outranked Pabst. If the doctor chose to exert his opinion on military matters, there was little Pabst could do.

The doctor spoke. 'The Reichsbehörde,' he said, 'is overdue for a recruitment drive.'

Klaus kept his expression neutral. He'd been expecting this, of course. The incubators and the new monstrosities meant the doctor expected a wave of test subjects in the near future. It was an open secret.

Pabst said, 'The doctor envisions a second generation of the Götterelektrongruppe.'

'My work has grown stagnant,' said the doctor at the window. 'I wish to circumvent my previous mistakes.'

This, however, caught Klaus by surprise. He wondered what that meant.

'Forgive me, Herr Doctor,' Reinhardt said. 'The war will be over many years before new subjects could be ready to join the Götterelektrongruppe. It will take too long.'

Von Westarp grew still. A moment passed before he said in a flat, angry voice, 'That remains to be seen.'

So many incubators. How do you plan to fill your crematorium, Doctor?

Pabst cleared his throat. 'The doctor believes' – again, that phrasing, distancing himself from this decision – 'that loyal families will gladly give up their sons and daughters when they see your magnificence on display.'

Ah. No more foundling homes, then.

Klaus barely remembered how he'd first arrived at Doctor von Westarp's orphanage. He had one hazy, dreamlike memory of riding in a horse-drawn hay wagon. He wondered if they truly had been orphans, or if a mother and father had given Klaus and Gretel to the doctor.

The meeting devolved into a planning session. Pabst discussed preparations for the attack Gretel claimed to have foreseen. After that, the doctor explained in great detail a touring recruitment effort. The sun was low in the sky by the time Klaus and Reinhardt were dismissed.

Reinhardt followed Klaus down the narrow stairs. He asked, 'He's not planning to replace us, is he?'

'I suppose that also remains to be seen.'

Heike's room abutted the stairwell on the second floor. Klaus heard sobs coming through the wall. So did Reinhardt.

He knocked on her door. 'Liebling, are you well?' No response. Only sniffling. 'I stand ready to comfort you.'

'Leave her alone,' said Klaus.

'Call when you need me,' said Reinhardt to the closed door. The sobbing resumed as they went downstairs.

Klaus took a simple dinner of stew and black bread while mulling the doctor's recruitment plan. He couldn't understand the expectation that parents would willingly give up their children to Doctor von Westarp. He and Reinhardt might have been strong arguments for greatness, but the wires attached to their skulls were bound to alarm parents and volunteers. Klaus's thoughts kept returning to the hay wagon. How had the doctor obtained his subjects the first time around?

He resolved to discuss these things with Reinhardt. The salamander was an arrogant ass, but he was no fool. And if he remembered how he'd come to be at the REGP, Klaus would want to hear that story. He didn't consider asking Gretel; no matter how much she knew, it would turn into a waste of time.

That night, Klaus dreamed of the hay wagon and a sickly towhaired boy.

Reinhardt proved difficult to find the next morning. He wasn't on the training ground. Nor was he in the mess, the machine shop, the library, the icehouse, the gymnasium, the laboratories, the briefing rooms. And it wasn't Sunday, meaning Reinhardt wasn't breakfasting with the doctor.

Klaus returned to the farmhouse to check Reinhardt's room again. He found Gretel sitting on the stairs above the secondfloor landing.

'Have you seen Reinhardt?' Klaus asked.

'He's in there,' she said, nodding at Heike's door.

'Really?'

'Truly.'

'How long has he been in there?'

'Thirty-seven minutes.' She paused. 'Thirty-eight.'

Klaus lifted his hand to knock, but Gretel said, 'I wouldn't.' He looked at her. 'He'll be out momentarily.'

And he was. Reinhardt emerged from Heike's room, smiling to himself as he buckled his belt. The smile disappeared when he saw Klaus and his sister waiting outside. His pale eyes widened in alarm. But he straightened his uniform, regained his composure, and went downstairs without saying a word.

Gretel called after him. 'Reinhardt.'

Reinhardt paused between the first and second floors, his back to them.

'Happy birthday,' she said.

Reinhardt trotted down the stairs.

Happy . . . ?

Reinhardt had left Heike's door ajar. Klaus knocked. 'Heike? Are you all right?' No answer. He knocked harder. The door swung open.

Heike lay sprawled on the bed, naked from the waist down. Her skin had a bluish tint. She stared at the ceiling, unblinking. She'd been dead for hours.

15 November 1940
Milkweed Headquarters, London, England

'We have the power to annihilate the Jerries *today*,' said Marsh. 'So why are we pissing about with defensive measures when we could be grinding them into *paste*?'

Floorboards squeaked underfoot as he paced. He looked

around the table, glaring at each person in turn. Six people had been summoned for this meeting in Stephenson's office. In addition to Marsh and the old man himself, Lorimer was there, as were Will, Hargreaves, and Webber.

Nobody met his eyes. Not even Stephenson. Marsh knew that his passion made them uneasy, as though they were made witness to things better left private. They treated him like a ghost. Like something that shouldn't be seen. It had been that way since Agnes . . .

Meaningful glances ricocheted through the trio of warlocks. They were a secretive lot. Even Will kept his own counsel more often than not these days.

All eyes turned to the warlocks. Seated together side by side, they looked like an illustration of the Riddle of the Sphinx. Will, with the dark bags beneath his bloodshot eyes, was morning's infant. Webber's eyes had long ago sunk into his skull; along the way one of them had become a colorless marble. He was the middle-aged man of noon. And Hargreaves, who'd lost more than an eye when fire ruined the left side of his face, was the old man of evening. It was like gazing upon a capsule summary of one man's life.

Marsh cracked his knuckles while waiting for a response. The bristles of a beard tickled the backs of his fingers when he pressed them to his jaw. It surprised him. He tried to remember how long it had been since he'd last shaved, but couldn't.

Will opened his mouth as if to speak, hesitantly, but didn't say anything until Hargreaves gave him the nod.

'It's more complicated than that, Pip.'

'Complicated? We're at war. Defeating the enemy is our one and only job,' Marsh said. 'I fail to see why this is so difficult for you to comprehend.'

Lorimer said, 'Moment ago you said "annihilate." Grinding them into paste isn't the same as defeating them.'

'They're annihilating *us*!' Marsh kicked his empty chair aside to stand over the Scot. His reflection in the polished cherrywood tabletop was that of a bellowing madman. Perhaps he was just that.

Stephenson pointed at Marsh. 'You. Sit.'

Marsh tossed the chair upright. 'This isn't bloody advanced maths,' he muttered, taking his seat again.

Stephenson looked at Will and the other warlocks. 'You three. The man has a point.'

Will waited for another nod before answering again. Ever since he had taken it upon himself to recruit the others, he'd been something of a liaison for them. But Marsh had never seen him act so deferentially to them. 'There are rules that limit what we can do. Certain actions that must never be undertaken.'

'Such as using the Eidolons to kill,' said Webber. The sound of his voice was surprising, almost alarming, in its normality. Marsh had never before heard the man speak English. Only Enochian. He wondered if warlocks ever spoke Enochian to each other, rather than to the Eidolons.

'What kind of shite is this?' said Lorimer. 'You lot did exactly that in the Channel.'

Hargreaves spoke for the first time. 'Bite your ignorant tongue and choke on it, Scotsman. We did no such thing.' The heat-glazed skin around the side of his mouth wrinkled in unpleasant patterns when he spoke. His voice wasn't quite so normal as Webber's. Enochian had etched itself into the soft tissues of his throat.

'Eat shit, you plug-ugly—'

'The Eidolons didn't kill those men,' Will interrupted. 'They altered the weather. Changed the wind and the sea. After that, events followed their natural course.' Looking at Marsh, he concluded, 'But the important point is that no man died through the *direct* action of an Eidolon. The Eidolons themselves did not shed a drop of human blood.'

Stephenson took a long drag on his cigarette. The smoke swirled up to join the growing cloud over the table. 'That seems a rather academic distinction.'

'Oh, it's not, sir. The Eidolons want blood. We mustn't give it to them.'

Stephenson frowned. 'Why blood?'

'Because blood,' said Will, 'is a map.'

Lorimer: 'What the hell does that mean?'

'Consider this,' said Will. 'What do we know about the Eidolons? Very little, but for two things. One: they are omniscient, omnipotent, omnipresent. And two: they don't like us. Our existence ... offends them in some alien way we can't hope to understand.' Will shrugged. 'They're beings of pure volition. Perhaps they're offended by the notion that anything as profoundly limited as we are could also express volition.'

Marsh thought back to the sensation of overwhelming malice he'd felt, the first time he'd experienced the presence of an Eidolon, the day he'd severed Will's finger. *We are pollution. A stain upon the cosmos. And we are not welcome here.* And then he understood Will's didactic point. *The Eidolons are godlike beings that want us dead.*

'How is it we're still here?' he asked.

'Exactly!' Will nodded vigorously, pointing at Marsh. 'That's precisely the point. They want to erase us. And yet, they haven't. Why? Because they can't *find* us. They know we exist, but they see every point in the universe. All of time, all of space, all at once. And it's all the same to them. So which points are *you*' – he pointed at Marsh – 'and which points are a distant star? They have no way of telling. Weeding us out is a virtually impossible task. Even for them.'

Marsh thought this through. Furrowed brows told him that Lorimer and Stephenson were doing likewise. The other warlocks looked bored and irritated.

'It's a problem of demarcation,' said Marsh.

'Yes. Imagine I told you all our problems could be solved by squashing one particular ant in Britain. How would you find it?'

'This is all fascinating, I'm sure,' said Stephenson, 'but what does this have to do with my question? What does blood have to do with any of this?'

Marsh nodded, feeling the same irritation. He shifted in his chair, trying to find a posture that eased the ache at the small of his back. Like his beard, he couldn't remember how long he'd had it. Since he started sleeping on the cot. When had that been?

'Blood is special. The blood coursing through your veins, around every crumb of your body, defines locus points in space and time that bracket your human experience. In other words, blood provides a map that directs the Eidolons to our very limited level of existence. It enables them to focus on us. To see us.'

Marsh thought back to how the Eidolons noticed him when he severed Will's fingertip. Gretel's nails had drawn his blood. It brought him to their attention.

They've given you a name.

Will said, 'That's why every negotiation begins with a token. We capture their attention with a combination of blood and Enochian. After that, well, every interaction with the Eidolons is a transaction. Every deed, no matter how small, carries a blood price.' Will raised his hand, displaying the stump where the tip of his finger had been.

Hargreaves frowned in disapproval. A grievous price for such a trivial negotiation. But then Marsh thought, *A fingertip? I'd give so much more than that, and gleefully, if it meant having Agnes back.* Expressing that thought sparked something in the back of his mind, but Marsh put it aside as Will continued.

'We barter for the lowest possible price. Once that's established, we carry out payment, and the Eidolon wills the deed into existence. Its volition shapes reality.'

'But they've seen plenty of your blood,' said Lorimer. 'Why haven't they erased you lot?'

'Because they're smarter than you,' said Hargreaves. 'They know that by eliminating us, they lose their access to the rest. But that is no good. They want us *all* gone. Every soul on Earth.'

Lorimer fell silent. He looked pale.

Stephenson crushed out his cigarette. Smoke eddied about his fingers. 'So they demand blood,' he concluded. 'The more you spill, the more people they see.'

'As far as they understand. To them, it makes sense: shedding a person's blood should give the Eidolons the map of that person's existence. But of course, it doesn't work that way because we—' he gestured at himself, Hargreaves, and Webber '—position ourselves as a buffer.' Will shrugged again. 'It must be rather frustrating for them. Or it would, if they had feelings.' His eyes clouded over, as though he were gazing upon a dark storm. Quietly, he added, 'And so their prices increase. Every day.'

Marsh shifted again, but the ache in his back wouldn't subside. He stood, stretched. Outside, sunset painted orange the barrage balloons over Pall Mall. Lengthening shadows inched across London's inconstant skyline. The Blitz kept the city in a state of flux.

'You want blood prices?' he asked. 'Thank the Luftwaffe for

doing your job for you. They're spilling our blood every miserable day.'

'Yes, Pip. Blood is spilled every day. But it has no bearing on our work.' Will shook his head. 'They don't know what blood is; only that they access it through us.' He gestured at the warlocks again. 'For that matter, we should be glad they don't understand our civilization any more than you understand the inner life of a bacterium. If they ever do understand us well enough to comprehend hospitals and blood transfusions . . . Well, that will be a very bad day.'

'I still haven't heard a compelling reason why you refuse to end this war overnight,' said Marsh. He pointed at the window. 'If we die, it won't matter if it's at the hand of Jerry or the goddamned Eidolons.'

'We're doing what we can. But we mustn't let the Eidolons start extracting prices on their own. We'd lose control over what information they obtain. Given enough information, they'll be able to fill in the gaps. They'd see all of us. And that would raise merry hob with, frankly, everything. It would all fall apart.

'So I hope you understand, Pip.'

'I understand that Agnes died for naught, and you lot are content to leave it that way.' Marsh slammed the door when he left.

The ache in Marsh's hip turned into a tingling pins-and-needles sensation along his leg. The cot frame creaked as he shifted his weight. He folded the thin pillow in half and propped it under his head. He'd roll again after the ache moved from his hip to his neck. He put his hands under the pillow to prop up his head. The stretched canvas felt rough against the backs of his hands.

A bead of water trickled down one corner of the storeroom. It was raining outside. Marsh crossed his arms across his chest to ward off the damp. Rainwater distilled the odor of mildew as it percolated through the stones.

The prisoner, Gretel, had slept here during her brief incarceration. Marsh had found reminders of her presence when he'd first started sleeping here. Long, black hairs draped across the pillow; the smell of a woman not his wife. Unlike Marsh, she'd had no trouble sleeping on the cot. But also unlike him, she'd been drugged.

Congratulations. It's a girl.

Why Williton? The question had become a lodestone aligning the iron filings of his thoughts. It made no sense. The only special thing about Williton, thought Marsh, was Agnes. And it was no coincidence.

But now he knew what to do. He didn't know how long the idea had been gestating at the back of his mind. It had crystallized during the long, restless hours he'd spent vainly trying to sleep after the maddening conference with Stephenson and the warlocks. It was strange, the way something so obvious had to simmer for so long.

The steady drip of water resolved into footsteps in the corridor. Marsh yawned and rubbed his eyes.

'I don't understand,' Will said from the doorway, 'why you won't accept my offer and stay at the Kensington flat.' He looked around the storeroom as he entered. He nodded at the mildew. 'I admit it lacks the same ambience. But I'd wager the sleeping arrangements are at least equal to what you're enjoying now.'

Marsh sat up on the edge of the cot. 'Hi, Will.'

Will's suit had changed. Now it was a royal blue herringbone pattern, as opposed to the charcoal gray he'd worn at the meeting. Neither combination included a tie, Marsh noted. Will had stopped wearing ties altogether.

Marsh added, 'Good morning, I suppose.' His own clothes hadn't changed since yesterday. Or was it the day before? Down here, day and night melted together into one sleepless blur.

'I didn't wake you, I trust.'

'No.'

Will used a toe to drag a stool from the corner of the room. It was far too short for him. He had to fold himself like a carpenter's rule in order to sit. His knees rested higher than his waist.

'Do think about the flat,' he said. He placed his bowler on one knee. 'Better still, go home to your wife.'

Marsh frowned.

'How is she?'

'I couldn't say,' said Marsh in what he hoped was a tone that implied the subject was closed. He didn't feel up to another argument.

He rested his back against the wall, letting his legs drape over the edge of the cot. Rough stone pressed painfully against the ripples of his spine. The cold and the discomfort helped to wake him.

'You look terrible,' said Will. 'Nip?' He opened his suit coat to reveal the tip of a silver flask tucked in the breast pocket.

'I thought it was morning. A bit early, isn't it?'

Will shrugged. 'Thought it might get you back on your feet.' He let his suit coat fall closed again. 'I came to see if what we told you yesterday made sense. Hargreaves would go off his nut if he knew I was doing this, but I wanted to make certain you understood our objections. I'm willing to discuss things further, if it will help.' He sighed. 'I'm sorry about the meeting.'

'Me, too, Will. I was wrong.'

'Don't concern yourself, Pip. We're all of us under tremendous pressure right now,' said Will, playing with the brim of his hat. 'Short tempers are the order of the day. No hard feelings.'

'Wrong about Agnes.'

'Oh?'

'She doesn't have to die for nothing. She doesn't have to die at all.'

Will stopped. Slowly, with great deliberation, he set the bowler back on his knee. He adjusted it twice. Then he sat up straighter. His chest swelled with a deep breath. He held it for several moments before responding. 'I don't know what you're suggesting, Pip.'

Marsh looked straight into the deep, dark things Will's eyes had become. 'Bring her back.'

The lines around Will's eyes disappeared. He stared at Marsh, wide-eyed but silent. His head drooped. He looked at the floor. He ran a hand through his ginger hair, massaged the nape of his neck. Still looking down, he said, 'I'm sure I didn't hear you properly.'

'Bring my daughter back,' said Marsh. 'Make the Eidolons give her back to us.'

Will ran his hands over his face. He sighed. 'Pip.'

'I'll help you. Anything you need.'

'I . . . I don't know where to begin—'

'The price doesn't matter. I'll pay it.'

'What if the price is your own life? Yours for hers?'

'I'd agree to that in a heartbeat, Will. I don't care what it costs.'

Will said, 'I can't believe we're having this conversation. This is monstrous.'

'More monstrous than having the power to save her life and not *using* it?'

'First of all, Pip, nobody – *nobody* – has the power to save her life,' said Will. He shook his head. 'I'm sorry, truly sorry, my friend, but she's forever gone. If I could, I'd undo it all for you and Liv. But I can't.'

'I knew you'd say that. But this isn't simply about me and Liv. It's our chance to thwart them, to stick it to von Westarp's brood.'

'Now I know I'm not following you.'

'Ask yourself, Will. Why Williton? What was so important about one insignificant little village in Somerset that Jerry had to bomb it into powder?'

'I haven't a clue. But I'm sure you'll tell me.'

'It was Agnes. They wanted her dead, Will. I'm sure of it. They wanted my little girl dead.'

'Oh, my God,' Will muttered. More loudly: 'Are you even listening to yourself? You sound like you've gone completely and utterly round the bend.'

'It's the only explanation that makes sense. We know they'd been watching us, Liv and me.'

'Do you realize what you're saying? Can you honestly look me in the eye and tell me you believe the Luftwaffe conducted a raid specifically for the purpose of killing one infant? And that now you want us to reverse her death?'

'I don't care how it sounds.' Marsh grabbed Will's arm. 'Bring Agnes back.'

'You should care, because you sound like a raving nutter. And as for Agnes, even if we went so far as to resurrect her body, I promise you, the thing inside it wouldn't be *her*. The thing that was Agnes has gone somewhere else.' Will shook his head. 'Ask the others if you don't believe me. They'll tell you the same, but they won't frame it so compassionately.'

He continued, 'I wish I had the power to undo things. I wish I had the power to breathe just one person back to life. To make up for . . .'

Click. It felt like a cog slipping into place. Separate parts of Marsh's mind came together and engaged.

Part of him still grappled with Will's objections. Marsh put that aside in a special place where he could go back to it later; he wasn't ready to consider that Will might be right. This was different, something new.

Cogs turned. And turned. And turned.

'Are you listening to me?' Will asked.

'I'm sorry, Will. What did you say?'

'Nothing at all. I was merely unburdening myself to you. It won't happen again.'

'No, earlier. Before that. About Agnes.'

'She's somewhere else now.' Will sighed again. 'You need to accept that.'

'That was it. You said she's gone somewhere else.'

'A figure of speech. What of it?'

Marsh cracked his knuckles against his jaw. 'You've just given me an idea.'

'Oh, bother.' Will crossed his arms over his chest. 'I'm listening.'

'You said yesterday that the Eidolons are omnipresent.'

'They are, insofar as nothing can be everywhere, I suppose. They don't relate to things like we do. If you imagine points in space and time as bricks in a wall, the Eidolons would exist in the mortar between the bricks.'

'In that case, let me ask you,' said Marsh. 'What prevents us from using them for transportation?'

Silence stretched between them long enough for another drip to become audible. Finally, Will said, 'Are you suggesting we should regard the Eidolons as our own private Tube system?'

'Like a Tube system with no distance between stops.'

Will said, 'This is the third mad thing you've said this morning. You need to start sleeping, Pip.' He stood. 'I don't like what happens to you when you don't.'

Marsh stood as well, feeling animated for the first time in days. 'Are you willing to tell me that nobody has ever thought of this before?'

Will's mouth opened and closed soundlessly for a few seconds. 'It – well – that is, there are *legends* . . .'

'So let's do something legendary.'

3 December 1940
Milkweed Headquarters, London, England

The window behind Stephenson's desk afforded Will a grand view of St. James' Park and the preparations under way there. Sleet pattered against the mullioned windowpanes, sounding like the impatient tapping of fingernails. It trickled down, slowly collecting along the sash like diseased hoarfrost.

The sleet had started out as a bone-cold drizzle within the fog that rolled off the Thames the day before. It was an unusual fog, but still a natural manifestation, rather than something wrought through prices and negotiations. Nobody complained. It kept the Luftwaffe at bay.

Down in the park, swaths of camouflage netting fluttered violently in a gust of wind. Moments later the same gust splattered a new layer of sleet against the glass. Will stepped away from the drafty window.

For the moment, he had the old man's office to himself. It smelled of winter rain, stale cigarette smoke, and Stephenson's brandy. Will helped himself to more of the last thing. He concentrated on pouring, but the liquid slopped over the side of his tumbler and trickled down the side of the desk.

'Oops,' he said to nobody in particular. 'Opps.' He giggled. 'Secret ops.'

He sipped again. The brandy burned on the way down, but the fire died when it reached the ice in Will's stomach. Nothing could melt that.

Outside, across Horse Guards' Road, a ten-foot privacy fence had been erected around two acres of royal parkland. Inside the rings of fences and sentries, under the camo, stood a jumble of tents. At least a dozen, but probably more by now. Will couldn't see well enough through the thickening weather to count them. But they'd been popping up like toadstools since the fog rolled in. There were one or two Nissen huts down there as well.

The encampment put Will in mind of a violent carnival. ('Carnival.' He giggled again. 'Farewell to the flesh.') Several tents had been erected to protect the machines that Lorimer and the science boffins had designed. One tent would soon contain a stone plucked from the lake in the center of the park.

All part of Marsh's ill-conceived plan to attack the Reichsbehörde. Marsh and his crusade.

The door opened, sending warm yellow light across the darkened office. Will's reflection appeared in the window. He looked like a haggard ghost hovering outside the Admiralty building, a revenant spirit condemned to wander endlessly through a landscape of winter fog.

'Beauclerk? What are you doing in my office?'

Will turned. Stephenson tromped in. Droplets of ice water sparkled in his graying hair. He shrugged off a sodden black mackintosh, flipped it off his shoulder with his good arm, and hung it on the coatrack in the corner in one practiced motion.

'Watching the festivities,' Will answered. He jerked his chin toward the window. It made the room spin. He shuffled sideways.

'Don't you and the others have more pressing issues to occupy you right now?' said Stephenson. The empty sleeve pinned to his shoulder flapped up and down as he kicked off his galoshes.

'I came to talk to you about that very thing.'

Stephenson turned on the light and joined him at the window. He looked pointedly at the bottle on the desk and the tumbler in Will's hand. 'Dozens of men down in St. James', working their arses off in this weather, and you're up here having a little party.'

'I'd offer to share, but . . .' Will took the bottle by its neck and waggled it upside down above the floor. Nothing dripped out. He set the bottle back in Stephenson's drawer, where he'd found it.

Stephenson looked around the room, assessing his office for further indignities. Will knew he'd left several strewn across the old man's desk. A finger's worth of spirits seeping across the blotter. A bent letter-opener. Scrapes and gouges in the finish along the edges of the drawer.

It had surprised Will to discover that the old man had taken to locking his desk drawer. Apparently he'd noticed the bottle slowly going empty.

'You're pissed. On my brandy.'

'Me? Heavens no. Empty stomach. Low blood sugar.' Will giggled again. 'Blood. Yes. That's the problem.'

'Beauclerk.' Stephenson shivered as he said it. Perhaps owing to the draft; perhaps not. 'I am wet, I am cold, and I am hungry. I wanted to come inside, dry off a bit, down a bracer to warm me, then go home and eat dinner with Corrie. You will note that nowhere on this list of desires did I include chatting with a soused toff.'

The room wobbled. Will plopped down in the wide leather chair behind the desk.

'And get out of my chair,' said Stephenson. He gave the chair a swift tug. It spun, and so did Will. Will lurched to his feet. Stephenson took the seat he vacated. 'What the hell is wrong with you tonight?'

'We need to talk. One Englishman to another.'

'Would knowing I'm Canadian born make you go away any sooner?'

Will waved away the objection. 'We're none of us perfect. Take me, for instance. Completely pissed.' He gulped from the tumbler. 'Runs in the family, you know.'

Stephenson sighed. 'How long have you been waiting?'

'I really couldn't say.' Will pointed at the empty bottle. 'How full was that when I found it?'

'Do I need to call a ride for you?'

'He's quite mad, you know.'

'Who's mad?'

'Your boy.' Will waved his arm at the window, slopping the remaining brandy with a gesture that encompassed the park and, by extension, all Marsh's works, and therefore Marsh himself. 'Marsh.'

'He's not my boy.'

'Oh, but he is. He is, he is. Perhaps not by blood, but – Ha. There it is again.' Beads of liquid splashed across the desk when he set the empty tumbler down. 'Can't get away from it, can I.'

'I wasn't jesting about wanting you out of here. Is this about Marsh?'

'It's about this whole bloody project.' Will pointed outside again. 'It's a terrible idea. Sir.'

Stephenson said, 'It's a brilliant idea.'

'Whatever it is that you and Marsh hope to achieve with this ploy, I tell you true, it will end badly.'

'We can hobble the Reichsbehörde in one stroke. We stand to obtain the research as well. Britain needs us to do this.' Stephenson looked outside, down at the park. The fingernail rattle of sleet against the window had tapered off; a handful of cottony snowflakes blazed in the office light as they eddied past the window.

'It's a brilliant idea,' he repeated. 'It's Milkweed's chance to balance the scales. And we have to take it now. At present they can't have more than seven or eight, perhaps a dozen at most, of von Westarp's creatures running around. But how long will it be until they number seven hundred? Seven thousand?'

'Have you forgotten that we don't even know what the woman, Gretel, can do? We had her, right here, and we still have no idea.'

'Marsh suspects she's some sort of mentalist.'

'All the more reason not to do this. If she is as he says, they'd only have to capture a few squad members to get a complete picture of the state of Milkweed.'

'Which is why every member of the team will be issued a cyanide capsule. Including you.'

Will rubbed his face. 'Look. Sir. You and I both know that on a typical day he's the smartest chap in the room. But what's escaped your notice is that he's *not* the smartest fellow right now. He's not thinking clearly. Hasn't been since Agnes died.'

'He's mourning.'

Will ran a hand through his hair. Too late he realized his fingers were sticky and smelled of very good brandy. 'Of course he is. But it's not just that. Did you know he's been sleeping down in the storerooms?'

Stephenson frowned, his head jerked back in surprise.

'They had a falling out. Liv and he.'

'When did this happen?'

'As best as I can determine, soon after they returned from Williton. He's fanatically private about his home life, you know.' Will shook his head. It hurt, getting cut out of somebody's life. 'It wasn't always that way.'

'They lost a child. Tragic? Yes. And yes, their marriage may falter. But he'll get the job done.'

Will said, 'You cold-hearted bastard. We stood there in your garden, you and I, while they said their vows.'

'I have larger concerns right now. And so do you. I recommend you go dunk your head in a bucket and pull yourself together.'

'I'm telling you, sir, he's not himself. And if you let him, he's going to take us so far off the fucking map that "Here be Dragons" will be a quaint memory.'

'Jesus, Beauclerk. You're raving—'

'He wanted us to resurrect his daughter. Bring her back to life. It's true. Practically fell to his knees and begged me to make it happen.'

'Can you *do* that?'

'Oh, not you, too. Of *course* not. The best result, the very best, would be nightmarish. But that's just it, sir: Marsh doesn't care.'

The outburst left Will feeling light-headed again. He took the chair across the desk from Stephenson. More snowflakes glittered past the window behind the old man. It was getting dark outside.

As if reading Will's thought, Stephenson rose and pulled the blackout curtains. 'He is very focused. Always has been. I'll grant you that much.'

'Focused? Was that your reaction when he pinched your motor car?'

Stephenson scowled. 'That was understandable, given the circumstances.'

'And yet you say he's not your boy,' Will muttered to himself. To Stephenson: 'You're not listening to me. He's fixated on one thing and can't be bothered to think past that result or the consequences of getting there.'

Stephenson turned. He pursed his lips, staring across the desk with narrowed eyes. 'You're frightened.'

'Of course I'm frightened. I'm not an imbecile.'

The old man sat again. 'Your colleagues are rather excited about this.' The unspoken word danced through the space between the two men like a snowflake: *teleportation*.

'They're eager to see whether or not it actually works. To them, it's an experiment. But they won't be the ones traveling piggyback on an Eidolon.'

'If it works, it will change the war overnight. We'll have the ability to send men and matériel anywhere we want, and to retrieve them just as easily. Without the Eidolons, this raid would be impossible. It would be a one-way trip for those men, assuming they made it as far as the farm in the first place,' said Stephenson. 'But with the Eidolons, nothing, nowhere, is beyond our reach. Imagine inserting a squad directly into the Berghof. Or sending a half ton of explosives to the OKW.'

'These actions aren't free. If we tried to make this our standard means of waging warfare, the blood prices ... well, we'd end up doing Jerry's work for him. And consider this. Every person who goes on this little jaunt, including most especially your lad Marsh (don't give me that look) will be giving himself to the Eidolons for safekeeping during the transition. And again on the way back. Assuming anybody comes back.' Will waited for his head to stop spinning. He summarized, 'It's a bit like using a pride of lions to escort a zebra across the Serengeti. Bloody daft.'

'I think you're overstating things just a bit.'

'Overstating? Understating. Here's yet another consideration for you: the blood price. Nobody knows what this will cost. This is so far beyond the pale that the others won't even hazard a guess.'

'The prices haven't been a problem thus far. I don't see why this would be any different.'

Will tasted blood. He'd bitten a chunk out of the inside of his lip. The blood seeped across his tongue, chasing away the brandy.

Not a problem? So that was it, then. The old man truly was an icy bastard. Will had first sensed it during the trip to Dover, where they'd seen the Eidolons in the Channel and the toll this took on local children. He'd hoped it wouldn't come to this. But it had.

Stephenson had an agreement with Hargreaves and the rest of the warlocks; he indulged their fanatical insistence upon keeping blood prices 'in the family.' Anything that threatened to breach the connection between the negotiator and the price – such as appealing for outsiders' help in paying it – was dangerous and therefore strictly forbidden. But the old man knew damn well what was happening. The escalating prices had forced the warlocks to seek out new tools and new training; Stephenson had arranged for their demolitions training with the Special Operations Executive.

Not a problem? The old man didn't consider the prices a problem, because he wasn't the one paying them. But that would change, if they stayed on this course.

'You know nothing of these things.' It was all Will could say, and perhaps even that was too much. He stood. 'Think about what I've said. Good evening, sir.'

Will paused in the doorway on his way out. 'What I tell you twice I tell you true, sir. This will end badly.'

ELEVEN

10–11 December 1940
Westminster, London, England
Reichsbehörde für die Erweiterung germanischen Potenzials

Sunrise was a dull glow peeking over Downing Street when Marsh entered St. James' Park. The sleet and snow of the past few days had tapered off after coating London with slush. But the clouds had remained, shrouding the sky like a wet wool blanket.

A pair of sentries stopped him at the checkpoint on the east side of the park, just across from the Old Admiralty building. They recognized him, no doubt, but they did their jobs just the same. One of the sentries, a thumb under six feet tall with a blotchy face, stepped in front of Marsh, rifle held across his chest.

'Can't let you through, sir. Password?'

Marsh said, 'Habakkuk.' And to the other sentry, he spoke the second half of the password: 'Rookery.'

The guards stepped aside, nodding their approval. 'Have a good day, sir.' They didn't know about Milkweed, or what it hoped to achieve from this impromptu base camp.

The park was silent. An early hour, and anybody with a modicum of sense would catch as much sleep as possible before tonight. Later, Marsh would go back inside and try to do the same. But not now.

Ice water drizzled from the camouflage netting as Marsh picked his way between the tents. It dripped into his hair, trickled down his neck, down his back. Throughout the staging area, tarpaulins and tent tops had bowed inward under the weight of water, occasionally dumping it all without warning in torrents that doused the unaware and muddied the earth.

He went to the largest tent, in the center of the staging area. Pain twinged in his knee, strong enough to evoke a grimace. Marsh felt, for a moment, like an old man. He gritted his teeth and shrugged off the pain. It receded to a dull throb. More water dripped on his head and neck when he limped inside the tent.

Two rows of chairs arranged in a semicircle faced a table, a lectern, and two blackboards. This was where they'd deliver the final briefing before tonight's mission.

Wood-and-Bakelite mock-ups of a battery were arranged along the table next to the lectern. These were models of the battery they'd taken from Gretel. Snipers had been training with these models for weeks, taking target practice on dummies wearing battery harnesses.

The battery they'd captured bore no identifying marks, not even a manufacturer's stamp. That by itself didn't rule out the possibility that the batteries were constructed under special contract by one of the chemical corporations within the IG Farben conglomerate. Agfa, perhaps, or BASF. But it seemed plausible, based on what little they knew of von Westarp and the massive construction work carried out on his family farm in the late 1920s and early 1930s, that he kept every aspect of the fiefdom under his direct control. So there was a possibility that the batteries were constructed on-site – perhaps by engineers on loan from IG

Farben – meaning Milkweed could destroy the Reichsbehörde's ability to make new batteries. Failing that, they'd eliminate the stores.

Objective: Destroy the technology.

Rows of photographs had been affixed to one blackboard. The first was an enlarged version of the single photograph in von Westarp's dossier. The photo was thirty years out of date, but it was, Marsh hoped, better than nothing. Beneath the photo, somebody with a steady hand had printed DR. KARL HEINRICH VON WESTARP.

Objective: Get the research; capture the researchers.

Only one photograph other than von Westarp's had a name printed beneath it: Gretel, the olive-skinned girl. Hers was the clearest of all the photos. They'd photographed her from every angle. It had taken an entire box of film just to map in detail all her surgical scars.

The remaining photos were grainy reproductions of still frames from the Tarragona filmstrip. There was a photograph for each person featured in the film. Each had a single question mark chalked beneath it in place of a name. Even under the shot of Gretel's rescuer. In a few places, a key word or two had been chalked in a different color: Flight? Speed? Fire? Invisibility?

Objective: Kill or capture the subjects.

A crust of snow crunched under Klaus's boots as he walked the perimeter of the grounds with Reinhardt, Buhler, Pabst, and Doctor von Westarp. The doctor called a halt every thirty or forty yards to consult a map of the grounds. The map contained annotations in Pabst's hand, based on intense debriefing sessions with Gretel.

'One ... two ... heave. One ... two ... heave ...'

They watched a handful of mundane troops struggle to erect klieg lights inside the forest at the edge of the complex. The block and tackle clattered while the men ratcheted upright the heavy mast supporting the lights. The cables sang in a rising wind that smelled of cold snow and diesel fuel.

'Put your backs into it!' yelled Pabst. 'I want these lights installed and tested before sundown.'

Farther back in the trees, more soldiers were busy hiding the generator that would power the lights. The bulk of the generator rested below ground level, in a hole they'd excavated. A buried cable ran from there to the lights. They'd also landscaped a fake thicket to hide the exposed portion of the generator.

In daylight, Klaus mused, the mess of boot prints and trampled snow around the thicket might have been a giveaway. But at night, in the pandemonium of combat, it wouldn't matter at all. The lights would stay off until the attackers arrived. Then the lights would illuminate their landing sites and make it impossible to hide.

Installations like these were going up on the south, west, and east sides of the Reichsbehörde. Each surrounded what Gretel claimed would be a landing site.

Assuming she could be trusted. Klaus had severe reservations on that point, but he kept them to himself. He'd known for months, at least since she had maneuvered to get herself captured, that she acted according to her own interests and motivations, whatever those might be. But until the failed invasion, and maybe even after that, he'd clung to the belief that her personal motives more or less aligned with the interests of the Reichsbehörde and the greater Reich. But what she'd done to Heike ...

When Rudolf had died, back in Spain, Gretel had used her

prescience like a blunt instrument. But now she wielded it like
one of Doctor von Westarp's scalpels. Heike's suicide had been
engineered: the culmination of subtle, devious psychological manip-
ulations that neatly excised the will to live from Heike's heart and
mind.

Von Westarp muttered to himself, nodded. He made a mark
on his map and then set off again through the blowing snow. The
tattered hem of a dressing grown dangled beneath his long
leather overcoat, tracing snake trails through the snow. Klaus and
the others followed.

Wind hissed through bare boughs, as though the oak and ash
trees were commenting upon the preparations. It carried a knife-
edge chill that pierced the tiniest gaps in Klaus's clothing. The
cold slipped through the buttonholes in his coat, sliced through
the seams in his uniform, raked his skin with ice. His breath
caught, trapped by the constriction in his chest.

He considered using his Willenskräfte, letting the snow and
wind pass through him by virtue of the Götterelektron, but the
relief would last only until he rematerialized to breathe. It would
waste his battery to no good effect.

No snow landed on Reinhardt, or in the steaming boot prints
left by his passage.

Reinhardt the necrophiliac.

He was as arrogant and cocksure as ever, except around
Gretel. Reinhardt avoided Klaus and Gretel as much as possible
these days.

Klaus kept trying to avoid his sister, too, after Heike's suicide.
Though it was somewhat pointless. She always knew where he'd
pop up.

Gretel had gone completely off the rails, and nobody knew it
except Klaus. And, he supposed, Reinhardt. After all, in the eyes

of Doctor von Westarp, Heike had taken her own life because she was weak. A failure. He spoke not of wasted resources, or of the decades squandered creating the now-deceased invisible woman. He spoke only of the mistakes he'd made with Heike, and how he'd avoid these in the next batch of test subjects.

Pabst cleared his throat. 'Respectfully, Herr Oberführer, I would like to reiterate my recommendation that we install gun emplacements. And land mines. The enemy may be more numerous than we expect.'

'No! Save the glory for my children.'

Buhler dug out a cigarette while the two argued. He struggled to light it in the cold wind. After a few moments he gave up, and glared at Reinhardt. Reinhardt smirked; the tip of the cigarette flared a brilliant ruby red.

In the end, von Westarp won. As of course he would. There would be no emplacements, no mines.

The inspection tour continued. Seeing the preparations was almost enough to make Klaus pity the doomed men who planned to attack his home. He'd walked among them; breathed their air. They weren't so monstrous.

No, he thought, watching Reinhardt. *This is where the monsters live.*

On any given evening, the train that passed along these tracks en route to Edinburgh carried perhaps a hundred passengers. One hundred souls: men, women, and children.

Hargreaves recited these details very matter-of-factly, like a physician listing a patient's medical history, while he and Webber fastened an explosive charge to the iron rail. Their breath formed long wispy streamers as they labored in the lengthening shadows of evening. Both men pricked a finger; dribbles of blood froze instantly to the rail.

Will stood a little way off, sheltering from the wind in a stand of fir trees. He would have preferred to stay in the car and avoid the cold, or better yet to have avoided this trip altogether. That, of course, was out of the question. He had necessarily been a participant in the negotiation of the blood price, and as such, here he was, seeing that it be paid.

The cold made him numb, but it wasn't the all-encompassing numbness he yearned for. He'd have hurried that along with drink, but he'd be damn busy in a few hours. Focus was important. He promised himself a treat if he made it through the night in one piece. A doubtful result.

'William!' Hargreaves beckoned to him. 'Come.'

'You know, it occurs to me,' said Will, tugging the bowler down over his ears as he stepped into the wind, 'that by watching this activity and alerting neither the police nor the Home Guard, I am, legally speaking, an accessory to this deed.' Hargreaves and Webber stared at him blankly. Webber's bad eye, Will noted, matched the color of the fresh snow that dusted the gravel alongside the train tracks. 'In other words,' Will continued, 'I am, through the agency of my tacit consent, already a participant in the payment of this price.' He looked back and forth between the two. 'You see.'

They didn't. Nor did they much care. The greedy bastards would butcher their own mothers if it meant half a chance to see a deed like the one slated for tonight.

Will crossed the country lane to where the others knelt. They had chosen this intersection thirty miles outside the city for its seclusion. Their chances of getting caught were quite low. The tall trees lining the road swayed, the wind in their boughs sounding for all the world like crashing surf. It felt like they were funneling the wind straight down the road. It was a suffocating wind.

He loosened the scarf around his neck until the ends flapped like pennants. 'In fact,' he added, 'you might say that by doing nothing, I've done quite enough.'

The shriveled skin of Hargreaves's face twitched as it often did when the warlock was irritated. 'Pull yourself together and do your duty,' he said. 'We must head back soon.'

Will sighed, tugged up his trousers, and crouched next to the tracks. He double-checked their work. They'd placed the charge at the seam between two lengths of rail. It was a small thing, not strong enough to topple a train by itself, but more than enough to pry the seam apart. All it needed was a trigger. Webber anticipated him and pushed a leather satchel across the ground with the toe of his boot.

In Will's grandfather's day, a warlock's bag of tricks contained knives, wooden bits, leather cords, and bandages. Will's carpetbag back at the Kensington flat still contained a pair of bloodstained garden shears. But this was not his grandfather's war. Warlocks served the king now – though His Majesty didn't know it – and their tools for spilling blood had grown in sophistication along with their understanding of Enochian.

It's a strange kind of inflation, Will thought, *always driving these prices up. Blades are outmoded, worthless; the ha'pennies of negotiation. Dynamite and priming cord, that's where the purchase power is.*

Will fished inside Webber's satchel until he found a length of cord and a pressure switch. It took several tries to affix the switch to the rail. The ice-cold steel shrugged off the adhesive putty. He layered it on until he could be reasonably sure that vibrations from the train wouldn't dislodge the trigger before the wheels touched it.

How is it that in order to serve my country I practically had to become a fifth columnist?

Which was exactly the result Stephenson wanted, the charming pragmatist. The warlocks' actions in paying the Eidolons' blood prices could be blamed as the work of fifth columnists. Nazi sympathizers. Jerry saboteurs. It had to be that way. A more direct path would have been to extract the prices from condemned prisoners and the like – so-called undesirables. But that would have required paperwork; it would have left a trail back to the Crown. And, given how expensive things had become, using prisoners to pay the blood prices would have quickly reduced the warlocks to executing people for shoplifting.

Webber and Hargreaves retreated along the road to where Will had parked the car.

Yes, you left the dangerous bit for me, didn't you? A frisson of paranoia jolted Will. Was this deliberate? Part of a secondary negotiation of which he knew nothing? Were they hoping for a mistake?

He took extra care while arming the charge. He did it just as he'd been trained by the SOE: one wire at a time, taking care to avoid stray static charges.

That finished, he nicked a finger and squeezed out a few drops of blood. They froze to the rail, mingling with the blood Hargreaves and Webber had already shed. The warlocks' blood was a bridge, connecting the negotiated blood price with this act of violence. They'd done their parts. Somewhere in Surrey, Will knew, Shapley, Grafton, and White were doing something similar. Together all six warlocks were co-negotiators. Co-conspirators, too, if anybody ever learned about this.

After that there was nothing left to do but give it a quick once-over and hurry back to the car.

A train whistle echoed faintly through the trees. Will gunned the engine to drown out the noise, and promised himself a single drink when they returned to the Admiralty.

*

The wind died around sunset. Darkness and silence together descended upon London. A deepening cold gripped St. James' Park. It leeched warmth from tents, turned metal Nissen huts to iceboxes, and aggravated the twinge in Marsh's knee.

He stuffed an extra packet of aspirin into his kit. The pain hadn't hobbled him yet, though it threatened to. He'd get a medic to look at his knee after he came back, but there wasn't time enough for that now. There was also the danger that he might be sidelined from the raid. And that was unacceptable.

Marsh counted through his gear. The ritual helped him to focus, to find his center.

One combat knife, six-inch blade. Six Mills bombs. Four white phosphorus grenades. One Enfield double-action revolver (No. 2, Mk. I). Five six-round cylinders for same. One Lee-Enfield bolt-action rifle (No. 4, Mk. I). Five ten-round magazines for same. One electric torch. One pair of handcuffs. One vial of ether. One garrote. Three magnesium flares. One compass. One medkit.

He filled the webbing pockets on his belt with still more cylinders and magazines. Then he rubbed burnt cork on the exposed skin of his hands and clean-shaven face, darkening himself until his flesh would blend into the shadows along with the black coverall he wore.

Throughout Milkweed's camp, he knew, dozens of men were going through the same ritual, if not with the same equipment. Mostly in groups, taking comfort in the camaraderie of false bravado, chasing off the collywobbles. Three huts, three teams. The plan was for the teams to retain the same geographical distribution – one each to the south, west, and east – when they landed in Germany.

Arrived in Germany. Marsh kept thinking of it as a landing, as though they were parachuting in, though he knew it was nothing of the sort.

He hefted the sack off the table and shrugged the straps over his shoulders. Then he checked his belt, slung the rifle over his shoulder, and stepped outside.

In peacetime, the glow of London, combined with humidity and smog, often erased even the brightest stars from the sky. But that was no longer the case, owing to the blackout and the crisp evening. Overhead, a wine-dark sky shimmered with points of blue and white. Even orange in places. The air felt so sharp, so crystalline, that Marsh found it easy to imagine there was nothing at all between himself and the stars.

The inconstant knee pain that had dogged him his entire adult life flared anew, sharper this time. Marsh leaned over to massage it. *Not now. Please, just through tonight.*

Footsteps squelched in the slush around the side of the tent. The noise was so subtle that Marsh wouldn't have heard it at all if not for the stillness of the evening. It sounded like somebody hesitating in the shadows, wanting to approach him without disrupting his solitude.

Marsh straightened up. 'Yes, I'm on my way, Will.'

No answer. Another squelch.

'Lorimer? Is that you?'

Something moved in the shadows. It created a rustling sound, like somebody brushing against a tent.

Marsh's hand went to the revolver at his belt. He crept forward. 'Who's there?'

The shadows moved again at the same moment he stepped around the corner. He found himself face-to-face with a stranger. Both men started in unison; both had their weapons drawn.

Marsh couldn't make out the other man's eyes, but he was

clearly surprised to see Marsh. A beard hid the stranger's face. Moonlight reflected wetly off a puckered furrow of scar tissue.

This wasn't one of Milkweed's men. The organization was small enough that Marsh knew every face, every name. Marsh knew that he'd never in his life seen this man, and yet there was something familiar about him. The revelation came in a flash: he'd heard this man's description before.

The intruder recovered before Marsh could raise his sidearm. His voice was a gravelly rasp. 'You'll thank me for this later.'

He pointed his own revolver at Marsh's leg, but his eyes widened in surprise as he pulled the trigger.

'No! Blood—' The stranger fired and disappeared in the same instant.

Pop. Marsh's knee exploded in pain.

Oh, God, Liv, I should have seen you this morning—

Marsh crashed to the ground, clutching his leg with one hand while swinging his firearm in a wild arc toward where the assailant had stood. But the man was gone.

So, too, was the pain. Just like that, it evaporated, leaving nothing behind, not even the original twinge. And not just tonight's pain, either; the constant trickle of discomfort from his knee, the ever-present ache that Marsh tuned out most of the time, was gone. The reversal was so complete that for a moment Marsh thought he'd gone into shock. But his hands were dry. No blood. And his coveralls were undamaged, with no hint of a bullet hole.

'Bloody fucking hell.'

Phantoms.

Marsh lay sprawled on the ground, panting. His breath sparkled. He flinched, expecting a surge of pain to follow every thud of his racing heart, but it never came. Only a slowly growing chill as the cold and wet seeped into him.

'Bugger me.'

He climbed to his feet, shakily, half-expecting his leg to give out. It didn't. But he did take a few moments to collect himself before joining the others.

All eyes turned to him when he entered the Nissen hut. Will, Hargreaves, and Webber stood around a workbench upon which rested a piece of Portland limestone somewhat smaller than a rugby ball. An iron chisel had been driven deep into the stone, not quite far enough to cleave it in two. The stone had been marked with a bloody handprint that straddled the fissure made by the chisel. A sledgehammer rested on the bench next to the stone.

Marsh understood that the stone was there for the benefit of the warlocks rather than for the Eidolons. It was an object to help them focus, in the same way that Will used fire. The cleaved stone would become a single object existing *here* and *there* simultaneously.

Waves of pent-up anticipation boiled out of the corner where the rest of Marsh's team milled around. Ten men: some younger, some older, every one a walking arsenal, every one replaying the Tarragona filmstrip over and over in his head. Marsh could see it in their eyes and in the hard, blank looks on their faces.

The snipers wore Ghillie suits, camouflage festooned with bits of foliage. The rest wore dark balaclavas to match their coveralls. The snipers carried Enfield rifles like Marsh's, with scopes; their spotters carried submachine guns. Everyone had corked their faces. It was the first time Marsh had ever seen Will in anything less than a suit.

Like Marsh, every man headed to Germany wore a small sticking plaster on the back of one hand: the warlocks had taken blood samples. The Eidolons had to see the men in order to move them. Marsh dreaded the thought of being scrutinized by those

monsters again, but he'd tolerate it for the sake of hurting the
Jerries.

Lorimer was inspecting the pair of tall, blocky wooden pillars
that flanked the squad. Lorimer called them his 'pixies.' Coils of
copper wire wreathed the narrower center portion of each
column. Ceramic endcaps covered the top and bottom of both
machines. The gadgets had been designed to be as light as possible, so that two men could carry one at a dead run.

Stephenson stared at the mud stains on Marsh's coveralls.
'What the blue pencil happened to you?'

Marsh shook his head. 'Forget it. It's unimportant.'

Will shot Stephenson a pointed look. The old man frowned.
He joined Lorimer.

Will came over. He didn't carry as much equipment as the rest
of the squad. The knife, the revolver, and the rifle all looked
absurdly out of place on him. The weapons were a last resort, in
the case of self-defense.

Marsh asked, quietly, 'What was that just now, between you
and the old man?'

'Bit of a disagreement. What did happen to you, Pip? You
took a fall, I can see that much.'

Marsh motioned him to a corner of the hut. He lowered his
voice to a whisper. 'I think I just saw your phantom.'

'My phantom?'

'The fellow you saw here in the park back in May, on the night
our strange little guest escaped.'

Will's eyes widened in surprise. It didn't, Marsh noticed,
soften the dark weariness in his features. 'You're certain? That
would be rather odd, you and I seeing the same apparition
months apart.'

'He matched your description. Down to the voice.'

'Hmm. The ghost of St. James'.' He shook his head. 'You know, Pip, there's still time to call this off . . .'

Stephenson clapped twice. 'Gentlemen. It's time.'

Will and Marsh joined Lorimer and the others. They stretched, limbered up, tightened their belts, checked their kit yet again. Marsh did the same. He clenched and released the muscles in his arms, legs, and back. He concentrated on his legs, banishing the cold so he wouldn't cramp up. His knee felt solid. The pain didn't return.

The elder warlocks launched into the shrieks and rumbles of Enochian. The earth seemed to shift slightly and assume an impossible cant, much like the floor in the Admiralty building had done so many times over the past seven months. An ozone crackle filled the room. And just for a moment, Marsh caught a fleeting whiff of baby powder.

Focus. Focus. He cracked his knuckles.

The rest of the squad watched and listened with expressions that ranged from hostility to something just short of abject terror. They'd all heard Enochian dozens of times, but tonight would be something different.

The stone spoke. Will cocked his head, as though eavesdropping on a hard-to-follow conversation. Which, Marsh supposed, he was.

The Eidolon's presence swept over them in a wave that threatened to rip the Nissen apart at the seams, so vast was the sense of its being. A boundless intellect swirled through the hut as though it were inspecting every atom. The men squirmed under its attention.

It lingered on Marsh for a microsecond eternity. The naked, inside-out feeling flashed through him again, just as it had when he'd severed Will's finger. More Enochian emanated from the stone as it withdrew.

Will inhaled sharply. 'There it is again.'

'There's what again?'

'Your name,' he said.

Marsh started to inquire, but Will shushed him. He nodded at the stone, and the chanting warlocks around it. 'Here it comes.'

The warlocks stopped. Hargreaves pointed at Will. 'Now,' he said.

Will lifted the sledgehammer. 'Ready yourselves, everyone.'

Stephenson said, 'Godspeed and good hunting, gentlemen.'

Will flexed his knees, preparing his swing. He counted backwards. 'Three ... Two ...'

On *one*, Will shouted something in Enochian, the hammer landed square on the chisel, and then—

Will felt the bifurcation of space in every particle of his being. His body was an impossible construct held together by the whim of an Eidolon. He was a riddle, a paradox, a rift in the cosmos within which *here* and *there* held no meaning.

He cried out. But sound, he discovered, did not carry through the crawlspaces of the universe.

'Ah.' Gretel put down her spoon.

'What?' said Klaus around a mouthful of black bread.

She dabbed her lips with a napkin. 'They're here.'

—darkness.

The Eidolon withdrew. Marsh occupied a single space once more. This space was colder and darker than the Nissen from which he'd departed, all those eons ago.

It took several long moments to regain his bearings, to become reacquainted with the claustrophobic confines of body and mind, space and time.

First, he noticed the breeze tickling his face, and the creaking of tree boughs. He looked up. Stars twinkled overhead just as they had in London. Wherever they were, their latitude hadn't changed appreciably.

Then he noticed moonlight on a snow-dappled field. Across the field, yellow light spilled from the windows of a three-story farmhouse perhaps a hundred yards away. Silhouettes paced behind gauzy curtains on the third floor. It appeared to be the same farmhouse featured in the photograph that Marsh had salvaged from Krasnopolsky's valise. The farmhouse and field were flanked by other buildings. He checked his compass. Marsh's team had arrived in the tree line along the south edge of the field, at the top of a U. The field constituted the center of the U, and the farmhouse was the base.

I'll be damned. It actually worked.

Only then did he hear the sobbing. He took a quick head count. Most of his men had come through looking pale and shaken. One member of the squad lay in the snow in the fetal position, crying and sucking his thumb. Another man – Ritter; he'd served with distinction in Norway – hugged his knees, rocking back and forth, muttering loudly, 'I can't exist. I can't exist. I can't exist.'

'Lorimer, where are you?' Marsh whispered.

'Back here,' said a voice in the shadows.

'Shut that man up or knock him back to his senses.'

'Damnation,' said Will. 'I tried to tell you this would happen.' He dropped the sledgehammer. It thudded to the ground alongside the cleft stone at his feet.

Lorimer's machines appeared to have weathered the passage with no ill effects. Marsh gestured at his squad. 'You two, and you two, get ready to move those pixies into position. Everyone else prepare to cover them.'

The first man had just grabbed a handhold on one of the pixies when a blinding white light flooded the world. Marsh reeled. At first he thought the transit had failed after all, and that they had ricocheted back to London.

Then he heard the yells emanating from across the field. *'Beeil dich!'*

They hadn't moved. But they were pinned under a ring of spotlights.

'Well,' said Lorimer, unslinging his rifle, 'I'd say we're fucked harder than an East End whore.'

The quiet night erupted into gunfire and explosions almost as soon as Pabst gave the order to activate the klieg lights. Doctor von Westarp waited for the lights before giving the order to attack. Otherwise, of course, he wouldn't have been able to watch the proceedings from the comfort of his parlor. And the cameramen wouldn't have been able to film the night's events.

According to Gretel, the attackers had arrived in three teams. Klaus, Kammler, and Reinhardt were assigned the defense of the west, south, and east sides of the Reichsbehörde, respectively.

Klaus charged through the icehouse, past Heike's remains. The doctor had dissected her, laying her open like the illustrations in an anatomy textbook as he cataloged the physiological alterations the Götterelektron had wrought upon her body.

He wore two batteries tonight, on a special double harness designed to distribute the weight evenly across his shoulders. It didn't. Every step jolted the batteries; it felt like getting punched in the kidneys.

He emerged through the west wall of the icehouse into blinding, deafening chaos. Light shone through the trees on the edge of the grounds, highlighting perhaps a dozen men. Some were curled up on the ground, unmoving. Others yelled to each other in English, or fired at the lights.

The men dived for cover, hands over their heads. The crack of a fragmentation grenade echoed back and forth across the grounds. Soil erupted from the forest floor near the base of one of the light masts. It toppled over like a great steel oak, making shadows swirl through the trees until it smashed its crown of glass against the earth.

The invaders didn't see Klaus. The men were too preoccupied with the remaining lights to notice that they weren't, in fact, under attack.

Well, at least this will be over quickly, thought Klaus. He sighed, wondering who would get stuck digging the graves for these men. Or perhaps the doctor would test the ovens on their corpses.

Klaus pulled out a grenade and rushed the invaders.

Marsh yelled, 'Somebody kill those goddamn lights!'

Will tried to untangle himself from his rifle. The light, the noise, the confusion and panic all melded into a fog. He fumbled with the rifle. How had the strap become wrapped around his arm like this? He couldn't unsling it gracefully. He gave up and took instead the revolver from his belt.

He stood, squinting up in the direction of the lights. Somebody tackled him. His shot *pinged* off the metal light boom and went caroming into the woods.

Lorimer bellowed in his ear. 'Don't! Stand! Up!' His hot breath cascaded over Will's face. 'Unless you want your chinless head blown apart, you worthless toff.'

Somebody yelled, 'Take cover!'

Will rolled over, face down, covering his head and ears with his hands, just as he'd been trained to do. There was a *crack* and then the ground shook. Clods of earth pelted him. He rolled over just in time to see one of the light booms lean over with much creaking and groaning. It stopped after tipping a few feet out of true. But the night was just as bright as ever.

He realized that part of the chaos filling his head came from elsewhere, a cacophony of gunfire and explosions. And screaming.

Is this what you had planned, Pip? Is this how you imagined it?

Will crawled on his stomach behind the line of men who had taken position at the edge of the tree line. Those who had recovered their senses after the transit from London lay under bare bushes, or hid behind trees, the barrels of their rifles and Bren guns pointed toward the buildings.

But they weren't, he noticed, firing. They were waiting.

A wave of dread swept over Will. *We haven't been attacked yet and this whole operation has already gone pear-shaped.* Snow funneled into his collar as he pulled himself across the ground. *Damn you, Stephenson.*

Somebody tossed another Mills bomb. The tilted light boom toppled the rest of the way, crashing to the ground in an eruption of glass and sparks. But two spotlights still highlighted their position.

Will scuttled over to where Lorimer and Marsh were huddled together. 'This isn't working,' said Marsh. 'We have to move out.'

'The pixies will make short work of those lights,' said the Scot.

Marsh shook his head urgently. 'They know our position. Tell the men to move out.'

'Aye.'

Marsh crawled over to Will while Lorimer spread the word. 'Where's your magic rock?'

Shit. Will cocked a thumb over his shoulder. 'It's, uh, back there.'

'Don't you dare lose that bloody thing!'

Marsh was right. Without the stone, they couldn't get back. Will turned and crawled back to where he'd come from.

Closer to the tree line, Lorimer yelled, 'Oy! You lot first! Then the pixies! Twenty meter—'

He crumpled up like a rag doll, shot into the air, and slammed back down again. The impact rattled Will's bones. Lorimer's body pounded the earth again before spinning off into the forest. It smacked into an oak tree, knocking snow from the boughs. What was left of Lorimer rained to the ground as an unrecognizable mass of bone and meat.

Marsh noticed, too late, two men standing in the center of the field. He recognized them from the Tarragona filmstrip. One wore a collar; the other stood behind him, yanking on his leash and screaming in his ear.

Marsh dived for cover. 'Fire on those two!' He ordered the squad. 'Aim for the battery,' he reminded the snipers.

They unleashed a volley. It achieved nothing. The rounds stopped in midair a few feet from the leashed man, and tinkled to his feet. The squad's cover started to disappear as trees and shrubs disintegrated explosively, showering them with splinters. The night smelled like sawdust and smokeless powder.

One man stood and lobbed a Mills bomb at the duo. It stopped a few feet over the leashed man's head, hovered, and then made a *snap* sound no louder than a Christmas cracker. The fragments of shrapnel fell unceremoniously to the earth.

Marsh reached for one of the phosphorus grenades on his belt. Just as he prepared to yank the pin, the man who had tossed the Mills got plucked from his hiding spot and rammed into the earth – headfirst – like a tent peg. Marsh opted to stay down instead.

Time for drastic measures. 'Fire a pixie!'

Lorimer had designed the pixies for use in the heat of combat. Which meant that each had a bright red Bakelite panic button on its base, where it could be tripped by foot or hand, depending on the circumstances. A sniper rolled over to the pixie and kicked the button. 'Everybody take cover!' he yelled.

The pixie emitted a high-pitched whine. The squad made a hasty retreat into the woods.

Marsh counted backwards. 'Ten ... nine ...' He grabbed Will, who was sprawled on the ground clutching the stone to his chest. 'Eight ... seven ...' Marsh shoved Will along in front of him. Trees erupted in their wake. 'Six ... five ...' More than one man screamed as he got caught up in the destruction. 'Four ... three ...' Marsh pushed Will down into the hollow behind a tree stump and landed next to him. 'Two ... one.'

Somewhere in the bowels of Lorimer's machine, an electrical relay clicked shut. It caused a capacitor bank to discharge its hoarded electrical energy through a wire coil. This turned the pixie, ever so briefly, into an electromagnet. A microsecond later, as special circuitry shaped the time profile of the electrical current, a second relay clicked shut. This activated detonators at both ends of a high-explosive cylinder in the center of the coil. This created a pair of convergent shock waves that squeezed the coil and crushed the magnetic field.

The end result was an electromagnetic pulse tuned to the electrical characteristics of the battery that Milkweed had obtained.

Bullets sprayed through Klaus's insubstantial body, pattering harmlessly against the brick wall of the icehouse behind him. He'd lobbied Doctor von Westarp for a new assignment, something *real* to do, for months. Now he had a new task, but it didn't fill him with pride as he'd hoped.

One of the attackers yelled, 'It's one of them! It's one of them!' as he fired. He watched, unbelieving, as Klaus approached the submachine gun leveled at his chest.

Klaus stopped just short of the barrel. He shot the panicky, trigger-happy soldier in the forehead.

He advanced on the rest of the soldiers. Though they'd watched him kill their companion, they continued to try to shoot him. Klaus imagined it was panic making them dull. Until he heard one of the British order his colleagues:

'Disable his battery!'

Somebody yelled something about a 'pixie,' but Klaus couldn't make it out over the noise of the gunfire directed at him. One man broke off and ran for a tall pillar of wood and copper wire that the British had apparently brought with them from England. He slapped a large red switch. The pillar started to whine.

Klaus pulled the pin and dropped the grenade he'd been carrying. It became substantial again when it left his touch. The grenade bounced in the slush at his ghostly feet. It had a four-second fuse.

The shooters dived for cover behind trees and underbrush. The man who'd gone for the pillar didn't see what Klaus had done. The concussion drove shrapnel through his chest and cracked the pillar in half.

A blinding flash erupted on the far side of the complex. It came from the east, like a sunrise, but Klaus knew it was Reinhardt blazing brighter than the sun. Klaus was too far away to hear the screams of the men he cooked.

He checked his battery gauge while the four remaining men climbed to their feet to renew the attack. The battery retained nearly 75 percent of its charge. That was more than enough to finish off these men.

First, he tried to goad them into shooting each other while he stood between them. To their credit, they didn't fall for it. He jumped through one man, spun, stuck his pistol through a second man's chest, fired at a third. The man through whom he'd shot dropped his gun, screaming incoherently as he stared at Klaus's arm protruding from his chest. Klaus withdrew and shot him in the back of the head. The two remaining men tried to empty their magazines into Klaus. He reached into one man's rib cage and squeezed. The dead man collapsed.

The lights went dead without warning, followed by the thunder of a distant explosion that shook the earth a moment later. A strange and painful surge from his battery left Klaus reeling. The sudden return of night disoriented him; his eyes had adjusted to the glare of the klieg lights.

The last man took advantage of the distraction and fled into the woods. Klaus tried to give chase by leaping through an ash tree.

And crashed facefirst into the bole.

The impact sent him sprawling backwards. He tasted blood, but not the copper tingle of the Götterelektron. All he could feel was the searing pain of an exposed nerve in his jaw. He'd cracked a tooth in half.

He rolled over to check his battery gauge. It was dead. It had lost nearly three-quarters of its charge in an instant. Head pounding, he climbed to his feet and switched over to his second battery. This one was low, too, but usable.

Klaus turned to run after the man who had fled. He stopped short, and almost fell for a second time, because Gretel had come up behind him.

'Careful, brother.'

'Gretel? What are you doing out here? It's not safe.'

'Kammler needs your help. Go, quickly now.'

As Klaus set off to cut through the battery stores, he said over his shoulder, 'Go back inside the farmhouse, Gretel. It's safe there.'

She might have responded with her accursed little half smile, but it was too dark to see for certain.

The pixie emitted a burst of violet light when it exploded. The spotlights died in the same instant. The combination left Will blinking furiously, trying to banish the spots behind his eyes.

The tree stump behind which he and Marsh huddled hadn't disintegrated yet. Nor had any of the adjacent underbrush.

Next, he noticed the smells: ozone, sharp enough to sting, and entrails. Poor Lorimer.

'*Scheisse!*'

'T-t-t—'

'SCHEISSE!'

Will peeked over the stump. The yellow glow from the farmhouse windows silhouetted their assailants. The pixies, he knew, were tailored to knock out the batteries. The farmhouse appeared unaffected. The spotlights had been much closer, and had taken the brunt of the EMP.

The leash-holder cursed in a constant stream of German while he fidgeted with something on the belt of the collared man. His battery, presumably. He was having trouble because the collared man wouldn't stand still. He ambled back and forth, stuttering.

Marsh took a shooting position. He rested his rifle on the stump and sighted along the barrel. He hardly seemed to breathe.

Will had seen men die tonight, and more men than that had died by his own hand these past months. Always at a distance, of course. But Marsh didn't flinch from killing. It showed Will a side of the man he'd never known. The same sense of focus was there, but now it was alloyed with something dispassionate, too.

No. Not dispassionate. A deceptively quiet rage. The man carried thoughts of his daughter. The look on his face made that much clear. It was a look that Will hoped Marsh would never direct at him.

Marsh fired. The side of the leash-holder's head erupted in a fine mist. He fell to the snow, unmoving.

'Damn it! Damn it, damn it,' Marsh muttered as he worked the bolt.

The collared man stuttered more loudly. It was a mournful, distraught kind of sound.

'B-b-b-b-b—'

Marsh prepared another shot. While he aimed, another figure emerged through the wall of a long, low building and dashed across the field. 'Kammler!' He leapt and grabbed the stutterer just as Marsh fired. A window behind the pair shattered.

The insubstantial man did something to the stutterer's belt. The stutterer – his name was Kammler, apparently – knelt next to the body of his companion. 'Bu-buh-g-g-g-'. It sounded like he was crying. He seemed to have lost his interest in fighting.

The insubstantial man turned and headed for Will and Marsh's position. Somebody behind and to the right of them fired – the squad had been whittled down three or four people by now – but it had no effect.

Will looked around for the second pixie. It was nowhere to be seen. It had been caught up in the destruction of the woods.

Marsh recognized the man advancing on his position. The

very same bastard had rescued Gretel, and in the process led Marsh on a wide-ranging chase through the Admiralty.

Marsh scanned through the mental list of things he'd learned from that experience. *Weaknesses: He can't breathe when he's insubstantial. He has to monitor his battery.*

Why didn't the pixie knock out his battery as it had with the stutterer? It seemed they were carrying spares. The man Marsh had shot – *why did I have to miss?* – must have been trying to swap out his companion's battery.

With luck, the pixie had taken a toll on the spare, too, although Lorimer and the science boffins had designed the pixies assuming the batteries would be in use when the pulse hit them. They'd have to drain it the hard way.

'Everybody, fire!' Gunfire echoed from two positions in the wood behind him. Marsh lobbed a Mills bomb at the advancing fellow, but of course it had no effect other than to force him to stay incorporeal.

'Maybe, Pip,' said Will, 'this would be a good time to leave.'

Will was huddled behind the stump, watching the man coming closer and closer. One hand held the cleft stone to his chest; the other held his revolver. Both hands shook.

If Will died, there'd be no going home for anybody.

Shit.

'Stay down,' said Marsh. 'Don't let them see you. And for God's sake, don't lose that bloody stone.'

Marsh stood.

Will said, 'Are you daft? What are you doing?'

'If you die, we all do. Now stay down and shut up.'

Marsh took off at a dead run along the edge of the wood. He hoped the Jerry bastard would recognize him, and that he had a taste for irony. He did. On both counts.

Marsh ran east, drawing his pursuer away from Will. His best hope – a feeble, fleeing hope – was to lose himself in the shadows between the buildings. With luck, he might find the battery store-house before they caught him.

Pop. Crack. A tree bole splintered above Marsh's head. Apparently the Jerry could still fire his gun while in his altered state. Marsh peeled away from the trees and headed north, along the east side of the complex. He squeezed off a couple of shots from his revolver now and then to keep his pursuer insubstantial and thus, Marsh hoped, desperate for air.

Once around the corner and out of sight, he took a phosphorus grenade from his belt and lobbed it toward the outer wall of the closest building. Toward where, if *he* could walk through walls, he would have taken a shortcut to catch himself. Toward where he'd probably take a deep breath when he emerged.

The grenade hissed out hot, dense white smoke that glistened like a pea-soup fog in the moonlight. Moments later a human figure emerged through the wall. The cloud eddied around him.

Marsh heard a gasp, a violent cough, and then his pursuer leapt back inside.

Hope you got a lungful, you son of a bitch.

A Mills could have finished the bastard off for certain, but it might have turned out to be a waste of good explosives. Marsh wanted to save what little he had left in case he could find the battery stores.

He set off to do that. And tripped over something very warm that crumbled under his weight. Marsh had to stare for a moment before recognizing it as a human body, charcoal-black and curled tightly in the fetal position. It smelled like charred pork. Bodies like this littered the field.

Somewhere, back toward where he'd first arrived, where he'd left Will, a roar shook the earth. The cacophony of gunfire and explosions started anew.

He considered going for the dead squad's pixies, but the ground had been seared into ash for fifty feet in all directions. No doubt their pixies had burned, too. But where was the man who had done this? He thought back to the Tarragona filmstrip, and a man with pale, pale eyes.

Marsh crept through a cluster of darkened buildings, looking for anything that might have suggested a storeroom. The thin layer of snow squeaked under his boots and left a record of his movements. He tried to step lightly, and he paid attention to the wind-shadows of the buildings where snow hadn't dusted the ground. He could tiptoe through these areas without leaving prints.

Watching the snow saved his life. Marsh was turning a corner when the snow in front of him evaporated. He leapt back. Flames erupted from the ground where he'd been about to step.

A man stepped around the corner, laughing, wreathed in blue fire. The light illuminated the adjacent buildings and made Marsh squint. He scuttled frantically backwards through mud that had been snow and frozen earth seconds earlier.

'You're quick,' said the burning man in English, over the crackle of his fiery aura. 'Quicker than your comrades. I'll grant you that much.'

Marsh emptied his revolver. The first shot went wide, scarring the bricks alongside the burning man. The second bullet flared purple when it touched the man's aura. The man took a step back to steady himself, still burning.

Marsh scrambled to his feet, trying to steady his hands so he could reload. But his assailant recovered before Marsh could pull out a new cylinder. The man clutched his shoulder, wincing.

'All done? I'd—'

A woman yelled: 'Reinhardt! Reinhardt, come quickly!'

Marsh knew that voice. It was Gretel. He had replayed it in his head countless times. *Congratulations. It's a girl.*

The burning man – Reinhardt – hesitated. Marsh ran. Behind him, he heard Gretel yelling, 'Reinhardt, please, this instant!'

Marsh weaved between a few buildings before pressing up against a wall and plucking a Mills from his belt, in case he was being followed. But the snow didn't melt behind him, and the earth didn't spit forth new flames.

By distracting Reinhardt, Gretel had inadvertently saved Marsh's life.

He took the opportunity to catch his breath and reload. He gulped cold winter air that chilled his throat. Rivulets of sweat stung his eyes with salt. He leaned against the wall, listening to shouts, dwindling gunfire, and the *whoosh* sound of disintegrating forest. The earth shook again. The remnants of his squad had engaged Kammler again.

He found himself staring up at the three-story farmhouse as he placed a new cylinder in his revolver. Von Westarp's farmhouse. A silhouette still paced in front of the windows on the top floor. Marsh couldn't see any details, but he had a hunch as to who owned that shadow.

More noise echoed across the grounds from the battle with Kammler. It gave Marsh an idea.

Klaus stumbled through a darkened laboratory, coughing convulsively. He fell to all fours. A tray of medical implements crashed to the floor when he banged against a surgical table.

The coughs came out so violently that they irritated the back of his throat and caused him to gag. He vomited rabbit stew on the tile floor of an operating room.

His eyes and sinuses burned. His throat burned, too, from the surge of stomach acids. But his skin wasn't blistering, and he couldn't smell garlic or fresh hay. So he hadn't inhaled mustard gas or phosgene. And the cloud had been white, not yellowish like chlorine.

The coughing fit receded. His eyes still burned, but he could open them now. It seemed he'd emerged in the middle of a smoke screen, but not into a poison gas cloud.

Sweat ran down Klaus's face, mingling with the tears from his watering eyes. Profuse sweating was a natural result of intense exertion while insubstantial; his body built up heat in that state and couldn't convect it away until he rematerialized.

But it was a cold sweat, too, because he knew he'd nearly killed himself. One little misstep, but he could have died. A terrifying reminder of his mortality.

Then again, Gretel would have warned him had he been in true jeopardy. *Wouldn't she?*

He had to pinch the tears from watery eyes several times before he could read the gauge on his remaining battery. Less than a quarter of the charge left; the needle rested just above the red. It was enough, if he was careful. It would have to be. There wasn't time to go to the stores.

Klaus wiped his mouth on his sleeve, trailing spit and vomit, as he headed for the conventional exit. He had to conserve his battery as much as possible. He stepped carefully; he didn't know the laboratory well enough to navigate it in the dark.

It was lighter outside than in the laboratory, owing to moonlight and the glow from the farmhouse windows. But Klaus's eyesight was blurry still. Cold air scraped at his raw sinuses, threatening to make him cough again. He doubled over, fighting another episode.

The night was alive with the noise of combat. Gunfire. Explosions. The ground rumbled. Kammler howled.

From somewhere off to Klaus's right came two reports like gunshots from a sidearm. Much like the revolver of the man Klaus had chased. Klaus headed in that direction.

'Reinhardt! Reinhardt, come quickly!'

Klaus skidded to a halt. His sister called for help from somewhere behind him.

She called again, more frantic this time. 'Reinhardt, please, this instant!'

Klaus hurried toward the sound of her voice.

Will watched all hell break loose after Marsh ran off.

First, another squad member came crashing through the woods from the west. He appeared to be the only survivor of that team.

Then the earth rippled. Furrows appeared in the field, racing across the ground at random. Snow, topsoil, and oak trees fountained into the air. Windows shattered. Will watched the tall metal masts of the dead spotlights coil up like so much ribbon on a spool. The screech of tortured metal was deafening.

Kammler howled. A cry of inchoate despair.

The new arrival fired wildly at Kammler. It achieved nothing.

Kammler jumped to his feet. Trees exploded into sawdust and splinters.

The rest of the men fired. Some lobbed their Mills bombs. All with no effect.

Before, there had been an orderliness to the destruction. It had been controlled. Logical. Methodical. But now, with nobody to control Kammler, it was chaotic.

Will retreated. So did the others. Random parcels of forest kept disintegrating around them. This was hopeless. They had to leave.

He had the stone. But what he needed was a quiet place to concentrate. How in the hell was he supposed to do that in the middle of a war zone? Another thing they hadn't thought through very carefully.

Marsh came around the side of the farmhouse, waving his arms. 'Hey! Over here!' The collared man turned. Marsh tossed something at the body of the man he'd shot.

Will jumped into a shallow streambed. He pulled his knife, sliced his hand, and concentrated.

The man called Kammler stood inside a maelstrom of devastation. Marsh understood why they kept him on a leash. Without someone to guide him, Kammler was capable only of unfocused destruction. There was no intelligence, no plan, no meaning behind it.

God almighty. How did they learn to control something like that?

'Hey!' Marsh waved his arms, trying to get Kammler's attention. 'Over here!' Kammler turned, the look on his face pathetic and puzzled. Soil, glass, steel, and wood swirled around him. The creature was too confused to understand that Marsh was a threat. All he knew was rage at the loss of his companion.

Marsh tried a different tactic. Instead of attacking Kammler, he attacked the dead man. He lobbed a Mills at the body and then ran like hell. Kammler automatically protected his dead companion, as Marsh suspected he would. The grenade imploded in midair, pulverized into dust with a little *pop*.

That got Kammler's attention. He followed Marsh, still wrapped in his furious cyclone. It tore a swath of damage through the grounds.

Marsh ran, turned, taunted Kammler, then ran farther.

That's it. Follow me.

Klaus followed Gretel's pleas for help around to the north side of the farmhouse. She was far from the action. Far enough that they could speak without straining to be heard over the combat noises.

Running in the cold had created a wheeze in his chest by the time he found her. He leaned over with hands on his knees to clear his throat and spit out the blood before he tried to speak. 'Gretel?' he panted, 'I thought you were hurt.' He caught his breath, then asked, 'Why are you out here? I told you to go inside, where it's safe.'

'I'm waiting.'

Reinhardt ran from another direction before Klaus could ask the obvious question. He stopped short when he saw the two of them.

'What the hell is this?' Reinhardt pointed at Gretel. 'I thought you needed help.'

'I'm waiting,' said Gretel.

'You crazy bitch. I thought this was an emergency. I *had* him, too—'

She put a finger to her lips. 'Shhh.' When she had his attention, she said, 'Reinhardt. I've given you the one thing you wanted more than anything in the world. Isn't that enough to make you trust me?'

She looked to Klaus, repeating, 'Trust me.'

'What are you waiting for, Gretel?' he rasped.

'That,' she said, pointing at the farmhouse.

The roof flew off. Bricks and timbers disintegrated along one side of the building, and then the rest collapsed like a gingerbread house beneath a hammer.

Will fought a rising tide of panic. He hadn't packed a lexicon, in order to prevent it falling into German hands. But he wasn't supposed to need one. Going home was supposed to be easy. It wasn't.

The return journey had been included in the original negotiation. It was a round-trip ticket purchased up front with a pair of derailed trains.

But now the Eidolons were changing the deal.

They spoke through the stone, the earth, the bare trees and the ice in the streambed. And Will couldn't follow what they were saying. Frazzled, terrified, shivering in the cold and half-deaf from the noise of the battle, he could pick out only bits and pieces from the stream of animus.

... DISPLACEMENT-REDRESS-SOUL-VOLITION-FUTURE ...

It made no sense. Soul? This was an impossible price. He couldn't hand over a soul, even if he wanted to. Future? Worse yet, they wanted to take their pound of flesh after all was said and done. They wanted free rein to extract their own price.

Will stammered. In Enochian, that felt like swallowing a shattered wineglass.

Negation-redress-satisfied-volition-displacement.

The Eidolons repeated their incoherent demand. Their intent included something else, too, but it was washed out by a tremendous crash. Will chanced a peek at the battleground.

Something had extinguished the glow from the farmhouse windows, so Will had only starlight and a sliver of moon to see by. A cloud of dust and smoke billowed from the far end of the field, near the farmhouse, where Marsh had been.

Pip? He squinted, straining to make out details. Darkness and distance confounded him.

For the second time that night, his eyes flared in pain as the darkness gave way to brilliance. Will squeezed his eyes shut and turned away. Purple spots danced in his field of view. He looked back at the scene slowly, in stages, to let his eyes adjust.

He thought it was another string of spotlights until he saw the source: a human figure, wreathed in fire, blazing like the midday sun. His nimbus illuminated the scene with sharp edges and deep shadows, like an endless camera flash.

The farmhouse had been reduced to a pile of rubble. Marsh stood a few yards off to one side. He raised his revolver, then Kammler sprawled backwards. Will heard the gunshot a second later.

The burning man and the insubstantial man advanced on Marsh from behind the ruins of the farmhouse. Their rage was evident, even at this distance.

'God in heaven.'

The Eidolons repeated themselves. *SOUL-VOLITION-FUTURE* . . . *Yes, yes, yes, fine, whatever you want, just get us the hell out of here. Agreement-volition-congruent.*

In the instant before the world fell away, Will finally heard the entirety of the Eidolons' demand. He heard *soul*, he heard *future*, and he heard *child*.

The soul of an unborn child.

'Wait!' He screamed, trying to refute this atrocity, but he was—

The air around Marsh shimmered with heat, growing warmer by the second. Reinhardt charged at him over the rubble pile of the demolished farmhouse. The air grew hotter still, like a blast furnace. It burned his sinuses. He couldn't breathe.

But then space peeled apart, and breathing didn't matter, because he had no body. He was an abstract concept sliding through the cracks in the universe.

Eidolons infused him; twined themselves through him. They sifted through his essence: past, present, and future.

—too late.

The cleft stone yanked Will back to its twin like a rubber band snapping back together. He was solid again. Substantial. The Eidolons had squeezed him back into what human beings called reality.

Where generations of children yet unborn would live and die. Except the one he'd given to the Eidolons.

'Beauclerk? What happened?' asked a voice he hadn't heard in eons.

Will studied his surroundings. The Nissen hut had blinked into existence around him. Stephenson, Webber, and Hargreaves stared at him.

Will dropped the stone. It sounded strangely insubstantial when it banged against the wooden floor of the hut. He walked to the door on unsteady legs.

'Where are they? Where's the rest?'

Somewhere, in the distance, a car horn blared.

Will paused at the door. He glanced over his shoulder. 'I brought them home,' he said. 'I brought them all home.'

Somewhere nearby, within the park, a sentry shouted.

Will wandered without purpose between the tents and huts. The first body he found had been charred beyond recognition. He kept walking. The second body he found had been crushed into a pulp. More shouts of alarm went up throughout the staging area as more bodies were discovered.

Down by the lake, Will found a body mostly intact. He flipped the dead man over and rummaged through his pack, searching for a medkit.

Will stuffed a morphine syrette in his pocket before heading off into the darkness.

INTERLUDE

Frozen earth meant shallow graves. Shallow graves meant easy picking. And so the ravens of Albion gathered along parapets and treetops while the men from the island quietly buried their dead.

Twenty-six holes, dug in neat little rows for bodies that weren't so tidy.

Some were sooty black things, curled tightly upon themselves; preternatural fire had charred these men to the core. This flesh, the ravens knew, wasn't worth the effort. Heat had seared away its nutrients; it was little better than eating charcoal.

Others had been crushed, their every bone pulped. These retained their man-shapes solely by virtue of their skin. Better than the scorched dead, but still too much effort. Meat mixed with bone dust and bile. Bitter, and difficult to digest.

A number of dead had succumbed to more familiar injuries, ones the ravens had seen time and again. Their bodies were perforated with holes both large and small, some that still contained metal. Bodies like these were strewn across the continent: the detritus of war.

But the best meat came from that handful of men who had died without apparent injury. These were the men who had traveled through places the ravens could never visit, whose souls and sanity had been lost in transit. Perfect, unblemished, lifeless bodies.

The ravens waited until the holes had been filled, until the men with shovels and spades left the valiant dead to their peace. Then, as one, they descended.

They picked at mounds of freshly turned soil while their cousins to the east, upon the Continent, did much the same in the field behind a ruined farmhouse.

Many years had passed since new burials had drawn the ravens to this farm. There had been a time when it was littered with tiny graves, each no larger than a sack of grain. But new burials had come less and less frequently, until they ceased altogether.

Thus with great interest did the ravens watch as bodies were pulled from the wreckage. Several had died in the farmhouse, but only one evoked tears and anguish. The ravens recognized this bald little man; his experiments had fed them well in bygone years.

His body did not join the others in the cold, hard earth. The mourners cremated him upon a hellish pyre that crumbled his bones to ash. Winter wind sent his remains aloft, beyond where the ravens circled, and farther still.

To the east, to the far edge of the Continent, where his ashes mingled with snow and fell in large gray flakes upon the armies converging there. Erstwhile partners in invasion now assessed each other warily, like lonely revelers eyeing each other across an empty dance floor. They watched for feints and missteps, waiting for new music, for a new dance to begin.

The ravens of Eastern Europe had watched this impasse take shape. Now they waited hungrily for the spring thaw that would rouse these forces into motion.

But the farmhouse and the events there had become a pivot, the fulcrum upon which politics and aggression hinged: twin levers that could move whole armies in new directions. Winter hadn't yet diminished when the would-be aggressors lost their appetite for eastern conquests. Instead, they re-evaluated. Consolidated.

The would-be defenders watched. And waited.

Spring came fitfully. The changing seasons were punctuated with savage, unnatural cold snaps.

Ravens everywhere huddled in their nests, to ride out the ice.

TWELVE

21 April 1941
15 kilometers east of Stuttgart, Germany

The supply truck toppled over, accompanied by the groan of creaking axles and the smashing of unsecured crates. Mud fountained up where the truck crashed in the ditch. The swath of cotton duck stretched over the cargo bed created a spray of slush when it hit the earth.

'God damn you, idiot.' Hauptsturmführer Spalcke, Buhler's replacement, yanked on Kammler's leash with both fists, hard enough to make the big man stumble. 'You stupid, shit-eating retard! I despise you.'

'T-t-t-' Kammler looked back and forth between the truck, now sprawled alongside the winding road to Stuttgart, and Spalcke. He moved awkwardly. A round from a British sidearm had shattered his clavicle in December. Ostensibly it had healed – the doctors said he no longer needed to wear the sling – but Klaus suspected poor Kammler would suffer an aching collarbone for the rest of his life. Especially when the weather fluctuated so wildly; the stumps of Klaus's fingers ached.

'S-s-s-s . . .' Kammler's face turned red.

'S-s-s-stupid,' said Spalcke. He savaged Kammler's leash again. 'S-s-s-pathetic.'

Kammler's wide confused eyes flicked back and forth. His face was turning purple.

Klaus stepped in. 'You're hurting him,' he said. 'He doesn't understand.'

'Of course he doesn't understand! He's a worthless turd of a human being.'

'You're making it worse. Give me the leash,' Klaus said. His tone turned the suggestion into a de facto order, though the hauptsturmführer technically outranked him.

Spalcke wheeled on Klaus, still enraged. 'Have you forgotten your place?'

Klaus let his overcoat fall open, so that Spalcke could see clearly the wire plugged into his battery harness.

'No. You have.'

The two men faced each other for a long moment. Spalcke looked away. He dropped the leash and stomped back to the second supply truck.

He passed Reinhardt, who watched the proceedings from a stand of cherry trees a little farther up the road. The previous day's storm had glazed the white blossoms with ice, freezing trees in midbloom. The ice on the boughs above Reinhardt melted, dripping water that flashed into steam when it fell on him. Behind him sparkled the terraced vineyards of the Rems Valley.

Klaus loosened the choke collar squeezing Kammler's throat. Quietly, so that Spalcke and Reinhardt couldn't hear, he asked, 'Are you hurt?'

Kammler rocked back and forth. He looked at Klaus. Normal coloration returned to his face. 'B-buh-b-b—'

'He's gone, Kammler. You need to understand that.' Klaus

kept his grip on the leash, but didn't pull on it. 'Now. Can you help me move that truck?'

The mud in the ditch was exceptionally thick. All across central Europe, winter and spring were engaged in a battle of their own, vying for supremacy. The seasons were not turning so much as brawling. Just as soon as the earth thawed and new buds sprouted on the trees, an ice storm or blizzard would come howling out of nowhere. But then the temperature shot up thirty degrees, the landscape erupted with new greenery, and the cycle began anew.

But the weather wasn't the worst thing about this trip.

After several tries, murmuring a constant stream of monosyllabic encouragements into Kammler's ear, Klaus eventually managed to get the truck out of the ditch, turned upright, and set back on the road. It wasn't so difficult, with a bit of patience. That much was obvious to Klaus, who had watched Buhler and Kammler for years. He wondered how Spalcke had been chosen for the job.

'Good job, Kammler,' said Klaus. 'Well done.'

He unbuckled the collar around Kammler's throat and checked the gauge on his battery harness. It was depleted. Klaus cursed to himself. It could have been dangerous, even deadly, had Kammler's battery died while he was levitating the truck. Lazy Spalcke wasn't keeping a close eye on his ward's battery. Klaus called to one of the regular troops in their entourage, an SS-Oberschütze who had trained as a rifleman with the LSSAH prior to his assignment at the REGP. The private jogged over, saluting.

'Tend to his battery,' said Klaus, motioning at Kammler with a nod of his head. 'And see that he's fed.'

He left the rest of the troops assessing damage to the fallen truck. They climbed onto the cargo bed, tying down the crates, and under the carriage, checking for damage to the axles and drive train.

Klaus squelched across the road to join Reinhardt. A low sun cast long shadows down the valley; he had to shade his eyes to see the Aryan salamander.

'We're behind schedule,' he said. 'The demonstrations will have to wait for tomorrow.' He tried to keep the relief out of his voice as he said it.

Reinhardt snorted. 'I shouldn't worry if I were you. Surely your sister would have *warned* us if it were a problem.' He spoke quietly, as though Gretel were within earshot and he didn't want her to overhear the venom dripping from his words. Perhaps she *could* hear them; perhaps she'd listened to this conversation long ago.

Gretel could have saved Doctor von Westarp. She'd known all along what was coming, but had refrained from saying anything. The doctor had died simply because she wanted him to. Or because she couldn't be bothered to care.

The OKW was furious. The Führer had raged for days on end upon receiving the news. Doctor von Westarp's genius had been the axle about which the Reich spun its plans for further conquests. But now he was gone, his body scattered to the winds, along with his plans for expanding the Reichsbehörde. Deprived of the second-generation Götterelektrongruppe he'd promised, the Reich was scrambling to revamp its entire strategy for the war.

Gretel had put everything on precarious footing. Yet nobody confronted her. Nobody dared.

The simplest questions colored every interaction with the mad seer: Is this what she wants? Am I doing her bidding? Has she seen this moment? Anticipated it?

Will I upset her?

Now everybody feared Gretel the same way Klaus did, though he didn't hate her as the others did. How could he? She was his sister.

Reinhardt continued, 'Anyway, who cares? I don't. This trip is a farce.'

'We have our orders,' said Klaus. He couldn't muster the energy to infuse the words with conviction. He hated this recruitment drive as much as Reinhardt did, though for utterly different reasons. *We're all orphans again. So why does he still hold sway over us?* 'We have to finish the doctor's work.'

'We should be on the front, tearing our enemies apart.'

'Just the three of us? How long do you think we'd last, outnumbered ten thousand to three?'

Reinhardt spat into the mud. 'I'm wasted here.'

'This is important work,' said Klaus. 'Valuable work.'

'Keep telling yourself that, Klaus. Maybe you'll start to believe it.'

'The farm will need volunteers once the doctor's work has been reconstructed.' Klaus shuddered, remembering the new machines. Machines for disposing of failed subjects.

The LSSAH men deemed the toppled supply truck to be in suitable shape for driving. Klaus and Reinhardt rejoined the small convoy as the trucks growled back to life, belching black smoke and diesel exhaust.

As Reinhardt climbed back into the cab of his truck, he said, 'We're all that's left, Klaus. We're all there will ever be.'

They entered Stuttgart at sunset. Klaus watched the glow of streetlamps move in a wave across the city as the setting sun plunged the valley into shadow. Handbills advertising the Götterelektrongruppe's demonstrations had been pinned or pasted to every public notice board their small convoy passed.

The mundane troops joined the local Waffen-SS garrison for the night. Klaus, Reinhardt, Kammler, and Spalcke were hosted by the Lord Mayor of Stuttgart. Birdlike Herr Strogan received them as honored guests, plying them with food, drink, and an atmosphere of strained goodwill. Yet throughout their dinner – roast duck, trout from the nearby Neckar river, white asparagus, and sweet wine from the local vineyards – his eyes wandered to Klaus's missing fingers, or Reinhardt's self-igniting cigarettes, or the wine dribbling down Kammler's chin.

The wrinkles at the corners of his eyes grew tighter, too, as Reinhardt charmed the young Fräulein Strogan. The mayor couldn't mask the look of impotent despair on his face each time his daughter laughed at one of Reinhardt's jokes, or gasped at his wildly exaggerated war exploits. Klaus wondered what Lord Mayor Strogan had been told about these strangers from the little-known Götterelektrongruppe.

That night, Klaus and Reinhardt slept in adjacent rooms. Klaus wrapped a pillow around his head to drown out Reinhardt's snoring and the fräulein's weeping.

There had been a time when he'd been accustomed to sleeping while others wept. What had changed? Reinhardt had grown more brazen with his appetites. That was it, Klaus lied to himself. The problem was Reinhardt.

When he did sleep, Klaus dreamed of blackbirds and a hay wagon.

They performed their first set of demonstrations in Stuttgart on the Schlossplatz, before the New Castle, the next morning. The Neue Schloss, the former residence of the kings of Württemburg, was an expansive construction of late baroque design. It was draped in so many flags that when the wind blew, it seemed the castle had been consumed in a red tide. Banners fluttered over-head (GREATNESS IS OUR DESTINY! YOU ARE THE FUTURE OF THE FATHERLAND!) while a gramophone blared the Deutschlandlied and the Horst Wessel song across the plaza. All this in the shadow of Concordia (the Roman goddess of unity, fittingly enough), whose statue watched from a perch high atop the marble Jubilee Column.

The morning smelled of fresh-baked bread from the nearby bakeries. Vendors sold fragrant Mandel-Halbmonde from push-carts. Klaus tried to buy one, but received it free with the baker's compliments. Honey, sweet and sticky, coated his fingers.

The spectacle drew a large crowd. Mostly fathers and moth-ers too old or weak to be of use, or children too young. But here and there, interspersed throughout the throng, teenagers and pre-teens watched the show with undisguised adoration. The members of the local Hitler Youth had turned out, and they watched the proceedings with expressions of rapture.

The Lord Mayor watched from the wings. His daughter was not in attendance.

The spectators *ooh*ed and *aah*ed appropriately as Kammler levitated an anvil, Klaus walked through it, Reinhardt reduced it to a puddle of slag. They embraced the suggestion that over-coming one's limitations was the province of all Germans. They clapped when the men from the Reichsbehörde demonstrated their immunity to small-arms fire, each in his own spectacular fashion. And they cheered the lie: how simple it was, how *pleas-ant* it was, to become more than human.

Klaus and the others took care to keep their wires hidden. They had learned in Munich that the prospect of brain surgery dampened people's enthusiasm.

Thirty-four men and women – some little more than boys and

girls, others adults who had until now opted to support the war effort in civilian roles – lined up to sign the roster afterwards. They received armbands marking them as cadets of the Götterelektrongruppe while parents smiled and a puddle of iron crackled. Parents and spouses received impressive stipends, plus the assurance that they were doing the Fatherland the greatest possible service.

Thirty-four. Back in the old days, Klaus knew, one or two of them might have survived the first round. He wondered how the reconstructed version of Doctor von Westarp's accelerated program would work, and if the survival rates would be any higher. But then he remembered the lime pits, and the ovens, and doubted it.

After all, if the procedure had been perfected, they wouldn't need to recruit civilians. Instead they'd take in trained soldiers. But only if it were reasonably quick, and the attrition rate low.

Spalcke took the roster of new volunteers. He signed it, stamped it, folded it, sealed it into an envelope, then stamped the envelope for special courier back to the Reichsbehörde. The REGP would arrange buses to collect the volunteers and distribute the stipends.

The crowd dispersed while the mundane troops disassembled the risers, pulled down the banners, and struggled with crowbars to pry up the iron slag. Klaus leaned against the base of the Jubilee Column, munching on another almond crescent. He felt disinclined to help speed along their next demonstration, which was scheduled across town at the Wilhelma botanical gardens that afternoon.

'Sir? Herr Officer?'

Klaus turned. A girl of perhaps fourteen or fifteen years stared up at him with wide blue eyes.

'Is it too late? I'd like to sign the roster.'

Klaus looked across the plaza. Spalcke was busy cursing out Kammler. He hadn't yet handed off the envelope containing the roster.

It would be a trivial matter for Klaus to pluck the roster from inside the sealed envelope, add a name, put it back. Doing so was his duty.

He looked back at the girl. She put him in mind of Heike, staring at nothing with her eyes of Prussian blue while Reinhardt had his way with her body.

'Go home,' he said.

'I want to do something wonderful,' she said. 'To make my parents proud.'

'It's too late. We're full.'

'I'm a good German.'

He took another glance across the plaza. The others were busy, casting no attention in his direction. Klaus beckoned the girl into the shadow behind the massive marble column. There he opened his coat, kneeled beside her, and tilted his head down.

'Look at me,' he said. 'This is what they'll do to you.' *If you survive.*

He watched the brass buckles on her red leather shoes, waiting for her eyes to trace the wires from his waist to his skull, waiting for the quiet gasp, waiting for the girl to stiffen and step back. She retreated again when Klaus climbed to his feet.

'Go home,' he repeated. 'The Reichsbehörde is no place for you.' He rebuttoned his coat while she ran away.

Klaus rode with Spalcke and Kammler on the way to the afternoon rally. It took but a trickle of charge from his battery to pluck the roster from the sealed envelope while the hauptsturm-führer was distracted.

He destroyed the volunteer roster. Spalcke sent an empty envelope to the REGP.

8 May 1941
Milkweed Headquarters, London, England

High tide had come, long, long ago. It had flooded the beach and rose higher still, a deluge that destroyed everything in its path. Will couldn't outrun it; it swept him along with the rest of the flotsam. There was no ebb tide. Just a crashing surf that echoed in Enochian.

He'd been the only warlock to attend the December burials. He'd also been the only person from Milkweed to visit the widows, the sons and daughters, to deliver the news of their loss. It started with Lorimer – Will had met the Scot's family, once. After that, it seemed that every family deserved to put a human face on their tragedy. And Will deserved their scorn. Perhaps not so much as Marsh did, but there was plenty of blame to spread about.

Thirty men went to Germany, and he brought all thirty back. Four of them alive. Three of them sane.

Perhaps only two. He wasn't his old self these days.

And then there was the soulless child. *That* was entirely his doing.

He leaned against the wall, listening to the litany of his colleagues' entreaties and the Eidolons' prices. Will's facility with Enochian had progressed to the point where he no longer needed to consult the master lexicon. Even in his current state, he could hear the strained desperation in the warlocks' voices. Nuances that would have been lost on him merely a year ago: the undertones of a human throat within the screech of colliding stars; the slightest trace of a heartbeat, of wet biology, within the ripple of starlight through empty space.

Since late winter the warlocks had found only sporadic success in their negotiations with the Eidolons. The ice storms, blizzards, and paralyzing cold never lasted past a fortnight before the Eidolons withdrew and the world snapped back to normal.

The warlocks had blockaded the Channel for months straight during the worst part of the Blitz. Yet now they were lucky to control the weather for more than a week.

Exert your volition in this fashion, said the warlocks.

Give us more blood maps, said the Eidolons. *More.*

We won't, said the warlocks.

You will, said the Eidolons.

The stump of Will's finger throbbed when he glimpsed the bloodstained floorboards beneath Hargreaves's seat. *Odd.* He shouldn't have been able to feel anything.

It was here in this room, almost exactly a year ago, where Marsh had severed Will's finger. It was here where Will had pleaded with him to do so. Here Milkweed had repelled an invasion, destroyed a fleet. Today the air tasted like the stones at the bottom of a centuries-old well. The bones of the earth steeped in tainted water and the shells of dead snails.

The warlocks tried again. Bartering, wheedling, chipping away at the Eidolons' demands. One soul. Two. A token reduction. Never enough. Everything cost so damn much these days.

The atmosphere in the room changed. Will caught a whiff of birch wood shattered by the cold that inhabited the void between the stars. This was the lowest blood price the warlocks would see today: fourteen souls, dead by drowning. They'd accept it, see it paid, and hope the Eidolons would hasten the war's end.

Nothing happened. Silence ricocheted through the broken reality of the room.

Grafton snapped at him. 'William!'

'Oh,' Will muttered. 'Yes. Of course.'

Correction: *He'd* accept it. *He'd* see it paid.

It was his turn again. (*Already?*)

Will braced himself. He called up his Enochian and gave a short, perfunctory response. *Agreement.*

It made him an agent of the negotiation; the Eidolons noticed him. They inspected him, poured through the gaps between the atoms of his body, then withdrew, disinterested. They already had his blood map, already knew the trajectory of his particular stain on time and space.

But that was enough. He was part of it now. It wouldn't work unless he did his part.

The suffocating presence of the Eidolons evaporated. The room returned to normal.

'Get it done quickly,' said Hargreaves. 'And take Shapley with you this time.'

Ah. He suspects. Well, it had always been just a matter of time. Nothing to do for it.

Will said, 'I'll need some time to prepare.' He started to look at his watch, but stopped for worry that the others would notice his tremors. To Shapley, he said, 'Give me a few hours.'

Shapley frowned. 'What am I to do until then?'

'I don't care. Say a maritime prayer. Or learn one.'

'And what will you be doing?'

'Preparing,' said Will as he stepped into the corridor, eager to get away, eager to kill the ache in his finger. Why wasn't he numb?

His voice echoed. This wing of the Admiralty still belonged to

Milkweed, though now much of it was empty. But for Marsh, they no longer had field agents. Just the warlocks, and a handful of technicians with nothing to do except tinker with pixies that would never see use.

He returned to his office and locked the door behind him. He didn't turn on the light. His chair, an ugly gunmetal-gray thing on squeaky casters, rumbled across the floorboards when he collapsed into the seat. The desk was bare but for a dog-eared, wire-bound copy of the master lexicon sitting on one corner. He'd spent much time here, hunched over that desk, compiling it from the disparate notebooks of the warlocks he'd recruited. It seemed eons ago; he hadn't cracked the lexicon since December.

Quietly, so as not to jangle the keys and announce his presence to passersby in the corridor, he fished the key ring from his vest pocket. He unlocked the bottommost desk drawer. The drawer where he kept his stolen morphine.

The syrette needles twinkled in the half-light leaking through the gap under the door. Half-grain dosages of miracle opiate, ready for use on the battlefield, for snuffing the most incapacitating pain. Yet they didn't work so well as they had in the past.

Will counted half a dozen left unopened. He counted again. Surely he'd had more than this? They had to last until Aubrey sent him more cash. He couldn't remember how long that would be. Not long. Not if he asked.

One dose wouldn't be enough to get him through the night. Not if he and Shapley were to spend it extracting another blood price for the Eidolons. He fished out two syrettes, placed them on the desk, and closed the drawer.

He pulled the hood off the first syrette, pinched the wire loop, and pushed the needle back through the foil seal at the narrow

end of the tube. Then he snapped off the loop, exposing the
hollow needle.

Will opened his vest and the lowest button on his shirt, just
above his waist. A small lump had formed beneath his skin at the
spot where he'd been administering the injections. He'd started
bleeding there, too, which tended to dilute the dose. An entire
dose had been wasted that way. (Yesterday? Three days ago?) He
picked a new spot, a few centimeters to the left.

The needle bit into his waist at a shallow angle. Will worked his
thumb and forefinger up the flexible tube, dispensing every drop of
the precious morphine tartrate into his bloodstream. The injection
stung for a few seconds, but then he couldn't tell if it ached or not.

He tossed the empty syrette back in the drawer. A second dose
followed the first. Warmth flowed through him like sunlight, like
molten gold. Through his belly, across his chest, into his heart and
out to the rest of his body. It washed away the pain in his finger,
quelled his shivering. He could breathe again. Even here, under-
water.

The second syrette slipped through his fingers. It hit the floor
tube-first, bounced, and then *plinked* as the needle wedged itself
between the floorboards.

There was something important he had to do.

Something about a barge on the Thames. Something about
the Eidolons, about a price. Something about a war.

10 May 1941
Walworth, London, England

Agnes's first birthday.

Candles and Liv singing, cake and streamers and a delighted, bewildered little girl. That's what today was meant to be. Instead, it dawned to find Marsh standing just outside the door of what had been his home, a key in one hand and an envelope in the other.

His shirt stuck to his back and shoulders. It bunched up when he moved, like a bedsheet twisted during fevered sleep or frantic lovemaking. Covering the final mile on foot – lest the taxi wake Liv – had left his covered skin moist with sweat. Yet the clamminess of predawn had chilled the exposed skin of his hands and face. The end result was a cold sweat.

It had been early when he finally abandoned the pretense of sleep. He'd gone upstairs and rummaged through the many empty Milkweed offices until he'd found a fountain pen and stationery. At first he'd intended merely to post a letter to Liv. But the date brought a new rawness to Agnes's death, ripped the scabs from that half-healed wound, leaving him tender and unprotected. The reality of the empty offices caught him unaware, forcing him to accept the reality he'd disregarded for months.

The offices were empty because of him. Milkweed had been decimated because of his mistake. Because there was no reasoning with the inarticulate rage he felt.

The same rage that had become a hammer pounding on the grief wedged between himself and Liv, driving it until they'd been thrown apart. She couldn't live in the margins of his agony. She needed her own space to grieve.

Now he stood in a sterile gray sunrise in front of his home. (His home? Liv's home?) He looked from the key to the envelope and back again, unsure of what to do.

His stomach gurgled. He wondered idly if Liv would plant new tomatoes next summer. Marsh had considered taking a cot out to the garden shed, or even sleeping in the Anderson shelter, though only in passing. It was cruel to stay so near to Liv. He had become a mirror for her sorrow, a looking glass that framed her loss.

As always, the envelope contained most of his pay. He saved what he could for Liv; his expenses had been minimal since he'd started sleeping at the Admiralty, and Liv needed the money more than he. She had a mortgage to pay. She'd rejoined the WAAF – once, he'd seen her leaving the house in her uniform – but he knew doing one's part for the war effort didn't always pay the bills.

Extra cash wouldn't dispel the grief that had taken root inside her, nor would it smooth the harshness that had taken root in corners of her eyes. But it would ensure that she could feed and clothe herself, and that she could keep the house if she chose to do so. Though he couldn't understand how she'd stayed there as long as she had, surrounded by hints of a family life that might have been. Liv had always been the stronger of the two of them.

The envelope also contained a letter. The first he'd written since before the new year. His chicken-scratch handwriting was an unworthy vehicle for laying bare tumultuous thoughts and feelings. Unworthy of Liv, too; it felt disrespectful, somehow, to send her something so coarse. He wished he had Will's penmanship, the elegant hand that came naturally to moneyed people.

He dropped the key back in his pocket. The cold metal flap over the mail slot creaked when he lifted it. He pushed the envelope through the slot, listening for the *pat-slap* sound as it fell to the vestibule tiles. The flap clanked shut when he released it.

Marsh was back at the walk, his hand on the wooden gate that had replaced the wrought iron, when the door opened behind him.

'Raybould?' Liv's voice made everything a song, even when she was confused and tired.

He stopped, suddenly feeling anxious, ashamed, cowardly. Like he'd been caught with his hand in the biscuit tin. He was afraid to look at her, but hungry for it, too.

Marsh turned. Liv stood in the doorway, one hand on the door and the other clutching the belt of a flannel robe. Her hair was shorter than he remembered. Curlier.

'Liv,' he blurted. 'It's early.'

'I couldn't sleep,' she said. 'Today, it's . . .'

He sighed. 'Yeah.' He shifted his feet, unsure of whether he should release the gate and step forward in order to see her better. He hadn't intended to speak with her, but now that she stood before him, he didn't want to drive her back inside.

She looked thin. 'Are you eating well enough?' he asked, nodding to the envelope at her feet.

The hem of her robe lifted slightly, revealing the bare ankles above her slippers as she shrugged. He'd kissed those ankles, long ago.

'The rationing,' she said.

'Yeah.' He couldn't meet her eyes.

A long hush fell between them. Birds twittered to each other. Somewhere, a lorry grinded its gears.

'I've miss—,' she said, at the same moment he said, 'I'm sorr—'

Another hush. Six years long.

Liv bit her lip. 'Do you . . .' She opened the door a little wider, unable or unwilling to voice the invitation.

His hand hovered on the rough wood of the gate. *Stay or go? Stay or go?*

The chasm between the gate and the house felt ten leagues wide, and his shoes full of lead shot.

Only when she had closed the door, and they were alone together, could he meet her lovely, lovely eyes.

'You're shivering,' she said.

'I . . . I've made so many mistakes,' he said.

'I've missed you terribly.'

'You're my compass, Liv. I understand that now.'

'It's my fault. I shouldn't have sent her away.'

'Hush, love. We did it together. Hush.'

'I feel so useless.'

'I wanted so desperately to punish them. The people who killed her.'

'You can't. It was done by people we'll never know.'

'Well . . .'

Liv's light touch, a fingertip on his lips.

'What?'

Quiet laughter, warmth in the dark. 'You were talking in your sleep again, love.'

'I'm sorry, Liv.'

Her breath tickled his earlobe. 'Don't be. I've missed it more than you know.' She laced her fingers through his.

'I'm glad I came back. I'm sorry it took so long.'

'So am I.'

*

That evening, Marsh studied the map of Europe tacked to Stephenson's wall. It bristled with more pins and flags than a hedgehog had spines.

He sipped from his tumbler. Brandy washed across his tongue and burned on the way down; it soothed his throat.

'I thought we'd decided this plan was dead,' he said in a voice made hoarse by daylong conversation with Liv.

'Not dead,' said Stephenson. 'Moribund.'

The plan was to lure the Soviet Union into the fray. Break the Wehrmacht's back, use the Eidolons to freeze the German war machine to death, and let Stalin's predatory instincts do the rest.

The enemy of my enemy . . .

Marsh cracked his knuckles. None of this speculation seemed to matter. He said so: 'Isn't this all a bit academic? The warlocks can't deliver.'

They'd scrapped the plan because the warlocks had failed repeatedly to produce the necessary results.

Stephenson dragged on the cigarette dangling at the corner of his mouth. Marsh took a marble ashtray from the windowsill and handed it to him. Stephenson placed it on a stack of papers. Construction manifests and requisition orders for building supplies, by the look of them.

Stephenson snuffed out his cigarette. The hunter-green Lucky Strike box bobbed up and down as he shook out another. American tobacco was virtually impossible to get via legal means these days. But with position came privilege, and the old man had many contacts.

'Well. As it happens, that remains to be seen.' He *skritched* a match along the edge of his desk. It released the sharp and unpleasant smell of sulfur. 'Had an interesting discussion with

Hargreaves and Shapley yesterday. They've unearthed the root of the problem.'

Marsh returned to the mullioned windows behind Stephenson's desk. The base camp for the December raid had long since been dismantled. St. James' was a park once more, and a greening one. Sunset glinted off the lake, causing Marsh to squint. The same lake from which Milkweed had fished several bodies after the raid in Germany.

I'm sorry, Will. I should have listened to you.

He sighed. 'It's Will.'

Behind him, Stephenson's chair creaked. 'He's become a liability.'

Marsh turned. 'What are you proposing?'

'Oh, relax, for God's sake. He's out of Milkweed, but we needn't do more than that,' said Stephenson. 'Though of course, we'll have contingencies in place. If he talks, we'll destroy him.' Outside, robins serenaded one another.

Destroy him? We've already done that, haven't we?

'I'll tell him.'

'It's my job. But I thought you should know.'

Quietly, Marsh said, 'I'm the one who brought him into this in the first place.' He shook his head again. 'It's my responsibility.' *I've made my amends with Liv. I owe Will at least as much.*

Stephenson harrumphed his assent. 'Very well. But see to it quickly.'

'Yes, sir. I will.' Marsh's voice cracked again. He drained the tumbler.

So. Milkweed would have at it yet again. Like a hound begging for a soup bone, getting kicked away time after time but still coming back for another try. He turned his attention back to the map.

Black pins and little swastika flags marked the known positions of Nazi army groups and divisions across the Continent. They weren't entirely static, but the overall pattern hadn't changed appreciably since the consolidation of forces in January and February. Pins moved most frequently in the region around the Balkans, where German and Italian forces dealt with the guerrilla tactics of Greek and Yugoslav partisans. Farther south, beyond the bottom edge of the map, the Afrikakorps had been much more dynamic. Britain had reluctantly written off North Africa as another casualty of the Dunkirk failure.

The locations of the red markers and hammer-and-sickle pennants on the eastern side of the map were a bit more speculative. Reliable intelligence regarding the distribution of Red Army forces was difficult to obtain.

Twin rows of blue map pins indicated corridors the warlocks would attempt to open in the weather by nudging the Eidolons aside, thus providing the Soviets with routes into Germany. Several of the corridors converged on Berlin. The weather would be peeled back as the Soviets advanced.

A single orange pin marked the location of the Reichsbehörde; there the Eidolonic weather would be strengthened into a bulwark that kept the invaders at bay.

It was a tricky balancing act. They needed the Red Army to strike deep into the heart of a paralyzed Reich, to deliver the killing blow that would end the war. But they also had to make damn certain von Westarp's farm didn't fall into the wrong hands. Which meant, given Britain didn't have an army on the ground with which to occupy it, the REGP couldn't fall into *anybody's* hands.

Hence the long-range bombers in southeast England. Britain's aircraft production was a pale shadow of what it had once been, but the RAF could scrape together enough bombers for one particular mission. The Luftwaffe was effectively grounded so long as the warlocks could keep the weather in place; Jerry's radar and anti-aircraft measures would be similarly blind.

But it all came down to timing. It required lifting the barricade around the REGP just before the RAF arrived to carpet-bomb the grounds. It was imperative the Soviets found nothing of value if they sent forces there.

The strategy hadn't changed since early spring, just before the warlocks' first attempt to shut down the Continent with endless winter. On paper, it made a desperate kind of sense. Except ...

Marsh cleared his throat. The brandy hadn't flushed the roughness out of his voice. 'The situation is more complicated now. We ought to reassess.'

Stephenson nodded, tapping his ashes into the tray. 'The recruitment drive.'

'If the Reichsbehörde has gone public, we can be certain old Joe knows about it. The Kremlin likely knows all about von Westarp's research by now.' The Soviets were rumored to have an extensive and aggressive spy network operating inside Nazi Germany. The Jerries referred to it as the 'Red Orchestra.'

'That's why,' said Stephenson, 'you have to be ready.'

'Sir?'

'If our ploy succeeds, I want you in Germany the moment the Red Army starts to move.'

Pangs of guilt and irritation jabbed at Marsh. He couldn't leave Liv alone again. He'd only just found her. He'd forgotten her scent for so long, but now he could smell her hair on the collar of his shirt.

'Sir. I doubt I could achieve anything that an RAF bomber squadron couldn't. I'm just one man.' A feeble protest, and he knew it.

Smoke jetted from Stephenson's nostrils, signaling impatience. 'I don't give a toss what you think. And you're the only man we have left because of your monumental cock-up in Germany. Your mess, you clean it up.' He dragged again on his cigarette. 'Flattening the REGP is only part of the equation. If the Soviets take Berlin, they'll get the files. Unless we destroy them first.'

Marsh sighed. Stephenson was right. This wouldn't be over until somebody destroyed the Schutzstaffel records of von Westarp's program.

And at the end of the day, it was Marsh's fault that Milkweed had been reduced to a single field agent.

At least he'd get to say his good-bye to Liv in person. He hadn't done so prior to the raid in December; he knew now with utter conviction that if he'd died in Germany, that regret would have been his dying thought.

Eddies of cigarette smoke curled around Marsh when he headed for the door. 'I'll start preparing.'

'There's one last thing.'

'Sir?'

'I'll need you to find new accommodations. Can't have you staying downstairs any longer.' Stephenson tapped the pile of papers beneath his ashtray. 'We're planning a bit of work down there.'

'That won't be a problem.' *I won't miss that cot.*

'Good.'

Marsh cocked an eyebrow. 'What sort of work?'

Stephenson picked up his telephone. Over the receiver, he said, 'Let me know when you've spoken to Beauclerk.'

Marsh turned to leave, pondering the new plan. Something about it still bothered him, tickled the back of his mind. Eidolons weren't tactical weapons. Weather savage enough to shatter the Wehrmacht would also freeze earth and rivers solid, kill fish and spring plantings.

The invaders would meet little resistance. If anything, they'd be welcomed as saviors, when the Great Soviet brought bread to the starving masses.

Marsh paused with his hand on the door handle. He turned. 'Question, sir?'

Stephenson paused in mid-dial. 'What?'

'What will we do when Soviet France is parked on our doorstep?'

'One problem at a time. We're long overdue for some good fortune.'

'And if fortune decides to kick us in the bollocks?'

'Then we'd better bloody well start things off on the right foot when we meet our new allies.'

THIRTEEN

11 May 1941
Kensington, London, England

Will decided, while packing up the Kensington flat, that his brother Aubrey might have been on to something with his ceaseless harping about the necessity of hired help. It rankled, the thought of taking on a valet. Will had always rejected the notion. *I can clothe myself, thank you kindly.*

But now half-empty boxes sprouted from every corner of the flat like corn poppies blooming on the grave of Will's old life. A knowledgeable hand to help prune the disarray wouldn't have been unwelcome. Perhaps what he truly needed was an undertaker.

He opted to leave the bone china. The notion of packing and shipping it back to Bestwood presented a headache he didn't care to indulge. Instead, he'd leave it for whomever succeeded him. A gesture of goodwill. And who knew? The next residents might be related to one of the many people he'd killed to satisfy the Eidolons' prices.

It occurred to him that his closet contained a ridiculous number of suits. He took a few shirts, some trousers, a pair of ties, and abandoned the rest. He left the paisley carpetbag sitting on the floor of the closet. Let the next residents make what they would of its bloodstained contents. He didn't give a damn.

The bell rang while he was emptying the bookshelves of Rudyard Kipling and Dashiell Hammett. Will peeked through the curtains. Marsh stood outside, his boxer's face hung low.

'One moment,' Will called. He rolled down his sleeves to hide the bruises and puncture wounds on his forearms. He buttoned the shirt and his cuffs, checking himself in the mirror above the umbrella stand. There was no hiding the bags beneath his eyes, but they could be attributed to a sleepless night. Or ten. The hollows beneath his cheekbones and the pale, papery skin were another matter.

He opened the door. 'Pip.'

Marsh removed his fedora, ran a hand through his hair. 'Hi, Will. Can I come in for a moment?'

Will stepped back, beckoning him into the foyer. Marsh stopped short when he saw the boxes. His nostrils twitched, and his hand started to move toward his face before he caught himself.

'Packing?' he asked, breathing through his mouth.

What – oh. The kitchen. *I'd forgotten about that. It hasn't been that long, has it?*

'I'm going away for a while,' said Will, leading him toward the den, where he hoped the smell wasn't so offensive. 'I've decided it's time for a change.' He tucked the eviction notice under a half-finished Sunday *Times* crossword puzzle, while Marsh perused the boxes. Then he tucked the crossword between two books, suddenly self-conscious of his shaky handwriting.

'In that case,' said Marsh, 'you know why I'm here.'

'I'm to be cut loose, am I?'

'Yes.'

'And then what happens?' Will asked.

'Nothing. You've served the country well. Go back to your life, Will.' Marsh paused. 'But please don't tell anyone about Milkweed.'

Will asked, 'If I do?' Marsh looked uncomfortable. Will waved his discomfort aside. 'No, no. I haven't forgotten poor little Lieutenant Cattermole, you know.'

'I know you won't reveal anything,' said Marsh. 'It had to be said. For the record.'

'Of course it did. Even so, don't let Stephenson make you his hatchet man, Pip. It doesn't become you.' Will perched on the edge of a chaise longue upholstered in long satin stripes of royal blue and sunflower yellow. He stretched his legs before him, exhaling heavily as he did so, and waved Marsh toward the matching chair.

Marsh sat. The chair creaked as he shifted back and forth, trying to find a comfortable position. He reached down into the gap between the cushion and the armrest and pulled out a saucer crusted with something black. It clinked against the glasses clustered on the coffee table when he set it there. His gaze drifted from the glasses to the empty decanter on the sideboard.

'I'd offer you something to drink,' said Will, 'but I'm fresh out.'

Marsh sighed. 'What happened to you, Will?'

'The war happened, Pip. I'm weary of it.'

'So are we all. But I meant ...' Marsh stopped. He sighed again, and encompassed the flat with a sweep of his arm. 'Will. This place is squalid. And pardon me for saying it, but you look like three-day-old shit.'

'As would you, had you done the things I have.'

To his credit, Marsh ignored the barb. He changed the

subject. Looking around the room, he said, 'Where are you headed? A change of scenery would do you good. You've earned a rest.'

'Here and there. Home, eventually. Bestwood.'

'I'd offer you a place here in the city,' said Marsh.

'I wouldn't hear of it, Pip.'

'It's just, right now ... Liv and I. Things are improving.'

Somewhere deep inside Will, a slender asp, green like emeralds, twined through his gut. *Even after all this, after all we've done, she still wants you, doesn't she.*

He forced a smile. 'That's good. I'm glad,' he lied.

Marsh fell quiet, looking at the wine-stained carpet. Finally, he said, 'You were right, Will. I should have listened.'

Will rocked back in his seat. 'Now this is rather surprising. What's happened to *you?*'

The other man shook his head. There was an air about Marsh, something new that Will hadn't seen. It wasn't exactly tranquillity, but rather an absence of anger.

No, not an absence. It was there, hidden deep in the caramel-colored eyes, if one knew where to look. But it wasn't bubbling away just a hair's breadth beneath the surface, as it had for so many months. And in that Will recognized Liv's influence at work.

Aubrey might have thought Will needed a batman. But what man could want for anything with Liv at his side?

'We should have dinner, the three of us,' Marsh said. 'Like we used to.'

At this, Will brightened. 'I'd like that.' Any chance to pretend the past year hadn't happened ...

'Though I don't know when. I might be away, traveling, for a while.'

'"Traveling," he says. Would this be related to the old man's grand plan?' Milkweed's bid to end the war.

'Yes.'

'Have you stopped to consider what we'll do if it works? It's trading one basket of concerns for another.'

'I have,' said Marsh, nodding. 'And I'd be lying if I said it didn't worry me. But I don't see that we have any choice. We'll deal with it when the time comes.'

'Do you know you *can* handle it? What if you can't?'

'We'll find a way. We have no choice.'

Will jumped to his feet. 'That's *exactly* the sort of cocksure attitude that got twenty-six men killed.' He paused, alarmed by his own intensity. He'd thought that by now any passions had long since drowned. 'Yes, you're very clever, but there are still some problems too great even for you to fix.' He sat again. 'Don't think you have it all sussed out, Pip. You don't.'

Marsh's puckered, knobby knuckles turned pale as he squeezed the armrests of his chair. But again, to his credit, the man held his temper. *Ah, Liv.*

'I've said you were right about the raid,' Marsh said in a quiet monotone. 'I'm well aware of the men we lost.'

Equally quiet, Will said, 'I notified the next of kin. All of them.' It was a statement of fact, a commiseration more than an accusation.

'You're a better man than I am, Will.' Marsh peered out the window, his gaze momentarily distant. He changed the subject again. 'Have you heard anything about some work going on downstairs? At the Admiralty.'

'I'm sure I'd be the last person to know anything.'

'Ah.' Marsh slapped his knees with the palms of his hands, and stood. 'Well. Need any help?' he asked, gesturing around the flat.

Will said, 'Thank you, but no. I'll send somebody for my things once I've returned to Bestwood.'

He showed Marsh to the door. As his friend descended the stairs to the street, Will called after him.

'Pip? I've—' He paused. *I've what? I've consigned a child's soul to the Eidolons? I've lost track of the men I've killed? I've forgotten who I am?*

It was all true, but none of it was right. He didn't know what he was looking for, what he was struggling to say.

'What, Will?'

'Never mind,' he faltered. 'See you soon, I'm sure.'

Will abandoned the Kensington flat. He called a taxi to Fairclough Street in Whitechapel. He took two suitcases; the one he'd packed, and another, smaller, empty case.

He had learned about Fairclough Street by following one of Stephenson's men. Stephenson couldn't come down here himself, of course, but the man did adore his American tobacco. And the only place to get it was on the black market. Almost anything could be found on the black market, if one had the money: Food. Extra ration books. Petrol. Cigarettes. Clothing. Even medicine.

Will traded almost the entirety of his month's allowance from his brother Aubrey, to fill the smaller case with syrettes of medical morphine. With the leftover cash he purchased a rail ticket to Swansea, and from there hired another taxi. The driver followed Will's directions through the Welsh countryside, and frowned with silent disapproval when they pulled up to a boarding hotel surrounded by landscaped acreage.

The working class took a dim view of funk holes. As well they should have.

Will, being not of the working class, knew of several such places. Places where those with enough money – more money than conscience, certainly – could wait out the war in comfort. The residents typically pooled their rationing books together, enabling the proprietor or proprietress to prepare more suitable meals. And in return for a not-inconsiderable fee, the residents spent their wartime years painting, punting, playing bridge, or listening to the wireless with a glass of sherry on hand while complaining about how Mr. Churchill had done everything so very wrong.

The driver sped off – grumbling about the well-to-do, his son in the Royal Navy, and his daughter in the Women's Land Army – as soon as Will had his suitcases out. From Will's vantage point there before the main house, he could see a tennis court, a fishpond, a whitewashed pergola, and a horse stable. A breeze carried the perfume of bluebells and hollyhocks blooming down in the garden.

It was, Will decided, a perfectly fine place to die.

22 May 1941
Bielefeld, Germany

The weather turned on them yet again. But it was different this time: a relentless, eyeball-cracking cold, equal parts ice and malice. And although this seemed impossible, or perhaps too disturbing to contemplate, Klaus felt as if the deepest freeze, the very worst of it, was following them. Dogging them. It seemed drawn to their uniforms, their regalia.

Klaus had never before in his life seen Reinhardt shiver. Now they all did it, constantly.

At night, when the temperature plunged and every snowflake became a crystalline fléchette, patterns emerged within the interplay of moonlight and shadow. Wind sculpted the snowdrifts into unknowable shapes. Phantom scents lingered like half-remembered dreams on a wind that murmured in a language too alien to discern.

But most disturbing of all were the rumors. Klaus had heard in each of the last two towns they'd visited that the local children had begun to act strangely. They babbled endlessly, and they babbled in unison, as though chanting to some unseen presence that lived inside the weather.

Klaus had heard reports from Channel weather spotters the previous year, during the run-up to the invasion of Britain. Those men had reported strange shapes, sounds, even scents in the fog. More than a few of those men had gone mad. Gretel had told him so. He believed her; her voice had carried an undertone of wry amusement, as though it were an inside joke to which he wasn't privy.

She'd also told him about the British warlocks, and the beings they commanded. This was their work.

Turnout for the Götterelektrongruppe's demonstrations had declined steadily as they performed their pointless road show in Heidelberg, in Frankfurt, and in the shadow of Cologne Cathedral. It was too cold for people to venture outside their homes, no matter the promised entertainments.

Their tour was forced to linger in Bielefeld – the birthplace of poor, martyred Horst Wessel – for an extra day when thigh-deep snowdrifts closed the road to Hannover. The mighty Götterelektrongruppe could have pushed through, had its members been so inclined. But after more than a month on the road, they couldn't stand each other's company long enough to discuss the issue. And besides which, they had only so many batteries.

Klaus took his dinner, alone, at an inn down the road from

where he and the others stayed. A late-spring sunset washed incongruously against frost-etched windowpanes, bleaching the room in diffuse white light. The décor was a thoroughly unconvincing re-creation of a beer hall. The stag heads, enameled tankards, and filigreed woodwork around the doorways would have been more natural farther south, in Bavaria. A true hall (Klaus had seen several; populous Munich had yielded many volunteers) required dark walnut paneling, stout ceiling beams, and casks of beer stacked behind the bar for fueling the *gemütlichkeit*. This place had none of these things.

It was the kind of place that didn't know itself, didn't know what it was meant to be. Klaus liked it. Though it was chilly, he felt more at ease here than anywhere else they'd visited.

The fireplace was empty and dark. Klaus inquired about a fire. He was told the flue had frozen shut soon after being closed to keep out vicious downdrafts.

He ate in a bubble of silence. All the other patrons stepped widely around Klaus's table. The wires unnerved people, but he was too weary of the issue to hide them any longer. People were polite when forced to interact with him, but jittery, too.

His meal was as slapdash as the décor. Gristle marbled the corned beef so thickly that Klaus was hard-put to carve out each mouthful. Brine squeezed out of the too-pink meat each time he sawed his knife through it. The water sloshed over the lip of his plate and made a ring around his glass of lukewarm cider.

But the beets weren't so terrible, and the venison sausage was edible if slightly gamey. Best of all was the black bread, which was warm enough to melt butter. It must have been made in-house; carrying it just across the street would have leeched away the heat, rendering the bread as cold and hard as a hearthstone in an abandoned house.

'Where are your companions?'

Klaus looked up. A short ruddy man stood across the table. He stood with elbows resting on the back of an empty chair, forearms extended over the table and fingers interlaced. He fixed a wide grin on Klaus.

'I beg your pardon?'

'Your companions,' said the stranger in a reedy voice. 'Especially the thin fellow.' He wiggled his fingers, raising his arms as he did so to mimic a blazing fire. 'Whooooosh! I'd be inclined to stick close to him, on a chilly evening like this.'

'You wouldn't, if you knew him.'

The stranger looked surprised. 'Oh. That's a shame.' He gestured at the empty chair. 'May I?'

Klaus's fork *tinked* against his dish when he set it on the table. 'Do I know you?'

'*Nein.* But I know you.' The other man untied the oyster blue muffler about his neck, unbuttoned his coat, and hung them on the hooks on the wall behind him. Under the coat he wore work boots, denim coveralls, and a flannel shirt over a thick white turtleneck sweater. 'I saw you in Augsburg several weeks ago. And your impressive friends.'

It was possible. That had been over a month ago, when the weather had still carried the potential for spring. They had drawn large crowds, large enough that Klaus wouldn't have remembered individual faces, even if they hadn't been on the road for so damnably long.

The man sat. 'Ernst Witt,' he said, hand extended.

Klaus took it. 'Klaus.'

'A rare honor, Obersturmführer Klaus.'

Klaus cocked his head in surprise. This man was dressed as a civilian laborer, yet he'd identified the insignia on Klaus's collar.

Few civilians knew the Waffen-SS well enough to correctly address an officer by his rank.

'How—?'

'I work for IG Farben. We do a lot of business with the Wehrmacht ... It's my job to know the military.' Witt's lips peeled back to reveal a gap-toothed smile.

That's one explanation, thought Klaus. *But there are others.*

'So you saw us in Augsburg, and followed us here?'

Witt laughed. 'No. Like you, my work sends me on the road. I saw flyers advertising a visit from the elite Götterelektrongruppe when I arrived yesterday. I hoped I'd get to see you and your companions in action again. Perhaps even meet you. One doesn't often meet such greatness.'

Klaus nodded at the fawning man. 'And why are you on the road?'

'What we sell to the Wehrmacht, we also fix for the Wehrmacht. That is to say, *I* fix. And with weather like this, many things need fixing.'

No, you're following us, Klaus decided. 'Is that so.'

'Oh, yes. You'd be surprised how brittle certain alloys can become, under the right conditions.'

'Really.' *Are you keeping an eye on us for the Sicherheitshauptamt?* If morale and discipline had declined at the Reichsbehörde after Doctor von Westarp's death, the SD Hauptamt, the SS Security Department, would want to know.

'Most people don't realize that a well-cast metal is actually composed of tiny crystals,' said Witt, warming to his subject. He spoke of atoms and dislocations and still other things Klaus neither knew about nor cared for. His eyes never lingered on Klaus's face, flicking instead to Klaus's collar and scalp whenever Klaus turned his head.

Witt trailed off. 'I've bored you. I apologize.'

'I lack your passion for science,' said Klaus.

'But German science made you the man you are today,' said Witt.

'I'm a soldier,' said Klaus, because it sounded true and needed no elaboration.

'And quite a soldier at that. You must be, to have been among the first recruits for such an elite project,' said Witt. His inflection might have breathed a subtle implication into the words, or perhaps not.

Klaus chose to let a heavy silence suffocate any implied questions. Witt didn't offer up anything else to fill the growing pause in the conversation.

'Things were different in the early days,' Klaus said, and left it at that.

'Yes, I suppose they were. You'll have raised an entire army soon! An army of men like you.'

'Perhaps.'

'I'm sure you've inspired many eager recruits.' Again, it might have been a question, and it might not.

'It varies from town to town. And with the weather.'

Witt nodded. 'I imagine so. You've been traveling for many weeks, it seems. Will you be returning home soon?'

'Soon enough.' Klaus drained the last of his cider, which had gone cold. 'And speaking of travel, I may be in for a long day tomorrow.' Witt again looked surprised. 'If you'll excuse me, I think I'll turn in early.' Klaus rose, shook Witt's hand again, and donned his wool overcoat.

As he buttoned it, he said, 'A question, Herr Witt?'

'Of course, my friend.'

'You said you entered Bielefeld yesterday. Yet the roads have been closed for the past two days.'

'I did? Well, then, I'm sure I meant Monday.'

'That explains it.'

'Yes. With weather like this, who can keep track of the days?'

'Safe travels,' said Klaus.

'Heil Hitler,' said Witt with a wave and another flash of his gap-toothed smile.

The cobbled walkway along the street had been reduced to an iced footpath trampled into thigh-deep snow. Wind sliced through the buttonholes of Klaus's coat and the seams of his shirt. It raked his skin, stippled him with gooseflesh. He hadn't gone twenty meters before his chest muscles ached with the effort it took not to shiver. A gust eddied around the side of the inn. Klaus slipped, landing painfully on the ice.

'To hell with this.' He stood, shook himself off, and embraced his Willenskräfte. The copper taste of the Götterelektron erased the last remnants of his drink, which was regrettable because he had enjoyed the hints of cinnamon in the cider. Armored in willpower, Klaus became a wraith untouched by the demon wind.

The change in his surroundings, in his personal microclimate, was immediate. The twin bulbs of a glass streetlamp shattered. Window shutters wrenched free of their hinges and exploded into matchsticks on the frozen street. The boles of the gingko trees along the boulevard cracked open.

The weather had been ferociously cold, but now it was nothing short of furious. By expressing his supreme volition, Klaus had enraged the elements.

He stood at the center of a maelstrom that tried in vain to assail him. Nor could the ice underfoot make him slip if such contradicted his Willenskräfte. He ran through snowdrifts and crashing icicles, impervious to one and all.

He ran because his invulnerability would last only so long as he could hold his breath. When he did rematerialize, just long enough to exhale and gulp down air, the arctic fury zeroed in on him. It savaged his throat, reached into his chest and attempted to freeze his lungs. He raced past the trucks parked outside, ghosted through the front windows of his inn, and released the Götterelektron before an ashen-faced desk clerk.

Klaus ascended the narrow stairs to his room on the second floor. Static and the high-pitched warble of a radio came through the wall; their LSSAH radio operator had the adjacent room. This arrangement suited Klaus. Anything was better than sharing a wall with Reinhardt.

When Klaus turned on the light over the washbasin, he discovered that his mouth and chin were caked with frozen blood. Inhaling the smoke from a British phosphorus grenade back in December had done minor but permanent damage to his sinuses. It left him susceptible to nosebleeds. Drawing a single breath from the blizzard outside had been more than enough to provoke one.

The blood had begun to thaw, but he was too numb to feel it trickling down his neck. The image in the mirror was that of a ravenous beast, an insatiable carnivore. Not a man.

He fell asleep in a chair, still in his uniform, holding a damp towel to his face.

He woke some time later to a commotion outside his window. Familiar voices, shouting, down on the street below. Klaus's hip twinged as he stumbled to the window; sleeping upright in a chair, with his battery harness still attached, had made for hours of awkward posture.

Though the sun rose early this time of year, most of the light on the street came from the few streetlamps that hadn't been destroyed during Klaus's sprint home. The wind had receded for

the time being, allowing fresh snow to fall placidly from a charcoal sky.

It might have been a serene picture, if not for the echo of
Spalcke's nasal voice as he yelled, 'Who are you? Who are you?'
The hauptsturmführer stood behind the third truck of their
convoy, hand on his sidearm. He was addressing somebody inside
the cargo bed.

Klaus suspected he knew who Spalcke had caught rummaging
through the truck. He donned his coat in the corridor as he once
again passed the hiss and warble of the radio operator's room on
his way back outside. Apparently Spalcke's tirade had awakened
most of the inn.

Reinhardt had made it down first. When Klaus approached,
he did a double take. 'What happened to you?'

Klaus checked himself in the driver's side mirror. His skin was
red and creased where he'd had the cloth pressed to it. Little
black flecks of dried blood peppered his upper lip and part of his
chin.

'Forget it,' said Klaus. He jerked his chin at Spalcke. 'Let's take
care of this so I can sleep.'

By then, Spalcke had sent one of the LSSAH troops into the
truck. The soldier emerged a moment later with the barrel of his
rifle nudging the ribs of Ernst Witt. Witt climbed out of the truck
and stood shivering on the street with his hands resting on his
head.

'Please,' he said. 'This isn't what you think.'

'Oh? Because I think you're a spy and a saboteur.' Spalcke
unbuttoned the flap covering his Walther.

'No, no!' Witt shook his head wildly. 'I'm, I'm an admirer. I
want to join you!'

Reinhardt said, 'By hiding away like a rat in our truck?'

Witt turned. His eyes opened wider when he saw Reinhardt, and his face lost a little more color. But then he saw Klaus, and his features softened. 'Klaus! Please, tell them! You know me.'

Spalcke turned. 'Is this true?'

'I met him last night. At dinner. I don't think he's a saboteur. He told me he works for IG Farben. I think he's—'

'Hauptsturmführer! Hauptsturmführer!' More shouting cut short Klaus's response. The radio operator, a twenty-year-old boy with jet-black hair and an ugly, crooked nose, came running from the inn.

Witt took advantage of the distraction and tried to run. The soldier who had flushed him from the truck reacted calmly. He leveled his rifle and shot the fleeing man in the back. Witt landed facefirst on the street.

'Are you out of your goddamned mind?' said Klaus. 'You've just killed an SD officer.'

The radio operator continued his clamoring. 'Hauptsturmführer Spalcke!'

Spalcke turned to him. 'Quiet.' Then he turned to Klaus. 'What did you say?'

'I tried to warn you. I think he was from the Sicherheitshauptamt. Keeping an eye on us.'

Spalcke turned pale. 'Why do you say that?'

'He kept asking about our work, the recruitment. Our training. My feelings about the program.'

'Oh.' Spalcke slumped against the truck. 'What do we do?'

'We?' Reinhardt laughed. 'This isn't my problem. That poor defenseless man was shot on your orders. You're the one who'll hang.'

Spalcke put his hands to his forehead. 'Oh, *Gott*,' he moaned. 'I knew this traveling circus was a bad idea . . .'

Klaus watched the steam rising from Witt's blood as it seeped through his coat onto the snow. His muffler was a brilliant blue. Klaus felt a pang of sympathy for the artless, tragically over-enthusiastic man.

The radio operator tried again. 'Please, Herr Haupt-sturmführer, it's urgent.'

'Oh, for Christ's sake,' said Reinhardt. *'What?'*

'I've been trying to tell you. The Soviets are moving west.'

'What?' Klaus and Spalcke said it simultaneously.

'They have armored columns pushing through Poland. They've already engaged our remaining forces there.'

Remaining? In the confusion of the moment, Klaus forgot about the weather. And then it sank in: *Oh.*

Reinhardt sneered at Klaus as he stalked over to Witt's body. 'He wasn't from the SD, you idiot.' He kicked the dead man in the ribs. 'He was Red Orchestra.'

22 May 1941
Berlin, Germany

Marsh was in the air before the advanced forces of the Red Army approached the Oder River, which, according to reports, was capped with four feet of ice. The warlocks moved the inclement weather as the Soviets advanced, opening a corridor straight to Berlin for Stalin's troops. And, Marsh hoped, maintaining a bulwark to keep them the hell away from von Westarp's farm.

His second trip to Germany proceeded via slower and more mundane avenues than the first. Marsh flew from Scotland to Sweden in an RAF Mosquito; rode two hundred bumpy miles in the cargo bed of a fisherman's truck, hidden under tubs of ripe cod; crossed the Baltic Sea to Denmark in a fishing boat cloaked by extremely heavy fog, courtesy of Milkweed; and finally entered Germany at Flensburg in the middle of the night. The Danish Underground had smuggled hundreds of Jews out of the country via much the same route in reverse.

All told, the journey took twenty-one hours. Far too long. The Soviets were moving faster than anybody had thought possible. The supernatural winter had proved more destructive to the embedded German troops than even the warlocks had predicted. But now the plan was in motion, and the time for fine adjustments had passed.

An avalanche goes where it will.

Eidolons are not tactical weapons.

In Flensburg, wearing the captain's uniform of an SS-Hauptsturmführer, Marsh commandeered a car from the sleepy local Wehrmacht garrison. Officially, of course, his uniform didn't give him that authority. But the Wehrmacht lieutenants knew better than to contradict an officer of the Waffen-SS. Particularly one with direct orders from Reichsführer Heinrich Himmler's command staff.

Marsh knew his best bet was to avoid dealing directly with the SS command structure for as long as he could. The experts in MI6 had done their best, but his papers wouldn't fool the most experienced officers. God knew he had a slim chance of fooling Himmler's staff, if anybody bothered to trace Marsh's cover story back up the chain of command.

Which was likely to become a problem. Himmler's interest in von Westarp's work extended from its earliest days, not long after his stint in the Thule Society twenty years ago. And Himmler, seeing the REGP as his own pet project, kept its records close at hand. Meaning the files Marsh sought to destroy were housed at 9 Prinz-Albrecht-Strasse: headquarters of the SS.

Thus, in addition to the counterfeit uniform, Marsh also wore Gretel's battery on his belt. When the time came, he'd attach the wires to the minute pieces of adhesive tape hidden on his scalp. The hopes were twofold: first, that most people in the SS still hadn't met a member of the Götterelektrongruppe in the flesh; second, that members of the Götterelektrongruppe received special consideration.

At the Flensburg garrison, he also commandeered an extra coat, hat, and gloves. But the deeper he drove into Germany, the less effective they became. The warlocks had summoned a cold unlike anything Marsh had ever experienced. They had infused this weather with the Eidolons' arcane hatred of man, creating a cunning and malicious entity. It slipped through every seam in his clothing. The rubber door moldings of his Mercedes lost their pliability, leaving gaps around the door through which entered the wind. His breath turned to frost where it touched the cold windshield glass.

Each passing mile found it harder to keep the heavy staff car on the road. His journey might have been altogether impossible had the warlocks not opened a corridor for him as they were also doing for the Red Army. But it also helped that the impending invasion had sent the Reich into chaos and panic. Every available soldier was converging on Berlin to aid in the defense of the capital. Convoys of heavy transports packed down the snow, leaving the roads slick but navigable by the Mercedes. Yet in places the roads were impossible even for the transports; Wehrmacht engineering detachments labored to clear downed trees from the roads with bulldozers and, in some cases, flamethrowers.

He made better time after falling in behind a panzer unit. The tanks' treads crushed the snow flat enough that his Mercedes could clear it.

Sunrise found Marsh entering Hamburg. He arrived not far behind two convoys awkwardly funneling themselves onto the city streets. The troop transports brimmed with soldiers trembling in their heaviest winter gear – those lucky enough to have such gear – as well as blankets and anything else they could find to ward off the chill. The convoys would pick up still more soldiers from the local garrisons before continuing to Berlin.

The high concentrations of military personnel made Marsh nervous. His hands trembled on the steering wheel. Exhaustion, cold, and nerves took their toll on him.

But, after thinking about it, Marsh decided to view the convoys as an opportunity. Protective camouflage. None of these men could peer through the fogged-up windows of his automobile and discern the spy within. No. His best course of action was to attach himself to one of the convoys as brazenly as possible. Which he did, sliding the Mercedes in a safe distance behind the final truck.

It took longer to traverse the city, following the convoy, but it vaulted him above suspicion.

Marsh was feeling a glimmer of optimism – *This might work. I could make it to Berlin.* – when two uniformed figures on the side of the road flagged him down. One kept to the shoulder, bundled in a heavy coat. The other stepped in front of Marsh's car, waving his arms. He couldn't discern any details of the two men without lowering the window, but he knew immediately from their coats and hats that they were SS.

Shit. Shit, shit, shit.

Stuck inching along behind the convoy, he had no choice but to stop. He pulled the parking brake with one hand as he loosened the holster of his Walther pistol with the other. Sweat trickled beneath his undershirt, defying the chill as it ran under his arms and down his ribs.

Marsh rolled down the window. The man in the road approached the driver-side door and saluted. 'Heil Hitler.'

It took a moment for Marsh's brain, running on a cocktail of fear and adrenaline, to process the rank insignia on his coat: SS-Obersturmführer. A lieutenant. Marsh outranked him. He returned the salute, relaxing.

The lieutenant said, *'Guten Morgen, Herr Hauptsturmführer.'* A cloud of his breath hovered between them in the still air. Black blemishes marred the man's face and nose. Frostbite.

'Be quick. I'm in a hurry,' said Marsh.

'Apologies, sir. But the standartenführer' – the frostbitten lieutenant indicated his companion – 'requires your vehicle.'

Standartenführer. Colonel.

Fuck! Fuck, fuck, fuck.

Marsh fought to keep his voice steady. 'I've been ordered to return to Berlin at once.'

'Berlin? Excellent! So has the standartenführer.'

'But – I must—'

The lieutenant called to his senior officer. *Their* senior officer. 'Sir, the hauptsturmführer has been ordered to Berlin as well.' He jogged around to the car's passenger side and opened the rear door.

Marsh was trapped. It was too late to don the wires and attempt to talk his way out of this. There was nothing he could do except wait for the officer to climb inside, and then drive the man to Berlin.

Or, actually, no. *He* didn't have to drive.

Marsh stepped out of the car and saluted the approaching

officer. 'Heil Hitler!' He played the moment for everything he was worth. *'Guten Morgen, Herr Standartenführer.'*

The colonel returned his salute with a half-hearted wave. 'Devil take these backstabbing Communists,' he muttered. 'Straight to hell. Every one of them.' His breath smelled of a stomach made sour by too much strong coffee and not enough food.

'Trust it to them to find their spine just now,' said Marsh. The colonel ignored him.

Marsh turned to the lieutenant once the colonel had settled inside. 'Take us to Berlin, Obersturmführer.'

'Jawohl.'

By the time the lieutenant had settled into the driver's seat and Marsh had settled into the front passenger seat, the convoy was on the move again. Loud snoring emanated from the backseat soon after the lieutenant had the car in gear.

They followed the convoy through the outskirts of the city. The streets were clear of all but military traffic and those vehicles, like his own, on Reich business. It was impossible to tell how much of this was by virtue of people opting to stay home, and how much by virtue of the fact that many of the civilians had frozen to death.

The flow of traffic slowed to little better than a brisk walk in several places; burst water mains transformed entire intersections, even major traffic circles, into skating rinks. They passed a house gutted by fire. A fire probably set by the residents themselves in a bid to stay alive. A truck from the local fire brigade blocked part of the road. The hoses had ruptured. The resulting geyser had coated the road and the truck itself in the instants before the water froze. One side of the truck was coated in inches of ice. So were the bodies of the fire brigade men, frozen in midscream.

My God, thought Marsh. *What kind of blood prices bought this? What is this costing us back home?*

They picked up the Elbe outside Hamburg, and followed the valley southeast toward Berlin. The river had become a glacier. It was frozen solid, from the surface all the way down to the riverbed. And the water had expanded as it froze, rising above its banks and ripping down bridges. The only way to cross the river was on the few temporary bridges the engineering detachments had erected.

Marsh closed his eyes. 'Wake me when we enter Berlin,' he told the lieutenant.

Liv's light touch, a fingertip on his lips.

'*What?*'

Quiet laughter, warmth in the dark. 'You were talking in your sleep again, love.'

'*I'm sorry, Liv.*'

Her breath tickles his earlobe. 'Don't be. I've missed it more than you know.' She laces her fingers through his.

'*I'm glad I came back. I'm sorry it took so long.*'

'*So are we.*'

Agnes fills the hollow between their bodies, nestled in the blankets. Marsh presses his lips to the fine, thin hair of her scalp.

Her skin is icy cold. She smells like baby and rot.

Marsh jerked awake.

The glare of sunlight on snow stabbed at his eyes; he squeezed them shut and then opened them slowly. They were still moving, though they no longer followed a convoy. They were driving through a large city.

'Hauptsturmführer?' The lieutenant took his eyes off the road for a moment. 'We've entered Berlin.'

Marsh's gut impression was of a venerable lady, a grande dame, never beautiful but handsome in a stern way, now ruined by illness and racked with tumors. If a city could contract cancer, this place was terminal. In some places the wounds were relatively small, embodied in the swastikas and Prussian eagles adorning everything. And in other places the Reich's philosophical malignancy had engendered severe art deco monstrosities like the Olympic Stadium. There were reminders of a healthier, more aesthetic time, and hints of old Europe, such as on the Potsdamer Platz, but even that was scarred with eagles and broken crosses.

The weather had changed while Marsh was napping. The ice caked to the edges of the windshield had begun to melt. And the roads were slushy. Compared with the rest of the countryside Marsh had witnessed, the capital of the Third Reich was balmy. Perhaps as warm as ten degrees Celsius. He could breathe without his nose freezing shut.

It meant the warlocks had completed their corridor to Berlin. Now the question was, where were the Soviets?

The lieutenant woke the napping colonel as they entered the central administrative district of the Reich. They passed the air ministry, which was a hulking square gray building with square black windows. Profoundly utilitarian.

The colonel's errand took him to the Reich Chancellery building, which occupied an entire city block on the Voss Strasse. It connected to the Foreign Office building, which stood around the corner on Kaiser Wilhelm Strasse, across from the Propaganda Ministry. The nerve center of the Third Reich had been shaped from countless tons of granite and yellow marble to create a monster of neoclassical and art deco construction topped with massive bronze eagles and bas-relief scenes of Aryan greatness.

It was all designed with an eye toward creating awe-inspiring ruins in some distant century, like those the vaunted Romans had left behind. Albert Speer's theory of ruin value at work.

Marsh began to sweat again. If the colonel gave the order to accompany him inside, his options would be severely limited. But the colonel stepped out of the car as soon as the driver brought it to a stop. He bounded up the stairs between the massive square pillars and disappeared into the Chancellery without another word for Marsh or their driver. He hadn't even closed the door.

Marsh released the breath he'd been holding. He moved to the backseat and told the lieutenant, who had apparently been left in his command, to drive to Schutzstaffel Headquarters. Then he took the opportunity while the driver was distracted to finish his disguise, pulling the wires from his collar and fastening them to the strips of adhesive under his hair.

The drive to the SS Haus was brief. The street directly in front of the headquarters building was clogged with trucks and other vehicles. The lieutenant parked next door, at Prinz-Albrecht-Strasse 8, formerly a school of industrial arts and crafts and now the headquarters of the Gestapo. Marsh imagined he could hear the special prisoners screaming themselves hoarse, confessing to anything and everything, in the basement cells.

Standing there in the nerve center of the police state, surrounded by thousands of the Third Reich's most dedicated servants, Marsh resigned himself to his fate.

I'm so sorry, Liv. I was a bloody fool. I should have gone back to you sooner. Why did I stay apart from you for so long?

What I do now, I do with a light heart, because I know you understand. You understand that I've loved you so fiercely that at times I've been unable to think rationally. You understand that everything I've done has been for you, and Agnes. Marsh touched the breast pocket of his uniform, felt the reassuring bump of the cyanide capsule hidden there. *Stephenson will look after you.*

In recent years, the trajectory of Marsh's life had orbited scenes of mass panic, of crowds bubbling with that barely contained animal instinct to flee, to lash out, to find cathartic release in the disorder of uninhibited emotion. He'd listened to its murmurings in Spanish, in French, in English. He'd walked amongst it in Spain, at the port of Barcelona; then again in France, where he heard it in the catch of people's voices and watched it in the way they moved too quickly; he'd smelled the sweat and fear again during the Blitz, in the shelters, and had seen the worry lines creasing every face in London. He had immersed himself in the panic, perhaps even indulged in it, at Paddington when he and Liv evacuated Agnes.

Thus, the scene outside Schutzstaffel headquarters held a surreal familiarity. The building itself, formerly the Prince Albert Hotel before Himmler commandeered it, was a four-story edifice that occupied most of the block. Here and there, hints of the building's old life could be seen in the reversed shadow of the old hotel sign on the weather-darkened granite, and in the clock atop the undulating cornices that overlooked the street. Marsh had seen the hotel only in photographs.

But the tension in people's voices as they barked out orders, the herky-jerky motions of their arms and legs as they hurried in and out of the building, the electric tingle of nervous energy: Marsh knew it well. Only the details differed. A constant stream of men flowed between the headquarters building and the line of trucks parked in front. Each man exited the building with an armload or hand truck of boxes, which he relinquished to other men loading the trucks. Everybody moved at a clip just below a dead run, just on the orderly side of chaos.

They're moving the files, Marsh realized. *In case the Soviets take the city. Jerry doesn't want his operational records falling to the Communists any more than* we *do.*

He watched the men hurrying into the building and rushing back out again with more crates. It all proceeded under the supervision of two officers who, with their steaming breath, suggested twin dragons looming overhead while medieval villagers scrambled to amass tribute.

Each load of boxes went to a different truck. Some, he imagined, were slated for destruction. But the most valuable information would be saved. Moved to bunkers, perhaps, or shipped out of the city ahead of the Soviets.

Somewhere in that mess resided the files that Marsh had come to destroy. The records of the Reichsbehörde für die Erweiterung germanischen Potenzials, and the Institut Menschlichen Vorsprung before that, and perhaps even of the orphanage before that. These were some of the Reich's most precious secrets and its vision for the future. They'd be moved to the most secure location possible, preserved until the bitter end, defended against all comers. Especially saboteurs like Marsh.

But the scene gave him an idea.

Strictly speaking, his mission wasn't to destroy the files. His mission was to ensure they didn't fall into Soviet hands. The ideal solution would have been for Milkweed to seize them, but that had never received serious consideration, since Britain lacked an occupying force with which to capture Berlin.

But as he watched the boxes loaded onto the trucks, Marsh realized they didn't *need* an army to seize the files. All he had to do was determine where the files were going, which truck they occupied, and steal the truck.

He breathed deeply and disregarded the chill as he opened his coat, rolled down the collar, and strode toward the hubbub. He counted over a dozen trucks, their cargo beds in various states of loading. Some were nearly full. He had to move quickly before the records he sought were moved out.

He joined the stream of men entering and leaving the SS Haus, quickening his pace to match the sense of urgency that surrounded him. The subordinate officers occupied with carrying and loading the boxes paid him no heed, except for the handful who noticed his rank and paused for salutes. These he returned with the same desultory air he'd received from the colonel. *Stay focused on your task*, his body language said.

They didn't question him; this was the last place anybody would expect to find a British spy.

Marsh made it as far as the entrance when one of the supervising captains lifted an arm to block his passage. Marsh stopped short, nearly bumping the clipboard in the other man's outstretched hand.

'You're late,' he said. Condensation from his breath glistened in his eyebrows and eyelashes. He held the clipboard out to Marsh again. Marsh took the board and flipped through the pages.

It contained a nine-page list, each page filled with pairs of columns of numbers. One column referred to the crates, while the other referred to the trucks. It was the list that determined which boxes went into which trucks. But it didn't specify the contents of the crates.

'You were supposed to be here half an hour ago,' said the second officer. Whiteness caked one corner of his mouth, and his runny nose had coated his upper lip.

Marsh ignored them. He also shifted his stance slightly, turning his head and neck toward the men without taking his eyes off the list. He made a show of inspecting the loading manifest, slowly perusing the pages while he waited for the men to notices his wires.

His accusers fell quiet; Marsh let the silence stretch into awkwardness. The buzz of activity swirled around them.

When he finally looked up, Marsh saw the supervisors looking at his battery harness, and then at each other. As he'd hoped, the battery spoke for him. The wire snaking up his collar and into his hair made his point more effectively than any words could have. These men knew the significance of the battery, knew that it commanded respect. Marsh hoped they didn't look so closely as to notice the sweat trickling down his forehead, along his scalp, and down his collar.

Marsh cleared his throat. 'I'm not here to relieve you,' he said, emphasizing *relieve*. *True, as far as it goes,* he thought. *Now for the lie, and the gamble.* He made an educated guess: 'I'm here to escort all Reichsbehörde records to the Führer's bunker.' He held up the clipboard, pointing at it. 'Where are they?'

It worked.

The men looked at each other. 'We only have what you see there, the crate numbers,' said one man. He nodded his head toward the former hotel building. 'We don't load the crates. You'll have to ask inside.' He paused before he added, tentatively and uncertainly, 'Sir.'

Marsh shoved the clipboard back at the first man, nudging him in the chest. 'Carry on,' he said. He turned his back on them and went inside.

The Prince Albert Hotel had been built long before the Nazis' rise to power. The original design of the lobby reflected that different time, but it had been subverted into the architectural bastard child of Albert Speer and Heinrich Himmler. Marsh imagined thick rugs covering the marble and parquet floor in the wings of the lobby, oak and leather furniture arranged cozily around low tables and the large hearth opposite what must have been the concierge desk at one time. A nicer space than the Hotel Alexandria in Tarragona. But now it was all gone, stripped down to bare marble polished to shining beneath the vaulted ceiling and the unblinking stares of bas-relief plaster eagles. There was no furniture, nothing to suggest comfort or welcoming, and certainly nothing to encourage loitering. The concierge station had been ripped out and replaced with a utilitarian desk, behind which sat an SS-Unterscharführer, a sergeant. Men streamed around him as they passed through the lobby, the rubber tires of their hand trucks squeaking on the marble.

Marsh stood inside Schutzstaffel headquarters feeling like Daniel in the lions' den. Yet nobody stopped him; nobody paid him any attention at all. It was as though the battery harness had rendered him invisible, like the blond woman in the Tarragona filmstrip. He wondered, fleetingly, where she was, and if she had participated in the decimation of Milkweed's strike teams back in December.

Wherever she was, the Reich had a fearsome assassin at its call. Perhaps, if his ploy worked and he obtained the Reichsbehörde's operational records, he could learn more about her. Although she wasn't his main interest.

Marsh followed a line of men returning from the trucks outside to a bank of elevators at the edge of the lobby. He and nine others stuffed themselves into an elevator. It was paneled with rosewood and lined with a brass rail at waist height, little remainders of the building's previous life. The men spoke little as it descended to the basement, instead taking the opportunity to catch their breaths where the air wasn't so cold. Some of the men had an unpleasant rasp in their chests, probably from working in chilly weather that had lifted only within the past day. They saluted Marsh as appropriate, and more than a few eyes widened in alarm when they glimpsed his wires.

The elevator dinged, the doors opened, and they poured into the basement. In times past, it had housed the laundry and other services. Now it served as an archive for SS records, a clearing-house for all information Reichsführer Himmler wanted to keep at hand.

That the operational records of the Reichsbehörde qualified as such was beyond question. The only issue was whether they had already been moved to a safe location, and whether Marsh would find them before his ruse fell apart.

Shelves had been installed in the former laundry, and the cor-ridors were dense with filing cabinets nearly identical to those back at Milkweed Headquarters. Stacks of crates, empty but oth-erwise like the ones Marsh had seen loaded on the trucks outside, occupied every spare inch of floor space. The shelves held boxes of files, which the men systematically loaded into the numbered crates for loading onto hand trucks.

The total amount of paperwork stored in the bowels of the former hotel was staggering. It seemed Jerry couldn't do anything without first completing a form in triplicate. And then again when the task was finished.

Marsh examined a random shelf. Some boxes were indexed with keywords and numbers, while others had dates printed neatly on their spines. But there was nothing to explain their con-tents.

He found the officer overseeing the packing procedure in a cavernous room carved directly from the bedrock beneath the building. Lightbulbs hung from cables affixed to the ceiling overhead, tossing harsh shadows between the vaulted brick arch-ways and casting the deepest niches into shadow. The hotel had once boasted an extensive wine cellar, but the casks and wine bot-tles had been replaced with row upon row of filing cabinets and metal shelving. Approximately two-thirds of the shelves were bare; many of the cabinets stood with their drawers open and empty. Doubtless the wine had long ago disappeared into the per-sonal collections of high-ranking SS officers.

The officer was tall, much taller than Marsh, perhaps even taller than Will. His long, thin face and large round eyeglasses made him look more like a librarian than like a soldier. Which might not have been far from the truth, Marsh realized.

He carried a clipboard upon which two high metal loops impaled a sheaf of papers. He walked among the empty crates, inspecting the shelves and cabinets that hadn't been packed yet, pausing to compare each label with something in his papers. He'd nod, make a note on his clipboard, and jot a six-digit number on the box or cabinet drawer with a grease pencil. The numbers corresponded to crates, showing the packing men which files went in which containers.

The archivist saw Marsh. He scowled. 'Don't stand there,' he said. 'Grab a crate' – he pointed to a stack in one of the shadowy niches – 'and get to work. But be certain to label your crate with the proper catalog numbers,' he added, pointing to the numbers on the file boxes. His attention turned back to his work.

Marsh cleared his throat. He stepped closer to the other man. He tried to keep his fake battery harness in plain view, but the shelves, low ceilings, and archways cast irregular shadows in all directions. 'I'm here for the Reichsbehörde files. Have they been moved yet?'

The other man shrugged, still studying his clipboard. 'Everything's getting moved today.'

'I don't care about everything else,' said Marsh. He stepped closer still. 'My orders are to escort the Reichsbehörde records. Where are they?'

The other man looked up, frowning. His eyebrows pulled together in puzzlement. 'I wasn't informed about this.'

'Of course not.' Marsh rested his hand on the battery at his waist, silently praying it would again make his point for him. 'The Reichsführer and the Führer themselves have a deep personal interest in our work. I'm here to escort the records. It's a special task, not something entrusted to merely anybody.'

'Still—' The archivist paused when he saw Marsh's battery. 'Oh, I see.' His gaze darted from the battery to the wires snaking up Marsh's neck. When it reached the collar of Marsh's uniform, his brows came together, and his mouth formed another frown. The sweat dampening Marsh's shirt felt clammy.

He studied Marsh's face. 'You're from the Götterelektrongruppe, then?'

'Yes, and I've told you why I'm here. Now, have the records been moved or not?'

'Let me check.' The archivist flipped through several pages on his clipboard until he found the one he sought. He tapped the page with one slender finger and looked up again. He took another look at Marsh's battery, then another at the polished *siegrunen* on his collar. Again, the furrowed brow.

Marsh didn't like the way this fellow was studying his uniform. He appeared to be looking for something, a patch or insigne that wasn't present. 'Is there a problem?'

'No,' said the archivist distantly. But then his demeanor brightened, and he tapped the clipboard again. He said, 'You're in luck. They're still here.' He ushered Marsh deeper into the cellar, toward shelves that hadn't yet been packed. 'That way.'

Marsh motioned the other man ahead of him. 'Show me.'

The archivist hesitated for the briefest moment, then cocked his head in a half-hearted nod. Marsh reached into his pocket as soon as his guide turned his back. He pulled out the garrote a second before the man reached for his pistol. With wrists crossed and arms outstretched, Marsh leapt forward to get the wire over the taller man's head. It caught briefly on the tip of the archivist's nose as he pitched forward, giving him time to drop the clipboard and get one hand up to protect his throat as Marsh frantically flipped the wire loop under his jaw and around his neck.

Marsh yanked backwards as hard as he could, straining until his shoulders groaned. His opponent made a wheezing, gurgling sound as his head was pulled back. But air still trickled into his throat because he'd gotten a few fingers under the garrote. And shorter Marsh couldn't get the leverage he needed to close off the man's trachea.

He backed into Marsh, using his greater weight to shove him bodily against a brick archway. The wire bundle taped to Marsh's scalp came loose. Pain ripped up his side. His ribs ached, but he kept pulling until it felt he'd sever the man's fingers.

Blood trickled from the wire-thin cut on the man's neck, making the garrote slippery. The wire and the blood together mingled into a hot, metallic, salty smell.

The man pitched forward again, lifting Marsh off the ground. They brushed a lightbulb. It swung wildly, casting kaleidoscopic shadows that danced around them. The archivist launched himself backwards, landing heavily atop Marsh. Air whooshed out of Marsh's lungs, leaving his chest painfully hollow. His ribs creaked almost to the point of snapping. A dark tunnel consumed his field of vision; he struggled to force air back into his lungs, but the

weight of the larger man atop him made it difficult. The tension
in the garrote loosened.

The man's gurgling, Marsh's gasping, and the hammering of
Marsh's heartbeat together sounded loud enough to alert the
entire building. He could hear the scuffing of boots, the rattle of
hand trucks, and men talking in another part of the cellar not far
away.

As the man atop him thrashed, Marsh worked one knee up
against the base of the taller man's leg and dug his opposite
elbow into the man's lower back, near the kidney. Then he flexed
his body, using those two contact points like fulcra. His opponent
arched his back, scrabbling at his throat with his free hand. The
gurgling trailed off. Marsh, quivering with too much adrenaline
to loosen his grip on the wooden handles of the garrote, struggled
to roll the archivist off him.

He kneeled over the man he'd just killed, panting as though
he'd run a steeplechase. It couldn't have lasted beyond a minute,
but the fight felt as though it had gone for hours. Marsh's ribs
ached, and his hands shook violently. He wrinkled his nose at the
mélange of sweat, blood, and panic.

Different parts of his mind followed disparate threads of
thought as he struggled to get his body under control. *Hide the
body. Watch out for blood. Something's wrong with my disguise. Find the clipboard.*

First things first. Marsh reaffixed the loose wires to the tape
under his hair. It took two tries because his hands trembled so
badly and his scalp was damp with sweat from his exertion. But
he managed to repair the gravest damage to his imperfect disguise.

Marsh heaved the dead man over his shoulder, careful not to
smear blood on his uniform. The man was thin but tall, and a

damn sight heavier than he looked. Marsh staggered into an abandoned wing of the cellar, where the shelves stood empty and where, he hoped, nobody would have reason to venture. He propped the body in a niche behind one of the brickwork arches, where the light didn't reach. He retrieved the garrote in case he needed it again. The wire made a wet slicing sound as Marsh pulled it out of the thin gash in the dead man's throat. After coiling the wire and putting it back in his pocket, he wiped his hands clean on the archivist's uniform. He listened for several long moments, to see if anybody in the cellar had heard the struggle. No shouts; no alarms.

The archivist had dropped the clipboard where Marsh jumped him. Marsh retrieved it. He scanned through half the pages before he found a sequence of entries marked 'REGP.' The Reichsbehörde records comprised a sequence of thirteen consecutive catalog numbers. He tore the sheet from the clipboard and folded the catalog page in his pocket. It took another fifteen minutes of searching the cellar before he found the cabinets marked with the same catalog numbers. They were empty, meaning the records in question had already been loaded on one of the trucks.

He rushed back outside, but was relieved to find the trucks still queued up. Marsh again scanned the supervising officers' cargo manifest – their replacements had arrived, while Marsh was inside – and traced his quarry to the fourth truck from the end of the queue. The lieutenant behind the wheel saluted when Marsh climbed in.

Marsh said, 'I'll be escorting our cargo to its new destination.'

The driver acknowledged this but otherwise said nothing. They passed the next half hour in silence broken only by shouts of the men loading the trucks. It took an effort of will not to

fidget, not to inspect himself in the mirrors. The truck occasionally bobbed up and down on its suspension as more crates
were loaded on the cargo bed. It rocked Marsh into half sleep;
the adrenaline rush evaporated, leaving him wearier than before.
But fear that the dead archivist would be discovered too soon kept
him jolting back to wakefulness.

Eventually, the stream of men filing in and out of the SS Haus
slowed to a trickle. One of the supervisors walked down the line
of trucks, loudly pounding his fist on each. One by one the trucks
belched exhaust. Marsh's driver turned the ignition, and their
own truck grumbled to life.

When the driver reached for the gearshift, Marsh said, 'Wait.'
Marsh watched the trucks in front pull away, and checked the
side mirror until the trucks in the rear had pulled around them.
When they had fallen to the end of the line, he said, 'Now.
Proceed, slowly.'

The lieutenant obeyed him without question. He didn't object
when Marsh directed him to take turns that separated them from
the rest of the convoy. They wove through Berlin, heading
roughly west.

Marsh waited until they were well outside the city before
ordering his driver to pull to the side of the road.

'Roll down your window, Obersturmführer.'

The driver hesitated. 'Sir?'

'Lower your window,' said Marsh. 'That's an order.'

Cold weather had left the window crank stiff and unrespon-
sive. The driver struggled with it, but managed to lower the
window glass.

Marsh pulled out his sidearm, pressed the barrel to the driver's
temple, and pulled the trigger. Blood, bone, and brain matter
exploded through the open window.

He dumped the driver's body under an ash tree, in a shallow grave of snow.

He parked the truck on a disused back road kilometers from the nearest town. The lingering glow of a late springtime sunset paled the sky while Marsh, working by the light of an electric torch, rearranged the cargo bed to free up the crates he sought.

His ploy had worked. Marsh had stolen the operational records of the REGP stretching back at least to the early 1930s. As he'd suspected, the project had used the Spanish Civil War as a playground for field-testing and training Doctor von Westarp's subjects.

Marsh skimmed through the files in roughly chronological order. He learned of a pair of psychic twins, rendered mute by the process that had forged them into bonded empaths, each seeing and feeling everything the other did. He learned that the ghostly man who walked through walls was named Klaus, and that Gretel was his sister. (Interesting: Klaus wasn't the first person to manifest the ability, but he was the only one to survive it longer than a few days.) Marsh also learned of a flying man named Rudolf, who had been killed in an accident weeks before the conclusion of the Spanish war. That fact was annotated with a footnote that led Marsh, after more searching, to a very thick folder: Gretel's file.

This last thing he read until the batteries in his torch died. Which was how he learned that Gretel had been roughly five years old when von Westarp had acquired her and her brother for his 'orphanage.' And how Marsh learned that through years of random experimentation, the mad doctor had created a mad seer, imbuing her with a godlike prescience.

Marsh sat up. 'Bugger me.'

He set the file down, absently, on the crate where he'd made his perch. He cracked his knuckles, staring into the distance while the cogs of his mind turned.

That single piece of information – *the girl's a bloody oracle* – was like a fingertip nudging the first in a long chain of dominoes. So many things fell into place.

That's how she knew me in Spain, though we'd never met. That's how she knew when Agnes was born. That's how she escaped so easily; they probably had the entire operation planned before I captured her. That's why they were ready for us, why our December raid never achieved the element of surprise. We never had a chance.

Click, click, click, fell the dominoes.

He remembered little things. Her tone of voice:

Try anything, anything at all, and I'll put a bullet in your gut.

No, you won't.

And the daisy: *For later.*

He took up the file again. As the years dragged on, the men who ran the IMV, and later the Reichsbehörde, had come to realize they could not control her. She was immune to their coercive tactics. Yet they tolerated her because her advice, when she deigned to give it, was invaluable. Marsh let out a long, slow whistle: Gretel had guided the Luftwaffe through the systematic destruction of Britain's air defenses.

But slowly, her handlers began to speculate that highly intelligent Gretel had her own agenda. Their speculations reached a crisis point after the destruction of the invasion fleet bound for Britain. Gretel's very existence should have rendered such a loss impossible.

Why would *she let that happen?* Marsh wondered.

And eventually they realized, however reluctantly and with no small amount of trepidation, that von Westarp had created a precognitive sociopath. The Reich's greatest weapon was a monster feared even by the Schutzstaffel.

'Jesus bloody Christ.'

But there was more. Marsh read further.

He discovered that the woman who had winked at him in Spain, who had become his willing prisoner in France, and who had first congratulated him on Agnes's birth, had also convinced the German High Command to obliterate Williton.

Gretel had looked through time and, for reasons known only to her, had orchestrated the death of his daughter.

The files offered no explanation as to why. In justifying the bombing raid, the OKW said only that their source – Gretel – had deemed the matter urgent and vital. They didn't know why she wanted Williton destroyed; the file made no mention of Marsh or Liv or Agnes.

She said we'd meet again, he remembered. At the time, during her escape from the Admiralty building, Marsh had assumed she was taunting him. But now he knew that wasn't it at all. She'd meant it as a statement of fact.

They'd meet again. He'd find her, and she'd explain herself. She'd explain herself, and then he'd kill her.

If the woman truly was what the records claimed, she already knew Marsh's intent. But he imagined a bullet would kill her dead just the same.

FOURTEEN

Mrs. Weeks objected to the term *funk hole*. Her establishment was an exclusive boarding hotel, nothing more.

She also disapproved of people who arrived unannounced, with no ration books to share and, most uncouth of all, with no cash and no checks on hand.

And she did not like Will. Not at first. But that changed quickly when she experienced his charm and, more to the point, learned his brother was a duke. From then on, Will enjoyed unlimited credit and boundless goodwill. He had the run of the place. Or would have, had he chosen to venture from his small but acceptably well-appointed room.

After the first several days, he started taking meals upstairs. He'd met the other residents and found them dreadful. Posh hypocrites who'd done nothing for the war but criticize it. They had no appreciation of the dirty reality, no conception of what it took to keep the island safe. He knew, in that corner of his mind that could still form a thought, that their view of him was likewise dim: exceedingly wealthy, embarrassingly unkempt, a drunken lout at all hours of the day. Even here, where the rich and cowardly convened, there were standards to uphold. And Will was letting the side down.

He abandoned sartorial conceits a week into his residence. After all, if he wasn't to venture past the threshold of his room, what point in clawing out of his bedclothes for a few hours each day? Far better to lounge beside the open window in his dressing gown. Breezes whispered through stands of hazel in the garden and rubbed his skin with warm silk. He dozed in the sunlight, inhaling the scent of hyacinths and listening to the occasional clack-and-murmur of a croquet game down in the garden. The smell of hyacinths made him think of weddings and the happier world of a lifetime ago.

His appetite disappeared not long after that. It was, he imagined, the bravest part of him, preceding him unto death. Will dozed, dimly aware of a quiet tapping and the clink of a dinner tray set outside his door. Time passed. It grew dark outside, then light, and over again. Will lost count. More dishes rattled in the corridor outside his room. He lost count of that, too.

And through it all, he floated in a pool of molten gold, drowning himself in a tide of his own design.

Yelling. Crashing. Splintered wood.

Will dreamt he was back in the glade on his grandfather's estate. Where a natural spring gurgled up through earth and stone, where no birds sang. Grandfather was there, yelling at him with juniper-berry breath while he and Aubrey kicked down the trees. Crack. Smash.

Then he floated. Out the window. Down a hole into the dark earth, because the faeries had come to spirit him away. Into cold, damp warrens, where all the lost children went. Will shivered. The faeries sang to him, but he didn't like their language.

Mr. Malcolm found him. Craggy-faced Mr. Malcolm, who had died long ago. He tore into the faerie mound with rough, strong hands. He lifted Will and carried him away, to hide him from grandfather, just as he used to do.

Motion. Darkness. Tires ringing on macadam. The smell of leather seats.

Daylight on polished walnut, flowing like honey through mullioned windowpanes. Ravens cawing in the distance.

Moonlight. Flannel. Ice water. The taste of stomach acid. A bucket. Strong hands.

Will woke in a four-poster bed, vaguely surprised to find himself alive. His head floated on a raft of goose-down pillows. He realized he was naked beneath a mound of blankets. Cool bed linens caressed him. He ran his hand through the sheets. Soft, fine: Egyptian cotton, high quality. It soothed the stump of his missing finger.

He cracked one eye open, but the room's walnut paneling was polished to such a high gloss that the glow of sunlight caused a flare of pain in his open eye. He squeezed it shut, satisfied that he knew this place.

His nose twitched at a whiff of something sweet. Attar. If he could have mustered the strength to look, he knew he'd find a decanter of rosewater and a porcelain bowl on the bed stand.

Somewhere off to his left, he heard the clink and gurgle of somebody pouring from a service. A few seconds later, his stomach did a somersault at the smell of strong Indian tea. This time he did attempt to turn his head, but the effort left him exhausted.

He woke again some time later. Minutes, perhaps, or hours. The scent of tea still wafted through the room, less intensely than before. The service had cooled. The light had moved, too, enough that it didn't hurt to squint.

A figure stood silhouetted before a panoramic bay window. Will couldn't tell if the yellow sunlight was from a sunrise or a sunset.

Sunset. These windows faced west, he remembered.

The man by the window held a saucer. He sipped from a cup, staring outside. Will recognized the way he held himself, the turn of his elbow and wrist as he sipped. Tense. Uptight. Even here, now, in his own home.

The tickle in Will's throat became a cough when he tried to speak. He worked up enough saliva to swallow down the gravel, and tried again.

'Good evening, Your Grace,' he croaked.

Aubrey turned from where he'd been staring out the window. 'William.' It came out as a sigh, betraying the slightest hint of relief and worry. 'I feared we'd have to call the physician back.'

Hunger clawed at Will. It wasn't a hunger for food, but for something else, something that would fill his body with liquid gold. *Yes*, Will wanted to say. *Call the physician, call the man with the painkillers*. The craving had been his constant companion for months. Will knew it intimately. Though strong and insistent, it was diminished from what it had been.

'How long—?' Will's voice broke into another raspy cough. He didn't have the energy to finish the sentence, but his brother understood.

'Several days.'

Aubrey moved to the bedside. He set his cup and saucer on the tea service and poured a second cup. Will's mouth watered. 'Here,' said Aubrey. 'Can you sit up?'

Will worked himself into a sitting position. The effort made his head spin, but he resisted the temptation to close his eyes again. Aubrey propped a spare pillow behind him. 'Here,' he said, offering the cup.

Will wrapped his fingers around it. It was the good china, the Spode pearlware. That must have been a mistake; the lustrous Spode was meant for honored guests. The tea warmed Will's fingers. It was strong tea, with lemon, the way he liked it. He wondered how Aubrey had known this, or if somebody on the kitchen staff remembered how Will took his tea. It soothed him, and eroded the burrs that scraped his throat.

After half a cup, he rasped, 'How did I get here?'

'The proprietress of the, ah, that place. She contacted us in quite a state.'

'Because I hadn't left my room in several days.'

'Because you hadn't paid. She said she had a, ah, guest on the premises who insisted, rather loudly I understand, that I would cover his expenses.'

'Oh.'

Aubrey sat in a century-old hand-carved oaken chair across the bed stand from Will. 'What were you doing there?'

Will took a long slow sip, thinking about how to answer his brother's question. 'I needed a change.'

'But why there? Why didn't you come home?'

'I'm rather unsure where that is these days.'

Aubrey quirked an eyebrow. Even during a heart-to-heart talk, or what passed for one, he strove for an elegant, understated

BITTER SEEDS 367

comportment. The man was so entrenched in his position that he looked upon everything, even himself, with utter seriousness. 'That's an odd thing to say. We grew up here, you and I.'

'We had different childhoods.'

Aubrey drained his cup. He poured the last of the tea for Will, then sent the service out with a servant whom Will didn't recognize. He supposed most of the household staff would be strangers to him. Who remembered the way he took his tea?

Sunlight on the near wall turned orange, then red, as it inched upward. The windowpanes crisscrossed the sunlight with thin shadows. Will nursed his tea. It was strong, astringent; it had steeped too long.

Aubrey's chair creaked when he uncrossed his legs. He leaned forward, elbows on his knees.

'What happened to you, William?'

'We had different childhoods.'

'That's not an answer.'

'It's the truest answer I have to give.'

The sun set. Aubrey turned on the lamps in opposite corners of the room. They spilled warm light across rugs that one of Will's forebears had obtained in India.

Will dozed off and on. Each time he woke, he was surprised to see that Aubrey had stayed. Will felt strangely pleased by this.

'I dreamt of Mr. Malcolm,' he said. 'Do you remember Mr. Malcolm?'

'Who?'

'Malcolm. Grandfather's steward, long ago.'

Aubrey shrugged. 'Of course.'

'That's good. He was a good man. He should be remembered.'

Aubrey pulled a pocket watch from his vest pocket. It clicked open. He read it, frowned, and put it back. He said, 'I'll have the kitchen bring you something to eat. Can you eat?'

Will's stomach gurgled. 'I shall try.'

'Excellent. Well, then.' Aubrey crossed the room, toward the door. 'I'm having guests tomorrow evening. I presume your convalescence will last longer than that.'

It wasn't, Will noticed, a question. 'Who can say? Perhaps I'll be on my feet sooner rather than later. Whom are you having?'

Aubrey hesitated. 'I think it would be better for all if you indulged in a few days of bed rest.'

'Ah. You'd prefer if I not make an appearance tomorrow. Is that it?' Will asked.

'It would avoid unpleasant questions.'

'Unpleasant?'

'My own brother in a, a, one of *those* places. What image do you think that projects?'

Will ignored the spinning in his head when he sat upright. 'I'm frightfully sorry to have inconvenienced you, Your Grace.'

'Don't be like that—'

'You wanted to know what had happened to me. Well, I'll tell you this. I've done far more for the war effort than you and your charities will ever manage.' Will's voice cracked. He had to clear his throat before continuing. 'I've done things you'd . . . I've been fighting a war and I'm exhausted beyond my capacity to express. I couldn't bear it any longer. Just like father.'

The mention of their father cracked Aubrey's imperturbable façade. Aubrey, being the older of the pair, remembered their father more than Will did. Sadness tightened the corners of his eyes. He shook his head.

Quietly, he said, 'No. Not like father. You'll get better.' His rueful smile diminished, but did not erase, the look of regret in his eyes. 'You'll be your cheerful, aggravating self once more.'

Will couldn't see his brother clearly, because his eyes were watery. 'I would like that very much.'

23 May 1941
On the road, near Magdeburg, Germany

They made decent time, rushing east from Bielefeld, but at the cost of rapidly depleted battery stores. The task of clearing the roads fell mostly to Reinhardt, who could vaporize the ice and snow as quickly as their three-truck convoy came upon it. In places they used Kammler, too, for tossing aside downed trees and other detritus, but Spalcke lacked his predecessor's finesse, meaning he couldn't make the telekinetic clear roads on the fly. This panicked, unscripted race wasn't a patch on the Götterelektrongruppe's perfectly choreographed performance in the Ardennes.

And it was a race; nobody denied that. Their destination was the point of contention. In the past three hours, they'd received several conflicting sets of orders over the radio.

Klaus rode in the lead with Reinhardt. He swapped out the other man's battery as their truck plunged through another cloud of steam. The vapor froze to the truck when they emerged onto another clear stretch of road. The windshield wipers rattled quickly across the window glass.

The driver cleared his throat. 'Herr Obersturmführer ...' He trailed off, obviously reluctant to address either Klaus or Reinhardt specifically. The two had been arguing all morning, which made the driver fidgety. Nobody wanted to be stuck in the middle when supermen fought.

The driver pointed. They were bearing down on a junction where several roads met. A signpost indicated the distances to cities in various directions.

'East,' said Reinhardt.

The familiar copper taste filled Klaus's mouth as he angrily called up the Götterelektron. 'South,' he said.

The driver bit his lip.

Reinhardt repeated himself. 'East. We're going to Berlin.' The air inside the truck became very warm.

Klaus turned to the driver. 'Pull over. Get out.'

The truck barely skidded to a halt before the driver jumped out.

Klaus ran a hand over his face. 'Reinhardt. There are three of us. Two and a half,' he said, jerking a thumb over his shoulder to indicate the truck containing Kammler. 'You think you're going through the batteries quickly now? How long will they last when you're fighting an army?'

'That's what we were MADE FOR!' Acrid smoke wafted up from the upholstery beneath Reinhardt.

Klaus dematerialized, willing his body transparent to the surging heat. He reached forward with one ghostly hand and unplugged Reinhardt's battery. It quenched the supernatural warmth. Klaus released his Willenskräfte.

Reinhardt's pale eyes frosted over with rage. 'Do you know how many ways I've imagined to kill you?'

'The Soviets were watching us,' said Klaus, attempting to deflect the threat with reason. Over the years, he had likewise imagined countless scenarios for dealing with Reinhardt, and even Kammler, should the situation arise. Few suggested a clear victory for anybody. 'They want the doctor's research. They're probably advancing on the farm right now, while there's nobody to defend it.'

Reinhardt grabbed the loose wire dangling above his battery. 'If that were the case' – *click* – 'surely your sister' – *snap* – 'would have given ample warning.'

He had a point. But Gretel had her own purposes, her own reasons for doing things. It was possible she had foreseen an attack and had chosen to stay silent; perhaps the best outcome came about when Klaus and Reinhardt arrived from the north, rather than being present when the attack came. Klaus expressed this to Reinhardt.

'You're making excuses for her,' Reinhardt said. 'Perhaps she wanted us on the road, so that we could get to Berlin when the invasion came.'

Klaus didn't voice his suspicion that Gretel worked according to her own plan, a blueprint to which the war was merely a side note. Instead, he said: 'My first instinct is to protect the Reichsbehörde. Gretel must know that. I am certain it's what she foresaw.'

'You can't bear to be away from her, can you?' Reinhardt sneered. 'You two always were overly close.'

The electric tingle of the Götterelektron surged back into Klaus's mind. 'This is perfect. I'm getting a morality lecture from a necrophiliac.'

The air around Reinhardt shimmered with another surge of heat. Klaus gritted his teeth, grabbed Reinhardt, dematerialized, and pulled him outside through the side of the truck before it went up in flames. They landed in a puddle, which instantly flashed into vapor. The contact with Reinhardt blistered Klaus's hands. It was painful.

'That's it,' said Reinhardt. 'You're going to smolder to death.' Mud bubbled beneath his boots.

Spalcke, who had been riding with Kammler in the truck

behind them, was standing on the road. 'What are you two doing? And why have we stopped? I gave no order to halt.'

To Spalcke, Klaus said, 'Shut up.' And to Reinhardt, he said, 'Just listen to me for a moment.'

Spalcke's lips moved silently while he clenched and unclenched his jaw. He appeared to come to the same conclusion their driver had, deciding it wasn't in his best interests to get involved if Klaus and Reinhardt fought.

Klaus turned his attention back to Reinhardt as the salamander was gearing up for an attack. He held up his hands. 'Wait! We're wasting time. This won't achieve anything, and it won't get you to Berlin any sooner.'

Reinhardt narrowed his eyes. 'You agree we should go east, then?'

'No. I propose we split up. You go to Berlin, and I'll return to the farm.' He pointed. 'You take one truck. I'll take another.'

This settled the matter because it gave Reinhardt what he wanted. After that, they quickly worked out the logistics over Spalcke's vocal but ultimately impotent objections. They split the remaining batteries evenly between the three trucks. Reinhardt took a driver, another one of the LSSAH men who'd been transferred to the Reichsbehörde and who knew how to swap out batteries. Spalcke, Kammler, the radio operator, and the third driver were consigned to the last truck. When Spalcke started to yell about insubordination and tribunals and courts-martial, the air around him shimmered briefly before he doubled over.

They were ready to depart for their separate destinations within fifteen minutes. As Klaus climbed into his truck – the one that stank of melted Bakelite – he said, 'Go find your glory, Reinhardt.'

'Go find your beloved sister.'

Klaus's driver put the truck into gear. A stack of charged batteries sat piled on the seat between them.

They turned right at the crossroads, heading south. They were followed by a second truck, which carried Kammler and Spalcke and the large store of depleted batteries. Klaus watched in the side mirror as Reinhardt continued east through the intersection. A few seconds later, the road curved, and Reinhardt's truck disappeared from view.

The south road was just as icy and snowbound as the roads they'd driven out of Bielefeld. Klaus urged the driver to greater and greater speeds. And to his credit, the driver kept them on the road, though nothing could have been fast enough for Klaus. Rather than clearing the roads as Kammler and Reinhardt had done, Klaus willed the entire truck insubstantial when they encountered snowdrifts, stuck automobiles, and other obstructions. Spalcke and Kammler quickly fell behind.

The weather improved as they neared the Reichsbehörde. Icy roads became slushy roads, then muddy roads, then roads. Snow-heavy tree boughs became naked limbs popping with green buds. It was as though they had traveled from the depths of winter to a pleasant springtime over the course of a hundred kilometers. Klaus massaged his aching fingers, waiting.

They were minutes from the farm, sunlight and shadow flashing over their truck as they barreled past oak and ash trees, when Klaus heard the first explosion. The ground heaved. A *crack* echoed through the forest.

The driver pushed his foot to the floor. Klaus checked the gauge on his battery, reassuring himself it held a complete charge.

They emerged onto the Reichsbehörde grounds. The facility hummed with frantic activity. Cargo trucks lined the gravel drive.

Mundane troops and white-coated technicians ran between the trucks and the buildings, loading the trucks with crates, filing cabinets, specialized electrical and medical equipment. A row of troop transports had been parked on the training field. Klaus realized they had brought reinforcements to defend the farm, and now the empty transports were being used to evacuate personnel. Klaus saw one of the Twins being pushed into a transport. There was no sign of Gretel.

They skidded to a halt in front of the icehouse. The staccato chatter of automatic weapons fire rippled through the forest on the eastern edge of the farm, along with the rumble of diesel engines and the rattle-clank of tank treads. Klaus saw movement and flashes of red in the trees.

He jumped from the truck and hit the ground at a dead run. The metallic tingle peculiar to fresh batteries buzzed into that place in his head where his willpower resided.

Another explosion. More gunfire, closer now. Close enough for Klaus to hear screaming.

Gretel wasn't in the first transport. Or the second. Or the third. She certainly wasn't loading equipment, and she wasn't advising the reinforcements. Nobody knew where she had gone.

Klaus found his sister in the barracks that had replaced their sleeping quarters in the demolished farmhouse. She was sitting on a cot, back to the wall, thin legs stretched out before her and ankles crossed, reading poetry. A rucksack lay at her feet.

'Gretel!'

The corner of her mouth quirked up. She dog-eared her current page, closed the book, and looked at him. 'Welcome home, brother.' The ground shook again. Gunfire chattered outside, followed by the *thump* of a mortar shell and more yelling. She scratched her nose. 'Did you have a successful trip?'

'We have to leave.' Klaus grabbed her hand and hauled her off the cot. 'They're evacuating the facility. We need to get to the training field.' He pulled her toward the outside wall.

'Wait,' she said. She pointed at the rucksack. 'We'll need that.'

The sack clattered like ceramic or glass when he lifted it. 'Don't worry,' she said. 'I've packed for you, too.'

They emerged on the training ground. Klaus half pulled, half dragged Gretel toward the waiting transports. He was just about to grab her waist and hurl her aboard when a line of tanks burst through the tree line. Klaus glimpsed red stars on the tanks as they maneuvered into a semicircle that blocked egress from the field. Their treads churned up clods of earth as they advanced on the evacuees. The Red Army had arrived at the Reichsbehörde.

Klaus swore. He pulled Gretel in a new direction. 'This way! I have a truck.'

The icehouse stood between them and Klaus's truck. He grabbed Gretel's wrist, invoked his Willenskräfte, and ran.

Twenty meters from the icehouse. Ten meters. Five.

And then—

WHUMP! WHUMP! WHUMP!

A chain of muffled explosions circled the facility in rapid-fire succession. They strobed the grounds with flashes of blue and violet like artificial lightning. The odor of ozone washed across the field thick enough to sting Klaus's eyes.

He recognized these explosions. He'd seen something like them once before, when the British had attacked the Reichsbehörde. *Pixies.*

His battery died, leaving the pair tangible and vulnerable. The Communists' operation was well-planned.

Soviet infantrymen emerged from the tree line. They jogged past the tanks, rifles at the ready. The evacuees raised their arms.

Klaus tried to slip away with Gretel, but they didn't get far before a trio of soldiers surrounded them. They stared at Klaus's battery harness and the wires twined through Gretel's braids. She squeezed his hand. One of the men called over his shoulder, something in Russian. An officer joined them. He looked the captured siblings up and down, consulted a clipboard, then barked an order.

The men took Klaus's sidearm and the rucksack, then stripped the siblings of their batteries. He felt naked.

The sounds of combat faded away as the Soviets established control of the Reichsbehörde. Klaus stood with his arms raised, wondering what would happen next. He knew they wouldn't be shot. Gretel would never expose herself to such danger. Unless it somehow suited her purposes.

He looked at her. As always, she observed the unfolding scene with perfect sangfroid. She noticed his attention, and winked.

A low drone echoed across the facility. It was so faint at first that Klaus mistook it for the rumble of idling engines. But it quickly grew louder, and soon his captors seemed to notice it, too.

Klaus looked up, searching for the source of this new noise. He found it in the western sky.

British Halifax bombers. The Royal Air Force had arrived at the Reichsbehörde.

23 May 1941
Reichsbehörde für die Erweiterung germanischen Potenzials

In a strange way, it felt like Williton all over again.

An eerie sense of déjà vu prickled Marsh as he sped toward the Reichsbehörde. This time, it was a German road cratered by

British bombs, rather than the other way round. But it was so similar: the cratered landscape, the smell of cordite, plumes of oily smoke rising in the distance.

Marsh's stolen truck teetered around the edge of a crater and seesawed over another rut. The transmission groaned in protest. The farther he went, the slower he had to proceed, and the worse his frustration.

Milkweed's plan appeared to have worked. The RAF had flattened the REGP, if the condition of the surrounding area was any indication.

Grand job.

It was a good plan, but they'd formulated it before they fully understood their enemy. A sick feeling had taken root in the pit of Marsh's stomach.

The girl's a bloody oracle.

Gretel was no fool. Mad as a hatter, but no fool. She wouldn't have stayed for the bombing. She'd have an escape hatch. He knew it with a certainty deeper than the marrow in his bones.

Marsh parked his stolen truck on the outskirts of what had once been the family farm of the von Westarp clan. The truck wasn't designed for this kind of terrain. Taking it any farther risked getting stuck, tipping over, or even snapping an axle. And he wasn't about to lose the files he'd worked so hard to obtain.

With Walther P38 pistol in hand in case he encountered survivors, he toured the ruins. It took an exercise of imagination to reconcile his memory of the layout, based on a single dark night in December, with the charred debris strewn across the clearing. What the RAF lacked in numbers it had made up for with munitions. They'd even dropped incendiaries. The smell of kerosene and phosphorus lay thick on the still air, overlaying the odors of burnt pork and hot stone.

Bricks. Bodies. Tongues of flame licking at shattered timbers. Just like Williton.

But there was other debris, other things that he and Liv hadn't seen on their fruitless search for Agnes. Dismembered Waffen-SS soldiers. Flattened trucks and heavy equipment. Dead men in white laboratory coats. Half a troop transport. A mangled tank turret, its paint blackened . . .

. . . but faintly visible, the suggestion of a sickle and hammer.

Another dead soldier, his body and uniform torched beyond recognition. So, too, the rifle in his hands. But . . . the length of the stock, the shape of the magazine . . . Had he been carrying a Tokarev?

The devastation was so complete, he hadn't noticed at first. But once he knew what to look for, he found subtle hints strewn everywhere. An officer's cap with a red star badge. Fragments of Cyrillic lettering.

Oh, no. No, no, no. You grotty little monster.

The sick feeling in Marsh's gut became an oily dread. He shivered, afraid that he'd found Gretel's escape hatch.

Simply leaving before the bombs fell, before the Soviets arrived, didn't suit her style. It was simple, but she leaned toward the baroque. The information in her file suggested as much.

Handing herself over to old Joe might have been a crazy thing to do, but it also ensured Marsh couldn't find her. And she knew he was looking for her. He knew this, felt it, with a certainty that he couldn't voice.

Some of the ruins still crackled with fire. Behind a toppled wall, Marsh found mounds of shattered glassware partially melted into slag and a metal gurney with what looked to be wrist or ankle restraints. This might have been a medical ward, or a laboratory; the dead here wore lab coats. These had died under falling debris when the roof collapsed, or perhaps from shrapnel when the windows blew.

Marsh checked every dead body for wires in the skull, or a battery at the waist. But he found none. His census of the dead turned up dozens of Germans and Soviets, but also a large number of bodies either in pieces or burned beyond recognition, or both. If those men and women had once worn battery harnesses, it was impossible to know.

He did find one survivor. It was a young man, no older than twenty, wearing the uniform of the Leibstandarte Schutzstaffel Adolf Hitler, the elite Waffen-SS unit spawned from Hitler's original bodyguard regiment. This didn't surprise Marsh; an operation like the REGP would have required a standing population of mundane soldiers who could keep their mouths shut. The boy had been thrown against a brick wall, part of which fell on him. His breath came in gasps, and his chest gurgled when he exhaled.

Marsh crouched in front of him. The boy looked at him with a dazed expression. After taking a moment to recognize Marsh's uniform, he attempted a salute despite the compound fracture in his free arm.

Elite, indeed, thought Marsh.

'At ease. What happened here?'

The dying soldier struggled to explain, pausing frequently to shudder or cough. 'Communists ... attacked. Tanks ... bombers ...'

The Soviets had bombed their own troops? Unlikely. The boy was understandably confused about what had happened. It was clear, based on what Marsh found in the debris, that the RAF bombers had arrived before the last of the Soviets had pulled out. But to somebody in the middle of the chaos, it could have seemed that the Soviets were dropping bombs.

Marsh didn't correct the misconception. His interests lay elsewhere. 'Was the facility evacuated? Did our people get away before the Communists attacked?'

'. . . loading trucks when . . . came through . . . trees.' The look in the boy's eyes became distant, unfocused.

Marsh jostled him. 'Hey! Stay with me. The medics are coming,' he lied. The boy coughed explosively. Marsh ignored the warm spray of blood that speckled his face. 'Did anybody get away?'

'I . . . don't . . .' Again, the slide into that unfocused stare.

Marsh shook him again, as hard as he dared. 'Gretel! What happened to Gretel?' But the boy shuddered, and then said nothing more.

'Damn it.' Marsh wiped the blood from his face.

Most of the Reichsbehörde staff might have died in the bombing, or been killed by the Soviets. Even Gretel. Perhaps she'd seen it coming, but it was inescapable.

He kneeled next to the dead soldier, weakened by despair. He and Liv would carry the sorrow of Agnes's death for the rest of their lives. And now he carried another sorrow, too. It was the shame of his inability to avenge her, to punish the people who had killed her. He'd tried, and failed, twice. What kind of a father was he? The kind that couldn't do a goddamned thing for his daughter. He hadn't even been there when she was born: he'd been with that raven-haired demon, Gretel.

Marsh stood, sighing. The Jerries would arrive soon to assess the damage. He had to leave.

I tried, Agnes. Lord as my witness, I tried.

Marsh drove his stolen truck toward Denmark, and home. He didn't look back.

*

It took most of a week to secure passage back to Britain for the stolen files. Marsh spent that time holed up with the crates in the secret oubliette beneath a Swedish fisherman's cottage. He passed those days thinking of Liv, sleeping, and reading the entire archive.

The more he studied Gretel's psychological profile, the more certain he became that she hadn't perished in the bombing. He absorbed everything they'd written about her, scrutinized it, read between the lines: Gretel excelled at twisting everything that happened to her own personal benefit. If the Red Army had occupied the REGP, he could be confident she'd found a way to take advantage of that.

The miserable bitch had gotten away with it. She'd killed his daughter, and then she got away with it.

Marsh stayed with the crates throughout the journey, even riding in the cargo bed of the truck that carried them all the way from his landing site in the Scottish highlands to Westminster. The files went into the same vault that contained the Tarragona filmstrip, a cloven stone, a photograph of a farmhouse, and the charred pages of a medical report. Marsh also returned Gretel's battery to the vault. He wasn't sorry to be rid of it; the ache in his back wouldn't subside.

Liv could fix that. But first he had to do something.

Stephenson wasn't in his office. He wasn't in Milkweed's wing of the Admiralty building at all. But he was in the building, and in the middle of a meeting when Marsh barged in.

Marsh recognized the lamps, the end tables, the smell of leather and tobacco. Daylight made the room much smaller than he'd remembered from his first visit. Back then when Stephenson had taken him here – Marsh's first trip to the Admiralty, back in '39, when the old man still held his position as the head of SIS's

T-section – the room had been cavernous, draped in shadows.

He entered on a tumult of voices raised in heated discussion. He recognized some of those, too. The same voices had said that Milkweed was a fool's errand.

Perhaps they were right.

Stephenson was seated at a wide oval inlaid table with six other men. Some wore suits, some uniforms. The discussion stopped immediately.

The old man's eyes might have revealed a hint of relief in seeing Marsh had weathered his mission. But he voiced nothing of the sort, not even a 'welcome back,' which told Marsh something about the nature of this meeting.

'Commander! If you please,' said Stephenson with a gesture encompassing the other men at the table. 'This is not a good time.'

'We need to speak. Immediately.'

'It will have to wait.' With a dismissive wave, Stephenson added, 'Find me tomorrow.'

'Oh, you'll want to hear this,' Marsh said quietly.

Several of the meeting participants turned to study the brash interloper who didn't know his place and didn't acknowledge when he was excused. One of the military men draped an arm across the back of his chair in order to crane his neck and see the source of the disruption. He was a big man, with thick caterpillar eyebrows perched over dark eyes and a wide, flat nose.

Marsh recognized his uniform. He'd seen several variations of it on dead Soviets at the Reichsbehörde.

Ah.

Stephenson sighed. 'I believe most of you gentlemen are already acquainted with Commander Marsh. General-Lieutenant Malinovsky, may I please introduce Lieutenant-Commander

Raybould Marsh of His Majesty's Royal Navy.' Then he looked at Marsh. 'Commander, please meet General-Lieutenant Rodion Malinovsky, who is here on behalf of our new allies.' The old man's gaze hardened into flint as he said *allies*.

Malinovsky nodded politely. In thickly accented English, he said, 'Commander.' His voice was a deep baritone.

Marsh returned the nod. 'Welcome, General-Lieutenant.' Then he nodded to Stephenson, too, saying, 'Tomorrow, then.'

'Yes.'

Marsh started to leave, but he stopped himself. He stopped himself because she'd killed his daughter. She'd killed his daughter, and now she was getting away with it. He turned back to Malinovsky.

'Where is she?'

Was there a pause, the slightest hesitation, before the Soviet officer cocked his head, frowning? 'I, I do not understand your question, Commander.'

Marsh locked eyes with him, stepping closer. 'Where. Is. She.'

The Soviet officer blinked, turning to address the rest of the table. 'My friends, please. Who is this "she"?'

'I truly couldn't say,' Stephenson said. The flint in his gaze had been knapped into arrowheads, all aimed at Marsh. 'I must apologize. Commander Marsh has been under great stress of late.'

Marsh gripped the back of Malinovsky's chair and heaved. In one quick motion, the chair and occupant slid away from the table and tipped over backwards before there was a chance to react.

Stephenson leaped from his seat. 'Raybould! Have you lost your bloody mind?'

Marsh ignored him. He loomed over the Soviet officer. Quietly, he asked, 'Where is she?'

Surprise and anger played over Malinovsky's face. He said nothing.

Stephenson skirted the table and grabbed Marsh while the others helped Malinovsky to his feet amidst a cascade of profuse apologies. The old man's single hand had a strong grip, which he clamped on Marsh's forearm to pull him from the room. His voice was like the first rumble of thunder from an advancing storm. 'With me. Now.'

He waited until they stood alone in the corridor, the door closed solidly behind them. Then he rounded on Marsh.

'What the hell has gotten in to you?' he demanded, his tone a shouted whisper. 'Have you any idea whom you've just humiliated? Have you any idea the damage you've done?'

'They have her.' Marsh paced, pointing back toward the meeting room. 'They fucking have her.'

'They have who?'

'You know damn well who!' This came out as a shout. 'The girl.' He pointed to his head, pantomiming wires and braids. 'Gretel.'

'My God. You're still obsessed with her. You have to let it go, son.'

'Let it go?' Marsh abandoned the pretense of being quiet. He didn't care who heard him. 'Let it go? She killed my daughter. I've seen the goddamned records.' He added an afterthought. 'They're in your vault now. Sir.'

That caught Stephenson by surprise. He faltered for a moment. 'The ... Oh.' He cleared his throat. 'Even if the Soviets have captured her—'

'They *did*. I was *there*.'

'—you seem incapable of grasping even the rudiments of this situation. Times are changing. It is imperative that we cultivate good relations with those people. And we absolutely cannot afford to act like hooligans. You've done more harm than you know.'

'I'll do more than that,' said Marsh. He headed for the meeting room door, rolling up his sleeves.

'No! You'll do nothing.' Stephenson blocked his way, shoving him back with a firm hand to the chest. 'Beauclerk was right. You've gone round the bend.'

He shook his head. 'You're done.'

'Not until I know why she—'

'You've done your service to the country.' Stephenson's tone was firm, if a little sad. His hand felt heavy against Marsh's heartbeat. 'But you've lost your objectivity. You're no longer fit for this work.' He shook his head. 'You're out. Go home.'

Long seconds ticked away while they stared each other down. Marsh swallowed down the rage, tamped down the urge to lash out. It left him feeling, for all the world, like a little boy caught stealing from a winter garden. He knocked Stephenson's arm away.

Stephenson returned to the meeting room. The door latched shut behind him, followed by the *snick* of a lock sliding into place.

Marsh went home. He didn't look back.

EPILOGUE

That summer, the ravens of Albion returned to the Tower of London.

Changing seasons brought longer days. Peaceful days. No more fire, no more rubble, no more shallow graves. The men and women of the island emerged from their shelters and rejoiced. The war was over. They had persevered.

They rebuilt. Day by day, a brick at a time, they rebuilt their country and plastered over the scars of war. And the ravens, knowing the cycle of all things, returned to their old perches. Those still standing.

At night, the cities and towns and villages and hamlets blazed with light. The night-time world had become a wine-dark sea to the ravens, with nothing but darkness below and the stars and moon above. But no longer. Light and joy returned to the world.

And the ravens, knowing the cycle of all things, returned to their old ways. They waited, and watched.

This is what they saw:

3 September 1941
Bestwood-on-Trent, Nottinghamshire, England

'You're looking dreadfully chipper for this time of morning,'

Aubrey said from the doorway of the breakfast room. The window behind him framed a trimmed hedge and a flock of blackbirds.

Will looked up from his breakfast. 'Today is an important day.' He shivered. 'Exciting, isn't it?'

Aubrey arched an eyebrow. He seated himself at the head of the long table. He lifted Will's teacup, which was half-empty, and sniffed the contents. Sunlight poured through the stained-glass rosette window, shattering into little rainbows that danced around the room when Aubrey also inspected the teapot.

It was the same ritual he'd performed every morning for the past two months. And every morning Will felt the shame a little less acutely than the day before.

'I trust you find everything satisfactory?' he asked.

Aubrey harrumphed. He opened the newspaper tucked neatly at his seat. The two brothers sat quietly, Will eating and Aubrey reading, while blackbirds screeched to each other in a shrubbery beneath the window.

As a rule, Will avoided reading the papers. Too frequently they dampened the nation's celebratory mood by mentioning the hundreds of Britons killed by pro-German saboteurs during the war, or calling for renewed efforts to find and punish the fifth columnists who had derailed trains, sunken ships, burned hospitals. The rhetoric was dying down, but it would forever be a sore spot on the British psyche.

The warlocks had returned to their secret, quiet little lives. They had gone into hiding.

Will called for Mr. Pantaiges, the current steward of Bestwood. Aubrey listened while Will described his plans for the day to Mr. Pantaiges.

Two hours later, Will stood panting in the glade where a

natural spring gurgled up through cleft granite. He'd discarded his vest and rolled his sleeves up to the elbow. His shirt was ruined, torn by the thorny brush through which he'd hacked a path wide enough for a wheelbarrow.

The exertion felt wonderful, like life was pumping through his body again. He relished the feel of sweat on his skin, the heave of his chest as he caught his breath, the rapid beating of his heart. Even the deep scratches on his hands and arms. Will imagined the sweat and blood wicking away any lingering traces of the poison in his body. Almost three months had passed since the phantom hunger had withered and died.

Will listened to the *whooshing* updraft from the bonfire. The blackbirds had fallen silent; they watched from the distant crenellations of Bestwood. His grandfather's personal effects released an exhilarating heat as flames consumed the pile. The fire wouldn't destroy everything, but Will would bury the ashes and anything left intact. The glade smelled of cleansing fire.

Mr. Pantaiges came crashing through the thicket, his wheelbarrow bouncing along the path of trimmings Will had left strewn through the surrounding copse. He set it down, close enough to the fire that Will could dump the contents into the fire: a walking stick, framed black-and-white photographs, and clothing.

'The last of it, sir.'

Will shook his head. 'I want you to gather everything. Nothing is to be spared.'

'I understand, sir. With apologies, I am quite certain these are the very last of His Grace's belongings, may he rest in peace. I've confirmed it personally, sir.'

Will sifted through the contents of the wheelbarrow. 'His papers, too, Mr. Pantaiges.' *Especially his papers.*

'Ah,' said the majordomo. A moment of awkward hesitation passed before he continued. 'I am afraid, sir, that the Admiralty men left nothing behind.'

The fire lost its warmth. Will shivered under a frisson of cold. He steadied himself on a granite outcropping and eased himself into a sitting position.

'What men, Mr. Pantaiges?' His voice was barely a whisper above the crackle of the bonfire and the faint booming of a distant surf.

'The men from the Admiralty, sir. They requisitioned all of the late Duke's papers. For the war effort, they said. And His Grace, being very keen to do his part for the country, as I'm sure you know well, sir, was quite emphatic that we should pack up every last scrap of paper for them.'

'I see.' Will fought to catch his breath. 'And when did this happen?'

'Many months ago, sir. This past winter.'

'Do you remember anything else about these men? Their appearances, or how they might have spoken?'

'No, sir. They seemed rather ordinary, if I may say so.' The majordomo paused. 'There was one thing, sir. Struck me as a trifle odd at the time.'

'Tell me.'

'I remember they were very specific. They asked several times if His Grace had kept any notes on child rearing. Can you imagine that, sir?'

An old memory floated unbidden into Will's mind, like a piece of flotsam carried on a rising tide. They'd been driving through the city, Pip at the wheel. Pip had asked about the lexicons, and Enochian, and how it all began. Will had tried to dodge the subject: *I had this very same conversation yesterday. Can't you have the old man explain it to you?* Will had tasted his first pint that afternoon.

And he remembered another, more recent conversation with Marsh. *Have you heard anything about some work going on downstairs? At the Admiralty.*

He stood. 'That will be all, Mr. Pantaiges. Please tell my brother I've gone to London for the day.'

The renovations had been so thorough that Will hardly recognized the space. The basement beneath Milkweed HQ had been rebuilt. Gone were the mildewed storerooms, the brick arches, the warren of corridors. They had been replaced with what appeared to be rows of bank vaults.

A pair of the heaviest steel doors Will had ever seen sectioned off each corridor. Lush, deep-pile chenille carpeting covered every inch of the corridors themselves, floor to ceiling, including the widely spaced doorways lining each wall.

The carpeting, he knew, was there to absorb sound. He knew it because of the placards, posted everywhere:

SILENCE, PLEASE!
CONVERSATION IS STRICTLY FORBIDDEN
AT ALL TIMES!
ABSOLUTELY NO LANGUAGE PERMITTED
ON THE PREMISES!

But the insulation wasn't perfect. If Will strained enough, he could discern the wailing of hungry babies.

He knew that if he waited, sooner or later the wet nurses would arrive, perhaps under armed escort, to enter the vaults. But he already knew what the vaults held.

Newborns, not more than a few months old.

War orphans.

3 September 1941
Walworth, London, England

The vines were thick and sturdy, their tomatoes tiny pale-green bulbs that would swell and redden into autumn. Marsh slowly worked down the row, inspecting every leaf for signs of blight or infestation. He trimmed a shoot edged with brown. The wet, loamy smell of the opened vine mixed with the aroma of Liv's bread baking in the kitchen.

Homemade bread was the only kind to be had in these first months after the war. Nobody complained. People were too busy celebrating. The war was over, and Britain had survived. No more air raids, no more gas masks. Life had mostly returned to normal.

But the rationing had become stricter. Bread was just one of many items that had been added to the list of rationed goods. Goods that would be sent to the Continent in a desperate attempt to feed the millions left starving by the unnatural winter. He knew, from listening to the wireless, that Stalin had invited Churchill and Roosevelt to Paris to discuss the situation.

He also knew that the Japanese had gobbled up the Kamchatka Peninsula and Sakhalin Island while the Soviets were busy dealing with scattered pockets of Nazi resistance in Europe. He wondered if that would be on the table for discussion in Paris. Churchill would have to step carefully around the issue, because—

No. Marsh grabbed the reins of his runaway mind, forced his galloping thoughts to a halt. *It's not my problem any longer. I don't do that work anymore.*

I'm done.

He would need to find a new situation soon. Before long, they'd have another mouth to feed. But he'd postponed the search for employment as long as possible. The summer had been for him and Liv. Marsh was back with the love of his life, and together they were building a new family.

Footsteps crunched on the gravel behind him. A shadow covered the sun, a miniature eclipse where he kneeled among the plants. For an instant, he tensed, remembering a ghostly figure in the shadows of St. James' Park. But he shook it off.

No. It's not my problem any longer.

'I'll be right in, Liv.' Marsh trimmed another shoot, inhaling deeply. He smiled. 'Can't wait for that bread.'

'Patience never was one of your virtues, Pip.'

Marsh started, turned. Will stood just outside the plantings, silhouetted by the sun.

'Will! This is a surprise,' Marsh said as he climbed to his feet, slapping the soil from his dungarees. 'When did you get here? I didn't know you were back in town.'

'It requires a lot of pruning,' said Will, pointing at the vines.

Marsh said, 'Not so much as I feared. They're—' He stopped himself, alarmed by the quaver in Will's voice, his tremorous hand. His old friend looked rumpled, gray. *Oh, no.* 'What requires pruning, Will?'

'Children. Many, many children.' Will's breath stank of juniper berries. 'Lean harvest, you know.' He giggled.

We'd heard Will was improving. But he's hardly coherent. He's fallen, hard. Marsh took him gently by the arm. 'Let's go inside. I think we should call Aubrey.'

This one is my problem. My fault.

He pulled Will's arm over his shoulder and led him toward the house. Liv must have glimpsed them from the kitchen, because she stepped outside as they approached. 'Will! It's so good to see you! It's been ages.'

'Olivia.' Will staggered against Marsh before righting himself. Liv made brief eye contact with Marsh, and he saw the frown of concern tugging at her freckles.

Will doffed his bowler and performed an unsteady bow. 'You are a vision as always, my dear,' he said, looking her up and down. His eyes widened when he saw the slight bulge of her stomach.

He turned. 'Pip?' His breath stung Marsh's eyes.

'We're starting another family, Will. Starting over.'

A dark reflection clouded Will's eyes, as though he were looking at something vast and dangerous. Marsh recognized the shadow, a legacy of Milkweed. The unhealthy pallor in Will's face deepened. Marsh saw he carried a wire-bound manuscript: a copy of the master lexicon.

'Unborn child,' Will whispered. He trailed off, his lips moving soundlessly. He turned to look at Liv again, mumbling to himself. 'Soul.'

'We've been discussing names,' said Liv with forced joviality. 'We thought that—'

'You have to get rid of it,' he blurted. 'Get rid of that baby. I know a doctor ...'

Liv's mouth fell open. Her hands went to her stomach, and she took a step back, the hurt plain on her face.

Marsh grabbed Will's elbow, spun him around. 'What did you just say to my wife?'

'Pip ...' Will wept incoherently.

Marsh took a deep breath, thought of Liv, and quelled his anger. He put a hand on Will's elbow. 'What's wrong, Will? Tell me what happened.'

But Will only shook his head, inconsolable, lost in a private anguish. He teetered for a moment before managing to right himself. 'It won't hurt.' He lurched toward the house. 'I know how to drown the pain. I'll teach you.'

Marsh sidestepped and positioned himself between Will and Liv. In a low voice, so that Liv wouldn't hear him, he said, 'I'm trying to help you. But if you won't let me do that, you have to leave.'

Will stopped, studied Marsh with glassy eyes. Then he started forward again, still weeping. 'Babies. Monsters. All of them.'

Now he was rambling. Will was utterly gone, making no sense. And he was upsetting Liv.

Marsh blocked him again. 'I mean it, Will. Leave. Now.' The last came out as a growl.

Will pointed past Marsh's shoulder, toward Liv. Now he wailed openly. 'Kill it, Olivia! Kill that thing growing inside you—'

That was all he said, because Marsh let his anger fly. There was a dull thud, and then Will collapsed into the tomato vines in a rumpled heap. A flock of blackbirds leapt for the sky with a commotion of flapping wings.

Behind them, Liv gasped. 'Oh . . .'

Marsh massaged his aching hand. 'Don't come back, Will,' he said. 'Stay away from my family.'

Will gaped up at him, hand to his face. He opened his mouth as if to say something, but stopped. The tears on his face glistened in the sunlight. So did the trickle of blood under his nose. He lurched to his feet, awkwardly collecting his hat and the lexicon from where they had fallen. For one long moment he stared past Marsh at Liv. The expression on his face was unreadable.

Hoping he wouldn't have to hit Will again, especially in front of Liv, Marsh tensed. But then Will shook his head sadly, turned, and stumbled for the garden gate.

Marsh waited until it latched shut. Then he put an arm around his wife.

'I wish you hadn't done that. He's our friend.'

'I'm sorry, Liv. I was afraid he'd hurt you.'

'Poor Will,' she said. 'How did this happen to him?'

'Let's go inside. It's over now,' said Marsh.

He was sorry about Will. But Marsh had his family and his garden, and he needed nothing more to be happy.

3 September 1941
Somewhere in the USSR

They were on the move again. It happened every few weeks. Klaus didn't know why, or where they'd go this time. All he knew was that each move took them farther east.

While others struck the camp, two soldiers motioned with their rifles, gesturing Klaus into yet another truck. Klaus knew that if he didn't cooperate, they'd connect the wires in his cranium to the AC generator again. The last time, he'd fractured a rib during the convulsions.

He climbed aboard the truck and took a seat on the hard bench next to Gretel, who was already seated and shackled. A soldier fastened manacles to Klaus's wrists and ankles, then locked his chains to an iron ring on the floor.

If only he had a battery . . . All he needed was a fraction of a second. A fraction of a second, the merest tickle of current, and he and Gretel could be free.

Klaus tried for the thousandth time to call up his Willenskräfte, to rouse that dormant part of his mind where the Götterelektron flowed. But it was useless. Without a battery, he was just another man.

Their captors dismantled the camp with swift efficiency. The truck rumbled to life. The captives' chains jingled as the truck bounced along a dirt road through a vast forest. Ravens flitted through the trees, flashes of black amongst the play of sunlight and shadow.

Klaus sighed, exhausted from his futile effort. He slumped on the bench with head hung low. Gretel patted him on the knee.

'I hope you know what you're doing,' he said.

She leaned close. Her breath tickled his ear.

'Incoming,' she whispered.

ACKNOWLEDGEMENTS

I am deeply indebted to my friends, colleagues, and mentors in the New Mexico Critical Mass Workshop: Daniel Abraham, Terry England, Ty Franck, Emily Mah, George R. R. Martin, Vic Milán, Melinda M. Snodgrass, Jan Stirling, S. M. Stirling, Sage Walker, and Walter Jon Williams. Without their passion for this project, I would never have attempted it; without their support, wisdom, and good humor, I could never have finished it. The weaknesses herein are mine and mine alone, but the good bits belong to Critical Mass.

I am likewise grateful to my companions at the 2007 Blue Heaven workshop for their excellent feedback on portions of this novel: Paolo Bacigalupi, Tobias Buckell, Rae Dawn Carson, Charles Coleman Finlay, Sandra McDonald, Holly McDowell, Paul Melko, Sarah Prineas, Heather Shaw, Bill Shunn, and Greg van Eekhout.

Thanks also to Mike Bateman for his peerless mastery of the whiteboard; Mark Falzini for sharing his wonderful collection of research materials from the Imperial War Museum; Char Peery, Ph.D., for critical reading and the lore of weird linguistic experiments in antiquity; Robert Bodor, Sam Butler, Brad Beaulieu, and Toby Messinger for critical reading; and B. K. Dunn for patient advice on German.

My agent, the fabulous Kay McCauley, has supported my

efforts with zeal and confidence from the very beginning. Thank you, Kay, for believing in me and believing in this tale.

I'd also like to thank my editor, Patrick Nielsen Hayden, for his enthusiasm for this novel, and for making it far better than it would have been otherwise.

Zoë Vaughter knew I'd become a writer long before I did. She's the best cheerleader anybody could wish for, and better than I deserve. I'll never be able to thank her properly for her unwavering faith, support, and patience over the years. Mere words will never be enough.

extras

orbit

www.orbitbooks.net

about the author

Ian Tregillis is the son of a bearded mountebank and a discredited tarot card reader. He was born and raised in Minnesota where his parents had landed after fleeing the wrath of a Flemish prince. (The full story, he's told, involves a Dutch tramp steamer and a stolen horse.) Nowadays he lives in New Mexico, where he consorts with writers, scientists and other unsavoury types.

Find out more about Ian Tregillis and other Orbit authors registering for the free monthly newsletter at www.orbitbooks.net

interview

The premise of *Bitter Seeds* – Nazi super soldiers versus occult powers conjured up by British Warlocks – is unusual, to say the least! What was the original inspiration behind the story?

A number of years ago, around 2002 or 2003, I read a magazine article about a little-known Allied secret project during the Second World War called Project Habakkuk. Habakkuk was conceived during the height of the Battle of the Atlantic, when German wolf packs were destroying Allied shipping convoys. The idea – and this is one of those wonderful places where truth is so much stranger than fiction – was to build ships out of ice. It sounds mad but it's actually a rather clever idea! Alas, for various reasons the project never made it past the prototype stage. (Maybe because it is just a little bit mad.)

But I couldn't get that image out of my head, of vast bergships plying the North Atlantic and changing the course of the war. So I began to wonder how the Axis might have responded if Habakkuk had been a success. A few days later, as I was driving to work, the answer hit me out of the blue: obviously, Ian, the Germans would have sent a pyrokinetic spy to sabotage the shipyards ...

The ice ship never made it into *Bitter Seeds*, but the pyrokinetic SS agent did.

Bitter Seeds is largely set in London in the 1940s with a comprehensive cast of English characters. Given that you are American, how difficult did you find it to tap into the British psyche of this particular period in history?

Extremely difficult. I won't make any claims about how well I did (or didn't) succeed, but I certainly tried my best. Without a doubt, it was the most daunting part of the entire project.

It's sometimes said that the past is a foreign country. If that's true, then when I tackled *Bitter Seeds* I found myself writing about people who were doubly foreign to me. Not only foreign in terms of country and culture, but also foreign in terms of the era. It was by far the most challenging part of the research process. By comparison, big historical events are relatively easy – that's what history books are for. It takes far more ground work to derive a reliable picture of the daily lives of people in a foreign country seventy years ago. Particularly the lives of Londoners during the Blitz, who endured terrible conditions with legendary resolve.

Luckily for me, I was able to scrounge up some wonderful research materials such as information packets from the Imperial War Museum and Norman Longmate's invaluable reference work, *How We Lived Then*.

I also mined the BBC People's War archive for bits and pieces of verisimilitude. I tried to read widely from writers of the period, like Evelyn Waugh. And I became a fan of *Foyle's War* along the way.

On a related note, how much research did you undertake in preparation for the novel – were there plenty of London field trips?

London is truly one of my favourite cities in the world. I love it there. I've been to London twice, but both trips were long before I started writing! At one point I did dig out my photographs from those trips, but they weren't very useful. I had to rely on historical archives, old photos, and contemporary descriptions. I was able to find a high resolution scan of a London map published in 1940, and that was a godsend.

Someday soon I'd like to return to London and visit the locations that I used in my books. But only when I know I won't die of shock and embarrassment . . .

In the course of writing *Bitter Seeds* and the sequels, I filled a bookcase with reference books and materials. Some pieces of information are relatively easy to find, such as the approximate date when Churchill renamed the 'Local Defense Volunteers' to 'Home Guard'. Other things are trickier, such as where a particular general was at a particular time on a specific afternoon.

Bitter Seeds **features an altered history of World War 2, with various changes to recorded events – some minor, others considerably more significant. How much fun did you have playing with history, and how difficult did you find it to make significant changes that nonetheless remained plausible given the internal logic of the story? In addition, did you feel some sense of responsibility not to dilute the importance of what remains a terrible conflict?**

I felt a very pressing obligation to somehow stay respectful of the real-life conflict, with all its heroism and horror, while fiddling with history to suit the story I wanted to tell. Whether or not I succeeded is not for me to say, but I was very aware of that tightrope while writing *Bitter Seeds* and its sequels. That included much contemplation of the atrocities of the Holocaust before I decided to tackle this project. I tried to make the atmosphere of *Bitter Seeds* the atmosphere of a world where something like that was possible, and was clearly happening just off the side of the page, even if we never see it directly.

Having said that, in terms of the general course of the warfare itself, it was a lot of fun to read up on the events and devise a secret explanation for everything that did (and didn't!) happen.

Once I knew how I wanted the story to unfold, and where I wanted it to go, choosing the pivotal events to change was fairly straightforward. I knew I needed a major event early in the war that was as close to Britain as possible ... And then I read about a very strange order given by Hitler himself during the Dunkirk evacuation – every history book I checked agreed that this happened, but to this day nobody understands why.

Once I knew what I was changing, and why, devising a mechanism for those changes was relatively easy. That's a benefit when one of your characters can see the future! (But it did require working out most of the trilogy in advance before I wrote *Bitter Seeds*.)

There are places in *Bitter Seeds* where I thought very carefully about exactly what changed, and how. But there are also places where I just winged it for the sake of the story. I wouldn't stake my life on the plausibility of my violence to history!

You've described *Bitter Seeds* as a novel in which 'good people do bad things'. By the end of the novel, the moral lines have become very blurred indeed. Was this a

deliberate move away from black and white depictions of good and evil, or did it occur naturally during the writing of the novel?

As a reader, I tend to connect most easily with characters who have a bit of grey about them. Human beings are complex. Nobody is purely good or purely evil. Everybody has good days and bad days, everybody has pangs of selfishness and moments of selflessness. I'm not claiming that in some folks the scales aren't tipped mighty far to one side or the other, but in general we're a complicated species. So I certainly wanted to avoid sharp delineations of black and white characterisation.

I also didn't want to fall into the cliché of portraying all the Axis characters as cartoonish villains and the Allied characters as flawless, noble, square-jawed heroes. That's why I found it fun to make the guy in the traditional hero role, Marsh, a bit of a jerk. And I tried to give our Nazi point-of-view character, Klaus, a well-defined character arc.

But I think the story would have turned out a little grey even if I hadn't wanted to play with the characterisations like that. It's hard to avoid at least a little bit of darkness when you have blood magic on one side and a precognitive sociopath on the other.

The story involves a variety of diverse characters, from the all-action Raybould Marsh, to the troubled aristocrat Will Beauclerk and the enigmatic Gretel. Was there a character you enjoyed writing more than the others, and if so for what reason?

Gretel is a very fun character to write. But the more I worked on *Bitter Seeds*, the more I discovered I had to dial back her physical presence on the page. Part of that was because of her precognition, which meant she knew as much as I did about what was going to happen next. When we first meet her as an adult in chapter one of *Bitter Seeds*, she's already thinking ahead to events in the final scene of *The Coldest War*. That made handling her scenes a little tricky.

So even though she's the axis mundi of the entire trilogy, I found her scenes worked best if I treated her like a spice to be used sparingly. And trying to see the world through her eyes was like piecing together a puzzle: if you could see many years into the future, and you could anticipate every action, every word spoken by the people around you, what would be the simplest, most efficient, most counterintuitive means of bringing those people from point A to point B? That's where I had the most fun: knowing what she was doing, and why, and then working backward to devise fun and intriguing ways to show her going about it without giving everything away prematurely.

You're a physicist by profession, which perhaps goes some way to explaining the science fiction elements in *Bitter Seeds*. This doesn't account for the dark, occult powers that the British warlocks consort with – what was the inspiration behind that, and how deeply did you need to delve into occult research in order to make the Eidolons the terrifying presence they are in the book?
The magic practiced by the warlocks in *Bitter Seeds* is more or less good old-fashioned demonology with the serial numbers filed off. A long time ago, when I was a kid, I read *The Devil's Day* by James Blish and I was struck by the notion that one might achieve magical ends by appealing to an outside agency. So I knew I wanted to do something with that.

I'm also interested in linguistics. I'm not particularly good at languages but I find the topic interesting nonetheless. So I'd read a bit about how scholars and theologians centuries ago strived to reconstruct the original language that Adam and Eve spoke in the Garden of Eden, the pre-Tower of Babel language. But it always seemed to me that the language of 'Let There Be Light' couldn't possibly be a human language ... And then I read about John Dee and his claim that he could talk to angels because he had learned their secret language, which he called Enochian.

It all came together when a friend of mine, a linguistic anthropologist, told me an ancient legend that involved raising infants such that they never heard any human language – the idea being to see what language, if any, they would speak by default in the absence of outside influences.

You're part of the New Mexico Critical Mass writing group, which includes many talented writers like Daniel Abraham and George R. R. Martin. How important was their advice and support to you during the writing of *Bitter Seeds*?

I'm extremely fortunate. Originally, I intended *Bitter Seeds* as a practice novel. An extended writing exercise, and nothing more.

But when I first brought the idea to the group (feeling a little embarrassed because I was convinced it was a terrible idea for a book), they were highly enthusiastic about it. And they immediately convinced me it was a trilogy instead of a single book. They were right. Also, as I've said, because of Gretel's precognition, which extends across multiple books, the trilogy took a fair bit of planning in advance. So the group got together one Sunday and, over the course of a long afternoon, we plotted out the whole thing on a whiteboard. The outline changed quite a bit over the course of writing the books, but that skeleton served me very well!

The group's encouragement and enthusiasm has been invaluable to me.

While *Bitter Seeds* is your first novel, you've written a variety of shorter fiction, including stories for George R. R. Martin's Wild Card series. How easy do you find it to switch between the two mediums, and do you prefer one over the other?

I'm not very good at switching mental gears – I don't like to multi-task if I can avoid it. So I find jumping back and forth between different projects rather difficult. I prefer to write short fiction as a palate cleanser between longer projects, but deadlines rarely work out that way!

I enjoy writing novels because I get a sense of accomplishment from finishing a manuscript. Even if it's a terrible first draft, I can look at the pile of paper and feel proud that I stuck with it to the bitter end. But I enjoy short fiction because while the sense of accomplishment isn't as large (for me personally), they take far less time to write and rewrite. The improvements become evident much more quickly when you're rewriting thirty pages instead of six hundred.

Both forms are very challenging to me. But I try to learn from my mistakes . . .

if you enjoyed
BITTER SEEDS

look out for

THE TROUPE

by

Rabort Jackson Bennett

CHAPTER 1

A DEPARTURE

Friday mornings at Otterman's Vaudeville Theater generally had a very relaxed pace to them, and so far this one was no exception. Four acts in the bill would be moving on to other theaters over the weekend, and four more would be coming in to take their place, among them Gretta Mayfield, minor star of the Chicago opera. The general atmosphere among the musicians was one of carefree satisfaction, as all of the acts had gone well and the next serious rehearsals were an entire weekend away. Which, to the overworked musicians, might as well have been an eternity.

But then Tofty Thresinger, first chair house violinist and unofficial gossip maven of the theater, came sprinting into the orchestra pit with terror in his eyes. He stood there panting for a moment, hands on his knees, and picked his head up to make a ghastly announcement: 'George has quit!'

'What?' said Victor, the second chair cellist. 'George? *Our* George?'

'George the *pianist?*' asked Catherine, their flautist.

'The very same,' said Tofty.

'What kind of quit?' asked Victor. 'As in quitting the theater?'

'Yes, of course quitting the theater!' said Tofty. 'What other kind of quit is there?'

'There must be some mistake,' said Catherine. 'Who did you hear it from?'

'From George himself!' said Tofty.

'Well, how did he phrase it?' asked Victor.

'He looked at me,' said Tofty, 'and he said, "I quit."'

Everyone stopped to consider this. There was little room for alternate interpretation in that.

'But why would he quit?' asked Catherine.

'I don't know!' cried Tofty, and he collapsed into his chair, accidentally crushing his rosin and leaving a large white stain on the seat of his pants.

The news spread quickly throughout the theater: George Carole, their most dependable house pianist and veritable wunderkind (or *enfant terrible*, depending on who you asked), was throwing in the towel without even a by-your-leave. Stagehands shook their heads in dismay. Performers immediately launched into complaints. Even the coat-check girls, usually exiled to the very periphery of theater gossip, were made aware of this ominous development.

But not everyone was shaken by this news. 'Good riddance,' said Chet, their bassist. 'I'm tired of tolerating that little lordling, always acting as if he was better than us.' But several muttered he *was* better than them. It had been seven months since the sixteen-year-old had walked through their doors on audition day and positively dumbfounded the staff with his playing. Everyone had been astonished to hear that he was not auditioning for an act, but for *house pianist*, a lowly job if ever there was one. Van Hoever, the manager of Otterman's, had questioned him extensively on this point, but George had stood firm: he was there to be house pianist at their little Ohio theater, and nothing more.

'What are we going to do now?' said Archie, their trombonist. 'Like it or not, it was George who put us on the map.' Which was more or less true. It was the general rule that in vaudeville, a trade filled with indignities of all kinds, no one was shat upon more than the house pianist. He accompanied nearly every act, and every ego that crossed the stage got thoroughly massaged by abusing him. If a joke went sour, it was because the pianist was too late and spoiled the delivery. If a dramatic bit was flat, it was because the pianist was too lively. If an acrobat stumbled, it was because the pianist distracted him.

But in his time at Otterman's George had accomplished the impossible: he'd given them no room for complaints. After playing through the first rehearsal he would know the act better than the actors did, which was saying something as every actor had fine-tuned their performance with almost lapidary attention. He hit every beat, wrung every laugh out of every delivery, and knew when to speed things up or slow them down. He seemed to have the uncanny ability to augment every performance he accompanied. Word spread, and many acts became more amenable to performing at Otterman's, which occupied a rather obscure spot on the Keith-Albee circuit.

Yet now he was leaving, almost as abruptly as he'd arrived. It put them in a pretty tight spot: Gretta Mayfield was coming specifically because she had agreed to have George accompany her, but that was just the start; after a moment's review, the orchestra came to the horrifying conclusion that at least a quarter of the acts of the next week had agreed to visit Otterman's only because George met their high standards.

After Tofty frantically spread the word, wild speculation followed. Did anyone know the reason behind the departure? Could anyone guess? Perhaps, Victor suggested, he was finally going to tour with an act of his own, or maybe he was heading straight to the legitimate (meaning well-respected orchestras and symphonies, rather than lowly vaudeville). But Tofty said he'd heard nothing about George making those sorts of movements, and he would know, wouldn't he?

Maybe he'd been lured away by another theater, someone said. But Van Hoever would definitely ante up to keep George, Catherine pointed out, and the only theaters that could outbid him were very far away, and would never send scouts out here. What could the boy possibly be thinking? They wasted the whole morning debating the subject, yet they never reached an answer.

George did his best to ignore the flurry of gossip as he gathered his belongings, but it was difficult; as he'd not yet made a formal resignation to Van Hoever, everyone tried to find the reason behind his desertion in hopes that they could fix it.

'Is it the money, George?' Tofty asked. 'Did Van Hoever turn you down for a raise?'

No, answered George. No, it was not the money.

'Is it the acts, George?' asked Archie. 'Did one of the acts insult you? You've got to ignore those bastards, Georgie, they can be so ornery sometimes!'

But George scoffed haughtily, and said that no, it was certainly not any of the acts. The other musicians cursed Archie for such a silly question; of *course* it wasn't any of the performers, as George never gave them reason for objection.

'Is it a girl, George?' asked Victor. 'You can tell me. I can keep a secret. It's a girl, isn't it?'

At this George turned a brilliant red, and sputtered angrily for a moment. No, he eventually said. No, thank you very much, it was not a girl.

'Then was it something Tofty said?' asked Catherine. 'After all, he was who you were talking to just before you said you quit.'

'What!' cried Tofty. 'What a horrendous accusation! We were only talking theater hearsay, I tell you! I simply mentioned how Van Hoever was angry that an act had skipped us on the circuit!'

At that, George's face became strangely still. He stopped gathering up his sheet music and looked away for a minute. But finally he said no, Tofty had nothing to do with it. 'And would you all please leave me alone?' he asked. 'This decision has nothing to do with you, and furthermore there's nothing that will change it.'

The other musicians, seeing how serious he was, grumbled and shuffled away. Once they were gone George scratched his head and tried not to smile. Despite his solemn demeanor, he had enjoyed watching them clamor to please him.

The smile vanished as he returned to his packing and the decision he'd made. The orchestra did not matter, he told himself. Otterman's did not matter anymore. The only thing that mattered now was getting out the door and on the road as soon as possible.

After he'd collected the last of his belongings he headed for his final stop: Van Hoever's office. The theater manager had surely heard the news and was in the midst of composing a fine tirade, but if George left now he'd be denied payment for this week's worth of performances. And though he could not predict the consequences of what he was about to do, he thought it wise to have every penny possible.

But when George arrived at the office hall there was someone seated in the row of chairs before Van Hoever's door: a short, elderly woman who watched him with a sharp eye as if she'd been expecting him. Her wrists and hands were wrapped tight in cloth, and a poorly rolled cigarette was bleeding smoke from between two of her fingers. 'Leaving without a goodbye?' she asked him.

George smiled a little. 'Ah,' he said. 'Hello, Irina.'

The old woman did not answer, but patted the empty chair next to her. George walked over, but did not sit. The old woman raised her eyebrows at him. 'Too good to give me company?'

'This is an ambush, isn't it?' he asked. 'You've been waiting for me.'

'You assume the whole world waits on you. Come. Sit.'

'I'll give you company,' he said. 'But I won't sit. I know you're looking to delay me, Irina.'

'So impatient, child,' she said. 'I'm just an old woman who wishes to talk.'

'To talk about why I'm leaving.'

'No. To give you advice.'

'I don't need advice. And I'm not changing my mind.'

'I'm not telling you to. I just wish to make a suggestion before you go.'

George gave her the sort of impatient look that can only be given by the very young to the very old, and raised a fist to knock at Van Hoever's door. But before his knuckles ever made contact, the old woman's cloth-bound hand snatched his fist out of the air. 'You will want to listen to me, George,' she said. 'Because I know *exactly* why you're leaving.'

George looked her over. If it had been anyone else, he would not have given them another minute, but Irina was one of the few people at Otterman's who could command George's attention. She was the orchestra's only violist, and like most violists (who after all devoted their lives to an ignored or much-ridiculed instrument) she had acquired a very sour sort of wisdom. It was also rumored she'd witnessed terrible hardships in her home in Russia before fleeing to America, and this, combined with her great age, gave her a mysterious esteem at Otterman's.

'Do you think so?' asked George.

'I do,' she said. 'And aren't you interested to hear my guess?' She released him and patted the seat next to her once more. George sighed, but reluctantly sat.

'What is it?' he asked.

'Why such a hurry, child?' Irina said. 'It seems like it was only yesterday that you arrived.'

'It wasn't,' said George. 'I've spent over half a year here, which is far too long.'

'Too long for what?' asked Irina.

George did not answer. Irina smiled, amused by this terribly serious boy in his too-large suit. 'Time moves so much slower for the young. To me, it is as a day. I can still remember when you walked through that door, child, and three things struck me about you.' She held up three spindly fingers. 'First was that you were talented. *Very* talented. But you knew that, didn't you? You probably knew it too well, for such a little boy.'

'A *little* boy?' asked George.

'Oh, yes. A naïve little lamb, really.'

'Maybe then,' said George, his nose high in the air. He reached into his pocket, took out a pouch of tobacco, and began rolling his own cigarette. He made sure to appear as nonchalant as possible, having practiced the motions at home in the mirror.

'If you say so,' said Irina. One finger curled down, leaving two standing. 'Second was that you were proud, and reckless. This did not surprise me. I've seen it in many young performers. And I've seen many throw careers away as a result. Much like you're probably doing now.'

George cocked an eyebrow, and lit his cigarette and puffed at it. His stomach spasmed as he tried to suppress a cough.

Irina wrinkled her nose. 'What is that you're smoking?'

'Some of Virginia's finest, of course,' he said, though he wheezed a bit.

'That doesn't smell like anything fine at all.' She took his pouch and peered into it. 'I don't know what that is, but it isn't Virginia's finest.'

George looked crestfallen. 'It . . . it isn't?' he asked.

'No. What did you do, buy this from someone in the orchestra?'

'Well, yes, but they seemed very trustworthy!'

She shook her head. 'You've been snookered, my child. This is trash. Next time go to a tobacconist, like a normal person.'

George grumbled something about how it had to be a mistake, but he hurriedly put out his cigarette and began to stow the pouch away.

'Anyway,' she said, 'I remember one final third thing about you when you first came here.' Another trembling blue finger curled down. She used the remaining one to poke him in the arm. 'You did not seem all that interested in what you were playing, which was peculiar. No – what you were mostly interested in was a certain act that was traveling the circuit.'

George froze where he was, slightly bent as he stuffed the tobacco pouch into his pocket. He slowly turned to look at the old woman.

'Still in a hurry, child?' asked Irina. 'Or have I hit upon it?'

He did not answer.

'I see,' she said. 'Well, I recall you asked about this one act all the time, nearly every day. Did anyone know when this act would play here? It had played here once, hadn't it? Did they think this act would play nearby, at least? I think I can still remember the name of it ... Ah, yes. It was the Silenus Troupe, wasn't it?'

George's face had gone very closed now. He nodded, very slightly.

'Yes,' said the old woman. She began rubbing at her wrists, trying to ease her arthritis. 'That was it. You wanted to know nothing but news about Silenus, asking all the time. But we would always say no, no, we don't know nothing about this act. And we didn't. He'd played here once, this Silenus, many, many months ago. The man had terribly angered Van Hoever then with his many demands, but we had not seen him since, and no one knew where he was playing next. Does any of that sound familiar to you, boy?'

George did not nod this time, but he did not need to.

'Yes,' said Irina. 'I think it does. And then this morning, you know, I hear news that Van Hoever is very angry. He's angry because an act has skipped us on the circuit, and is playing Parma, west of here. And the minute I hear this news about Van Hoever today, I get a second piece of news, but this one is about our young, marvelous pianist. He's *leaving*. Just suddenly decided to go. Isn't that strange? How one piece of news follows the other?'

George was silent. Irina nodded and took a long drag from her cigarette. 'I wasn't terribly surprised to find that the act that's skipped us is Silenus,' she said. 'And unless I'm mistaken, you're going to go chasing him. Am I right?'

George cleared his throat. 'Yes,' he said hoarsely.

'Yes. In fact, now that I think about it, that act might be the only reason you signed on to be house pianist here. After all, you could've found somewhere better. But Silenus played here once, so perhaps he might do so again, and when he did you wished to be here to see it, no?'

George nodded.

Irina smiled, satisfied with her deductions. 'The famous Silenus,' she said. 'I've heard many rumors about him in my day. I've heard his troupe is full of gypsies, traveled here from abroad. I've heard he tours the circuit at his choosing. That he was touring vaudeville before it was vaudeville.'

'Have you heard that every hotel saves a private room for him?' asked George. 'That's a popular one.'

'No, I'd not heard that one. Why are you so interested in this man, I wonder?'

George thought about it. Then he slowly reached into his front pocket and pulled out a piece of paper. Though its corners were soft and blunt with age, it was very well cared for: it had been cleanly folded into quarters and tied up with string, like a precious message. George plucked at the bow and untied the string, and then, with the gravity of a priest unscrolling a holy document, he unfolded the paper.

It was – or had once been – a theater bill. Judging by the few acts printed on it and the simple, sloppy printing job, it was from a very small-time theater, one even smaller than Otterman's. But half of one page was taken up by a large, impressive illustration:

though the ink had cracked and faded in parts, one could see that it depicted a short, stout man in a top hat standing in the middle of a stage, bathed in the clean illumination of the spotlight. His hands were outstretched to the audience in a pose of extreme theatricality, as if he was in the middle of telling them the most enthralling story in the world. Written across the bottom of the illustration, in a curling font that must have passed for fancy for that little theater, were three words: THE SILENUS TROUPE.

George reverently touched the illustration, as if he wished to fall inside it and hear the tale the man was telling. 'I got this in my hometown,' he said. 'He visited there, once. But I didn't get to see.' Then he looked at Irina with a strange shine in his eyes, and asked, 'What do you remember from when he was here?'

'What do I remember?'

'Yes. You had to have rehearsed with him when he played here, didn't you? You must have seen his show. So what do you remember?'

'Don't you know the act yourself? Why ask me?'

But George did not answer, but only watched her closely.

She grunted. 'Well. Let me think. It seems so long ago ...' She took a contemplative puff from her cigarette. 'There were four acts, I remember that. It was odd, no one travels with more than one act these days. That was what angered Van Hoever so much.'

George leaned forward. 'What else?'

'I remember ... I remember there was a man with puppets, at the start. But they weren't very funny, these puppets. And then there was a dancer, and a ... a strongwoman. Wait, no. She was another puppet, wasn't she? I think she might have been. And then there was a fourth act, and it ... it ...' She trailed off, confused, and she was not at all used to being confused.

'You don't remember,' said George.

'I do!' said Irina. 'At least, I *think* I do ... I can remember every act I've played for, I promise, but this one ... Maybe I'm wrong. I could've *sworn* I played for this one. But did I?'

'You did,' said George.

'Oh? How are you so certain?'

'I've found other people who've seen his show, Irina,' he said. 'Dozens of them. And they always say the same thing. They remember a bit about the first three acts – the puppets, the dancing girl in white, and the strongwoman – but nothing about the fourth. And when they try and remember it, they always wonder if they ever saw the show at all. It's so strange. Everyone's heard of the show, and many have seen it, but no one can remember what they saw.'

Irina rubbed the side of her head as if trying to massage the memory out of some crevice in her skull, but it would not come. 'What are you saying?'

'I'm saying that when people go to see Silenus's show ... something happens. I'm not sure what. But they can never remember it. They can hardly describe what they've seen. It's like it happened in a dream.'

'That can't be,' said Irina. 'It seems unlikely that a performance could do that to a person.'

'And yet you can't remember it at all,' said George. 'No one else here can remember, either. They just know Silenus was here, but what he did up on that stage is a mystery to them, even though they played alongside it.'

'And you want to witness this for yourself? Is that it?'

George hesitated. 'Well. There's a bit more to it than that, of course. But yes. I want to see him.'

'But why, child? What you're telling me is very curious, that I admit, but you have a very good thing going on here. You're making money. You are living by yourself, dressing yourself' – she cast a leery eye over his cream-colored suit – 'with some success. It is a lot to risk.'

'Why do you care? Why are you interested in me at all?'

Irina sighed. 'Well. Let me just say that once, I was your age. And I was just about as talented as you were, boy. And some decisions I made were ... unwise. I paid many prices for those decisions. I am still paying them.' She trailed off, rubbing the side of her neck. George did not speak; Irina very rarely spoke about her past. Finally she coughed, and said, 'I would hate to see the same happen to you. You have been lucky so far, George. To abandon what you have to go chasing Silenus will test what luck you have.'

'I don't need luck,' said George. 'As you said, I can find better places to play. Everyone says so.'

'You've been coddled here,' she said sternly. 'You have lived with constant praise, and it's made you foolish.'

George sat up straight, affronted, and carefully refolded the theater bill and put it in his pocket. 'Maybe. But I'd risk everything in the world to see him, Irina. You've no idea how far I've come just to get this chance.'

'And what do you expect will happen when you see this Silenus?' she asked.

George was quiet as he thought about his answer. But before he could speak, the office door was flung open and Van Hoever came stalking out.

Van Hoever came to a halt when he saw George sitting there. A cold glint came into his eye, and he said, 'You.'

'Me,' said George mildly.

Van Hoever pointed into his office. 'Inside. Now.'

George stood up, gathered all of his belongings, and walked

into Van Hoever's office with one last look back at Irina. She watched him go, and shook her head and said, 'Still a boy. Remember that.' Then the door closed behind him and she was gone.